The Devil's Jigsaw

Nigel Lampard

A Bardel Publication

Published by Bardel 2015

First Edition
The Devil's Jigsaw

This is a work of fiction. Names, places, businesses, characters, and incidents, are either the product of the author's imagination or are used fictitiously and any resemblance to any actual persons, living or dead, organisations, events or locales, or any other entity, is entirely coincidental.

Cover designed by Bardel
Image taken from www.123RF.com

Part One

July 1994

Chapter One

Amy Carpenter wasn't her real name.

She looked like an Amy. She had shoulder-length blonde hair, an almost clear complexion, a small turned-up nose, high cheek bones and the sort of big blue eyes that would hold the attention of most men, but only when they could drag their gaze away from an equally attractive figure.

Having been told on numerous occasions that her long slim legs appeared to go on forever, she was never sure whether it was meant as a back-handed compliment or not. Did such comments mean the rest of her was out of proportion? At just over five and a half feet tall, she felt that her height was an asset – not too tall and not too short.

He had chosen the name Amy Carpenter for her because of the way she looked. She still didn't understand why she needed to change her name and why the way she looked suggested her name might be Amy.

His logic was questionable but she hadn't questioned it too often. She was Leah Carmichael, she would always be Leah Carmichael, but she accepted that when she got there she would have to be Amy Carpenter; she just hoped she had the wit not to slip up when the time came.

She normally exuded self-confidence, her prettiness matched by her intelligence. But for perhaps obvious reasons to some, her intelligence did not always prove to be an asset. Another woman once told her that a good-looking female with a brain was the most dangerous creature on earth.

She was a predator to beat all predators.

Although Leah didn't regard herself as that good looking, she did not want to come across as being dangerous, so more often than not, and especially when in male company, she tended to keep her opinions to herself. Whether that was the right thing to do, she didn't know.

As for being a predator, that was the last thing she was. She didn't want to prey on anybody else for anything and she certainly didn't want to be preyed upon. Appreciating her naivety might be an added attraction; she used it whenever necessary.

She also appreciated that some of her assets – if that's what they were called – were difficult to hide but others she could conceal. Coming across as a dumb blonde sometimes worked to her advantage, but when the time was right she often used her intellect to her benefit, and to the disadvantage of the person who was doing the patronising bit. This tactic worked more often than not, especially when she needed to point out – with a smile and sometimes a pout – just how supercilious some men, and women, could be.

At this particular moment though, Leah did not feel overly self-confident. She felt lonely, nervous, apprehensive, worried and just a little scared. As individual sensations they were not feelings she felt that often, but when grouped together they were certainly unusual and unsettling.

Looking out over the English Channel on a clear, hot, beautiful summer's day was enough to make anybody feel good, but not so for Leah. She knew what awaited her arrival on the other side of the water.

Well, she thought she knew.

Other than the little she did know she had no idea what really awaited her on the other side. Actually, her imagination was proving to be her own worst enemy. She remembered his words: "The less you know the better. What you don't know you can't repeat."

He hadn't meant to be nasty or anything, in fact he had been smiling as he said it to her, but the message was clear.

A little knowledge was a dangerous thing.

Her argument was that if it all turned into a guessing game it could be even more dangerous. In response, he had smiled that smile and told her that all would become clear once she was there.

With a couple of hours to waste, she had found her way to the National Trust White Cliffs car park above Dover harbour. Having been here once with her parents when she was in her early teens, she had remembered the magnificent view. Now, resting her arms on the open car door, her last cigarette – well, she hoped it was her last – smouldering between her fingers, everything should have seemed normal.

At this time in the morning there were only half a dozen other cars parked here. In the two nearest cars, she could see elderly couples looking out over the Channel as they munched on whatever they were having for breakfast, and in both cars the plastic cups of coffee or tea placed on the dashboard resulted in the windscreens steaming up. It made Leah wonder if they were thinking about something entirely different and didn't realise their view was obscured.

Were they reliving their pasts, wondering what they should say to each other, or were they worrying about their futures? They might be wondering why time passed so much more quickly as they got older. Perhaps they had sons and daughters who were giving them enough trouble to stop them thinking about their own worries.

That was what Leah was doing.

Worrying.

It was all in her mind, but maybe if she stopped to think logically she would realise she was letting the products of her imagination get the better of her.

She must stop asking why she had accepted the responsibility in the first place especially when she didn't know the truth … it was too late now to go back on her promise.

Of course she wanted to prove herself to him; after all she was in love with him, wasn't she? However, even if she was in love, accepting more responsibility than she could perhaps cope with was, in retrospect, probably unwise.

She was getting herself into a state and she wasn't even there yet.

Allowing a smile to cross her lips she remembered her father looking over his left shoulder while driving and saying, "Will you stop asking if we are nearly there yet?"

Although she could see France, she was nowhere near her destination. By her estimation, she was at least two hundred and fifty miles away from where her responsibilities would really start.

Perhaps they had already started.

She had been responsible for getting herself this far, and now she needed to get to her final destination. Looking down, there was something unexplainable but absolute about the cross-channel ferries she could see leaving the port beneath her: it was as though they were sailing into a mist of insecurity, not knowing what lay beyond.

An ominous shiver ran down her spine, making her scrunch up her shoulders.

She could not believe that such a narrow stretch of water could be so busy. As she drew on her cigarette for the last time before stubbing it out with her booted foot, she really wished she hadn't decided to stop smoking. Why when faced with this amount of stress had she decided to give up the one thing that could help her? Perhaps she ought to give up drinking as well and really punish herself.

In an attempt to steady her nerves she counted the number of ferries she could see. At least seven. She could also see all the way to the French coast. Well, she assumed it was the French coast because she couldn't think what else it could be; it wasn't low cloud or just a heat haze, it had to be the French coast.

She was being silly.

When she drove onto the ferry in a couple of hours' time, she would feel the same as she always did when she boarded an aircraft. As she took the final step into a plane, she always said 'goodbye' wondering if she would ever set foot on mother earth again. She wasn't scared of flying, nor was she scared of being on a ferry, but she still said 'goodbye'.

She wondered if she was alone with such thoughts.

Stepping into the British Airways Embraer 170 on the internal flight from Newcastle to Heathrow yesterday, she had wondered exactly that.

Was she unusual?

With a slight shake of her head she told herself she was being stupid. If he had confidence in her then she really ought to share that faith. If he did not believe she was capable of doing what he had asked then he would not have risked giving her such a mammoth task. He certainly would not have been able to convince them, whoever *they* were, that she was capable of doing it.

Of course she was capable so of course she would do it.

She reached into the car to recover the empty packet of cigarettes she had thrown on the floor, praying that there was still one in the packet.

There wasn't, so she rifled through her shoulder bag and smiled when she found an old packet containing two cigarettes.

She would give up – eventually.

Exhaling skywards she thought about how all this had come about.

Late October 1993

Chapter Two

His name was Peter.

They met for the first time one Sunday in the autumn of last year. Leah was reading psychology for her first degree at Durham University. Peter was there to do some research for a doctorate in clinical psychology, or so he said.

It was such a lovely autumnal day that she decided to go for a walk by the River Wear to get some inspiration from somewhere; maybe the ripples, eddies and currents in the river would help straighten out her own mind. She had an awkward essay to write on whether people's personality profiles could determine what career they ought to follow, rather than deciding without any reference to their psychological make-up.

Not even sure what she thought about personality profiles, or how she supposed psychologists thought up the right questions to pigeonhole people, she found a suitable spot by the river and sat down to reflect on the question. The grass looked floppy and sad, the trees sorry to be losing their leaves – although the colours were magnificent – and the fast flowing water looked cold and uninviting.

Nothing she was looking at was inspirational ... just depressing.

She was sitting with her back against a tree trunk, her knees drawn up and a note pad resting on her faded jeans. Tapping the end of a pencil against her teeth she gazed down towards the river.

Quite a few people were about but as she was well away from the main path, she remained undisturbed.

She did not want any intrusions.

Looking up, she saw a lone man coming towards her, and he was deep in thought.

"Damn," she muttered, "why can't he stick to the proper path like everybody else?"

Leah was wearing a black leather jacket with the fur collar turned up, jeans, black boots with grey socks folded over the top and fingerless black woollen gloves. On her head was a pink woollen hat she had pulled down over her ears, her long blonde hair tucked under the hat. With a thermal vest on under the jacket she felt warm, but she was still having trouble in concentrating.

She glanced to her right. The man was getting closer.

He was kicking at the leaves, his hands thrust deep into his jeans pockets and he seemed to be unaware that he was being watched, albeit furtively. Leah looked down at her notepad and pretended not to notice him. She turned her head away and tapped her pencil on her teeth again, hoping he would just walk on.

He didn't.

"A picture of total concentration," he said as he stopped a few feet away from where she was sitting.

Without answering, she slowly lifted her head towards him, shading her eyes from the weak sun.

"I'm sorry, I didn't mean to interrupt your work," he said as he squatted down and rested his arms on his thighs.

Leah felt compelled to say something. She turned towards him, screwing up her face. "What? Were you talking to me and if you were, who are you?"

She wasn't normally rude but he had intruded into her space.

He was standing with his back to the sun so she couldn't see him properly. "Yes, I was and I am a passing stranger," he said. "But I'm sorry the sun is in your eyes." He moved round to her other side and squatted down again.

He smiled and Leah felt a little of her initial wariness leave her. In fact, if she were being honest with herself, she felt goose pimples on parts of her body covered by at least three layers of clothing.

"Well, passing stranger, perhaps you'd better carry on passing, I'm trying to –"

"I know," he said. "And I'm sorry to have interrupted you, but something made me stop and say hello."

"At least you're original. I haven't heard that one before." She looked down as she felt herself colour under his gaze. She didn't normally blush in men's company.

"What are you doing?" he asked.

"I'm trying to write an essay, and I came here for peace and quiet and for inspiration, but not to be sociable."

"That's me told," he said, the smile still on his face. "Sorry. I didn't mean to pry or interrupt."

"You did both," Leah said, but she was actually pleased when he didn't stand up and move away. "You just stopped to say hello, that's what you said."

"That's right."

"Well ..."

"Are you here, at the university?" he asked.

She carried on with her assessment of this stranger.

He wasn't too tall, six feet maybe, with longish but well cut dark brown curly hair, a dark complexion, grey-green eyes, and – the thing she approved of most – clean shaven, except for the designer stubble he probably had to take care of every day. He had dimples when he smiled, which made him appear slightly boyish for thirty. She was guessing at thirty, but he couldn't be any younger.

His jeans were a good quality and the dark tan Burberry boots and Barbour jacket suggested he might have a bob or two, not that having money was necessarily a factor in her assessment ... but it might be a bonus. She liked what she saw so she decided to prolong the conversation; it was certainly better than trying to write an essay.

"Yes," she said, "I'm at the university. And you?"

She was surprised when he said, "Yes."

"What are you –?" they asked at the same time, laughing as they suddenly stopped.

"You first," he suggested.

"Psychology," she said. "I'm in my third and final year, thank God."

"I'm surprised I haven't seen you before. We must have passed in the night."

"Why?"

"I'm here doing a bit of research for my doctorate and I spend quite a lot of time with you first degree psychologists, or are you a sociological spy?"

The smile slipped from her lips. "What do you mean?"

"Nothing, just thinking of a joke I was told the other day."

"I see."

During a few seconds of silence, he looked over the river towards the golden yellows and browns on the other bank, while Leah continued her scrutiny.

Yes, she concluded, she liked what she saw.

Doing his doctorate, he had said. Should she be impressed?

As she looked at him, he seemed to come to a sudden decision.

"I know this is a bit banal and just a little forward," he said, "but it's such a beautiful afternoon, would you like to go somewhere for a cup of tea?"

He stood up and she saw him wince as he straightened his legs.

Lifting her hand to her mouth she sniggered.

"It's not only banal and forward, but it's old fashioned too. The last time I was asked to go somewhere for a *cup of tea* was by my mother when we were out shopping."

"Lucky mother," he said.

"Now that *is* unoriginal." Lifting the pencil to her lips, she tapped it again on her teeth. "But, on this occasion I think, yes, I would rather like a cup of tea."

"Oh, that's great. I'd better introduce myself, my name's Peter, Peter Bennett."

He held out his hand.

"Mine's Leah Carmichael." Taking his hand she held on to it as he helped her to her feet. His grip was firm and reassuring but once she was on her feet he let go immediately.

She brushed the back of her jeans.

"I'm not really dressed for afternoon tea. Mother wouldn't approve," she said.

"And what does mother expect you to wear for tea?"

He was watching her as she pushed the pad and pencil into her shoulder bag. "A twin-set and pearls if she had her way," Leah said, screwing up her eyes slightly, still looking and assessing.

He smiled.

Yes, she really did like what she saw. His infectious smile was very attractive and he seemed to have a sense of humour too.

She thought she might enjoy having a cup of tea with this tall, dark stranger.

July 1994

Chapter Three

Leah snapped out of her reverie when she realised there was movement ahead of her.

While she had been thinking about how she had met Peter, she had almost subconsciously driven away from the white cliffs, crossed over the A2 and followed the signs to the ferry terminal. She tagged onto other cars, the drivers of which looked as though they knew where they were going and what they were doing.

If asked by somebody to describe the short trip from the cliffs to the terminal, she would have difficulty. However, she hadn't been driving in a complete daze because she did remember that during the entire booking-in process nobody had checked her passport.

Finding her way to the correct ferry had been more by luck than judgement. Although she had been on cross-channel ferries with her parents many times, she had never driven herself onto one.

The call to board the ferry happened after she had been waiting in the queue for about twenty minutes; the cars in front of her moved and she followed. She had needed the loo the moment she parked up but hadn't dared to leave her car just in case.

Just in case of what?

If she had left the car there wouldn't have been much anybody could do about it other than wait for her to return, but it was too late now. She was sure she could hang on until she was on the ferry.

Now, concentrating on the car in front of her, she didn't forget to say 'goodbye' as her own car bumped over the join between the loading ramp and the ferry, the reason for her being here temporarily forgotten as she followed the instructions given to her by a disinterested man in a yellow safety jacket and a silly-looking blue bobble hat. Waving his arms at her as he guided her into the right-hand lane on the boat, he was simultaneously having a conversation with another guide over in the other lane.

Her guide remained disinterested until she got closer and as he looked at her through the windscreen of her car, his gesticulations stopped momentarily.

Here we go again, Leah thought.

The man smiled now that she had his undivided attention ... the smile quickly turning into a salacious grin.

She was used to it and ignored him.

After pulling up her red Peugeot 206 behind an expensive looking Mercedes she scanned her boarding pass again to see whether she should leave it unlocked, in gear or what? Sure that she had read somewhere that she ought to lock the car, she collected her shoulder bag from the front passenger seat, got out, locked the car and followed the other drivers and passengers up the steep stairs to the decks above, pleased when she saw the toilets at the top of the steps.

A little later, she found a seat with a small table in the corner of one of the bars and settled down for the ninety-minute crossing to Calais. Peter had given her all the necessary details and a route card for the journey from Calais, through France, Belgium and Holland and then on to Germany.

After yesterday's flight from Newcastle to Heathrow she had picked up the car from the long-stay car park where Peter had left it. Having checked the documents in the glove compartment – the insurance, registration book, and driving licence – she was pleased but not surprised to see that, as promised, they were all in the name he had given her: Amy Carpenter.

Having scrutinised the documents with an untrained eye she couldn't see anything wrong with them, but Peter had assured her that anyone who looked at them – and that was unlikely – would only give them a cursory glance. Also in the locked glove compartment was a sealed envelope that contained a British passport in the name of Amy Carpenter, with the recent photograph she had taken a month or so ago. She had carefully inspected the passport because that *would* be looked at, but could see nothing wrong with it. Once again, Peter had told her not to worry; her new passport and everything else was perfect in every way.

The envelope also contained a thousand *Deutschmarks,* which she calculated was approximately three hundred and thirty pounds in mixed used notes. All the documents and money were now in her shoulder bag.

On a slip of paper, she found the details of a bank account opened for her at the *Commerzbank* in a town called *Brüggen,* which was just over the Dutch border in Germany. This was her final destination and where Peter had rented a flat for her for the next six months.

As her passport wasn't checked when she drove through the port of Dover towards the ferry, she remained concerned because Peter had told her checking was more likely when she disembarked in Calais.

However, he assured her she wasn't to worry.

Other than the two medium sized suitcases, one of which she had needed to put on the back seat because the car boot wasn't big enough, all her other belongings were locked away in a container in secure storage in Durham, all arranged by Peter ... and in his name.

He had been incredibly efficient but now that she was alone, now that she only had her own resourcefulness to depend on, she felt the apprehension return. If everything went to plan, she would not be seeing him for at least three months.

He had even told her where they would meet, on what day and at what time.

As she glanced about her at the other passengers, apprehension took over once again and she prayed she would live up to his expectations. She was being silly again ... it wasn't as if she would be hopelessly lost once she got to her destination.

And after all, she had agreed to it.

In an attempt to reduce the worry engulfing her, she picked up her mug of coffee, settled back in her seat, and let her mind go back to that first cup of tea.

Late October 1993

Chapter Four

"I haven't been in here before," Leah remarked as a waitress guided them towards a table at the far end of the long narrow restaurant. "I've been in Durham for over two years and this must be one of the few places I haven't eaten in."

"I'm not surprised, looking at the prices," Peter said, glancing at a 'specials' board as he followed her between the tables.

Leah stopped. "If it's too –"

"No, that's not what I meant," he said smiling. "I meant that it's not the sort of place poor undergraduates can afford to patronise."

"You don't know that I am a *poor* undergraduate," she said before acknowledging the waitress who was standing at an empty table for two. "What a lovely view." Leah looked out of the window to the river far below and smiled.

Yes, she thought, *the next hour or so could be quite enjoyable.*

"Will a cream tea be all right?" Peter asked, studying the menu.

"Why not? If a girl can't indulge herself once in a while there's little point in sticking to salads and fat free food for the rest of the time," Leah said, turning back towards Peter.

"Two cream teas," he told the waitress, who became quite flustered when Peter added a smile.

Once the waitress had gone, he looked across the table at Leah. "So," he said, "this is an unexpected pleasure. One minute I'm walking by the river wondering why I'm feeling so bored, then in less than thirty minutes I'm sitting having tea with a very pretty young girl who I don't know from Eve. So who are you? Tell me about yourself."

Flicking a couple of crumbs off the white tablecloth, Leah wondered what she should tell him. How were two people supposed to get to know each other if one didn't take the initiative?

"Girl?" she said, smiling. "That's not very PC. Are you a handsome man or a good looking boy?"

"Whoops, sorry." He lifted his hand. "That wasn't a very good start. I meant a very pretty young woman," he added with a grin.

"No. I prefer girl to woman."

Her mother certainly would not approve of what was happening. She would say that ladies of Leah's age waited to be introduced by a third party to eligible men, assuming Peter was what could be regarded as eligible. He might be married with four kids for all Leah knew, but that sort of question could wait a little longer. She loved her parents dearly, particularly her mother, but she lived in a different age, probably in a different century.

"Well?" Peter asked, breaking into her thoughts.

She looked up. "What do you want to know?"

He shrugged. "I don't know ... where you're from and your background." He shrugged again. "Tell me whatever you are happy for me to know."

Leah was still wearing her pink woollen hat so she pulled it off and shook her head. Her blonde hair cascaded over her shoulders and she heard an audible gasp from Peter.

"Wow!" he said.

She cocked her head to one side. "What?"

"How did you get all that under a woolly hat?"

"Practice," she said.

"Makes perfect," he replied.

"You're very previous with your compliments."

"Am I?"

"No."

They both laughed.

The waitress arrived with their tea and Peter poured.

"So, come on, at least tell me something," he said. "Milk and sugar?"

"Yes, I think I can reveal that much," she said mischievously. "I like just a spot of milk please, but no sugar."

She studiously cut her scone in half and applied some cream and jam before saying, "I was born in Hong Kong in 1972, where my father was stationed at the time. At the age of eleven I went to a boarding school in Surrey, from where I eventually got the necessary 'A' Levels to come to Durham, which thrilled me because it was always my first choice. I first took a year out and did Australia with a couple of girlfriends, after which I came here in September 1991 to study psychology."

She stopped talking and popped a piece of scone into her mouth.

"The life of Leah Carmichael in one sentence," Peter said, smiling. "A sentence that generates more questions than it answers."

"Ask away then." Leah wiped some jam from her chin. "I can never eat these things properly … and if I want to answer your questions then I will, but if not you will hear a stony silence. All right?"

Peter ignored the immediate challenge. "I don't think there is a proper way of eating them," he said. "So let's go back to the day you popped into the world. Hong Kong, you said, that must have been exciting."

Peter's scone was still untouched on the plate.

"I didn't know much about it, but I have been back there since and I was shown the BMH I –"

"BMH?"

"British Military Hospital. It was called BMH Hong Kong."

"So your father was in the Army?"

"Yes, he retired a couple of years ago. He and my mother live in Marshfield near Bath now and he works as a consultant in the Bristol area."

"Did you spend a lot of your time abroad?"

"Indirectly. As I said I went to boarding school from the age of eleven. After Hong Kong my father spent most of his time in Germany so I went to military primary schools there and in the UK." She looked down at Peter's plate. "Aren't you going to eat your scone?"

"It looks a bit sweet to me," he said. "You have it," he added pushing the plate across the table.

"Are you sure?"

"Positive. Where in Germany did you live?"

"Oh, we lived all over. *Rhinedahlen*, *Berlin*, *Heidelberg*, *Paderborn*, all over," she told him absentmindedly as she piled more cream and jam onto her second scone. At last she looked up. Peter was frowning as though he was weighing up various possibilities in his mind, but when he saw her puzzled gaze he smiled again and refilled their teacups.

"So did you learn to speak German?" he asked.

"Yes, and if I say so myself, I do speak it quite well. I learnt it at school but of course I was able to practice it when I went home on school holidays, when Daddy was stationed in Germany that is. I think I learnt more during holidays than I did at school."

Peter looked at her over the rim of his cup.

The same expression was there but just as she was on the point of asking what the matter was, his face softened and he asked, "So a potential psychologist who speaks the language of the founder of psychoanalysis. That's a bonus."

"Founder, a German?" she said. "Who are you referring to?"

"Wilhelm Wundt, of course."

"I thought Rene Descartes started it all off. Didn't he create a bit of a stir when he disassociated the mind from the body?"

Peter smiled. "Just testing," he said. "Actually the Greeks are believed to have started it all off as they did with most things."

“Are you trying to be superior?” Leah asked, a mischievous smile on her lips as she enjoyed every moment of this stranger’s company.

“Trying?” he said. “Not in the slightest, especially when I intend asking you if you would like to have dinner with me this evening.”

July 1994

Chapter Five

The port of Calais had not changed as much as she thought it might have done, but Leah still wished she had paid more attention when she travelled with her mother and father.

She hoped it was simply a case of follow my leader.

Either side of the two lanes of cars that had left the ferry ahead of her, there were four police officers scrutinising all the cars, but they were not stopping every one. Leah knew she would be one of the unlucky ones. No, it wasn't a question of luck – or bad luck – because it happened every time anything needed to be checked. She was always stopped and she knew why.

She edged forward, her fingers caressing the passport on the seat next to her.

Although Peter had told her she had nothing to worry about because the passport was perfect in every way, she could feel the hairs on the back of neck prickling. Regardless of what he might have said, it was still her photograph shown against a false name.

Looking down at the passport, she remembered what he had said when she asked why she couldn't be who she was rather than assuming a different identity:

"It is for your safety," he said. "By becoming Amy Carpenter you will become a different person in more ways than one. Believe me, it is for the best."

"I don't understand," she had told him. "You're talking in riddles."

"Trust me," he said. "All will become clear."

Even though she didn't understand, she had accepted his explanation but she was fed up with being told *everything would become clear.*

It was the fact that he was able to get her a proper passport, a driving licence, insurance documentation and even the logbook for the car in her new name. Perhaps he already knew an Amy Carpenter and it was just a question of matching her photograph. He had assured her that all the documentation would withstand the closest scrutiny and she was not to worry.

"Bonjour, Mademoiselle, your passport please," the middle-aged gendarme said through the open window.

Leah handed him the false passport, offering him a 'bonjour' and a smile in return.

"To where are you going, please?" he asked, looking from the photograph to her, his face expressionless.

"Germany."

"Av' you anyzing to declare, Mademoiselle?"

"No," she said, although she wasn't sure whether carrying so much cash was actually allowed.

"Proceed," the gendarme said with a slight wave of his hand, "and Mademoiselle, drive carefully and on ze right of ze road."

"I will and thank you."

"*Mon plaisir*," he said, allowing a slight smile to creep on to his face.

Leah selected first gear then swore when she stalled the car. She looked at the gendarme feeling her cheeks flush as she turned the ignition key. The gendarme's smile broke into a grin and Leah guessed that he was used to people feeling nervous in his presence.

"I'll drive carefully," she said.

"Bon!" he replied, with another wave of his hand.

After navigating the roundabouts on the other side of the port, she picked up the main Paris to Bruges *autoroute*. Having accelerated to the national speed limit she settled down for the three and a half hour drive to Germany.

Feeling a little more confident, she reached for her sunglasses from the passenger seat, and after switching on the radio she pushed a cassette into the recess.

Roy Orbison's unique tones filled the car.

The forty cigarettes she bought on the ferry were lying on the passenger seat. Selecting one from the open packet she lit it and exhaled through the open window.

Giving up would happen, but not yet.

She smiled as her thoughts went back to that first day ... and night with Peter.

Late October 1993

Chapter Six

Leah agreed to have dinner with Peter.

She had previously arranged to go for a drink with a couple of friends but she was sure they would understand. Peter was far too good an opportunity to miss. As she walked back to her digs she could not help smiling when she realised that during tea she had done all the talking which meant she actually knew nothing about him. He asked all the questions and she provided all the answers.

There were no stony silences.

She would find out more about him during the evening.

The house she shared with three other undergraduates seemed to be empty when she opened the front door, but then she heard voices coming from the communal living room down the corridor.

Leah's bedroom was supposed to be the dining room but the landlord had made it into a bedroom so that he could get the maximum rent. She did not mind because it was actually the biggest room in the house but it could be a bit noisy when she was trying to work.

Before deciding what she was going to wear this evening, Leah went into the kitchen to make herself a coffee. She certainly hadn't looked her best when Peter met her by the river this afternoon.

"Oh! Hi Leah," Sandy said, coming into the kitchen. "Your mother called."

Leah's hand shot up to her mouth. "Oh, shit!" she said. "She always calls at five o'clock on a Sunday and I forgot."

"There you go," Sandy said, flicking on the switch for the kettle that Leah had just boiled.

There was no love lost between Leah and Sandy.

They had shared the house with two others since the start of the second year, and initially they all got on magnificently well, but then some money went missing and it created an air of distrust among them. A few weeks later, Leah could have sworn somebody had been in her room and rifled through her drawers. Then one of the other girls was sure her mail had been tampered with.

By a process of elimination, the culprit had to be Sandy, and it was Leah, chosen by the other two as their representative, who pointed the finger of suspicion at Sandy. Nothing was ever proved, but Sandy never forgave Leah and the air had been icy between them ever since.

"I've just boiled that," Leah told her.

Sandy shrugged. "Sorry for living," she said.

Leah had learnt to ignore Sandy's childish behaviour so she carried on making her own coffee. Anyway, she had an evening with Peter to look forward to.

There was no way she was going to get into an argument.

"Is Maggie in?" she asked, popping a couple of sweeteners into a mug. She never had sugar in tea but always put sweeteners in coffee because she found the taste quite bitter.

Unlike her relationship with Sandy, Leah and Maggie got on extremely well. She was one of the group Leah was supposed to be going out with this evening.

"No," Sandy said.

"Okay." Leah picked up the mug of coffee and walked out of the kitchen just as Maggie came in through the front door.

"Hi, Maggie," she said, indicating her room with her eyes. Once inside she said, "I see Sandy's in one of her moods."

"When isn't she?"

Maggie was everything that Leah wasn't.

She was tall, large, and dark – her mother was Spanish. She was also one of the kindest and most genuine people Leah had ever met. Maggie sat on the bed as Leah put her coffee on the dressing table before sitting down so that she could peer at herself in the mirror.

"Do you mind if I cry off tonight?" Leah said, putting her finger on an almost invisible blemish on her cheek.

Maggie leant back against the wall.

"Who is he?" she said, her voice resigned.

Leah turned round, smiling.

"What makes you think it's a he?"

"When isn't it? You have every man in the town drooling over you. You're so lucky, especially after you've just dumped Mark."

"I did not dump him. We reached a mutual understanding."

"A mutual understanding my fat bottom, you told him to get lost. Anyway who is this unfortunate gullible male?" she added before Leah could comment.

Leah hesitated. "I don't really know. I only met him a few hours ago. His name's Peter, Peter Bennett, but he *is* rather nice."

Leah's eyes were wide open.

The ceiling was a dim grey haze above her, and she couldn't hear a thing.

Why had she done it?

Why had she broken the one cardinal rule that up to that point was, for her, so important? She hadn't drunk too much, taken drugs or been simply swept off her feet, but she did know from the moment she met Peter this evening for dinner that they would end up in bed.

And she was right.

No matter how often during the preceding few hours she told herself she would be doing the wrong thing, she knew her willpower would let her down. It had never happened before, and she was sure it would never happen again.

So why had it happened this time?

What was so special about Peter bloody Bennett?

Damn him.

It wasn't even his fault. She could not blame him and nor did she want to. There was nobody to blame but herself.

Fault?

Blame?

Why was she thinking these words? It was she who suggested she would like to see the inside of his flat, who invaded his personal space, who kissed him first. And it was she who did not resist when he responded as any man would have responded.

Now the chase was so dramatically over in less than seven hours, would he disappear? Would he promise to call her, a call that would never happen? Would he look at her as though she was just another conquest, a cheap thrill, an unbelievably easy lay?

She deserved whatever he did, thought, or said.

Perhaps he would say nothing; maybe he would simply ignore her.

She could still feel her body glowing under the duvet, the aftermath of the most exquisite experience she had ever had … not that there were that many to compare him with. There was Mark, with whom she had split less than a week ago, and Alan, although she had thought Alan was her future husband but perhaps seventeen had been a little young to make such decisions. She remembered going home after the first time with Alan and she was sure her mother guessed what she had been doing.

Was that why she felt the way she did?

Was it guilt?

Was she supposed to feel this way after she had initiated what had happened?

As Peter unzipped her dress, he did ask her if she was sure and without hesitating she said yes, and she was. As he led her into the bedroom when she was clad in only her bra and pants, he asked again and she said yes again, this time with some impatience.

God, had that really been her?

He treated her as though she was the most delicate porcelain vase; his hands and fingers were like feathers on her skin. When she felt the time was right, did she really straddle him in anticipation? He looked up at her and asked again if she was sure, and after she nodded he proceeded to make her feel sensations that no man had ever made her feel before. She floated on air and wished he would never stop.

He did stop but only after he made sure that she could not want for more … when every nerve ending in her body quivered with absolute desire. He put a fingertip on her lips in an attempt to silence her but this had only generated a new sensation, a new discovery and a new awareness of her own betrayal.

Yes, her body glowed and no, she did not regret what they had done, but also she did not want him to reject her, to take what she was so willing to give and then just walk out of her life.

Leah turned her head slowly so that she could look at him in the dim light. She felt his thigh against hers, his hand resting gently on her tummy and the warmth of his breath against her shoulder, but she did not expect to see his eyes watching her as she fought with her conscience.

"Hello," he said, a flicker of a smile on his lips as his hand moved across her tummy, his fingers tickling her.

She did not know what to say. Should she say she was sorry? She wanted to say that she regretted what they had done, but she would not have meant either lament, so instead she said nothing. She actually wanted to say thank you – to thank him for the most fantastic and sensual experience she had ever had.

But that would not have been appropriate either, so she continued with her silence.

His fingers glided over her rib cage, moving on her skin like silk in a breeze. She closed her eyes, the tip of her tongue moistening her lips as she struggled to stay calm, though inwardly she was screaming at him to touch her again, to make her feel as though she was the only woman he had ever cared for, the only woman he ever wanted.

"Open your eyes," he said, his index finger now gently tracing a line between her breasts.

She did as he asked.

He was still smiling. "Anything I might say would be an understatement, so shall we just accept that if neither of us ever makes love to anyone ever again, it wouldn't matter? That was something else and may never be repeated except between us?"

Leah nodded slowly, thinking what a lovely thing it was to say.

"I didn't bite your tongue off, did I?" he said.

"No … no, not my tongue," she said, as a smile came to her own lips and to her eyes.

His hand drifted upwards to the side of her face, and then behind her neck as he slowly pulled her towards him, his lips on hers, his body against hers.

Leah fell in love for the first time.

Maybe it was because she felt this way after knowing him for less than twelve hours that gave her such a conscience. Maybe having sex with him was minor by comparison and was just part of how she felt.

July 1994

Chapter Seven

An hour after leaving Calais, Leah crossed the border into Belgium. Although told she would have to leave the uncompleted *autoroute* at *Ghyvelde*, cross the border and then rejoin the *autoroute* at *Veurne*, she thought she was lost.

The road she was on ran alongside a canal and for some reason it was not what she expected, so it wasn't until she saw some buildings in the middle of the road, which she assumed was the French/Belgian border, did she begin to relax.

She smiled to herself.

Seeing the end of the first stage of her journey made her feel more relaxed. In Dover, and as she left the ferry in Calais, she had felt nervous but now she was pleased to see the next passport check. Close enough to see the border police stopping cars ahead of her she was, this time, unconcerned … but hopefully not complacent.

Unexpectedly, the French border police waved her through without even a glance in her direction. She still had her passport in her hand and kept it there while in the short piece of no-man's land between France and Belgium. The Belgian border policeman at least looked at her, but then with a disinterested wave of his hand indicated that she should proceed.

For once luck was on her side.

She relaxed even further, deciding that her concern was more to do with driving on the right-hand side of the road than feeling lost.

She had driven on the *autoroute* since leaving Calais so driving on the wrong side of the road had not been a problem, but once she left the motorway and with cars passing her only feet away to her left, she found it frightening and unnerving.

She shrugged and peered through the windscreen expecting to see at any moment the sign that would take her back onto the *autoroute.* She kept checking her mirror because she knew she was driving more slowly than she would in England.

It was a strange car, on a strange road in a strange country. Perhaps because it was right-hand drive with British number plates, other drivers would make allowances ... especially when they saw that she was young, blonde and female!

Let them think what they wanted.

After ten minutes she saw a sign for the *autoroute.* As her confidence returned she accelerated a little.

Not far to go now.

Well, maybe another couple of hours but Peter had told her that once she was in Belgium it was motorway all the way to Germany and it was only the last couple of miles that would be on normal roads.

There wasn't a lot of traffic on the Belgian *autoroute* so her mind rushed back again, back to how she had felt after she and Peter made love for the first time.

All he had done that afternoon was ask her to have tea with him and they had finished up in bed.

October - December 1993

Chapter Eight

After lying in bed on that first night wondering what she had done ... well, she knew what she had done but wasn't sure why she had done it ... Leah did not subsequently feel the need to regret for one second, her early – very early – sexual encounter with Peter.

If anything, the magic that occurred that first time simply went from strength to strength and to such an extent that at one stage she wondered if she was ever going to complete her degree.

She became so besotted with him that her mind could not concentrate on anything else.

When she was supposed to wax lyrical about a particular aspect of human behaviour, she found her mind wandering back to the last time she and Peter had made love.

At last she admitted that she was totally and utterly smitten.

Every second she was awake she thought about him and just before she went to sleep, and when she wasn't with him, she willed herself to dream about him. Even when she could feel the warmth of his body next to hers, she prayed that in her dreams he would be there.

She accepted and he would have to learn that she was head over heels in love with him.

She moved in with him after only four weeks.

Maggie told her she was being stupid but Sandy just smirked, her envy very obvious. Leah never questioned, nor did Peter ever tell her, how somebody working towards his PhD could afford such a nice flat in North Bailey at the top of Saddler Street, one of the most expensive areas of Durham. She did not ask because she did not want to know. She found out later that he didn't tell her because he did not want her to discover the truth. If she had asked he would have told her that he had inherited a lot of money from a maiden aunt who had thought the sun shone out of wherever he might have been.

But as Christmas approached all was not as rosy as she hoped it would be. Her disappointment came from a suggestion that during the Christmas break Peter might like to spend a couple of days with her at her parents' house in Marshfield. Peter declined and asked her to accept it was too early in their relationship for him to meet her parents.

"I've fallen in love with you, Leah," he told her, "and I want to be with you all the time, but let's wait until you've finished your degree. When I meet your mum and dad I want them to accept me for what I am and not somebody they think might just be using you while you are vulnerable."

"Me vulnerable? What do you mean? They wouldn't think that ..."

"University relationships, that's what I meant ... they happen. And are you so sure they would understand? I'm nearly ten years older than you. I've been out there and seen life, while you're still closeted in this constant academic environment. Let's get that over and then perhaps it'll be the right time to move on."

"You might be ten years –"

"I know what you're going to say but trust me on this one. We are only talking a matter of months before you get your wish."

Reluctantly, Leah agreed with his logic and spent most of the Christmas break feeling utterly miserable. She tried her best for her mum and dad but she knew from the looks her mother kept on giving her that she was aware that something was wrong, that there was something on her daughter's mind. Her father, bless him, remained in blissful ignorance no doubt putting her moodiness down to a mixture of her approaching final exams and a cycle that for him explained every female oddity.

If Peter thought she had been closeted in an academic environment he would see reality when he eventually met her father. Although now retired from the army, he was still a military man from the top of his head to the tips of his toes and her mother had become, as far as Leah was concerned, a military clone. They both lived to standards that were more applicable to the turn of the last century than being only a few years away from the turn of the next century.

One day, Leah believed, she would be grateful for the strict upbringing but now was not the time. In many ways, her desire to take Peter home for Christmas had been in satisfaction of her need to show some rebelliousness. She generated her own embarrassment when she imagined what her parents' reaction would be if they knew what their daughter had been doing.

Sleeping with a boy once would be bad enough, but with a man ten years older than her and every night – except when he was away that is – well, that just wouldn't be happening.

Each time she tried to understand her feelings she became so confused that she resorted to a non-explanation. Her previous relationships had involved a lot of groping, experimentation and quite a lot of amusement but they had all been part of growing up, of maturing. She really liked some of the boys, because that is all they were, boys. But they had never been anything special, anything that made her swoon; none had kept her from her sleep at night … or her studies.

None had made her scream.

Until she met Peter.

He was different.

He was so different, so unbelievably different that immediately after the first night they slept together Leah decided she would have done anything for him. She had been so worried, so concerned he would regard her as having been easy and discard her as quickly as … as what? She couldn't think of a word that fitted properly into her thoughts. He had been marvellous, absolutely incredible. And her worst fears were dashed the moment he looked at her and asked her to open her eyes, saying exactly the right things as if he knew what she was thinking.

Regrets?

No, she did not have any regrets and nor would she ... ever.

July 1994

Chapter Nine

Christ!

She must concentrate.

Leah almost missed the signs that told her to slow down as the *autoroute* swung round to the right to merge with the Oostende – Bruxelles motorway. She couldn't say she wasn't warned about this junction: her lane merged with the fast lane of the other road. *Nincompoops*, she thought, *why can't they design things so that they are driver friendly*?

Then again, where the M40 merged with the M42 south of Birmingham was the same, but at least there she was on the right side of the road. She shrugged when she realised the right side of the road was on the left!

Having quickly but not that easily crossed into the inside lane of the new *autoroute*, she returned to her reverie.

April 1994

Leah was disappointed when Peter turned down the invitation to spend Christmas with her and her parents, but she accepted that perhaps he was right: maybe it would be best for them to wait. As compensation, he did suggest they go away for a few days during the Easter recess and Leah jumped at the opportunity.

She would remember those five days they spent together ... forever.

Dreams did come true.

They flew to Miami for a very long weekend and Peter paid for everything. The hotel was small but beautiful and he forked out the extra for a room with a view, and what a view. She stood at the window watching the world go by for what seemed like hours, wishing that it would never end. The traffic and pedestrians below were noiseless, but intriguing … and being able to see the blue of the Atlantic Ocean above the row of palm trees made it all so special.

They ate, drank and danced the five days away and when they weren't out, they enjoyed each other. One thing they did not have was much sleep.

Leah cried when the aircraft took off for the return flight.

It was during their few days away that Peter first introduced the possibility that after she had graduated she could take a bit of time out and do him a big favour. At first she thought he was joking ... maybe not exactly joking, but certainly not serious.

Sitting in an Italian waterside restaurant, thinking they didn't have a care in the world, Peter suddenly asked: "Leah, how good is your German?"

She smiled. "What?" she said as she sipped her red wine. "Why do you suddenly ask that?"

He shrugged. "I'm interested in everything about you, and I remember you telling me the day we met that you spoke German. I think we were having tea at the time."

"I told you lots of things that day and you told me absolutely nothing, and I still don't know that much about you. I know you're thirty years old, I know you are an only child, I know both your parents are dead, and I know you originate from the Winchester area, but other than that I don't know a lot more. We seem to have talked about me a lot, but very little about you. I don't even know anything about previous girlfriends." She paused. "I've never asked you before, I just presumed, but you're not married, are you?"

"No," he said, smiling, "I'm not married and I'm surprised you think I would bring you here for a long weekend if I were."

"Yes, I'm sorry, but have you ever been married?"

"No."

"So why didn't you tell me?"

"Tell you that I wasn't married?"

She nodded.

"Because I didn't think it was necessary. I didn't tell you I don't like tripe, black pudding or haggis either, did I?" he said, smiling. "And anyway, you're a lot more interesting than I am. I'm just me, a boring researcher who ought to find a proper job. Well, I have a job but because of the research I'm doing it's more on a consultancy basis at the moment rather than full time. And that's what I want to talk to you about, but I think I'm being boring."

"You're not boring, and if you've got the sort of money that means coming out here for a week is just a drop in the ocean, then you're *certainly* not boring." She smiled and put her hand on his to let him know she was only joking.

"I might have borrowed the money," he said.

"No! That flat in Durham, the car you drive, your clothes. Everything about you smells of money. The rich aunt you told me about eventually must have really taken to you."

"An only child, whose parents were killed in a car crash, a widowed aunt whose husband left her a fortune, generated a not unacceptable windfall."

"A *windfall* he calls it," Leah said.

Peter smiled. "Anyway that's enough about me. This proposal I have for you isn't dependent upon you being able to speak German but it would help. So how good is your German?"

Leah narrowed her eyes playfully. "You tell me what this proposal is and I might, just might, answer your question."

She was intrigued.

There had been a number of occasions, even at the very beginning of their relationship, when she was aware that he was assessing her. She had wanted to ask what it was all about but had decided he would tell her when he was ready.

It now appeared that the time had come.

He slowly picked up her hand and let his fingers play with hers. The smile left his face. "There's something you might be able to do for me."

"What? When?" Leah asked in a rush, eager to please.

"The *what* will have to wait and the *when* will really be up to you, but it won't be until after you've finished your thesis and handed it in."

"Can't you even give me a clue?" She looked at her hand in his.

Peter took a deep breath. "It would be in Germany and it could involve you using their language. That's why I need to know."

He let go of her hand as the waiter brought their main courses. He ordered another bottle of wine and they started to eat. Both had ordered lasagne and salad.

"I'm intrigued. What could I possibly do for you in Germany?" Leah said, lifting the fork to her mouth. "Umm, this is delicious."

"I can't tell you much more at the moment but I do need to know –"

"How good my German is," she said. "Well," she continued after taking another mouthful of lasagne and catching with her napkin a little melted cheese as it dripped down her chin. "I'm sorry. I wouldn't say that I could pass as a German, *aber mein Deutsch ist sehr gut, verstehst du*?" He nodded and smiled. "I think I told you I did it at school ..."

"Did what?" he asked.

"Behave," she told him.

He inclined his head knowingly, his smile so infectious that Leah smiled too.

"I think I told you on that first day, daddy was in Germany a lot and I really picked it up from there."

Peter became serious again. "Would you say you could understand technical German?"

She stopped eating. "Technical German?" Her eyes widened. "What? Engines and things?"

"No, it would be more general than that."

She frowned. "I think a lot of it is probably pretty much the same in any language, especially if it's to do with computers."

"So you think you could cope?"

"Well, yes, I suppose I could, but it's not easy to be certain without knowing what you've got planned." She held Peter's eyes for a second. "It's nothing illegal, is it?"

He grinned. "Good Lord no, but as I said you're going to have to wait for the detail." He put his knife and fork down on an empty plate. "I need to talk to a few other people and get their go ahead."

"Sounds absolutely intriguing, and what are you smiling at?" she asked, finishing off the last of her salad.

"Just thinking how lucky I am."

"That's a nice thing to say."

"It's a nice way to be," he said.

"What shall we do for the rest of the evening?"

He looked at his watch. "It's just after ten. We've got three days of our holiday left. We were dancing last night, so what about strolling along the beach for an hour or so and then having an early night?"

"What sort of early night?"

"That sort of early night. You know – you and me and, well, not a lot else."

"Sounds good to me," Leah said with a little smile on her face.

About thirty minutes later they were walking hand-in-hand along what Peter had referred to as a sidewalk, when it happened.

They were on the Lummus Park side of Ocean Drive when Leah said she needed to get some cigarettes. They crossed Ocean Drive near 8th Street and cut down a side street to look for a drug store.

Perhaps they had walked too far.

The street lighting wasn't as good as it had been on the main drive and that is when out of a dark alleyway a couple of figures appeared and blocked their way.

Peter and Leah stopped.

The two men were only feet in front of them. They were wearing dark clothing but had not bothered to cover their faces. One of the men was white and the other black.

The white man was holding a gun and the black man a knife.

The black man spoke.

"Give us yo' fuckin' wallet, man," he said.

As Peter took hold of Leah's arm and slowly moved her behind him, a scene from the film *Crocodile Dundee* immediately leapt into her mind followed instantaneously by the incongruity of her thought processes.

She was terrified.

The muggers were looking very nervous, the sweat gleaming on their faces.

"Yo' fuckin' wallet, man," the black man ordered again.

"And why should I do that?" Peter said calmly.

Leah was cowering behind him, her fingers gripping the sleeve of his shirt.

The white man lifted the gun so it was pointing at Peter's head.

"'Cos if yo' don't, man, yo'll be did, man, then we'll have fun wid the liddle lady before she gits slotted."

The black man was the taller of the two, about the same height as Peter, and was also the more nervous. He kept on glancing at the white man, who, from the look in his eyes, was high on drugs.

What happened next was over as soon as it started.

Peter kicked the gun out of the white man's hand and before his accomplice could move he crumpled to the ground without making a sound. The black man lunged at Peter but he too finished up on the ground.

"Have you got anything to tie them up with?" Peter said, his voice still calm.

"What?" Leah asked, leaning against the wall, not believing what she had just witnessed.

"Are you all right?"

"All right? Yes … yes, I'm all right. Peter, what … what did you do?"

Peter shook his head. "They were easy."

The white man groaned as Peter turned him over and pulled the belt from his jeans. He tied the man's arms and hands behind his back then turned to the prostrate black man and did the same.

There had been nobody else about during the exchange, but as Leah looked up she could see a police car approaching about two hundred yards away. She stepped off the pavement into the road and started waving her arms. Peter stepped out after her and took hold of the hand she was waving.

"No, don't Leah. We don't want to get involved."

"But they tried to –"

"I know what they tried to do." He pulled her back onto the pavement.

The two men, hidden from the road by a parked car, were both groaning.

"Come here," Peter said.

He took Leah in his arms and kissed her.

The police car slowed down but then moved on down the road, sounding its siren once as if in approval of what its occupants had seen.

"Why didn't you –?"

"If the police got involved we would be needed as witnesses and we fly back to the UK in a couple of days. These two aren't going to be causing any more trouble tonight." He bent down and picked up the gun. "It's real enough," he said. He ejected the magazine and Leah wondered where he had learned to do that. "And there are bullets," he added, "real ones." He tucked the gun in his belt under his shirt before picking up the knife.

"Yo' fuckin' –" the white man shrieked as Peter stepped on his exposed ankle.

"Just stop the noise and listen carefully," Peter said in a conversational voice. "You are both lucky I didn't do you any permanent damage."

The black man just stared at him.

Peter dragged them one by one into the alley they had appeared from and dumped them next to some overflowing dustbins. He used a length of flex he found to tie their ankles together.

"Have a good night's sleep and all being well you'll be found before they come to collect the rubbish. Then again, they might treat you as the trash you are anyway."

Peter put the knife in his belt and joined Leah who was standing with her mouth open having watched but not believed what she had seen.

He took her arm and together they walked back the way they had come.

"The cigarettes can wait," he said.

After a couple of minutes' silence, she asked, "Where ... where did you learn to do that?"

Her voice was shaking.

"With a couple of amateurs like that, you don't have to know a lot. Let's just say I'm quite capable of taking care of myself. Would you like a drink?"

"Yes, I think I would."

"Let me just get rid of this gun and knife and then we'll find a bar."

Chapter Ten

An hour later when they walked into the hotel Leah felt in a complete daze and just a little drunk. Consuming too much alcohol too quickly probably wasn't the answer, but as she had finished her second whisky and dry ginger, she reasoned that it was the only way she could cope with what had happened, so she had a third drink.

Peter on the other hand seemed to stay completely composed, drinking little by comparison, neither stopping nor discouraging Leah from her binge drinking.

"That will have been pretty traumatic for you," he said as he closed the door to their hotel room. "I acted the way any man would have done. You were being threatened and I had to defend you," he added.

Leah narrowed her eyes. "I … I think most men would have simply handed over their wallets."

Peter shook his head. "Didn't you see the way that white guy was looking at you? My wallet and its contents were necessary but incidental to what he had planned for you. We were both going to be the losers and in a big way."

Leah began to shake at the very thought of what could have happened.

Regardless of the anaesthetising effect of the alcohol the shock was setting in. At the time of the attempted mugging she felt completely useless, knowing that if she tried to help she would have only got in the way. She screwed up her eyes as images of what could have occurred shot into her mind.

"I need a hug," she whispered, her eyes still closed.

"I think we could both do with a hug," Peter said, crossing the room and closing the curtains.

Leah stared at his back. Rather than waiting for him she walked towards the bathroom, stripping off her clothes at the same time.

"I thought you wanted a hug," Peter said from behind her.

"I do," she told him without turning round, "but it's more than a hug I need." As she reached the bathroom door she stopped. "You can get rid of those," she said pointing at her jeans and T-shirt on the floor. "And these," she added, removing her underwear. "Get rid of them all, please. Just looking at them will remind me."

She went into the bathroom, closed the door and rested her hands against the wash-basin. The mirror didn't help. She looked and felt drunk: her eyes were bloodshot and her skin had a pallid sheen.

She didn't normally drink that much, well, not as quickly. But she had needed the effect the whisky would have on her. She had never experienced anything as upsetting as this before. What would have happened if Peter hadn't disarmed both men as he did? And where did he learn to do things like that?

But he was right: their attackers had not stood a chance.

Going into the shower cubicle she turned the water on, adjusting the temperature to the hottest she could stand. Three times she washed her hair and body in an attempt to cleanse herself of the thought of what could have happened.

They made love slowly.

It was at the pace she needed.

At first she shuddered as Peter touched her but gradually she relaxed until she needed him completely.

"No," he said as she rolled onto her back. "I think you need to feel dominant on this occasion."

She moved so that she was sitting astride him.

"Are you using your advanced psychological theories on me," she said, smiling down at him.

"I don't think men are your flavour of the month at the moment," he said running his hands along her thighs.

"Aren't you being rather presumptuous?"

"Just get on with it and we'll see," he said, smiling.

Ten minutes later Leah collapsed exhausted next to him.

"You were half right," she said sleepily as she snuggled up to him and closed her eyes.

"I won't ask which half," he said.

"You shouldn't have to," she said.

"Then I won't," he said.

July 1994

Leah was becoming more confident.

Surprisingly, she was finding driving on the continent more predictable than in England. Lane discipline seemed better and although drivers tended to drive a good deal faster she felt they were more aware of what was going on around them. But then again perhaps that was why she was feeling more positive.

She picked up the signs for the Antwerp *autoroute* well in advance and was prepared when the filter took her in a sweeping curve up and over the Bruxelles *autoroute* and onto the road for The Netherlands and Germany.

After concentrating for the next ten minutes so that she was sure she was still heading for Antwerp rather than Ghent – a none too easy accomplishment for first-timers Peter had told her – she thought back to what had happened once she and Peter returned to the UK after their eventful short holiday.

Late April 1994

Each time she attempted to find out why Peter had been so self-assured when dealing with the two muggers, he became dismissive of not only what had happened but also his own actions.

He kept on saying: "It's what any man would have done."

In her mind it certainly wasn't but after several attempts she gave up and put it to the back of her mind until such time that she would tell her friends what a hero he was.

"So, have you had your exam results?" Peter asked her one evening when they were back into the routine of university life. "You seem to be acting particularly smug this evening."

"Smug?" Leah retorted. "I've never been accused of being smug before."

"It's not an accusation," he said, "but I think there's something you're not telling me."

Leah broke eye contact, annoyed with herself for not being able to hide her news from him: he had seen straight through her planned ruse.

"Maybe there is and maybe there isn't," she said.

She picked up her mug of coffee.

They were sitting in the kitchen in Peter's flat.

It was still Peter's flat not *their* flat.

Initially she had kept on her room just in case things changed, but after returning from Florida she moved out completely. She did not have any trouble finding somebody to take her place and therefore pick up the rent, and despite Maggie's protestations and declarations that Leah would live to regret the decision to move in with Peter, she did it anyway.

There *were* no regrets, Leah told herself constantly: she just wished Peter would let her into his real life and not just the one he wanted her to see. All she knew was that as well as being a mature student he also did this consultancy work. But what sort of consultancy it was she did not have the faintest idea other than it might have something to do with Germany, and she might be able to help him in some way.

She would simply have to be patient.

"I see," Peter said with the hint of a smile creeping onto his face. "You're still looking smug so I can only presume it is good news."

"All right," Leah said, putting her mug on the table. "I did pass all my exams, and," she added, holding up a finger as Peter leaned across the table towards her, "I also got the required grades to go on to my dissertation for an honours."

"That's great," Peter said, kissing her across the table. "What a clever girl you are!"

Leah believed it was as a result of her high spirits and the subsequent celebratory meal they went out for, that he chose that evening to give her the outline of what he was asking her to do.

She had three months to complete her thesis and then she would be ready.

Well, as ready as she would ever be.

Chapter Eleven

"I don't understand," Leah said, screwing up her face. "Are you telling me that all this PhD and stuff is a cover? You came to Durham looking for ..." She turned away from him. "Not only do I not understand, I don't bloody believe it either. I feel used," she said, sulkily.

Peter ran a finger down her spine, slowly tracing each individual vertebra. She loved the feeling his touch generated in her and she didn't want him to stop, but she felt it was a ploy to get her to agree to what seemed to be a harebrained scheme.

His finger reached the base of her spine before moving upwards again.

Why had he told her he was researching for his PhD?

"Will you stop doing that," she said.

He didn't.

Except for the Christmas after they first met, she had spent nearly every hour possible with him, but he had also been away a lot, sometimes for four or five days. She gave up asking where he had been because all he ever told her was that she would find out, but not yet.

His fingers reached her neck and then started their downward journey again.

"Peter, I said, will you stop doing that."

"Forget I ever broached the subject," he said quietly as his fingers tickled the base of her spine. "Meeting you was not planned. I didn't go looking for you. When I saw you sitting down by the river I was immediately attracted to you, and I wanted to get to know you. It was only after you told me about yourself that –" He breathed in deeply. "No," he said. "Forget it."

He fell silent.

His hand slipped over her hip onto her thigh.

July 1994

Leah slowed down as she saw brake lights going on ahead of her.

She could see the outline of the Kennedy Tunnel in the distance as the queuing traffic disappeared into it like a long red glow-worm into a hole.

Every lane was nose-to-tail with cars and lorries.

She smiled.

He had even been right about this, she thought.

"You'll find the traffic lighter than in the UK but when they do have a hold-up they do it in big style. You'll be okay until you hit the outskirts of Antwerp but that could be the first place you'll meet a problem."

She could remember his every word.

Late April 1994

His fingers were moving up the inside of her thigh.

"How … how do I know you're not just saying that?" Leah mumbled into the pillow, almost on the point of tears but still enjoying his touch. "How … how do I know our entire relationship hasn't been a sham?"

"You don't," he said, his fingers stopping their movement. "But I thought we'd moved on from that sort of thing. That's why I –" With tight lips he glanced up at the ceiling. "Look, Leah, I said forget it, so let's do exactly that and pretend I didn't even mention it to you."

He took his hand away and rolled onto his back.

"Forget it," he said again.

Leah twisted her body towards him. He was staring at the ceiling, his hands behind his head.

"But it's spying! What you're asking me to do is industrial espionage. You're asking me to do something illegal."

He turned his face towards her and smiled, shaking his head. "I wouldn't ask you to do anything that was either illegal or dangerous. This is neither. All I was going to ask you to do was keep your ear to the ground and if you heard anything that might be of use, just to let me know. But as I said let's …"

"We'd also be apart. You said it could take up to six months or even longer."

He took hold of her hand and kissed her fingers. "Yes, if you went ahead with what I ask, it could take that long. But –"

"And why do you need somebody like me?"

"That's simple to answer. I've already been over there asking questions myself, so my face is known. I would have to keep out of the way and to allay suspicion we could never be seen together. If you did do it, nobody would know the connection between us. Obviously you must never mention my name. In other words we would never have met … in theory. But we would be able to meet every now and again … but well away from –"

"But isn't it illegal?" Leah asked. What he'd described sounded illegal.

"No, it most definitely is not, not in any way, shape or form. And I'm just a little upset that you think I would involve you in anything like that."

"So why did you lie to me about doing research for your doctorate?"

"I didn't lie. It is something I want to do and that's why I'm in Durham. I know it sounds bizarre but I'm researching what research would be necessary to see if I can fit it in around the other things I do."

"That doesn't make sense … and what do you do?"

"As I told you, I'm a consultant," Peter said.

"That tells me nothing. I'm totally confused."

He shrugged. "I'm sorry but I'm very limited as to what I can tell you."

He rolled onto his side.

As he looked into her eyes, he moved his hand so that his fingers stroked her breast.

"That's pretty obvious," she said as she took a deep breath and closed her eyes. "And … and you reckon I'll be able to … to … will you stop doing that, Peter. I can't think."

Peter took his hand away but Leah immediately grabbed it and put it back.

"Look …" he started to say.

"All right," she said huskily, "I'll do … I'll do it … but only because it's you and only if … if you promise that …"

"Promise what?"

Leah opened her eyes. "Only if you promise that afterwards you won't just dump me."

"There's no chance of that. You're too important to me."

Moving closer to him she tried to see beyond what those grey-green eyes were telling her.

She wanted to believe him but more importantly she wanted to be with him, so she had to take the risk and do what he asked.

July 1994

Half an hour after entering the tunnel Leah was still stuck between a lorry in front of her and a white van behind her.

In the UK she would have tuned into a local radio station to find out the reason for the hold-up, but although she spoke German fluently, her Walloon (French) was poor and her Flemish (Belgian variant of Dutch) almost non-existent.

She lit another cigarette and listened to the Charlie Landsborough tape that was playing.

What he had asked her to do seemed a simple enough task – after she managed to get herself a job that is. She was more than willing to do what he asked but as its success depended on her getting a job it made the whole thing just a little reckless.

She was amazed … no, that was wrong because nothing Peter did should surprise her anymore because his planning and grasp of the detail were … incredible. However, it would all fall on its face if she did not get a job. It wasn't that she doubted her own ability, and she understood now why she needed to speak German, but if there were no jobs on offer then what was the point?

She selected first gear and moved forward a few yards.

The driver of the car to her left looked across at her and shrugged. As a smile crossed his face she smiled back at him. He reminded her of her father and her thoughts went back immediately to when she had gone to see her parents to tell them what her plans were.

June 1994

"Why do you want to go off to Germany?" her father asked while conducting some form of minor operation on the bowl of his pipe. "I would have thought you'd spent quite long enough over there when you were a child."

They were sitting in the garden in Marshfield.

It was a lovely house and when Leah first went to Durham, she would lie in bed thinking about what she had left. Even though she had been to boarding school and got used to being away, for some reason she was terribly homesick once she arrived in Durham. There was something grown-up about going to university. She missed her cosy bedroom, which was at the top of the house in Marshfield. From the small window she could see the church, and at night she used to lie in bed and listen to the church clock chiming every thirty minutes.

She missed her mother's cooking.

She missed Rory, their King Charles Spaniel, and she missed the smell of her father's pipe. When he worked up a full head of steam, she could smell that pipe even when she was in her bedroom with the door closed and he was downstairs in the drawing room.

"I was eighteen the last time I went out there, Daddy. I was hardly a child."

Her father's head shot back as his lighter seemed to take on the guise of a flame-thrower. "Still a child," he muttered, after getting the flame under control and dipping it into his pipe.

"I could be going a lot further away," she informed him. "Some of my friends are going to Australia and New Zealand ... I went to Australia during my gap year. Remember?"

Her father peered at her over his reading glasses. "It's Germany I don't understand."

"What are you two talking about?" her mother asked, coming up the steps from the house carrying a tray with a pot of tea, cups and saucers and a plate of her homemade scones.

"Germany, again," Leah said, raising her eyebrows and looking at her mother.

"Leave her alone, Bartie, she could be going a lot further afield ... again," her mother said.

"That's what I told him," Leah said, clearing a space on the table for the tray.

"I was simply asking why Germany, that's all. It seems a strange place for a young gel to go after university."

Leah had told them very little of the detail. They also knew nothing of Peter, and even though she had moped round the house the previous Christmas, her mother, who was the more astute, hadn't asked any questions.

After Peter had explained what he wanted her to do, he had asked her if she understood now why he could not do the normal thing and meet her parents.

Once she had moved in with Peter, she had been worried sick that her parents would turn up in Durham unexpectedly. She arranged with Maggie that if they did, she could pretend that she was still living in her old room. Her plan had many flaws, so it was rather fortunate that other than for her graduation, they had been unable to make the trip at any other time during her last semester.

Withholding the fact that she needed to be in Germany just a week after her graduation, didn't seem right but they would find out soon enough anyway. Fortunately Peter wasn't able to be there at the ceremony as he was needed in Germany, and at least Leah now knew that was where he had been going when he disappeared for days on end.

"We're in the EU now, Bartie," her mother said, fussing with the cups and saucers.

He took off his glasses. "What's that got to do with it?"

"Well, EU citizens can all work in each other's countries, can't they?"

Leah saw her father shake his head in the way that meant he was about to be defeated by female logic.

"Mummy is right, Daddy," Leah said. "I speak the language, and I just want six months or so on a sort of working holiday before I settle down to a career."

"What career?" her father asked, resuming the attack on the bowl of his pipe.

"Bartie," her mother said, looking genuinely shocked. "Don't start that again."

"Well, she hasn't had any job interviews and she doesn't even know what she wants to do."

"I'm still here, Daddy. You don't have to talk about me as though I'm already on the other side of the channel."

Her mother handed them each a cup of tea. "Just because you were in the army when you were twenty doesn't mean to say your only daughter is a lost cause because she doesn't know what she wants to do at nearly twenty-three."

"I prefer twenty-two, Mummy," Leah said as the two women exchanged smiles. "But I do know what I want to do. I've told you. I want to work for a couple of years to get a bit of capital and then go back to university to do my Masters."

"Is that what they call a mature student?" her father asked.

"Daddy, why are you being so horrid and hostile? I am an adult, and I know my own mind."

"He's not being hostile, darling," her mother said. "He's just showing how ignorant and intransigent he can be."

Mother and daughter exchanged knowing looks and they smiled again.

A change in the tone of her father's voice suddenly had her attention as he said, "I'm being neither of those things. I just want the best for you, Leah, that's all."

"I know you do, Daddy, and I want you to be proud of me, but I just need a break."

"But why Germany?" he asked again.

"It's quite simple. As I said, I speak the language. I should be able to get a job and I'll have a bit of independence."

"It's perfectly understandable, Bartie," her mother said. "Leah's got to learn to stand on her own two feet."

"I know she has, but ..."

Leah was quite surprised because she had expected a harder time from her mother rather than her father. She didn't like lying to them, although she wasn't really lying, she just wasn't telling them the whole truth, that's all. There was no need for them to know everything. How could she be independent if she told them everything? In six months she would go home and start looking for a job, a career. Maybe his reluctance was because she was so keen to do her Masters.

"Where are you going to live, darling?" her mother asked, helping herself to another scone.

It was the question that Leah had been dreading, but one she had expected. “I’ll find somewhere and there are plenty of *Gastättes* I can stay in until I do.”

“And who is going to pay?” her father asked.

“We are, Bartie,” her mother said. “Once Leah has found a job she can pay us back, can’t you darling?”

What could she say?

She was going to have thousands of *Deutschmarks* in the bank and she would be living rent-free. Nobody else would understand, let alone her parents.

“Of course I will. Just don’t worry about me,” she said.

Her mother smiled wanly. “We won’t, darling.”

Leah knew what her mother was actually saying was that they would worry about her all the time.

July 1994

Chapter Twelve

The traffic began to move.

Once out of the tunnel Leah quickly moved over to the inside lane to be sure she would be ready to take the right exit. She was looking for signs to *Liège* and then *Eindhoven.* The jam she was in seemed to disperse as quickly as it started and within five minutes she picked up the signs and her confidence returned.

She understood now.

Peter told her it was not only the fact that she could speak German extremely well but also because her father was an ex-senior officer in the British Army so she knew the jargon and her way about. She could not involve her father but there was bound to be someone she knew in the Joint Headquarters in *Rhinedahlen* near *Mönchengladbach* who could pull a few strings if it ever became necessary. It would have to be a last resort though, and Peter must never know that if she did find somebody she would revert to her proper identity.

She now had two passports: one as herself, Leah Carmichael, which she kept hidden in a zipped compartment in her bag, and the other as Amy Carpenter. She wished she had ignored Peter and used her proper identity from the beginning; she couldn't see what difference it would have made. Unbeknown to Peter, she still had her army dependant's identity card. She had kept it for sentimental reasons, telling her father that when it was time to hand it in, she had lost it and fortunately, after she spent hours searching for it, she discovered that it was still valid for another eight months. She smiled when she found it and thought of the doors it might open.

Anyway, now that she was nearly on the other side of Antwerp, she needed to think a little more about what Peter had asked her to do.

June 1994

"So all I have to do is get a job at this British Army ammunition depot and … what's it called again?" she asked. They were in the Gardener's Arms, a pub not far from Peter's flat. It was the evening after he first broached the subject in more detail.

Peter sighed openly. "3 Base Ammunition Depot," he said slowly. "It's a couple of miles from the flat I've rented for you in *Brüggen*."

"So somehow I've got to get a job in this 3 Base Ammunition Depot and then simply listen to all the local gossip and report what I hear back to you?" She did in fact know where the ammunition depot was because she had gone there once to watch a rugby match when she was on holiday from boarding school.

Peter shrugged. "In a nutshell, yes, that's all there is to it. As I told you, it'll be closing down in eighteen months or so as part of the British Army's withdrawal programme from Germany. Basically the Army and the Royal Air Force are downsizing and the closure of this depot is part and parcel of it all."

"And the real-estate will all be handed back to the Germans?"

"Yes. There are or were three RAF flying stations almost on the Dutch border – RAF *Wildenwrath* in the south near *Limburg* has already closed, RAF *Laarbruch* near *Weeze* in the north is due to close in 1999 and RAF *Brüggen* not far from *Roermond* in the centre and near where you'll be living, will close in a few years' time. This ammunition depot though, is the one I'm really interested in."

"Why?" Leah asked.

"The old RAF stations are likely to be used for a similar privatised or governmental function, you know, be kept as airfields, and there is a possibility that some remaining British Army units might move into RAF *Brüggen*."

"You seem to know an awful lot."

"I'm paid to know a lot."

Leah sipped her wine. "So with this depot, it's all to do with future commercial exploitation?"

"I know it sounds all a bit underhand but everybody is at it, so why should we be any different?" Peter said.

"By *at it* I presume you mean spying on each other. So who exactly is this *we* you keep on referring to?"

"It's best you don't know. As I told you, there is no need for you to know. It allows you to remain innocent should –"

"Innocent? I thought you said there was nothing illegal about it?" she asked, her apprehension returning.

"There isn't anything illegal about it but it's still better if you don't know."

"All right," Leah said a little reluctantly, "but how do I know what I should find out if I don't know who I'm doing it for?"

"You're doing it for me," Peter said. "The depot covers a vast area. It's bigger than the area occupied by Heathrow Airport and it's been shut off from the outside world for nearly fifty years. Once it's handed back to the Germans they'll be looking to develop the land. It's in a perfect position for another Euro-Disney site for example, and we want to –"

"Ah!" Leah said, narrowing her eyes. "Your first slip. You work for Euro-Disney," she added triumphantly.

Peter smiled. "No, I don't but my work is not dissimilar to what they do."

She narrowed her eyes again. "And this *we* you work for that is not dissimilar to Euro-Disney, puts people into universities in England to find gullible females to exploit their business potential, do they?"

"I've tried to explain to you what that was all about so in answer to your question, in a way, yes."

"In a way, yes?" She shook her head "You're going to have to do better than that I'm afraid. Your explanation of why you picked me up that day last autumn is still whirling round in –"

"I didn't pick you up as you put it. It was a case of mutual attraction –"

"Believe that if you must," she said with a smile. "I might be a gullible blonde female but I do have a few brain cells and what you're asking me to do coupled with the way you're asking me to do it, just doesn't compute. As I said earlier, is what you are asking me to do called industrial espionage?"

Peter returned her smile. "Not what I'd call it but in a way you're right. It's just a means of obtaining a little inside information, that's all. As I told you last night, there's no danger involved and certainly nothing illegal."

"And in a matter of weeks I've got to –"

"You haven't *got* to do anything," he said.

"I appreciate that. But in a matter of weeks I've got to worm my way into whatever organisation there is in this depot and get to know people sufficiently well for them to tell me what might be happening after the depot is handed back to the Germans."

"Yes. That's precisely what I'm asking you to do."

"And there's no other way you could find out what you need to know?" Leah finished her wine, looking at Peter with eyebrows raised.

He reached for her glass. "There are but ..."

"I was too good an opportunity to dismiss."

Peter's chair scraped on the floor as he stood up to go to the bar. "Once again, not how I would put it but if you were to say I'm making best use of the resources available, then I would agree."

"Oh, I'm a resource now, am I?"

Peter bent down and brushed his lips across hers. “I’m joking but you’re a resource in more ways than one, believe me.”

July 1994

Chapter Thirteen

Leah drove at seventy miles per hour.

Because she was getting closer to her destination, she found her apprehension increasing again. Peter had told her where she should collect the key to the flat and that she would find the fridge and cupboards stocked with the essentials. Everything appeared to be thoroughly organised but she still felt her nerves getting the better of her.

The identity switch was beginning to worry her more than anything else. Everything had gone smoothly so far but there was still that damn question ... why did she need to have another identity? She had known lots of British wives and some teenage children who had worked on the military net, so just because she was returning to Germany for a few months, why did she need to be someone else?

When she asked Peter for the umpteenth time about the passport, driving licence, bank account and all the other things that were in her pretend name, he had dismissed her concerns by saying, "Your dad was in the area wasn't he? It would be best if no-one who might have known him makes the connection. It's just a safeguard, that's all."

"It's a hell of a lot to do for just a safeguard, and my face goes with my proper name, surely –"

"You will have changed a lot since then, so what I'm doing is not for you and actually not for me either, so just accept that's the way it is. Take my word for it, a change of identity is necessary."

Dismissing questions about where he managed to get the false documentation he smiled, tapped his nose, and said, "Need to know."

So her protestations that it was all too much simply to avoid the chance of somebody making a connection came to nothing, and the suggestion that she might bump into somebody who did recognise her whether she had changed or not, got the same reaction. Each time he told her that if she didn't want to go ahead with what he was asking her to do she only had to say so.

But her feelings for him were still the same, which meant she didn't say no.

He was such a kind, gentle and considerate man, she would probably have done anything for him and she could not even add *within reason.* She loved being with him, she loved the way he treated her when they were out, the consideration he showed towards her when they were making love and how secure she felt with her life because he was part of it.

Everything she loved about him would explain to anybody who wanted to know, why she was in love with him.

Except there was nobody to explain it to; there was nobody who needed to know but her.

There was nothing about him to dislike, but she still did not really know him. He had only told her the bare minimum. Why? Had she really fallen in love with him? Maybe. But did she know what being *in love* meant? She had to assume that she did.

She loved her parents but that sort of love was different.

If he wasn't there for her in six months' time, in a year or whatever, then she would put it down to experience but an experience she would not have missed for the earth. Any new man in her life was going to have to be rather good to live up to what Peter had given her. Why was she thinking so negatively? He said he would be there, so why didn't she believe him?

Because she was so bloody nervous, that's why.

Leah moved into the outside lane to overtake a line of slower moving vehicles and immediately there was a Mercedes sitting almost in the boot of her car. She pressed down on the accelerator and saw the speed slowly build up to nearly ninety miles per hour, but still the Mercedes was there. She thought her car was a bit sluggish when she first drove it, but hadn't wondered why because she wasn't that technical.

The Mercedes was so close she could see the driver tapping his fingers on the steering wheel. She pulled in after passing the sixth lorry, glancing sideways as the Mercedes whooshed past her, its driver shaking his head as much as to say she had no right to be on the road.

She passed the signs for *Eindhoven*, hoping she would soon see *Venlo* signposted. She really was getting close. What she had left behind in England seemed now to be on the other side of the world, but because she had been to Germany so often, she did not feel as though she was going to a foreign country. Yet things would be different, especially after spending nearly three years in Durham. She would have to get used to the idiosyncrasies of German life again, but regardless of her current nervousness she accepted that maybe she was actually looking forward to it.

She hoped the flat would have a decent shower.

She remembered the bathroom in the last Army quarter in Germany her parents lived in. The water used to come out of the tap as though a jet engine was propelling it, and the shower was the same. She loved the way the water had bitten into her skin. She always felt cleaner after a shower in Germany than she ever did in England.

Leah smiled to herself as she realised how disjointed her thoughts were becoming. She ought to know why but she could not remember the detail of the lecture she'd attended on thought-association. Anyway, she must stop thinking of herself as Leah Carmichael because she was now Amy Carpenter. Her new name was not that difficult to remember; at least her surname started with the same three letters. Amy Carpenter: she wasn't sure she liked it but Peter had said she looked like an Amy.

What does an Amy look like?

There must be thousands of women called Amy and not one would look the same, so what did he mean?

She checked her rear view mirror.

She could only see a couple of cars behind her.

Chapter Fourteen

He was about a mile behind her.

Only a mile had separated them ever since she left Calais. He knew which ferry she was on so waiting for her in the car park beyond the French customs complex wasn't a problem … tedious but not a problem. Her car was easy to spot. His concern increased a little when he saw from a distance that it was low on its shock absorbers, but maybe he thought that was because he knew the reason. No matter. He smirked and shook his head when he saw her stall the car after the *gendarme* waved her on … silly bitch! Watching as she drove hesitantly out of the ferry terminal, he waited five minutes before following – there was no need to keep her in sight because he knew her destination. If she broke down, or if she was in an accident he wouldn't get involved.

"You don't exist, do you, Leah?" he said out loud. "You're just a stupid, gullible little bitch."

Peter Bennett smiled to himself.

Late October 1993

Spotting her that Sunday afternoon at a time when he actually wasn't looking, listening and waiting for the right person to come along who would satisfy the criteria he had set, was a bonus.

He was a patient man.

There had been any number of previous candidates from other universities but for one reason or another, they had all fallen by the wayside. They all fitted the bill with regard to looks, but didn't come up with the goods in other areas.

The criteria were quite straightforward.

Whoever it was had to be English, young – between twenty and twenty five would do – pretty but not beautiful, have a good figure, be of average height, but above all she had to be intelligent, innocent and very gullible.

Where better to look for such a girl other than in Britain's finest universities. He had decided that Warwick was due to be his next port of call having already tried Cambridge, Oxford and Bristol. It had been an interesting exercise but time was now a limitation.

He had been due to leave Durham the following day because his visit was only to check out his bolthole and make sure it was ready for him when the time came. Why hadn't he thought of Durham? Maybe it was too close to home although its university was above Warwick's in the league table.

So, taking an autumnal stroll by the River Wear below the castle walls and wondering whether he was wasting his time ... perhaps he ought to look abroad but no, his choice had to be English. Seeing Leah – as she was then – sitting by a tree and seemingly oblivious to what was going on around her was a very pleasant and welcome surprise. Close to home or not, if he was anything he was flexible.

The pink woollen hat with tufts of blonde hair sticking out, the turned up collar, the fingerless black woollen gloves, the long slim legs and the profile were like a magnet.

Before he even spoke to her, she was an immediate contender.

Going for an innocent cup of tea had worked so well before. What could be less threatening than having a cup of tea mid-afternoon on a sunny autumnal day? Even before he found out that she could speak German and daddy had been in the Army, he had almost made his choice. However, the innocence oozing from every pore attracted him the most.

She was perfect and could be ready in less than ten months, which fitted beautifully into his time frame.

July 1994

The overhead sign told him that *Venlo* was only twenty kilometres away, but as he had driven this route so many times before, he could have described every sign, every *autoroute* and *autobahn* exit and almost every tree.

Had he expected to go to bed with his choice on that very first night?

His plan had always been to seduce his victims verbally and then wait. With all of them it was going to happen, but not necessarily on the first night; that was an added bonus. With a couple of the others it had taken only a few days, and with one it had never happened ... her leanings had been elsewhere and he hadn't detected them. Charlotte had been ideal in every other way and nobody would have guessed ... she enjoyed his company but the moment he moved onto physical seduction, he discovered she wasn't even bi-sexual.

However, with Leah it was that very first night and his plan hadn't needed to wait.

From seeing her sitting under the tree down by the River Wear to watching her screw up her face in delight – he presumed it was delight but it didn't matter if she was faking it – all within twelve hours was totally unexpected. What was more, she was the one who made it pretty bloody obvious what she wanted: the others had taken a little gentle persuasion but eventually they had let him move on to the next stage.

Even when earlier they were having a cup of tea and a scone, he could tell by the way she looked at him that she was immediately infatuated with him. That wasn't a problem because words were words. When the time came, and to keep her on his side, he might have to reciprocate and tell her that he was in love with her too. She would want to justify what she had done, so the word *love* had to be the explanation.

He liked Leah, and he had liked the others too, but once he dismissed them their futures stayed within their own control. Girls like her were easy to like, but he knew what really lay under the surface of their pretty facades and their accepting bodies. The part of him that found the female of the species attractive was controllable; it had to be and to some extent it helped.

Fortunately, it was just a small part; the rest of him really controlled his needs.

However, even when he imagined Leah's final few seconds of life and he saw in her eyes the realisation that she was about to die, he found her a very difficult girl not to like. She was different and he didn't like the risk that accompanied his feelings. Love was never an option for him with any other woman ... his mother was the only woman he loved, although he accepted that it was a different sort of love. Whether he liked Leah or not had to be an irrelevancy, but if he was going to be with her for a while, perhaps liking her helped. He accepted that any emotional attachment from his point of view could generate a problem or two, but when the time came it wouldn't matter one way or the other.

This time he just knew that his choice was right.

In fact, she really was perfect.

She had a very bubbly personality and was genuinely a very nice person – on the surface. In the first five months they were together, he could not remember her being in a bad mood. All right, she went into sulks every now and again but they lasted minutes not hours or days. He understood why she was so miffed when he had not taken up her offer to go to Marshfield for Christmas to meet her parents, but doing something like that was totally and utterly unthinkable. Even meeting any of her friends was also out of the question. You do not find somebody like Leah and then pop down to mummy and daddy's for Christmas.

Eighty per cent of what he needed was already in place, already in Germany and would remain so until he was ready. Finding Leah had simply completed his list: she was the final twenty per cent, the final fifth, the last of five. The others were already there, so Leah was the final piece in the jigsaw puzzle and she was the only piece he had needed to go out and find.

Understandably, Leah was inquisitive but he was used to lying. In fact, he was better at telling lies than the truth. The ruse that he was researching for his PhD was the same story he had used with the others as a means of introduction, although he hadn't got as far as telling them that the truth had been twisted just a little. His final choice – Leah – was the only one privy to that admission. Getting her to agree to go to Germany had been easy. The time it took didn't matter because he had all the time in the world.

Perfect planning and execution were more important than time.

Changing the identity of his final choice was necessary. Out of the other four waiting in Germany, two were already operating under false names given to them by their respective controllers, and with the other two, it didn't matter. They could be who they really were for just a little bit longer.

Getting the false documents for Leah was not a problem. He had his contacts and if he gave them the right money they could produce anything he wanted, and perfection cost money.

Setting up the flat, getting her the car, opening the bank account and partially preparing the ground for her to get a job with the British Army was all easy by comparison.

The flowers, the toothpaste and soap would keep her on his side for the time being.

He deliberately moved a lot closer now because he wanted to make sure she took the right exit.

Seeing her brake lights come on, he presumed she was checking the overhead road sign. It wasn't much further now. It had been so easy to get the car and its contents this far, and he couldn't see a problem in getting it to its final destination either. He smiled as he remembered Leah telling him that when she finished her degree she was looking for adventure before settling down to ... whatever.

Except for the career she might have chosen, she was certainly going to get what she wanted.

It would be the adventure of a lifetime, never to be experienced again.

He could guarantee that.

Chapter Fifteen

The business with those two bloody muggers in Miami was a mistake but not one too far. This time he'd been able to recover.

He had reacted instinctively; his training had cut in immediately.

'*Don't wait for the enemy to make the first move because it will be the only move. You must act first and ask questions later,*' the instructor had said.

At the time, he was sure the gun was real and it was loaded. Whether or not its owner knew how to use it was immaterial. They were a couple of druggies who wanted money for their next fix, and that was all they were. If they were high on drugs, they did not see the situation in the same way. He and Leah were not victims in their attackers' eyes: they were merely another source for their continued release from reality.

On this occasion though, the attackers became the victims.

By reacting instinctively, his own defences were down temporarily, which was something he definitely did not want to happen again. Without thinking twice, PhD students did not normally go around neutralising two armed men. In the given scenario there was no alternative, but afterwards he needed to play it cool, lead her away from the obvious, and bring her back to the reason why she was there. She would think about it and even dream about it and no doubt she would tell her friends, but she certainly would not know the truth behind his actions.

Nobody must know the truth.

Not yet.

He remembered in the hotel afterwards picking up Leah's discarded clothes when she was in the bathroom taking a shower because she wanted to rid herself of anything associated with them.

He smiled ruefully.

Two complete jerks might have set his plans back a month or so, but maybe not. Regardless he would recover the situation and he would get things back on track but it had all been so unnecessary. She was right; he should have just handed over his wallet. It contained no more than fifty dollars. He had locked everything else away in the room safe.

Yes, he had reacted instinctively, not having time to give the consequences of his immediate reaction any thought.

But it must not happen again.

Suggesting to Leah that their attackers really did have other plans for her was merely his way of trying to convince her that his actions were justified. In reality and in retrospect the white man was probably incapable and the black one too nervous. If either of them had tried something like that, it would have been the last thing they ever did. Leah was his to do with whatever he wanted – not anybody else's.

The muggers had been lucky.

A month's delay was probably an exaggeration.

She seemed to get over what had happened quickly, or she may have just buried it in her mind somewhere. At least this meant he could approach the subject of the job in Germany again and earlier than expected. He thanked God there had been nobody else about; no witnesses. The police patrol car had been too close for comfort. It would have been a different story or even worse if the police had become involved. They would have carried out a cursory background check on both him and Leah. Even a superficial check would mean he'd have had a lot more explaining to do. He had kept his own identity because when the time came he wanted people to know who was responsible; only after the events he had planned would he become somebody else and disappear. All he needed was already in place.

Because of Leah's unexpected bloody questions, he came close at one stage to dropping her completely, but otherwise she was too perfect. If he did drop her, it would have spoilt some of his plan, though it wasn't critical to the final outcome.

However, on the evening of the attempted mugging she had walked out of the bathroom and told him that she would do whatever he wanted … and more.

"Short term or long term," she said with a salacious smile on her lips and in her eyes.

"I can see what you mean by short term," he said, "but long term?"

"Whatever you need me to do, I will do it."

She had made the decision for him.

Following her taillights as she approached *Venlo* and the turning that would take her into Germany and to her final destination in more ways than one, meant that everything would very shortly be in place and he could start what for him would be the culmination of over a year's planning.

Yes, the girl driving the car up front was ideal but ideals have a habit of kicking you in the teeth when you are not looking. When you least expect something to go wrong.

In the end, she would be the easiest of them all but he must not become complacent.

He dropped back a little but kept her car in sight all the way to *Finkenweg.* He watched her park, take her shoulder bag off the back seat, and with his directions on a piece of paper held in front of her, she went to find the address.

He would go back to his own flat and give her another thirty minutes or so before he rang her.

Chapter Sixteen

The flat was not what she expected.

Having collected the key from a *Frau* Schmidt who lived on the ground floor of the apartment block, Leah climbed apprehensively up the stairs to the top floor. She decided to leave her luggage in the Peugeot, which she parked in the small car park in *Finkenweg* fifty yards away, until she could see what the flat was like. She didn't have any choice really, but seeing the flat first made her feel better.

The sweet scent of fresh flowers hit her as she opened the door. Her brief conversation with her landlady – she assumed *Frau* Schmidt was her landlady – had not prepared her for what she saw. As she wandered through the flat, there were flowers everywhere, mixed bouquets and beautifully arranged.

Leah went to the balcony door and opened it.

It was just after three o'clock on a beautiful summer's afternoon. There wasn't a breath of wind and when she added the silence she would have expected on a Sunday, it was almost as though the world was standing still.

Going from room to room, Leah met with surprise after surprise. The small kitchen was modern and equipped with every conceivable utensil and gadget. The fridge contained more than just the essentials Peter had mentioned. On the bottom shelf was a whole chicken plus steaks and sausages. The bottom drawer was crammed with salads and vegetables, and the upper shelves were stacked with cartons of milk, bottles of white and rosé wine, water and mixers.

In the bathroom, she found fresh smelling towels, shampoo – the variety she liked – soap and even a tube of her favourite toothpaste. The bedroom and living-room-cum-dining area were no different – everything was immaculate. She sat down on the two-seater sofa and looked around with her mouth open. If her mother and father could see her now ...

Her mother and father – she must let them know she was safe.

She went over to the small table by the kitchen door, picked up the receiver and dialled her parents' number.

She heard her mother's voice after the second ring.

"Mummy, it's me."

"Hello, darling, where are you?"

"In *Brüggen*, Mummy. I just thought –"

"*Brüggen*? But that's ..."

"Yes, Mummy, it's not far from where you and Daddy were."

"But why *Brüggen*?"

"Mummy, I'll explain later, but I just thought I'd ring to let you know I've arrived."

"Well, thank you, darling, but …"

"Mummy, I'm sorry but I've got to go. I'll ring again in a couple of days. Give my love to daddy."

"Darling, I –"

"Got to go, Mummy. As I said I'll ring again shortly."

Leah put the receiver down gently, hating herself for not being able to tell her mother the truth. She believed her mother understood why she had wanted to come to Germany, but now that she was here she was not so sure.

Everything was perfect. Too perfect.

Although it was warm, she felt a chill run down her spine.

Something was not right.

After uncorking a bottle of ice-cold white wine she took a full glass out onto the balcony and watched a few pedestrians window shopping below her and thought some more about what Peter had said one evening not long ago.

"As I've mentioned to you on so many occasions, nothing was further from my mind when I first met you. It was just that every time you told me a little more about yourself you became the missing piece in this jigsaw puzzle."

"I never realised big business was so bizarre," Leah said. "No, that's not the right word, I mean … what do I mean? Underhand, that's the word, underhand."

"It's the way business is conducted nowadays: it's big fish eat little fish for survival, believe me."

"I'm sure it is but ..." Leah saw that she didn't have his attention. "Hello, is there anybody in there?" she said, cocking her head and smiling.

"Sorry, I was –"

"Daydreaming, that's what you were doing. Would you like some more coffee?"

"Please," Peter said.

"I just can't believe that little old me could be the lynch pin in a multi-million pound deal," Leah said, pouring the coffee. "Why me? I know, I know," she added quickly, holding up her hand, "it's because I speak

German, my father was in the Army so I know the jargon, I've lived in Germany, etcetera, etcetera. But …"

Peter reached for his mug. "Are you nervous?"

"Of course I'm bloody nervous. This isn't what I quite intended after leaving university."

"You can still –"

"Don't you dare bloody well tell me that I can still pull out. I've got two days to think about it before I go and the more you tell me that I can still pull out the more likely I am to do exactly that."

She didn't pull out.

It was Sunday evening.

She was in a strange town – she had been here before but not to live – she was alone, she was apprehensive. No, not apprehensive, she was scared and … and she was hungry. Looking down from the balcony, she could see the neon sign for a Pizzeria – Da Marcello's. Perhaps she would have a pizza.

The phone rang.

It must be Peter.

Nobody else knew where she was.

"Hello," she said apprehensively.

"You're there," was all he said.

"About three hours ago, yes, but –"

"Was the journey all right?" he asked, his voice sounding strange.

"There was a hold-up at the Kennedy Bridge in Antwerp as you said there would be but other –"

"You know what to do tomorrow?"

"Of course I do, you've told me often enough. Peter, I –"

"I'll ring on Wednesday to –"

"Peter, this flat ..."

"Is there a problem?"

"No, not a problem but …"

"Good. As I said, I'll ring on Wednesday."

"Peter, I love –"

"What?"

"Nothing," she said feeling her eyes watering.

She was listening to the dialling tone. She closed her eyes as a tear trickled down her cheek. He had been so abrupt, so distant. What was going on?

Opening her eyes, she stared at the receiver in her hand. She was being stupid. He was probably as apprehensive about what she had to do as she was.

Yes, she was being stupid.

She went into the bedroom to get changed.

Leah lay on the bed and cried.

She had gone to the car to get her cases and they were now lying on the other side of the double bed. She had stripped off but only got as far as undoing one of the cases to select something to wear before she filled up with tears again.

She wanted him to be with her, wanted him to hold her, to tell her that she really was being stupid. There was no need for her to feel so scared. They had spent nights and days apart when she went to see her parents, and when he needed to be away, but there was something final about what was happening now.

It could be months.

He sounded so close on the phone but for the first time he also sounded so business-like. They only exchanged a few words, and as was usual he did not let her tell him the way she felt. She had tried to tell him before but each time he didn't seem to want to know. Was he being wary of the way he might feel or did he simply not want the commitment that love might bring.

He had said that he loved her but only once, and that was when they were in Miami ... but there had been nothing said since. She could only assume that he did love her because of the way he touched her, the way he seemed to care more about satisfying her than himself. Love wasn't just physical: it had to be in the mind too.

Leah curled up into a ball, wishing she could feel him next to her, and wishing she had not agreed to this crazy venture.

What did the future really hold for her, she wondered.

Chapter Seventeen

Peter slammed the receiver back onto the cradle.

She was going to tell him that she loved him. He did not need her love and he didn't want her love. If she thought she loved him then that was her choice. They were her emotions and he had thought it might happen. Women use the word love too freely anyway: they become infatuated with somebody and they think it has to be love to justify what they are doing to express that love and the feelings that went with … whatever.

With women, everything was an extreme.

They either loved or they hated; there was no in-between. She could do what the hell she liked with her love, her emotions, but he wasn't interested.

He checked his watch.

It was nearly six-thirty in the evening.

Ursula would be here soon; she was normally on time whenever it was time for them to meet.

He lay down on the bed, resting his head in his hands and smiled as he thought back to the last day he had with Leah in the UK.

He could see them sitting in his kitchen enjoying a cooked breakfast, a rarity and luxury for them both. It was the day before Leah was due to fly down from Newcastle to Heathrow, where she would collect the car and drive to Dover. He was now confident that she would do it; she was still asking questions – they were inevitable – but she would still do it.

She was well and truly hooked by him and the thought of the adventure he promised her. The intrigue was like a drug to her; it was the same as watching a horror film: you screamed, you shouted, your flesh crawled but deep down you knew you were perfectly safe, so you enjoyed the experience rather than being scared witless.

Afterwards you wondered what all the fuss was about – they were only actors and the blood wasn't real. For Leah it must be a game, just a game. If it remained a game then she would play by the rules – his rules. As long as she came up with the goods then he could make up his own rules.

As he looked at her across the table that last time, he admitted he still liked her, but not too much. She was fun to be with, but not too much fun.

She was pretty, but not too pretty. She had a good figure, but not too good. She was skilful in bed, but not too skilful. As long as she remained like that then she remained expendable. What was one more life? In the blink of an eye more lives could be lost than were imaginable.

Leah would be but one more life snuffed out in a few seconds. What was one in five? Here one second gone the next. The blink of an eyelid, the snap of her neck, the look of death in her eyes and she would be gone … never to return. When he killed her he would make sure she didn't suffer. There were times when pain was essential. Pain made people realise their mistakes, and they would tell others.

Leah wouldn't feel any pain. She wouldn't have time.

Looking at her on the other side of the breakfast table on that final day, he wondered if she would look so pretty, so gullible, so innocent in death.

Now he lay staring at the ceiling in his flat, only a few miles away. He could see Leah moving round her new but temporary home. She really was no more than a sweet, gullible, naïve child. She had been overprotected for too long. She radiated innocence. It was time she found something out about the real world, about life. The incident in Miami was nothing compared with what would be waiting for her.

Arranging for the flowers, the food, the wine and the toiletries was a small price to pay for the thrill she would bring him when it happened.

He was distracted from his thoughts by a slight tap on the door and he became immediately alert. Reaching under his pillow he felt the cold metal of the 9mm Browning automatic pistol slip into his hand.

He rolled off the bed, crossed to the door and peered through the spy-hole.

It was Ursula.

"Hello, Peter," she said as he opened the door.

"Hello," he replied standing back to let her walk into the room. As she brushed past him, Ursula's perfume wafted into his nostrils. Before closing the door, he checked that the corridor was clear – an unnecessary precaution but it was something he always did.

"You look very pleased with yourself," she said in German, looking at him. The slight dip of her head and the sparkle in her eyes was a sure sign she was playing with him.

"I'm a creature of habit," he said, also in German, although Ursula's English was faultless.

"That could be quite dangerous in your line of business," she said as she turned away and dropped her bag onto the bed. "But I hope one of your habits is still the same," she added, undoing the top button of her yellow shirt. "And you can put that gun down before I come anywhere near you."

Peter narrowed his eyes as he tossed the automatic pistol onto the bed next to Ursula's bag. "And what makes you think that I want you to come anywhere near me?"

"Because I am also a creature of habit and it's been a long time," she said, undoing the last button on her shirt.

"Too long," Peter said.

Walking across the room towards him, she let the shirt fall onto the floor, followed by her bra.

She put her arms round his neck and stared into his eyes for a few seconds before their lips met.

"Well," Ursula said twenty minutes later. "You have lost none of your technique. That was worth waiting for. Thank you."

"You're not trying to tell me there hasn't been anyone else since we last met, are you?"

Peter lay on his side, looking at her profile. Ursula was in her late twenties but looked older. Her high cheekbones, tanned skin and almost black eyes gave her a mixed Slavic-Mediterranean appearance. Her black hair and the way she applied her make-up added to her mystery.

"Why do you want to know if there's been anybody else?" she asked.

"What about Manfred … that so called husband of yours?" he said, his voice full of sarcasm.

"Him? You must be joking … he will never touch me again."

"Has there been anybody else?"

Whether she had been with anybody just to have sex wasn't the problem. It was *who* she had been with that mattered. If it was a one-off then so be it, but if she had started an affair with another man – or a woman – this could generate a complication. Ursula was a very physical woman and he was sure her needs exceeded what he could give to her when he was in the country.

"Of course not," she said, pouting. "With you there is always something different so I don't need anybody else. And when you're not here, well, I am quite capable of looking after myself."

"I'm not sure how I am supposed to take the … *something different* comment."

"As a compliment," she said, stubbing out the cigarette in the ashtray on the bedside table. She always had a cigarette immediately after they had sex. He hated the smell but was willing to put up with it for the time being.

She would be the fourth.

"Is everything in place?" he asked, becoming serious. He smiled as Ursula pulled the single sheet over the lower part of her body. The fun was over and he wanted to be serious – she was a good girl.

"As far as things can be in place then, yes we are ready. Will she do as she is told?" she asked. "I presume she arrived in one piece."

"She did. I watched her go all the way into the flat and I've spoken to her."

"She still suspects nothing?"

"Nothing at all," he said. "And you're sure the job isn't going to be a problem?"

"If it was, you wouldn't be here, would you? I told you, Manfred will do as he is told."

"Are you hungry?"

She smiled. "Yes, for everything."

"Restaurant or here?" he asked, ignoring her innuendo.

"Here."

"I'll go and get a take-away," he said, getting off the bed and picking up his clothes.

"When do you go back to England?" Ursula asked, watching him pull on his jeans.

"On Thursday."

"So I wait until then."

"That's the plan, yes."

"No problem," she said, moving her hand under the sheet as she looked at him, a smile on her lips. "Don't be long."

Chapter Eighteen

This early in the morning there were only two other cars in the small car park outside the Chinese Restaurant, which was mid-way between the small towns of *Brüggen* and *Bracht*. Peter parked between the cars and waited. The restaurant was on the corner of *Brüggenerstraße* and *St Barbara Straße*, which led down to the ammunition depot.

He did not have to wait very long because Leah's little Peugeot came along the main road from *Brüggen* right on time. When she scanned the cars in the car park while waiting to turn left, he slipped a little further down in his seat.

Her mind would be on other things. She would be nervous and in any case she thought he was in England. Wanting to make sure that she hadn't backed out at the last moment, he smiled as her car disappeared from view. Everything was in place and after he left for England on Thursday, Ursula would keep an eye on her.

In all other ways, Leah was on her own for a while now.

She would cope.

"Hello, Miss," the young guard said, without trying to hide his appreciative smile. "What can we do for you?"

Leah looked up at him. Although he was smiling, the rifle he held across his chest was quite intimidating. He was a big man and she suddenly felt nervous. "Erm, I … I am looking for the civil labour office," she said tentatively, remembering what Peter had told her to ask for.

"Are you now?" the soldier said. "I see." He adjusted the rifle again before squatting down so that he was at her level. "It's not in here, I'm afraid, love. It's down the other end of the camp past the football pitch, but you can get a pass in the guardroom." He pointed beyond the barrier. "If you park over there and then come with me, we can do the necessary, all right?"

"Yes fine, thank you."

The soldier stood up and with one hand lifted what looked like a very heavy barrier.

Leah drove through and parked where he had pointed. Picking up her bag, she got out of the car and locked it. She was wearing a light grey business suit, sensible shoes and her hair was tied back in a ponytail, but the way the soldier was looking at her she might as well have not worn anything. Why did some men make it so obvious?

"Follow me, love," the soldier said as he led the way. Once in the guardroom he said, "Sarge, young lady here is looking for the civil labour office."

The sergeant looked up from checking what looked like some sort of register. His eyes widened on seeing her and as he jumped to his feet he knocked his chair over. He tried to ignore the crash, but Leah couldn't help noticing his embarrassment as the chair hit the floor.

"Oh, right," he said as he approached the counter. The soldier who had taken Leah to the guardroom stood to one side, looking her up and down. "All right, Chalkie, you can go back outside," the sergeant said. "I'll look after Miss, Miss … er?"

"Carpenter," Leah told him, looking down. It was the first time she'd had to use the name and she had almost said Carmichael.

"Miss Carpenter," the sergeant repeated. "Chalkie, I said you can go back to the gate, and you can put your tongue away as well," he said, puffing out his chest. "Sorry about that," he added, turning back to Leah before Chalkie had actually left the guardroom. "Now what can I do to help? My name's Sergeant Brown by the way."

Leah put her bag on the counter in anticipation that she would need to show her passport.

"It's quite a long story," she said hesitantly, "but basically I'm in Germany for a few months and I need a job."

"A job?" Sergeant Brown looked surprised. "What sort of job?"

"Anything."

"Oh," he said, a little flustered as he reached for a form from behind the counter. "Can you give me a few details, Miss?"

After the form was completed and he had given her passport a cursory glance, Sergeant Brown handed Leah an orange temporary car pass on which he had written the number of the Peugeot. "Show this at the bottom gate and they'll direct you where to park. Do you know where to go from here?"

Leah shook her head.

"Okay, turn your car round, go back through the gate, turn right and follow your nose – and a very pretty one it is if you don't mind me saying so." When Leah didn't say anything, he added quickly, "You'll go past the football and cricket pitches on your right, over the speed ramps and you'll see the barrier ahead of you. Pull up there and show this pass and they'll do the rest."

Ten minutes later Leah sat in the chair outside the Civil Labour Officer's door. His clerk, a very determined looking woman in her fifties who had introduced herself as *Frau* Spinks, tapped away on an old-fashioned typewriter behind her desk in the corner. She glanced up every now and again, peering over her glasses at Leah, who had tried without success to break the ice by smiling.

After a further fifteen minutes the door to her left opened and a tall, thin, bespectacled man in his early forties looked across at her.

"*Fraulein* Carpenter?" he enquired, his eyes travelling slowly from her face to her feet.

Leah stood up, smoothing her suit skirt. "Yes."

"Please come in."

As she entered his office he was resuming his seat behind a desk that was far too big for the room.

"Please sit down," he said, adjusting the glasses on his nose. "My name is Manfred Dorf and I am the Civil Labour Officer for this depot." He spoke slowly and very precisely, his accent strong but his English good.

"Thank you for seeing me. I –"

"I understand that you are seeking employment," he went on, his head bowed as he flicked through some papers on his desk.

"Yes, that's right, I –"

"This is most unusual," he said almost absentmindedly, "most unusual."

"I –"

"However," he added, looking up and taking his glasses off, "although I cannot promise you anything I am willing to listen." He then steepled his fingers and waited, his face expressionless.

Leah took his silence as a signal that she could now speak. "May I thank you, *Herr* Dorf, for seeing me." He inclined his head, but only slightly, his eyes flicking to her knees. Leah clasped her hands tightly on her lap, trying to hide her nervousness. "My name is Amy Carpenter and I have just finished my degree in England. I have been to Germany before on holiday but I have always wanted to stay longer. I thought before settling down to a career back in the UK, I would take six months to a year out and come to your country for a break and some experience."

Herr Dorf smiled for the first time. "I would not say that this part of Germany is the most scenic. We do not have many tourists around here. I would have thought Bavaria or the Black Forest area would have been more appealing." The smile disappeared as he changed from English to German. "The form *Frau* Spinks asked you to complete tells me that you speak my language. Is this so?" he said quickly.

Leah took a deep breath. "Yes, that is correct," she told him, also in German. "Like many others I learnt German at school but then used the holidays to improve it and to learn the colloquialisms."

"From what you have said so far, you did very well. Not many foreigners know the word *umgangssprachlich* let alone how to use it."

"Thank you, I –"

"I presume," he continued, "that you can read and write German as well as you can speak it?"

"Yes, I think so, although I haven't had much cause to write a lot."

Leah's confidence increased slightly, and she crossed her legs so that her skirt rode up her thigh a little further. As she expected, *Herr* Dorf's eyes followed the movement. She had never used her obvious attractiveness and sensuality in this kind of situation before, but Peter had told her to use every trick in the book to secure any form of employment.

"And how are you socially?" *Herr* Dorf asked. When he saw Leah's frown he added, "I mean, are you happy in all sorts of company?"

She shrugged. "I think so, but never having worked properly before I haven't really had much experience. Why do you ask?"

"In this depot as well as the two hundred British soldiers, we have nearly a thousand workers. Most are German but in all we have nineteen different nationalities. For example there are two Americans and two Russians." If *Herr* Dorf had expected Leah to look surprised he was disappointed. "Some of the workers are from the lower classes but they are very good at what they do. Others? Well, let me just say they are happy to work with the anonymity that this depot gives them, and perform well under their ability so that they do not risk becoming too well known elsewhere."

This time Leah did look slightly taken aback. "I would have thought that an army depot of this sort would have warranted tighter control, with security I mean."

Herr Dorf smiled ruefully. "Some of the jobs are very demeaning and we have to rely on foreign workers, but we keep a careful eye on them. Without them we would not get anyone else to do the work."

"I see." Leah wanted to know whether there was an opening for her or not so she decided to ask a direct question. "*Herr* Dorf, do you think you have something for me? I would be willing to work anywhere."

He leant back in his chair and rubbed his chin with his hand. "There may be some temporary work, yes, but," he referred to the form again, "this address in *Brüggen*, it is also temporary, no?"

"I have taken a six-month lease on it. It's a small flat."

"And you need to work to pay the rent?"

"And eat," Leah said, smiling as she re-crossed her legs.

Herr Dorf nodded. "In that case, perhaps I can offer you something but as I said, it is only short-term."

"How short is short-term, *Herr* Dorf?"

It was Leah's longest conversation in German for well over three years, but she was comfortable, her confidence increasing by the second. Peter would be pleased with her.

"*Frau* Weissmüller, our translator, is on maternity leave and will not be back for three months. I thought we would be able to cope without a translator for a while but circumstances have changed. The closure of this depot in 1996 has been announced which presents me with unprecedented problems and I need a translator. I could take you on as *Frau* Weissmüller's temporary replacement but I am afraid the pay would not be too good, I could only offer you a casual labourer's rate."

"And that is?"

It was *Herr* Dorf's turn to shrug. "Maybe two and a half thousand Deutschmarks per month. I doubt if that would be enough to pay your rent and feed you."

"I have some money of my own. If you are making me a formal offer, I would like to accept."

Herr Dorf raised his eyebrows and took off his glasses. "All right, normally translators are locals who can speak English, so this is setting a bit of a precedent. But when can you start?"

"As soon as you need me, but won't you have to do a security check on me first?"

"As I said, we have people working here whose backgrounds would not necessarily stand up to any in-depth investigations. You have a British passport, so I think we need only conduct a cursory check." *Herr* Dorf began shuffling the papers on his desk. "If you see *Frau* Spinks she will complete the necessary paperwork. Come and see me at eight o'clock in the morning and I will give you your programme."

"Thank you, *Herr* Dorf, you have been most kind," Leah said as she stood up.

"Kindness does not come into it," he told her, also standing up. "Due to *Frau* Weissmüller's absence, your availability is a convenience for me.

After they had shaken hands and Amy Carpenter had left his office, *Herr* Dorf picked up his phone and tapped out a number. He smiled as he heard the ringing tone: the interview had gone better than he thought it would. Even if Ursula had not told him what was required he would have offered *Fraulein* Carpenter the job anyway, but there was no need for Ursula to know that. Perhaps now she would be a little more accommodating.

"Yes," Ursula said.

“It is done,” Manfred Dorf said before replacing the receiver.

Having sat in the car park for over an hour, Peter smiled as he watched the Peugeot stop at the T-junction before turning right for *Brüggen*. He switched on the engine of his car, waited a few seconds for Leah to disappear beyond the pub on the other corner, and then moved slowly out of the car park.

He turned left and headed in the opposite direction.

He was still smiling as he joined the autobahn to the east of *Bracht* and headed south for *Mönchengladbach.*

Everything was coming together beautifully and it was the culmination of a lifetime of planning, although it was only after the incident in Northern Ireland that the way in which he could be released from his torment was given to him ... the voices had waited until then.

Now they were silent.

But their silence didn’t mean they weren’t there ... waiting.

Part Two

Chapter Nineteen

Peter Bennett always wanted to be in the army.

His mother, Anne-Marie, once told him that when he was just over a year old, contained within his limited vocabulary was the word *tholder*, which took only a short while to interpret, and she settled on *soldier*. She said that she could never work out why there was this early fascination with the Army because there were no military connections in the family. Her father had been a fireman and therefore not called up for the Second World War, and her grandfather had polio when he was only ten, so he escaped for the first debacle.

When she told him the story, Peter was never too sure why his mother used the word 'debacle'. War was an honourable diversion from politics, or so one of his history teachers told him. In fact, very early on Carl von Clauswitz became a bit of an icon when the same history teacher quoted him as saying: 'war is the continuation of politics by other means'.

Later she said that she put his fixation with the Army down to when they were living in Aldershot. After-all, it was the home of the British Army. When he was still in nappies she used to push him down Queen's Avenue in his buggy as often as she could, so that he could see the soldiers on the playing fields, in the stadium and then further down the avenue, watch them on the drill-square, sometimes in their ceremonial uniforms and with bands playing.

It was the only time Peter was as good as gold.

"You wouldn't utter a word," she said. "You sat perfectly still with your mouth slightly open. For me it was utter bliss … well, peace and quiet. There were times when you and I made up a loyal crowd of two and even some of the soldiers got used to us being there, winking at you as they marched by … although I always hoped they might be winking at me."

"Perhaps they were," Peter said.

"Maybe, but how I wished it could be three of us watching the soldiers – you, me and … your father."

It wasn't until he was settled into secondary education that she told him the truth about his father. He remembered his mother ignoring his early questions and changing the subject very quickly. When he was a little older, eight if he remembered correctly, he did at least get a response.

"Mum, where's my dad?" he recalled asking for the umpteenth time.

"Abroad, he's working abroad," she said, appearing disinterested.

"Why does he never come home to see me?"

"He's a very busy man."

"But I've never seen him … not ever," Peter said.

"He wants to see you but he doesn't come here because of me," his mother told him.

"Why, what do you mean?"

"All these questions," she said. "It's simple. We're not friends anymore."

"Why aren't you friends anymore?"

"You're too young to understand. Go and watch television."

Later when Peter was eleven, she decided that he was old enough for the truth. "I don't know who your father was, Peter."

He was immediately confused. How could she not know who his father was? "But Mum, you must know."

"I didn't say that very well. I know who he was but I don't know where he is."

"Why not?"

"You'll understand one day," she said.

"I want to understand now. One minute you're telling me he's abroad, the next it's because you aren't friends anymore and now… now you're telling me you don't know."

His mother put her arm round his young shoulders, pulling him close to her and hugging him.

"Many years ago, mummy did something that she was ashamed of but she is very proud of what came from it."

"I know where babies come from, Mum. I know how they are made," he said.

"I'm sure you do. Your dad and I were together for a very short time …"

"But long enough to do it."

"Yes, Peter, for long enough to do it."

"Other children at school call me a bastard."

"It's just a word, Peter. You are my son and I love you so that's all you need to know."

Only a few weeks later she told him exactly what had happened.

He remembered sitting and taking in every word she said.

He didn't like what she was saying but at last she was telling him the truth … well, he hoped it was the truth.

Anne-Marie would have been more than happy if Peter's father had been around when he was born.

At seventeen she was a pretty girl but socially very naïve.

He told her his name was Francis but afterwards she doubted whether anything he told her was true. Going to The Swan Hotel in Alton with a few girlfriends was an adventure; they had never been there before, believing it was out of their league. Anne-Marie responded when a very handsome, well-spoken and charming young man showed an interest in her. She accepted not only the offer of his company and champagne but also his invitation to go and admire his Jaguar E-Type sports car. She felt very grown up and could see she was the envy of her friends who watched her from the other side of the bar as she left the pub.

Peter's conception happened fifteen minutes later on the brown leather front passenger seat of a very expensive car parked in darkness behind The Swan Hotel in Alton. Francis – if that was his real name – didn't even ask for her telephone number.

Afterwards she walked back into the pub and boasted to her friends about what had just happened. They giggled and nudged each other especially when Francis looked across at them and smiled. He was standing at the far end of the bar with another man. Anne-Marie thought he would certainly come over to them once he finished talking to the man he was with, but after draining his glass he walked out of the pub and out of her life with just a nod and another smile.

Just over six weeks later, she discovered she was pregnant.

After Peter was born, he and his mother lived with her parents for a while in Farnham, but, and she wanted to be completely honest with him, it was Peter who was the cause of them having to move out.

"You were diagnosed as being hyperactive and also something to do with attention-deficit something or other," she told him … she could never remember the relevant string of letters. "I never understood what was really wrong with you and I thought you were far too young to be diagnosed with anything. All I knew was that you were a little bugger. You screamed, shouted and threw yourself about. You were a real handful."

Peter smiled.

"You can smile, young man" she said, "but then again you were all I had. I was eighteen-years old with you, an uncontrollable one-year old little monster in tow. There was no chance of me having any form of social life, and even if I did find somebody, who was going to take a little monster and me on board? You don't mind me being this honest, do you Peter?"

"No … no, Mum, I would prefer to know the truth. I'm sorry I was so awful but I don't remember, well, not everything."

"Of course you don't, you were far too young," she said. "I never resented or hated you, Peter. I want you to know that. No matter how bad you were, I always loved you. Somebody once told me that I was a devoted mother. I made it my mission to control your behaviour so that you could have a better start in life than I ever had. Would you like another squash?"

"No, Mum, thanks. I just want you to tell me the rest."

"Well," his mother continued, "by the age of five, your behaviour was much improved. I have to admit during your early years there were times when I could quite easily have either walked out for good, or pushed you under the bath water, but then you would look at me and smile, and I hated myself for even thinking of leaving or harming you. Once you were getting better I did have a couple of male friends, ones I met through work, but as soon as they found out I had a kid – and it was nothing to do with what you had been like – they didn't want to know. The money I earned paid for the crèche I put you in and we were left with just enough to keep us above the bread-line."

"What's the bread-line," Peter asked. "I've heard others say it but …"

"It means there were no luxuries and the food we ate was very basic. I got clothes for both of us from charity shops. I would have been better off on the Social but I needed to work, and I'm sorry to say this, Peter, but I needed a break from you or else I would have … well, we won't talk about that … but I must add very quickly that when I was at work I just longed to see you again."

"So there was a good side to me?" he asked.

"Of course there was, silly. I did quite well at work. I managed to get a couple of promotions and we moved from a studio flat, which in our case was a quaint name for a one-room hellhole. The landlord, who lived on the ground floor, threatened me with eviction every time you whimpered let alone had a tantrum, but when I had more money coming in, we moved to a flat with a separate bedroom in a nicer area of Aldershot. Although you were much better by this time, you still had your moments and your teachers told me that there were times when you were uncontrollable. They thought you ought to be going to a special school but I wasn't going to have that. Whenever I tried to talk to you about your behaviour at school you said you couldn't remember being naughty so that might explain why you can't remember it now."

"But I can't, Mum, I'm not lying."

"No, I know you're not," she said. "But it wasn't me that stopped you from being sent to a special school, it was you, yourself."

"Me? How could I …?"

"It was your academic progress. As well as threatening the most grotesque and painful of punishments whenever you threw a tantrum – threats they never carried out – your teachers marvelled at the speed with which you learnt. By the time you moved to the local Grammar school last year having sailed through the eleven plus ... well, you know the rest ..."

"Thanks for telling me all that, Mum. I'm sorry I was such a –"

"There's no need to apologise, Peter. You've more than made up for it since."

"I'll never let you down again, Mum. I promise."

"I'm sure you won't, Peter."

Chapter Twenty

Anne-Marie Bennett was so proud when Peter, as he had promised, didn't let her down again. It seemed that when he moved to secondary school it was not only the turning point for him but for her as well.

After eleven years of loneliness, heartache and times when she thought the only way out was suicide – such thoughts were momentary and she always chastised herself after thinking such a thing – she met a man who was different.

Happenstance brought Michael into her life.

It had to be by chance; planning was out of the question. Previously, if she gave the slightest indication that she was going out and leaving Peter with a baby-sitter, the screaming and head slamming would start.

Although she didn't have a social life, Anne-Marie didn't let herself go to waste.

Rather vainly and surprisingly, and except when she was having one of her depressive moments, she found that looking at herself in the mirror was one of her remaining pleasures in life. She kept her auburn hair short because she could not afford to go to the hairdressers more than once every two or three months. She also ensured that her diet was sensible, and late at night, after Peter had at last settled, she would exercise. She would strip-off and do her aerobic exercises in front of a full-length mirror she bought especially for the purpose. She was young and believed that there was always a flicker of hope that one day she would meet somebody. She hoped that by keeping herself presentable it would prove worthwhile.

At just over five feet tall, she considered herself tiny, but she had what others referred to as an old-fashioned figure. Seeing so many hipless and what she thought were shapeless models in magazines made her proud of her figure, although other than her experience with Francis in his Jaguar, nobody else ever saw it. Her legs were not long, but they were slim and in proportion with the rest of her body. Yes, she was pleased with what she saw each time she looked at herself in the mirror: with a pretty face, big green-blue flecked eyes and what she thought was a cheeky smile, there was always a chance.

At twenty-eight, the same year Peter started secondary school, her sexual experiences still only comprised having lost her virginity to a spotty-faced schoolboy in the long grass beyond her school playing fields when they should have been attending a double-maths session; and Peter's father, Francis.

It was therefore an absolute miracle when Michael walked into her life … or to be precise, drove into her life.

She had taken a day off work to visit her parents in Farnham. Her mother was not very well. It was only a short distance so she could have taken the bus, but she had recently bought a rather old but supposedly trustworthy Mini 850 and she wanted to enjoy her newfound independence.

Unfortunately, just after joining the A31 there was a coughing and a spluttering from the car's engine and it suddenly lost power. She had to pull over into a rather convenient lay-by where the engine coughed once more before stopping completely. She hadn't joined the AA, RAC or any of the other similar organisations – she couldn't afford it and she never drove far enough to warrant the expense anyway. She certainly could not afford to call out recovery from the local garage so that was a definite non-starter in more ways than one.

She sniggered at her own joke, shrugged and got out of the car.

She lifted the bonnet and looked at the engine, assuming the clicking sound was the hot engine cooling down. The array of wires, pipes and metal bits meant absolutely nothing to her at all. Cars were whooshing by on the main road but none even slowed down let alone stopped. After twenty minutes of worry, she had just decided to start walking when this very shiny but even older car pulled in behind her Mini. The front door of the car opened the wrong way, and a tall willowy man in his early thirties got out, smiling as he did and adjusting his glasses on the bridge of his nose.

"Are you a damsel in distress?" he asked in a soft and very educated English accent. He walked towards her and stopped as he reached the front of his car.

Anne-Marie had been in the process of locking her car when he arrived. For some reason, she was immediately concerned about the image she presented. Most people were enjoying an Indian summer. It was a hot Wednesday morning and she was wearing what could only be described as short shorts, a vest, no bra and a pair of old sandals … after all she was only going to see her mother.

After hesitating for a second she said, "It just stopped."

The man smiled the most engaging smile she had ever seen and then adjusted his glasses again before resting his hand on the bonnet of his car.

"Stopped? Would you mind if I take a look for you?" She stepped back and hesitated but he just smiled again. "I can assure you, Miss, I am not a marauding sexual deviant. I was just taking Bessie out for a spin. I know something about cars and I may be able to help."

"Erm, I suppose … yes, if you wouldn't mind. Thank you," she said.

He smiled again as he moved next to her. He was wearing a pair of pristine cream trousers, a yellow shirt with the sleeves rolled to mid-way up his forearms, and very expensive moccasins. His hair was a light brown, cut short and he was clean-shaven. His face, although thin, was aristocratic which went with his voice and the way he was dressed. When he smiled, it was with his entire face.

"Of course I wouldn't mind," he told her.

Moving past her to get to the front of her car, she thought he smelt clean and unruffled.

"Would you mind opening the bonnet for me?" he asked.

Anne-Marie unlocked the door, leant into the car and pulled the lever. At least she knew where that was. "Be careful," she said, concerned about his clothes, "it's not very clean."

He looked at her as he lifted the bonnet, the smile still on his face. "Worry not," he said, "hands and clothes can be washed."

She looked at his hands as he began to fiddle with the wires that meant nothing to her. They certainly were not a manual worker's hands; his fingers were long and he had manicured nails. She thought he might be a musician.

"It just stopped," she told him again. "It lost power, coughed and then stopped."

He glanced at her sideways. "Would you mind not standing there?" She was between the car and the road. "Come round this side. You'll be safer and you'll also be able to see what I'm doing."

She did as he asked. "I might be able to see but I won't understand," she said, smiling.

"I will explain everything," he said.

As she bent forward to look into the engine, the front of her vest fell away so she quickly brought her hand up and pressed it against her chest.

Modesty suddenly seemed very important.

The man continued to fiddle for a few seconds.

"It's probably the carburettor … these old Minis are notorious for having such problems."

He fiddled with other bits and pieces for a few more seconds.

"Can you try to start her?" She began to move round him. "Be careful, the road," he said indicating speeding cars with a nod of his head.

Anne-Marie got in the car and turned the ignition. The engine whirred, coughed and then whirred again. She saw his hand at the side of the bonnet telling her to stop. After getting out, she joined him at the front of the car.

"Yes," he told her, "it's the carburettor."

"Can you fix –?" She stopped, realising it was a bit of a cheek to ask him such a question.

He nodded. "Yes, I think I can." He came out from under the bonnet. "Look why don't you go and sit in Bessie while I have a fiddle?"

Without hesitating, she followed him to his car where he opened the passenger's door for her. The car smelt of leather and it was spotless. The smell took her back to her experience with Francis, Peter's father, but she dismissed the thought immediately.

Her saviour smiled at her once again and then disappeared to the back of the car and opened the boot. She watched him walk to the front of her car with a small toolbox in his hand before he vanished under the bonnet.

She looked around the inside of his car. Everything was immaculate and she blushed as she thought about the inside of her car ... it was a mess. Glancing down she saw a pair of expensive sunglasses on the driver's seat, so she moved them in case he sat on them when he got back in. He must have changed his glasses when he stopped, she thought. Other than the glasses, nothing else told her anything about him.

She saw him move from the front of her car a couple of times and heard him turning the engine over. After about ten minutes he looked at her and nodded his satisfaction but indicated that she should stay where she was. He lowered the bonnet, put the toolbox back in the boot of his car and wiped his hands on a cloth.

"As I thought," he said, "you had a blockage."

Anne-Marie put her hands on her thighs, aware of just how short her shorts were. She thought about making some witticism about having a blockage but decided it wouldn't be appropriate. "Will it get me to my mother's?" she asked.

The moment she asked the question, she realised just how stupid it must have sounded.

"It depends whether your mother lives just down the road or in Scotland," he said, his eyes on hers.

She noticed that he only ever looked at her eyes. Even when he walked from his car to hers the first time, he had not looked her up and down, as most other men would have done.

"That was a silly thing to say," she said, blushing. "It's just up the road."

"Then you'll be all right but I do suggest you have your car serviced very soon."

"How can I ever thank you?"

He stopped wiping his hands. "I would be more than willing to overhaul your engine for you." When he saw her surprise, he added, "It's a hobby of mine, old cars. Bessie is a Rover 90 and she was in a mess when I bought her."

"That's very kind of you but it is hardly saying thank you," she said.

"There is a catch, I'm afraid."

"What's that?"

"When I've finished, would you have lunch or dinner with me?"

"Yes, of course I would. That would be lovely," Anne-Marie said, not believing her ears.

He smiled again. "It's been very remiss of me but I haven't introduced myself. My name is Michael Warburton." He reached across the short space between them and took her hand. "And you are?"

"Anne-Marie Bennett," she told him, watching as he lifted her hand and brushed his lips against her fingers.

Chapter Twenty-One

Anne-Marie and Michael were married a year later almost to the day. She gained a husband, a lovely house on the outskirts of Farnham, and a father for Peter.

She could not have been happier.

It wasn't until she took her car to his *house* for the promised engine overhaul that she appreciated just who and what her knight-in-shining-armour was. Michael came from a rich family but he had made his own fortune as a stockbroker in London. He still commuted to his office three days a week, but for the rest of the time he worked on his collection of old cars – he had five – played golf, and, Anne-Marie was delighted to discover, played the piano.

When she confessed on their fourth date that she had an eleven-year old son, Michael did not bat an eyelid, which meant he really was too good to be true. He asked all the right questions, and when he and Peter eventually met, they became friends immediately.

Once Anne-Marie and Michael were married, and after a short discussion, Peter insisted on keeping his mother's maiden name, which was a great disappointment to her.

After going to bed, she lay with her head against Michael's shoulder, and wept.

She so wanted them to be a proper family, all with the same name.

"Give it time," Michael said. "Rather than forcing the situation, give it time."

Peter's academic progress stayed on course and he showed a particular preference and ability for the sciences, especially chemistry and physics.

However, it was a mutual love of the internal combustion engine that threw Peter and Michael together even more. Anne-Marie often took mugs of tea or coffee out to the garage and her greeting was a pair of bottoms emerging from under the bonnet of yet another car undergoing restoration.

The other marvel was Michael's parents.

Anne-Marie was understandably apprehensive but they took to her straight away, and they were delighted when told that Michael had asked her to marry him. Their joy could not have been more genuine. When she expressed her surprise, Michael told her that the family motto was *Beatitudinem* which was Latin for 'Happiness', and as she made him happy, they were happy too.

That is how things remained.

In twelve months, Anne-Marie and Peter went from a small flat to absolute comparative luxury, but neither wanted such a change for anything else other than their respective love for Michael.

As she expected though, her own parents were a little cynical about the marriage.

"Why would somebody like 'im marry somebody like you? You with a brat and all," her mother asked in one of her more hurtful moments.

"Because he loves me," Anne-Marie replied, embarrassed by her mother's attitude. "And don't call Peter a brat."

"Because you're his only chance more like," her mother said, ignoring her daughter's rebuke.

"That's a horrible thing to say."

"But it's the truth," her mother said.

To clear her mind of her mother's doubts she asked Michael that same day, "What was it about me the first time we met that made you ask me out?" She was actually wondering if there was some truth in what her mother had said.

"What, as well as thinking that you were gorgeous?" he said, smiling.

Anne-Marie also responded with a smile. "Yes."

"When you leant under the bonnet of the car to look at what I was doing, you held your top to your chest," he told her, smiling. "That could have meant so many things."

Anne-Marie looked at him quizzically. "You weren't looking anyway."

"I was but only when you weren't looking at me."

"And what about when I told you about Peter?"

"I've told you before how I felt, I was worried that you wouldn't have time for me."

Anne-Marie leant across and kissed him on the lips.

Her parents' attitude didn't last long though. Once they got to know Michael, and more importantly discovered that they were included in on the deal, their manner changed.

Anne-Marie decided she shouldn't have been surprised.

Peter told her that from the day they moved into the Farnham house, which was located in Moor Park Way, he had set himself an objective. He would make her the proudest mother on earth because he was going to succeed in everything he did and there would be no looking back.

"And what about Michael?" she asked. "Don't you want to make him proud too?"

Peter looked at her without smiling. "He's my elder brother, so of course I do," he said.

Anne-Marie did smile when she heard Peter calling Michael by his first name. She had told Michael what Peter had said and he told her that being an elder brother was a good substitute.

Five months later Anne-Marie had some news that she thought would please everybody in her new family.

She was pregnant.

Everyone in both families was delighted – except Peter.

On the evening she told him he looked at her blankly and said nothing before going to his room. Minutes later the noise she and Michael could hear was terrifying. They rushed to Peter's room and could see straight away that he was having a fit. It was the first one for over six years and the worst his mother had ever witnessed.

She honestly believed that if it had not been for Michael's quick reactions and the speed with which the paramedics arrived, Peter could have done himself some very permanent physical damage.

For each of the three days Peter was in hospital, his mother was with him for most of each day. She took a break when he was taken away for more tests, but she was there waiting for him when he returned to the ward.

Michael joined her at the hospital whenever he could.

When the nurse informed Anne-Marie at the end of the third day that she could take Peter home, Michael took Peter down to the cafeteria to get a Coke while Anne-Marie went with the consultant to his office. The conversation they had was brief.

"So what's the matter with him?" she asked, hesitantly.

The consultant looked sideways at the young female doctor who had accompanied him. "It's difficult to say," he said.

"What does that mean?"

"You told us when your son was admitted that nothing like this had happened for six years," the consultant said. "Is that right?"

"Over six years," Anne-Marie said. "His behaviour was very difficult almost from the day he was born but from the age of five, nearly six, he seemed to come out of whatever he was in. I think –"

"And what were you told could be the problem?" the consultant asked.

"I never really understood," Anne-Marie said. "But hyperkinetic something or other was mentioned and autism, but because he seemed to settle down after he was six I thought –"

“That is confusing, Mrs Warburton.” The consultant and the young doctor exchanged looks again. “Mrs Warburton, what we are dealing with here is not an exact science –”

“I’m sorry. What are you saying?” Anne-Marie asked.

“It means that like a lot of areas of medicine – human behaviour, biology, disease etcetera – we are far from fully understanding everything there is to know. We do our best with the knowledge we do have but … well, if we got everything right then longevity would become the norm, if you see what I mean.” The consultant paused and for a few seconds inspected the fingernails on his right hand. “From what you have told me and what I have learnt from his doctor’s notes, I find your son’s situation very confusing. He certainly had all the symptoms of autism when he was a lot younger. You see, autism can come with a range of challenges in making sense of the world, but it can also give people advantages, such as in memory or in concentrating on tasks. The autism spectrum is also very broad. Some people have language or intellectual difficulties but do engage with others. Other people on the autism spectrum, such as those with Asperger Syndrome, may have very good or even advanced language skills but find the rules governing social behaviour hard to fathom. On the other hand –”

“Doctor,” Annie-Marie said, trying to control her exasperation, “please just tell me what is wrong with my son.”

“I don’t know what’s wrong with your son. He has gone six years without demonstrating the ongoing – and it normally is ongoing – symptoms of autism.” The consultant took a deep breath. “Mrs Warburton, I would put down what happened the other day to … to a one-off unexplainable tantrum. All the tests we have conducted suggest your son is not only perfectly normal, but he is also highly intelligent. His social skills are excellent and,” the consultant smiled before adding, “Peter could give me the material for a full day’s lecture to all my learned colleagues, and at the end they would be as confused as I am now.”

“But it was when I told him I was pregnant that he –”

“It was going to bring change, Mrs Warburton,” the consultant said. “For him it would mean he was going to lose some of you when the baby was born.”

“I don’t understand.”

“Mrs Warburton, as I said we do not have all the answers, but you have been Peter’s lifeline –”

“I’m his mother.”

“Yes, but you are more than that. He sees in you … well, let me put it this way, he obviously dotes on you.”

"Thank you," Anne-Marie said. "So, you don't think I have anything to worry about?"

"No, Mrs Warburton, I would say you have something to marvel at rather than worry about."

Anne-Marie nodded. "Thank you, doctor."

Chapter Twenty-Two

Peter watched as his mother's happiness and tummy grew almost by the day.

He felt confused by his feelings towards what was happening. Every time he looked at his mother, he wanted to do something that would take them back to how it used to be … just the two of them. Although he fought against it, his feelings for Michael had changed. After going to bed, he often lay awake until he heard his mother and Michael come upstairs, and a few minutes later he would go and listen at their bedroom door. Sometimes the noises he heard puzzled him and he wanted to burst into the room to see what was happening. When he heard his mother scream he wanted to protect her, but then there was laughter and much shushing and that was equally bewildering.

The day his mother told him – told them – she was pregnant was a day he would never forget. He felt a sudden rage, he wanted to lash out and tell her she was lying. Something happened inside his head; it hurt and he wanted the pain to go away. He remembered rushing up to his room, screaming, and banging his head against the wall to get rid of the awful stabbing pain. In the hospital, they gave him some medicine and he felt better afterwards. They asked him many questions and gave him some simple tests to do, but after a few days it was over and he went home.

Having seen how worried his mother was that day he didn't want to hurt her again, so he learnt to control his feelings and devote more and more time to his homework and his further studies. There was one further incident after his sister, Rebecca, was born. At first his mother used to take the baby into her bedroom at night, but after a couple of months she was put into a cot in the newly-decorated nursery next to Peter's room. During the early hours of the morning when everything in the house was quiet, Peter crept into the nursery and looked down at his baby sister. The night light in the wall gave a mysterious glow to the room. Picking up a cushion from the chair his mother sat on when she was breastfeeding the baby, Peter went back to the cot. Just as he was placing the cushion over the baby's face, there was a noise, and then his mother's voice.

"I can't sleep, darling," he heard her whisper. "I'm going downstairs for a drink."

Peter went to the nursery door and saw his mother going down the stairs. Looking back at the cot he smiled.

"One day," he said quietly, "one day."

After the incident with Rebecca, Peter was determined to regain his mother's full affection and make her proud of him. Watching her going down the stairs when he had been on the point of suffocating his baby sister made him realise his feelings were perhaps temporarily misguided. Although there were strange voices in his head urging him on, he managed to take control and stop himself from doing something that would have brought great sadness to his mother's life. There would be other opportunities and he would be there to take them.

The next seven years passed without further incident. Throughout secondary school, Peter knew he was different because he didn't want to socialise with any of the other boys and girls, and later young men and women. He was more than happy in his own company and this made him a prime target for bullying, but when a couple of the boys who tried it on finished up the worse off, they left him alone. Peter was a handsome young man, tall and well-built so a few of the girls also tried it on for different reasons, but they soon got the message … he wasn't interested. For a while he became a talking point but the others soon lost interest, which suited him perfectly.

His excellent exam results got him into Cambridge University from where he achieved a 1st Class Honours in Biochemistry. Along with his academic success and his continuing love for cars, he also kept himself very, very fit. Despite his anti-social tendencies, he played junior county level rugby, and then after choosing the Army as his career, he played for the Military Academy, the Army and then the Combined Services rugby teams.

He was also an excellent cricketer, athlete and swimmer.

When they were sitting in the garden during a summer break and enjoying an early evening Pimms, his mother told him that she could not believe he had turned out the way he had. She explained what the doctor had said after Peter's admission to hospital when he was twelve having thrown a fit. She made it clear that she didn't want to take anything away from Peter's successes but she did put a lot of what had been achieved down to Michael's influence. It was something Peter didn't want to hear, but for his mother's sake he agreed.

When the time came for him to decide what regiment he wanted to be commissioned into, a number of the high profile infantry and cavalry regiments approached Peter, but much to everyone's surprise he chose the

Royal Army Ordnance Corps (RAOC). Although the explanation he gave for his choice satisfied the inquisitor's curiosity, in reality he knew he would have more of an opportunity to work on his own. Peter didn't bow to the ribbing he got from the other cadets about officers in the RAOC being called 'blanket stackers' because he knew that he was going to specialise in something that was far more dramatic than blankets.

"We thought you would have gone for one of the better-known cavalry regiments or even the Guards," Michael said to him.

Peter didn't think Michael was being openly critical, but his surprise was genuine so he smiled and said, "The sciences have always fascinated me, Michael, you know that. Without being overly boring, the chemistry of explosives is a science beyond all sciences. From when the Chinese first invented gunpowder in the 9th Century to the atomic bomb in the 20th, what could be more fascinating?" Peter didn't miss the look that passed between Michael and his mother. "So, the need to know more automatically pointed me towards being what is known as an ammunition technical officer or an 'ato' as they are called in the RAOC. I could have joined the Royal Engineers but their involvement is more conventional and less scientific, although they would dispute that."

"Darling," his mother said, "I'm sure Michael understands what you are saying but I'm afraid I don't."

"I know and I'm sorry. All I can say is that the RAOC have accepted me with open arms especially as I'm in the running for the 'Sword of Honour'," Peter said, his pride swelling his chest.

"What's that?" his mother asked.

Michael beamed from ear to ear. "It's the award that goes to the top cadet of the intake. "And –"

"And you could get it?" Anne-Marie said.

"Yes, Mum. I'm confident I will get it."

And he was right.

Peter was awarded the 'Sword of Honour' and on the day of his passing-out parade at the Military Academy his proud parents were given front row seats to watch the ceremony. Rebecca, who by now was ten years old, was also there having been taken out of school for a couple of days.

After a short inaugural tour in the rank of second lieutenant and then lieutenant as a platoon commander with an Ordnance Company in Germany, which he hated, Peter attended the Ammunition Technical Officers' course. Although he found elements of the course just a little tedious, he once again came top in everything. Because he excelled in the bomb disposal phase of the course, his first posting was to the Explosive

Ordnance Disposal (EOD) Company (Coy) in Hereford, and soon after he arrived, he went on his first operational tour of Northern Ireland.

When he defused one of the most dangerous and intricate terrorist devices the Province had seen for a very long time, he made Anne-Marie, Michael and Rebecca even more proud because the 'system' acknowledged his outstanding bravery with the Queen's Gallantry Medal (QGM).

Before going to Northern Ireland, Peter's Officer Commanding – Major Matt Constable – had told him that he had already seen in Peter attributes that warranted special treatment. He considered Peter to be an exceptional young officer whose career in the army was set in concrete. In other words he was a major general of the future.

When Peter returned from the Province and after some well-earned leave, his OC called him into his office. "Sit down, Peter, would you like some coffee?" Matt Constable asked him.

"No, thank you, Sir," Peter said as he sat down. "I never drink coffee, and tea only on rare and special occasions."

He fixed his boss with one of his looks.

Matt Constable sat down in the other easy chair. "Many congratulations for a superb tour, Peter. You did brilliantly. The General is coming over next week and he wants to see you. Have you been told when you'll be going to the Palace to get your gong?"

"No, not yet, Sir," Peter said. He could do without a bloody General's visit and a visit to the Palace.

"You've brought a lot of kudos to the Corps, Peter."

"I'm pleased to have been able to do so," Peter said as he wondered how many others would use his successes for their own advancement … including the General.

The two officers talked about Northern Ireland for a short while when Peter yet again related the details of 'The Castle Court Bomb' – the name given officially to the device he defused. Although Peter wasn't mentioned by name in the papers, when his decoration was published with many others as a Northern Ireland Gallantry award, it would be pretty obvious who had dealt the Provisional IRA – who claimed responsibility for the bomb regardless of it being defused – a bit of a propaganda blow.

After listening to Peter's account, Matt Constable said, "I had a chat with the CO of 22 SAS about you."

The OC suddenly had Peter's attention. "Why?" then remembered to add, "Sir?" to his question.

Matt Constable smiled. "I just thought you might like to have a crack. Things might be a bit mundane on the mainland after your last four months."

"I must admit I haven't thought about it," Peter said.

If he were being truthful, he had thought about little else and he intended applying anyway. Perhaps Matt Constable was a little more astute than Peter thought.

"Well, what do you think?" his OC asked him.

"I'll certainly give it a go."

"Great," Matt said, clapping his hands together. "Because they're so close, I've arranged for you to pop over later in the week to have a sneak preview."

Chapter Twenty-Three

Except for the worrying interludes when his mother told him she was pregnant and then when he came so close to smothering his baby sister, Peter didn't look back. What was going on in his head then and since was his very personal world and he never mentioned it to anyone.

The voices were his guides and he normally followed their advice.

Having started when he was eleven, the voices had become part of his daily life. At first he wasn't sure how to react. He tried wearing earphones when he could, and listening to loud music, but when that didn't work he began to pay attention to what the voices were saying to him and to his delight he discovered they guided him through some of the more difficult aspects of growing up but also helped him stand out from his peers. Sometimes the voices were supportive, congratulating him on doing something well, at other times they were angry and urged him into dangerous situations ... he was aware that the angry voices were often responsible for some of his achievements that others shied away from, telling him what to do next. The voices encouraged him to do better, run faster, hit a ball harder, and stay awake until three o'clock in the morning swotting for his exams.

When he passed SAS selection with flying colours, not only was he considered one of the best candidates for the Special Forces, he was also immediately earmarked for probable permanent transfer and to become one of the future Commanding Officers of the regiment … a significant accolade and another stepping stone towards his eventual aim.

The evening he heard he had passed selection, Peter smiled when he remembered his mother telling him that at a very early age she discovered he was supposedly suffering from an attention-deficit-disorder problem. How providential then that since a couple of weeks after his mother met Michael until now at the age of twenty-five, he was happy to have received all the attention he could have hoped for.

The voices were his, and he believed he was not alone in receiving subliminal guidance, so why make a mother overly worried for years when all medical science observed then was a child's development. Peter read up on hyperkinetic impulse disorder, discovered it was now called attention deficit/hyperactivity disorder (ADHD) and came down on the side of the critics who said it was not a straightforward psychiatric disorder. They referred to it as nothing more than a social stigma given to a child who was difficult to handle. Medication should not be allowed to replace good parenting; his mother told him that she never gave him any of the prescribed Ritalin (methylphenidate) believing that if she couldn't control his behaviour herself she would have felt she had failed him. In addition, she was worried that even at such a young age, Peter could become addicted ... and nobody could tell her what other side effects there might be.

He loved his mother for putting trust in not only herself but also in him. As a result they had both come through the traumas of his very young life a lot stronger and closer. He had and would make sure he never let her down – his successes were testament to how much he wanted to please her.

However, he wasn't anybody's fool.

Up until he passed SAS selection most of the competition he had come up against was either weak or lacked commitment. Peter learned very quickly that when serving with the cream of the crop, any chinks in an individual's armour might endanger his future.

He was determined to stay on top and watch his back every step of the way.

Nobody would ever know that he had secrets.

There was one particular individual who Peter quickly concluded was worth watching far more closely than the others. The critical and immediate trust wasn't there.

It was obvious from the outset that Staff Sergeant Stan Powers did not like him. During one 'off the record' exchange, Stan Powers told him that he had met some bloody good officers in his time but he believed that everyone, regardless of rank, had to earn the respect from their subordinates. Such an accolade did not automatically come with rank or background ... and he'd been in the Army long enough to smell the bad ones.

Peter quickly checked Powers' background.

Staff Sergeant Stan Powers was detached from the Royal Signals. He had also done extremely well during the Special Forces selection and had been with the regiment for eight years – a lot longer than expected – when Peter joined it.

At thirty-four years of age, Stan was one of the older members of the Regiment but also one of its most experienced and highly thought of operators. At only five and half feet tall, he was one of the shortest men in the Regiment. Although small, his wiry frame hid a body of immense strength and energy. Peter learned that Stan Powers could put an fifty-pound pack on his back, walk undetected for fifty miles, move into an Observation Post (OP) for forty-eight hours and then walk back again. That might not sound a particularly great achievement, Peter surmised, but when in hostile country – as Stan Powers had been on many occasions in the Middle East, Africa and Northern Ireland – there were times when it was a miracle that he and his 'brick' went undiscovered.

That was why Stan Powers earned the nickname, 'The Invisible Midget', and he was proud of it.

If he were on side, Powers would be a tremendous ally, but as an enemy, he would be ruthless.

Although Peter was an officer, the pecking order afforded by experience was well recognised. After being assigned to Stan Powers' 'brick' – a colloquialism for a four-man operating team – he learned to control what others deemed as arrogance, but he was determined to make his mark and stamp his superiority straight away. He had to watch his back but at the same time he had to make sure the others knew who was really in charge.

The voices advised caution.

After a couple of early verbal confrontations, Stan Powers was as open as the system, and Peter allowed him to be. He told Peter that he would bide his time. He had come across cocky officers before, both in and out of the SAS, and he had eventually turned them into what they should have been in the first place. If they didn't come up to his expectations, he broke them and he hadn't failed yet.

In response to the threat, Peter smiled and winked at him.

Powers might think he was the king but all kings were eventually deposed, and Powers' unseating would be rather pleasurable.

July 1992

Chapter Twenty-Four

Regardless of the ill feeling that existed between Peter and Stan Powers, their first few assignments together went well, mainly due to Peter holding back from anything that might cause dissension. He had to bite his tongue on any number of occasions, but it was something he was willing to do for a while.

The voices continued to advise caution.

Their fourth mission involved a covert observation in bandit country a few miles south of Carnagh in South Armagh. They were overlooking the border with Ireland and their task was to observe cross-border traffic movement and, in particular, to watch an isolated farmhouse, which was, they believed, used by the Provisional IRA as a safe house.

Briefed on exactly what was expected and what information was required, they were just leaving the briefing room when Peter's OC called him into his office.

Major Sebastian Fowler – the 'boss' – was an ex-Grenadier Guards officer and if asked, Peter would have reluctantly said he was the first officer for whom he had the utmost respect and would have followed anywhere.

Seeing the stern look on his OC's face, Peter knew straight away it wasn't going to be good news.

"It's your father," the boss said. "I'm afraid he's been killed in an RTA."

The shock didn't register straight away and all Peter could say was, "He's not my father. He's married to my mother, but he's not …"

The boss shrugged. "Well the news is the same."

"What happened?" Peter asked.

"Not totally sure but it seems he was crossing the road and was hit by a car."

"Right," Peter said, "thanks for letting me know."

"What about this mission you're going on? If you –"

"Don't even think it, boss," Peter said. "I'll go but I'll ring my mother first."

"If you're sure," the boss said.

"I'm sure."

"What happened, Mum?" Peter asked as he tried to calm his mother down. She was sobbing at the other end of the phone but Peter didn't have the time to call back later.

"He … he went into … into Farnham to get a few things for me … Rebecca's not well … she's off school. He was crossing the road near the Chemist in … in the High Street when this maniac of a woman driver completely ignored the pedestrian crossing and ploughed into him … he didn't stand a chance, Peter, not a chance."

"And the woman responsible?" he asked as calmly as he could.

"The police … the police are looking for her … she drove off, but witnesses said she must have been doing over forty miles per hour." There was a long pause. "It was murder not an accident … what am I going to do, Peter?"

Peter suddenly felt very strange.

It was almost as though he was outside his own body and looking down on Michael lying broken and bloody in the middle of the road. He also saw the car speeding away. His imagination pushed him into the car and he saw the maniacal smile on the woman's face, and he could smell the alcohol on her breath. This woman had taken from his mother the only other man she really loved, and from Peter the man he regarded as his brother … a brother he loved dearly regardless of his earlier misgivings.

Ignoring his mother's plea he said, "I've got to go, Mum. I have a job to do. I'll call you when I get back."

"The funeral –"

"Yes, the funeral," Peter said. "Mum, I can't explain but I might not be able to be there."

"But the arrangements … who will –?"

"His parents … and his sister, she's in Guildford, isn't she?'

"Yes, but –"

"Mum, believe me, if I can be there I will, but … I've got to go. Ring this number when the details are known." He gave his mother the Chief Clerk's telephone number. "I'm sorry, Mum. If they get the woman she will pay for what she's done."

He put the receiver down.

Chapter Twenty-Five

Peter took up his position with the other three on the edge of a large wood. Their location was above and about two hundred and fifty hundred yards from the farmhouse, and they could also observe the main road leading to the border as well as the house. They were due to be there for two days before they were withdrawn to be replaced by another 'brick', depending on what the first group discovered.

They were there to observe, nothing else.

Those were their orders.

It was a task that none of them liked but appreciated it had to be done. They watched the farmhouse day and night, taking it in turns to get some sleep and to eat.

At two fifteen in the afternoon on the second day, two cars turned off the main road and headed for the farm. All four members of the 'brick' were awake and observing, although one was in depth and watching their rear. It was the first movement near the farm they had seen for the thirty-eight hours since starting the observation.

The cars, one a dark blue saloon, probably a Mazda, the other a black estate and easily identifiable as a Volvo 760, were travelling quickly, throwing up a blanket of dust in the hot July afternoon. They disappeared behind a small hill, on which a few bedraggled looking sheep were grazing, before reappearing about fifty yards from the entrance to the farm. Once at the farm the cars slewed to a halt by the side of the main house. Two men and a tall woman got out of the first car – the saloon – and then three more men from the estate. Two went to the back of the saloon, opened the boot and bundled a large object wrapped in a dark sheet from the car to the house.

"A body," Stan Powers whispered to Peter Bennett.

"And it's light," Peter added, his own powerful binoculars trained on the group making him feel as though he was standing only yards away from the men.

"Maybe female," Stan said. "He threw whoever it is over his shoulder with ease. It's a pity we're here just to observe."

"I'm well aware of that," Peter said.

After the five men and the tall woman went into the house, the door closed behind them.

The SAS troopers, now joined by their rearguard, waited and Peter made sure that at all times one of them had his binoculars focussed on the house.

He was bored.

Although it wasn't his first task since moving to the Province, he found it tedious. He was very aware of Stan Powers' continuing hostility towards him, but little men like him, Peter thought, needed keeping in check. He believed the hostility was now because Powers realised how good Peter was, and nobody liked to be wrong.

Although he had been on a few assignments in the UK and one in Germany, he hadn't had the opportunity to show this little shit who was really in charge, but his moment would come. The other two members of the 'brick' knew exactly where they stood, but Stan Powers thought he knew it all because he was the most experienced.

However, Peter was no fool: he would use Powers' experience to his own advantage. He was glad he was with the regiment, but he didn't want to stay too long. More than a couple of years would interfere with his planned promotion programme. He wanted to be a Lieutenant Colonel by the time he was thirty-five and he knew he was capable of achieving his aim. Little people like Stan Powers were not going to stand in his way.

Yes, he was bored.

If the cars hadn't appeared, he would be asleep now – it was his turn. A couple of hours, that's all he would need. He closed his eyes for a few seconds. Immediately he saw Michael lying in the road, his body broken and bloodied. He also saw the car that had hit him, speeding away from the scene. He heard people screaming as they witnessed the horror of what had happened.

He was sorry he had to speak to his mother the way he did, but Michael was dead and nothing would bring him back. If they caught the woman who murdered the only man he and his mother loved so dearly, Peter wondered if some smart-arsed lawyer would get her off and she would escape the suffering she had inflicted.

Real screams permeated their way into his tired and confused mind.

It was a female's haunting cry for help. The creature who had been dragged into the building was being tortured. Glancing at the other three members of the 'brick', it was obvious from their expressions that they had drawn the same conclusion. Peter was surprised at first by his reaction. If it had been a man or even an animal he would have wanted to put them out of their misery, but it was neither; it was a female crying for help. Rather than wanting it to end, he found the thrill he was getting from listening to her cries exhilarating. He frowned when a wry smile came to his lips. Why was he smiling? Of course, the woman who had murdered Michael … he imagined his killer was suffering and feeling the pain he must have felt. The voices were there, telling him that what he was hearing was just.

It was what she deserved.

The screaming stopped suddenly.

Peter closed his eyes once again and waited.

Half an hour later, the back door opened. It led onto a small courtyard surrounded by a low wall.

Peter lifted his binoculars.

Two men carrying Armalite rifles left the building, looked all around and then indicated to whoever was just inside the door. Two more men emerged carrying AK47s and dragging a naked female between them. Her hands were bound behind her back and a hood covered her head, but there was no mistaking that she was a female.

Peter adjusted the focus on his binoculars.

The men took the woman into the middle of the courtyard and forced her to her knees. She was alive and able to support herself ... just. Kneeling in the middle of the yard, her bare buttocks resting on her calf muscles, her small dirty feet at a slight angle, her breasts pointing towards the ground and her head bowed, her bruised and bloodied body looked pathetic. Compared with the men who had dragged her out, she was tiny.

Her fate was sealed.

Peter reached for the Heckler and Koch sniper's rifle.

"No, boss," Stan Powers whispered next to him, putting his hand on Peter's arm. "There's nothing we can do."

Looking through the telescopic sight, Peter shrugged off Powers' arm. It was the first time Powers had called him 'boss' – he had won. The girl's covered head came into view. He adjusted the sight and switched to the four men, lining up the cross hairs on each of their heads in turn.

"Boss, no!" Powers repeated next to him. "We are here to observe not to fight."

"They are going to kill her," Peter said through clenched teeth, his eye never wavering from the telescopic sight. The other two troopers were a few yards away but Peter was aware that they were watching the exchange intently.

The voices were loud, telling him he was doing the right thing.

"Yes, they are," Powers said in a hushed voice. "The poor kid looks half-dead anyway. There's nothing we can do."

"Maybe not you, but –"

Sensing further movement, Peter swung the sniper's rifle towards the back door through which the tall woman and the fifth man were emerging. The man was carrying another AK47, and the tall woman had a silenced pistol hanging loosely at her side. When the group had first arrived, Peter did not get a good look at her, but this time he could see her quite clearly. She was pretty in a rugged sort of way, tall, slim, only an inch or so shorter than the man who walked beside her, black hair in a ponytail, blue jeans, trainers, a dark green T-shirt and a pair of wrap-around sunglasses.

Peter put the cross hairs onto her head and took the first pressure from the trigger of the rifle.

"Boss, you'll compromise the whole fucking operation. We are here to observe not to –"

"Tell me we're here to observe once more and I'll –"

He broke off again as the tall woman slowly crossed the courtyard and stood behind what he believed was her intended victim. The other four men moved away, each lifting their rifles to their shoulders and looking around the surrounding area. Peter saw one of them look directly towards their position, but his eyes moved on. 'The Invisible Midget' had chosen the spot well, Peter admitted but reluctantly. The fifth man stayed with the woman but to one side, his eyes never leaving her.

The tall woman bent down as she held the pistol out to one side before pulling the hood from the naked woman's head. Peter saw the naked woman lift her head, her eyes slits as the sudden light blinded her. She had very short brown hair and a long neck.

His grip tightened on the rifle.

The voices urged him on.

"Boss –"

"Shut up, Powers," Peter said through clenched teeth.

"You mustn't –"

"Shut up and get ready," Peter said.

He indicated which of the armed men in the back yard were to be their individual targets, and then secondary targets. He saw the other troopers slowly reach for their rifles and put the butts to their shoulders, their loyalty now divided: Peter was the officer.

The tall ponytailed woman yanked back the naked woman's head by her hair and said something into her ear. Tears fell slowly down the naked woman's cheeks as she unhurriedly shook her head. Dried blood crusted her nostrils, and all round her mouth. He could even see the cigarette burns on her breasts and abdomen.

Her head jolted forward as the tall ponytailed woman released her, at the same time moving the pistol so that its silencer was resting against the back of the naked woman's skull.

The voices were saying, “Now, now, now.”

Peter centred the crosshairs on the tall ponytailed woman’s head.

He opened his left eye and he could see the men in the yard were now all watching what was happening.

“Boss –” Peter heard Stan Powers say just before he pulled the trigger.

The tall woman crumpled, a single black hole appearing at her temple, her sunglasses flying off, a mass of blood and bone spouting from the other side of her head. For a split second, a look of utter surprise appeared on her face and then she slumped to the ground. The two men furthest away, and the man next to the executioner, fell almost simultaneously, quickly followed by the other two as bullets ripped into their bodies.

It was over in seconds.

The sound of the rifle shots echoed round the surrounding hills and then died, as six people had just died. All Peter could hear was the breeze in the trees above him, and the scrawny sheep bleating in the field on the hill to their left.

He took aim.

The naked woman’s body wasn’t moving and there was blood under her head. He hadn’t shot the tall woman to save the one he was now aiming at; he had shot her for revenge. The smirk on her face had been so arrogant, so superior, just like the one who had killed Michael.

The voices were congratulating him.

He took the first pressure on the trigger but then stopped.

Slowly he lowered the sniper’s rifle, and picking up his binoculars he swept them across the scene of carnage. There was no movement. The naked woman was lying on her side; her lower jaw had almost disappeared and the pool of blood at the back of her head was getting bigger.

“You silly fucking bastard,” Stan Powers said as he indicated to the trooper with the radio to call for extraction.

Trooper Bill Green spoke into the microphone strapped around his neck. “Hullo, Zero Charlie, this is One Two, extract in forty minutes, over,” quickly followed by, “forty minutes, out.”

With Stan Powers in the lead, the ‘brick’ moved swiftly and silently rearwards from their position, and nobody said a word until they were on the other side of the wood thirty minutes later, and twenty-five yards from the extraction rendezvous point. They automatically moved into all-round defence as they waited for the Lynx helicopter.

Stan Powers looked across at Peter Bennett and said loud enough for the others to hear, “Yours will be the shortest tour with the regiment ever, you fucking idiot.”

Peter Bennett ignored him.

“What the fucking hell did you think you were doing?”

Peter remained silent.

The voices had encouraged him to kill for the first time.

They were there now, as he lay trying to blank out Powers' words. They were there talking among themselves and telling him he had done the right thing. He had killed evil and that had to be a good thing. They kept on using the word ... revenge.

"You stupid fucking bastard, Bennett. Have you any idea what you've done?" Powers' said, sneering. "This is the end for you."

"Shut the fuck up," Peter said, "or you'll be the next."

Turning to locate the source of the sound of the helicopter's rotor blades, the realisation of the truth behind what Powers' was saying hit him. He was not in control – not this time. The enormity of his actions would mean the end of …

What an idiot! Why had he listened to them?

They had been there to observe.

But he didn't have any choice because he had to do it. The voices had always been right before.

Nobody would ever understand.

Nobody understood when at twelve years of age he threw that tantrum on hearing his mother was pregnant, so why would they understand now?

He must regain control.

The voices had always been right ... but this time?

There must be a way of ridding himself of the power they had over him..

Chapter Twenty-Six

Peter wasn't surprised when within twenty-four hours he was flown out of Northern Ireland, by-passed his unit in Hereford, and was sent to an RAOC unit – 154 Forward Ammunition Depot (FAD) near *Wulfen*, located between *Münster* and *Wesel* in *Nordrhein-Westfalen* in Northern Germany.

It wasn't what he expected – he thought things would be kept within the ranks of the Special Forces. He didn't understand.

The Commanding Officer of the depot was Lieutenant Colonel Mark O'Connell. Peter was under no illusion concerning the trouble he was in but he knew the CO wouldn't be told the real reason he was being sent to Germany. When the authorities informed the CO of the move, it was because there was a need to relocate an officer quickly for disciplinary reasons and he had drawn the short straw. There was no need for him to know any more at this stage.

Flown by military aircraft from RAF Aldergrove, Belfast, to RAF Northholt near Ruislip in England, a scheduled RAF commuter flight subsequently took Peter to RAF Brüggen, where a car was waiting to take him to his destination.

On his arrival in 154 FAD, and once he had unpacked his bags in his room in the Officers' Mess, he was called for an immediate interview with the CO who tried unsuccessfully to extract some more information from him.

The two men did not shake hands.

"I know who you are and I'm aware of the reason why you are here," the CO said.

"With respect, Sir," Peter replied, standing in front of the CO's desk with his hands behind his back, "you might know my name and a bit of my background, but you do not know why I'm here and it's unlikely you will ever know."

Peter knew of the facts transmitted by Staff Sergeant Sam Powers in his verbal and written reports to the CO 22 SAS in England. The facts could not be disputed. The CO immediately flew to Northern Ireland, and he was in the General Officer Commanding Northern Ireland's office when Peter arrived. There was no defence to offer and Peter had little choice but to corroborate Powers' account. After expressing their gross disappointment, his superior officers ordered Peter out of the Province and told him where he would go until dealt with officially … probably by court martial.

But why Germany?

The speed with which things happened meant Peter did not have time to contact his mother, and even if he'd been given that courtesy, he wouldn't have tried. He had no idea when Michael's funeral was, but under the circumstances, he would not be there. His mother would be devastated but the situation was not under Peter's control.

The voices had fallen silent.

But during his journey from Northern Ireland to Germany, Peter had time to reflect.

His mother didn't know he was in Northern Ireland and she certainly was not going to know that his future and therefore his career were now in tatters. Also on reflection, he didn't regret what he had done, and although the voices controlled his actions he couldn't get over the elation he felt at the time of taking that female's life ... nor afterwards.

He felt exhilarated … with the power over life and death.

He saw again the naked woman kneeling on the dried earth in the courtyard of the farmhouse: the silenced pistol held to the back of her head, and her female executioner's own head exploding as the 7.62mm high velocity bullet passed through her brain.

He had executed the executioner and more importantly, the female executioner.

The voices in his head might have urged him on but he would have done it anyway. He was wrong to question the wisdom of the voices, they had been right.

And he would do it again.

It was not over because there would be more; there had to be more.

He wasn't sure what the outcome of any court martial would be when he was charged with gross negligence and disobedience of a lawful command – but he was sure the court martial would be held 'in camera'. It had to be. There was too much at stake for it to be anything else. Nothing would be allowed to become public.

But he did know he wanted out of the army completely and as quickly as possible. Accepting his career was over was not as difficult as he expected, but if he could make it easier for the authorities to accept his resignation rather than go through the embarrassment of what might be said at a court martial, then that's what he would do.

A female who worked in the Officers' Mess helped his cause.

The woman concerned was Mrs Sandra Davies, the wife of Corporal Trevor Davies who worked in the control office in depot headquarters. She was a pretty woman in an earthy sort of way, and she caught Peter's eye straight away and from her reaction to the attention she thought he was giving her, it was obvious to him that she would be a willing participant in his plan.

However, his immediate future wasn't the only thing he needed to consider. When he looked into Sandra Davies' eyes for the first time, the voices came to life; they saw death, and therefore so did he. At that moment, he had no idea why he felt this way but he was sure the voices would tell him and then guide him.

For the time being, he needed to keep away from the other officers living in the Mess. He would eat his meals late and if there was anybody in the dining room he would make sure he sat down well away from them. If they tried to strike up a conversation, he would ignore them. It didn't matter what they thought ... what anybody thought.

But with Sandra Davies it was different; befriending her was necessary.

The papers which arrived late that morning – the day after they were published in the UK – had in one way or another all referred to a *Massacre in South Armagh.* The bodies of five men and two women had been discovered at Stonehouse Farm near Carnagh, all the victims had been shot. There was no mention in any of the reports that the SAS had been involved, in fact editorial speculation suggested that Loyalist paramilitaries were responsible.

He read the reports over lunch, the voices congratulated him.

As he left the dining room after lunch on his second day he noticed Sandra Davies was in the bar clearing up. He introduced himself and started flirting with her. Within a few minutes of meeting him, she was telling Peter that she was bored with life, with her marriage, with her job, with being stuck out in the middle of no-where in Germany, and bored with the lack of attention her husband was paying her.

"At thirty-one I feel more like a fifty year old," she said as she put the used glasses on a tray.

"So why do you stay with him?" Peter asked.

"Because," she said, "until I find somebody else who can look after me properly then I'm stuck with him."

She went on to tell him that she had managed numerous affairs since she and Trevor had married twelve years ago, some of which he knew about but none of which he cared about. Her husband was of the opinion that if she wanted more than he could give, then she could make a fool of herself if that was what she wanted, but just let her try getting one penny out of him if she ever decided to run off permanently with another man.

Mrs Sandra Davies was being rather obvious and her message was clear; and Peter would make full use of what she was saying. They talked for another five minutes before she needed to go. It was her afternoon off and she had things to do.

"Which room have they given you?" she asked just before she left.

"Why do you ask?" Peter said.

"I'm on 'earlies' tomorrow so I'll be bringing your tea in the morning –"

"I rarely drink tea," Peter said.

"Coffee then?"

He shook his head and smiled. "No, I don't drink coffee at all."

"There's got to be something I can bring you. What about orange juice or lemon?"

Peter nodded. "Orange would be lovely."

"I'll leave you till last," Sandra said, smiling.

The next morning Peter was awake when she tapped on the door and opened it without waiting for his response. He pretended to be asleep but was aware she had come into the room and closed the door. The single sheet was only covering the bottom half of his body. He opened his eyes and saw from her expression and smile that she was unabashed by his semi-nakedness.

"Your orange juice," she said, a little huskily.

She stared at him.

"Haven't you seen a naked man before?" he asked, quietly amused.

The military academy, sport, the courses he had attended, and then SAS selection and training, had been his priorities; he didn't have time for relationships. He didn't want a relationship – his mother could never be replaced by any other woman. When he needed a female for purely physical reasons he paid for sex if necessary but was always discreet. He ensured the women's discretion because before they were paid he explained precisely what would happen to them if they were ever to kiss and tell. Most of them were shaking by the time he finished, but not one ever told.

"Of course I have," Sandra said, looking a little embarrassed. She was still holding the glass so she moved to the other side of the bed and put it on the writing desk.

"Then why were you staring?"

"It's not every morning you see … well, you know. You're so different and so –"

"If you'd waited after you knocked, you wouldn't have seen anything."

He kicked the sheet away, got off the bed, went over to the wash basin and looked in the mirror. She was still staring at him.

He turned round to face her.

"Oh," she said. "It's not that I don't see things, I don't mind seeing things, it's just that they don't normally look like you do." Her eyes drifted down his body.

"So, Mrs Sandra Davies, deliverer of tea and coffee and orange juice in the early morning to naked and frustrated officers, what are we going to do next?"

He moved away from the wash-basin and walked over to her.

Putting his hand under her chin, he traced a line with a finger down her throat, between her breasts to the waistband of her jeans. He undid the button fastener and slowly lowered the zip.

She stood perfectly still as though paralysed … or hypnotised.

"What ... what are we going to do next?" she whispered as the tips of his fingers played beneath the elastic of her pants.

He leant forward, withdrew his hand and kissed her on the forehead.

"I'm going to have a shower, that's what," he said, as he reached for the towel on the back of a chair. Sandra Davies didn't move. "Won't the others be wondering where you are?" he asked, wrapping the towel round his waist.

She shook her head. "Yes … yes, of course."

Opening the door, Peter bowed. "Then you had better go." As she passed him, he said, "I'm not that stupid but it doesn't mean to say I'm not interested. We'll need to agree a few ground rules first."

Sandra stopped on the other side of the door.

"Who are you?" she asked, screwing up her face.

"Captain Peter Bennett," he said. "Room 12, neither tea nor coffee, just a glass of orange juice."

"No, I mean who are you really?"

"It would be best if you never found out," he said.

After showering and before going down to the dining room for a late breakfast, Peter sat down at the desk in his room and wrote his letter of resignation. What he had done and what he intended doing were sure to see him out of the army reasonably quickly, but if he added his resignation into the pot it would give the authorities cause for thought ... an easy and quiet exit strategy for everybody.

Over a passable full English breakfast he decided that he was not going to be humiliated by ignoramuses … they wouldn't get any satisfaction out of watching him being judged by idiots who would make up a court martial.

The voices agreed. He was doing the right thing.

He would eventually tell his mother where he had been and that he had decided the army was not for him after all: he would go back to university as a mature student and then choose a career where his talents would be recognised and appreciated.

The summons came the day after Peter had given the sealed envelope containing his resignation to the CO's PA. Previously, he had kept out of everybody's way, either by staying in his room or going into the public rooms when nobody else was about. He also went for a couple of runs in the depot. He needed to maintain his fitness.

"Sit down, Peter." Mark O'Connell stayed behind his desk. He had Peter's letter in his hand. "I think we need to discuss this before I send it into the system, if indeed that's what happens."

Peter hoped the look in his eyes communicated his contempt. "There's nothing to discuss, Sir."

"When an officer of mine decides to resign then of course there is something to discuss." Mark O'Connell let the letter fall from his hand onto the desk.

"Sir, you have my letter of resignation. I am not one of your officers. I am no more than an irritation to you so you should be pleased with my decision, and that letter contains my decision. I would prefer it if you would just put it into the system. As you can see I've asked to be released as soon as possible."

"The system might decide that they won't accept it," he said. "I understand that a court-martial is in the offing for whatever it is you did. I can assure you any disciplinary action will take precedence over your own personal needs."

Peter had been deliberately insolent and his senior officer was angry. He was going to play on that anger. "The system will accept it. I can assure you of that. I will not be court-martialled because I will not come out of such proceedings the worse off."

Mark O'Connell sneered. "And why are you so sure of that?"

"Sir, there are things you don't know about and have no need to know. In fact, I doubt whether your clearance is to the right level for you to know even an inkling of what I am talking about. My resignation will be welcomed and I see no need to sit here and discuss it any further with you," Peter said and stood up.

As expected, Mark O'Connell exploded. "Sit down, you insolent little shit!"

Peter didn't move. "Sir, for you that letter is a formality. We both know what you should now do with it. I would be obliged if you would do exactly that."

Mark O'Connell was almost puce with rage. "You –"

"Sir, if I stay in your office any longer you are likely to have a fit. By talking to you the way I have, if you didn't already have my resignation you'd have every right to ask me for it. I've saved you the need to ask."

Peter put his hat on, saluted, and walked out of the CO's office.

The voices in his head cheered him on.

During the next week, and to make his life a little less tedious as he waited for the bureaucratic wheels to turn in his favour, Peter Bennett took Sandra Davies up on her rather obvious offer. She had become part of his plan.

It was seven-thirty on Friday morning.

Fifteen minutes after taking him his orange juice, Sandra was lying on his bed, one leg hanging over the side, wallowing in the aftermath of her reawakening to what having sex can really mean.

Peter was standing at the wash basin, watching her in the mirror. He hadn't done anything special, would give her five out of ten but possibly a six if he took her enthusiasm into consideration. She lacked finesse, but as a means of satisfying his needs and as a source of amusement, she would do. He would also make sure the right rumours started because they would speed up his departure. When he had looked down at her a few minutes ago, he once again saw her eyes staring up at him in death.

"You'd better carry on with your early morning calls," Peter said, turning round and leaning against the wash basin.

"You were the last," she said without opening her eyes.

"Then the other staff will be suspicious." Having taken what he needed from her, he wanted her out of his room. He felt disgusted with himself but it was how he always felt after having sex: disgust and confusion generated by a lack of understanding as to who he was and what he was – thoughts that always chiselled into his brain.

Sandra opened her eyes. "Is that it then?" She levered herself up on her elbows.

"Until the next time, yes," he said.

"There will be a next time, will there?"

"When I'm ready, yes."

"You're pretty damn sure of yourself."

"And you didn't want it to happen?"

"Yes, but –"

"Then we're both happy, but I think you should get dressed and leave now."

Sandra swung her feet onto the floor, and stood up. "Is that all I am to you?"

"You are to me what I am to you." Peter said, getting annoyed.

Sandra picked up her pants from the floor and stepped into them. "And what are you to me?" she asked as she pulled them over her thighs.

"A solution."

"Yes, you certainly are damn sure of yourself," she said, fastening her bra.

"Are you denying it?"

She thought for a moment but then smiled. "No."

"Then think yourself lucky ... for the moment."

As she left the room, the voices came to life.

Peter heard a deep, penetrating almost metallic voice take precedence. "*In the bible,*" it said, "*six symbolizes man and his weaknesses, the evils of Satan and the manifestation of sin. The figure six will therefore signify your release. You have killed once, there must be five others and then we will release you. The woman who has just left will be the second, and you must choose four others. When you have killed your sixth victim, you will be free.*"

Peter smiled.

He had direction.

Chapter Twenty-Seven

Two weeks later and after Sandra had given Captain Peter Bennett her *special morning juices* as she called them on a further four occasions, she was watching television with her husband when he said, "So who is it this time?"

She heard him but ignored his question.

"I asked you who it is this time?" Trevor Davies persisted.

"I'm watching the TV," she said angrily.

"Fuck the TV. I asked you a question."

She turned and glared at him. "What makes you think there is a *this* time?"

"When isn't there? Who is it?"

Sandra looked at her husband with disgust. He was sprawled in an armchair wearing the same joggers he always wore, his vest grubby with food stains, and the same smelly slippers. He was overweight, needed a shave and she knew if she got too close, he would smell. But he was her meal ticket, and until she found somebody better he would have to do.

"You've never wanted to know before," she threw at him.

"I've always known before. I've always known who you are shagging, but this time –"

"What do you mean you've always known? You've never known." Sandra began to feel a little worried.

"For me to know and you to find out," he said childishly.

"You've never fucking known."

"So who is it?"

Their eyes were still on the television screen, but it was probably the longest exchange of words they had managed in days. "If you're so good, you tell me."

"I have my suspicions."

"Do you? So why on this occasion do you want to know from me?"

Trevor looked at her for the first time. "Because … because whoever it is, is making me jealous."

"Jealous! You jealous? And what about all the fucking sluts you've been with over the years. I suppose you think I didn't know about them."

Trevor shrugged. "Maybe."

Trevor Davies loved his wife. In fact, he loved her so much he would die for her. He would do anything to keep her but he was on a knife-edge. Regardless of what he said, he hadn't the faintest idea who she had slept with and who she hadn't, but if it meant that she stayed with him, then he was willing to overlook her adulterous behaviour.

The night before their wedding he discovered she had slept with his best man so it wasn't as if he didn't know what he was letting himself in for. He never questioned why he believed his fiancée – or his best man come to that – would do such a thing so he just accepted she would. There had never been anybody else for him; he just let her think there had been to perhaps ease her own conscience a little.

It wasn't because he hadn't wanted to or because the opportunity had never arisen, it was just that he couldn't. He loved his wife and regardless of what she did, he couldn't do the same. He accepted that he was being spineless, but nobody would ever understand how he really felt.

Sometimes when she was out, whether just for the evening or the whole night, he would cry himself to sleep but he never let on about the effect she had on him. He would rather be with her under the worst of circumstances than not at all.

This time it was different. This time he was worried. She was taking extra special care of herself. She was even taking longer to get herself ready in the mornings. This morning he had watched her at just after six-thirty putting on her make-up, sitting at the dressing table, her bare back as tantalising as ever. He pretended to be asleep, but he was watching her. Whoever it was, he must be local ... maybe even a work colleague. Was somebody laughing at him behind his back? At least with the others it had been in her own time, not when she was supposed to be at work.

"So who is it?" he asked again.

"Somebody who knows how to treat a woman," she spat at him. "Somebody who dresses properly, somebody who has manners, somebody who has a bath more than once a week, somebody who –"

"Is it more than just sex? Do you love whoever it is?"

Trevor closed his eyes because he was dreading her answer. She didn't love him, although she stayed with him, but he wasn't stupid enough not to know why. If she found somebody else, somebody she might even love – if she were capable of love – then the knife-edge he was balancing on wouldn't exist.

He might lose her completely and he didn't want to think that was a possibility.

Thrown by the question, Sandra was temporarily stuck for words.

The word love hadn't been mentioned for years, so why was he suddenly talking about it?

Love?

What the bloody hell did that word mean anyway? Did she love Peter Bennett? She loved what he did to her: she loved the way he made her feel, but real love? She wasn't sure what real love was. If she went to his room on Monday morning and found him gone, would she feel as though part of her had gone with him?

She wasn't sure.

He had never answered her question about who he really was, but she was sure he wasn't who he said he was; there was something odd about him. Could she love somebody she didn't know? He never asked her out. They could have gone somewhere miles away, met up some place or other where nobody would see them. If he did ask she would go, she would go anytime and anywhere.

There was something about him that mesmerised her. There were rumours of course; one of the cooks in the Mess told her that he was in some sort of trouble but she had added, "Does it really matter if you're in trouble when you look like him?"

Sandra had agreed.

When she went into his room all he did when he wanted her was nod his head. He didn't even smile. In fact, she'd never seen him smile. His nod told her to take her clothes off and get into bed with him, which of course she did every time.

Was that love?

No, that was sex – nothing more, nothing less. He wanted her and she wanted him … for sex.

Is that what she should tell Trevor? Should she tell him anything?

She didn't hate Trevor: she would never have married him if she thought that one day she would hate him, but she certainly did not love him. She liked him enough to be there for him, she understood his needs, and even that was all right as long as he took a bath or a shower first. In fact, the previous Tuesday when the mysterious Peter Bennett and Trevor had both had sex with her on the same day, she had got quite a thrill out of it. That had never happened before, having two men on the same day.

She would do it again, as long as it was Peter first.

She stopped, surprised by her own thought process.

Since mysterious Peter Bennett had been having sex with her, she realised she had wanted her husband more than before. Now there's a turn up – or even a turn on – for the books. She let a whimsical smile cross her lips, amused by her own thoughts.

The smile was not lost on Trevor.

"Why are you smiling? Are you thinking about him?"

She let her eyes drift in his direction. "I think you're becoming paranoid."

"Paranoid? I think I've every right to be fucking paranoid."

Chapter Twenty-Eight

The rumours reached Lieutenant Colonel Mark O'Connell's ears the same day they spread like wild fire round the camp, and this time he had to do something about it. He had put up with enough from this bloody officer, and he wasn't going to let it get to him any longer.

"Tim?" Mark said, "It's Mark O'Connell here."

"Morning Mark, how's the smallest ammunition depot in Germany?" It was the same banter whenever they spoke on the phone.

"It's still holding more ammunition than that wasteland of yours." Then before his fellow CO could carry on he said, "Tim, I think I'm going to need your help. I'll clear it with the Brigadier before we go firm but I just wanted your agreement in principle before I speak to him."

"Shoot," Timothy Smithers said.

"You know I told you that I'd taken on Captain Peter Bennett?"

"Yes. I felt for you."

"Well, something has reached my ears that could mean I'm going to have to move him pretty quickly."

"That could only mean one thing," Timothy said.

"It's only a rumour at the moment but he's coming to see me at nine this morning in …" he looked at his watch, "... in ten minutes. I just wanted to have a plan in place before I see him."

"My officers are as perplexed as anybody else as to why Bennett was sent to you in the first place. So, somebody's wife is it?"

"Worse than that, a bloody corporal's wife."

"A corporal? Bloody hell, that could be a court martial offence to add to whatever else he's done, and knowing this Brigadier … actually he might go for the soft alternative."

"Just sack him you mean?"

"Yes."

"But we'll still need to keep Bennett in Germany until a decision is made."

"Christ, as if I haven't got enough with Clive Benton," Tim said. "I told you about him, didn't I?"

"Yes, you did. Is he behaving himself?"

"So far." There were a few seconds silence. "Well, I suppose one more won't make that much difference."

"Thanks, Tim."

"Why can't these young officers keep their willies to themselves, or at least put them in places that don't matter?"

"Search me, but it keeps us on our toes."

"You're right there, Mark. When are you going to phone the Brigadier?"

"After I've seen Bennett … oh, did I tell you Bennett's submitted his resignation?"

"No. When did he do that?"

"Couple of weeks ago," Mark told him.

"What a prat. The system might have allowed him to go quietly even after … well we don't know after what, do we? Now look at him. Says a lot for sword of honour winners, doesn't it? QGM, SAS, he had everything going for him. He must have … no, I won't speculate, not on the phone, but have you discovered anything else? Yes or no will do."

"No, Tim. Just that it was something in Ireland."

"How the mighty are fallen, eh?"

"Exactly."

"Let me know if the Brigadier agrees with the move, Mark."

"Will do, Tim, and thanks."

As Mark O'Connell put down the phone, there was a tap at his door.

"Come in," he said.

Captain Penelope Ward, his Adjutant, peered round the door. "Captain Bennett's here, Sir."

"Thanks, Penny. Give me five minutes, then send him in."

Mark O'Connell sat back in his leather chair. He knew he had to be careful how he handled this. Bennett had already demonstrated what a bloody smart-arse he was. Whether there was tangible proof or not about this affair, the rumours were sufficient to move him. He was sorry to be shifting the responsibility to Tim Smithers – he liked Tim – but it would be best to keep it in the family. He was sure the Brigadier would agree.

Five minutes later, Peter Bennett was standing in front of his desk.

"Do you know why you're here, Captain Bennett?" Mark asked. There were going to be no informalities, not this time.

"No, Sir."

"I thought you'd say that."

"Then I didn't disappoint you –"

"Don't you dare speak to me like that –"

"Like what, Sir, I was just agreeing with you?"

"You think you're really smart, don't you," Mark O'Connell said, trying to keep control of his temper.

"No, Sir, I –"

"That wasn't a question."

"Oh, right, Sir."

Mark O'Connell closed his eyes momentarily. The interview hadn't lasted a minute and Bennett was already getting up his nose. He took a deep breath and opened his eyes.

"I have been reliably informed that you are having an affair with a corporal's wife. Are you?" He spoke as calmly as he could, knowing that he was going to have a battle on his hands and he had to stay in control.

When Peter Bennett gave him his reply, he almost fell off his chair.

"For once, Sir, your information is accurate." Peter Bennett was standing rigidly to attention, looking at a spot about a foot above his CO's head.

"What? You admit it?"

Peter lowered his head and looked directly at Mark O'Connell. "Yes, Sir, I admit it, but I wouldn't say I've been having an affair with Sandra Davies, more a, how can I put it? More a rather special early morning call, Sir."

"What does that mean?"

"It means that when she brings me my orange juice in the morning, she stirs it for me."

"Orange juice?"

"Yes, orange juice, Sir."

"What the hell are you talking about?"

"It means she gives me an interesting wake up call, Sir, accompanied by a glass of orange juice."

"You've been doing it in my Mess with her?" Mark O'Connell said through clenched teeth.

"When I arrived, Sir, one of your officers, I won't mention his name, told me what a boring hell-hole your Mess was. So, I'm afraid I took him rather literally, Sir. And perhaps you ought to ask your Adjutant what she gets up to in your Mess, Sir."

"Who, Penny?"

"If she's your Adjutant, Sir, then yes. Penny."

"That's typical of you, Bennett, trying to involve somebody else. You're in deep shit and I'm going to recommend to the Brigadier that he adds insubordination and insolence to a charge of behaviour unbecoming of an officer, and bringing the Army into disrepute."

"If it gets me out of your Army of disrepute earlier than my resignation would have done, I'll plead guilty to whatever you want."

"You can pack your bags and be out of my depot in six hours, Bennett. You're to report –"

"They are already packed, Sir. I can leave earlier if you would like."

Mark O'Connell shot out of his chair, rising to his full height of five and half feet.

"Bennett, you are to report to the CO of 3 Base Ammunition Depot in *Bracht* at oh-nine-hundred hours tomorrow morning."

"Of course, Sir. Is that all?"

"Get out!" Mark O'Connell shouted.

Chapter Twenty-Nine

Peter Bennett's introduction to 3 Base Ammunition Depot (3 BAD) was similar to his arrival in 154 FAD except that arriving at just after eleven in the morning, he didn't even have the chance to find his room in the Officers' Mess before he was summoned to the CO's office. The driver of the Landrover that had brought him from *Wulfen* dropped him at the guardroom and then did a quick three-point turn before disappearing.

The guard on the gate, a young female, approached Peter and smiled. “Can I help you?” she asked.

“The Officers' Mess, please,” Peter said, taking a deep breath.

The female guard straightened up and eyed him a little warily. “The Officers' Mess,” she repeated. “Are you Captain Bennett, Sir?”

Peter nodded. “Yes, I am.”

“Would you mind going in the guardroom, Sir. I think Sergeant Thompson has a message for you.”

“Sergeant Thompson,” Peter said. He picked up his two bags and went into the guardroom.

The sergeant had obviously been watching the exchange from the window because as Peter walked in he said, “Captain Bennett?” Peter nodded. “Sir, the CO would like to see you straight away.”

“And where is the CO?”

“Down the bottom, Sir.”

“Down the bottom,” Peter said. “And where precisely is 'down the bottom'?”

“Sorry, Sir, in depot headquarters, about half a mile down the road.”

“And how am I supposed to get there? Walk?”

“No, Sir, the duty driver will take you,” Sergeant Thompson said. “You can leave your bags here.”

Ten minutes later Peter was sitting in the CO's PA's office. Sam Cox was her name and she told him the CO's name was Timothy Smithers and he was interviewing another officer at the moment. Peter Bennett was to be next in. She then went back to her typing.

Out of her office window, Peter gazed at a large area of hard-standing on which a few vehicles were parked, and beyond that the perimeter fence that must run all the way round the ammunition storage area of the depot. A couple of stationery Landrovers stood at the security check gate that led into the depot, but what was going on was of little interest to him. He looked at Sam Cox and wondered if she was going to be one of the five.

Every now and again her dark brown eyes flicked in his direction. She was nervous under his scrutiny. A brunette in her early to mid-thirties, her thick ponytail was held in place by a blue band and she was wearing very little make-up. He couldn't really see what her figure was like as most of her body was hidden by her word processor.

The voices had been quiet most of the way from *Wulfen*, and he'd allowed his own thoughts to wander as he did now. He would be back because he had Sandra Davies to deal with. She would be the second female he had killed and to a great extent a good test ... his first victim had been over two hundred yards away from him when she died. But Sandra Davies' death would be very personal, very close-up; when she realised she was only seconds away from death – he would see her eyes.

Sam Cox's intercom bleeped, breaking into his thoughts.

"Yes, Colonel?" she said.

"Has Captain Bennett turned up?" a metallic voice asked.

"Yes, Colonel, he's with me now."

"Send him in please, Sam, and can you bring us some coffee?"

"Yes, Colonel."

"You can go in now," Sam Cox said. "Oh, how do you like your coffee?"

"I don't drink coffee," Peter said, before leaving her small office.

As he had travelled from *Wulfen* in civilian clothes there weren't going to be any unnecessary military formalities. He just wanted it all over and done with so he could get the hell out and plan what he now knew he must do. Sam Cox wouldn't be one of his victims because he didn't see death in her eyes.

Peter closed the door and stood in front of the large desk which was to the left as he went in. To his surprise a tall, lean, dark-haired officer stood up and held out his hand.

"Timothy Smithers," the officer said.

Peter shook hands. "Peter Bennett," he said.

The CO indicated a couple of easy chairs round a coffee table. "Shall we sit over there? Sam will bring us some coffee."

"I don't drink coffee," Peter said, sitting down.

"Oh, right," Timothy Smithers said. "What about tea?"

"No, thank you."

The CO shrugged. "Okay, have it your own way." He sat down and looked straight at Peter. "When I agreed to take you on while you waited for a decision to be made about your future, I decided I had a choice. Either I made things very formal, even placing you under Mess arrest, or I could trust you to behave yourself and we could then deal with things quietly and without the entire camp knowing why you're here. Which option do you think I should go for?" he asked.

Peter tried not to show his feelings. This officer was different from the others and he would play on those differences. If he kept him on his side he might just be able to speed up the process. "Obviously it's up to you, Colonel, but I would prefer to be away from here as soon as possible."

Timothy Smithers nodded. "I'm not going to ask what you've been up to other than what went on at *Wulfen*, but would I be right in saying your behaviour there was an attempt to get out of the Army as soon as possible?"

Peter smiled for the first time: he was right about this officer. "I thought it might help, yes." In the same way he hadn't expected to be sent to Germany, he also hadn't anticipated the move to the BAD, so he certainly didn't intend starting all over again. He had victims to find, and here was as good as anywhere.

The CO nodded. "I'll come clean with you, Peter. Your college commander at the Academy and I are old friends, and I will admit I did ring him and ask what he really thought of you. Would you like to know what he said?"

Peter shrugged. "I have a feeling you are going to tell me anyway." He saw Timothy Smither's eyes narrow slightly.

"Yes, I am. He said you thoroughly deserved the sword of honour because you were by far the best cadet both academically and militarily that he had seen for a very long time, but ... but he wouldn't trust you as far as he could throw you. What do you think he meant by that?"

"I've no idea, Colonel. We seemed to get on reasonably well."

"He said you were a loner, that socially you had a lot to learn but social awareness was something that could be drummed into you later ... he used the words 'on the ground'. But they wouldn't be my choice," he added.

Wondering where this conversation was going, Peter decided to refrain from any comment that might anger his senior officer, so he said, "I'm sorry he felt that way about me. He never mentioned it."

"That's a maybe," Timothy Smithers said, "and it actually doesn't influence what I've decided to do with you, but his reference to not trusting you does." Pausing while he sipped his coffee, the CO stared at Peter. "I make my own decisions and sometimes, but rarely, allow other people's opinions to influence what I decide. You had any number of cavalry regiments champing at the bit for you to join them, but you chose the RAOC. We might be re-badging as the Royal Logistics Corps next April, but that's irrelevant. You still chose the Ordnance Corps. You became an ammunition technical officer, earned yourself and the Corps tremendous kudos when you were awarded the QGM, and then even greater standing when you were selected for the SAS."

Peter watched the CO drain his coffee cup, but didn't say anything. He was surprised by what had been said and the way in which the conversation was going. It wasn't what he had expected.

"Somewhere down the line," Timothy Smithers said, slowly replacing his cup in the saucer, "you have been badly managed by somebody. You don't start off at the pace you did but then come to a grinding halt without there being some sort of external influence. I'm not going to hazard a guess what happened and where, but I am going to give you the benefit of any doubt that precedes you into my unit, regardless of any admissions you might have made." The CO took a deep breath. "I am going to treat you as though you are one of my officers. I have a few projects that need looking at so you won't be idle while we're waiting for decisions from above. If worse comes to worst, and you are court-martialled, then I'll have to come clean with the other officers but until then, well, it's up to you."

"They'll have heard about what happened at *Wulfen*, Colonel." Peter wondered why he was referring to this man as 'colonel'. It was less formal than 'sir' and used to be reserved for senior officers for whom he felt some respect. There hadn't been many.

Timothy Smithers smiled. "Between us we'll fend off the rumours for the time being."

"Thank you. This is not what I expected, Colonel, but you are assured I won't do anything to make you regret your decision."

"We will see," the CO said. "This evening we'll have an opportunity to assess whether my decision was the right one. We have an informal dinner in the Mess and I'd like you to attend. My officers and their wives will be there and no doubt you will agree that wives hear things long before their husbands do."

"I look forward to it, Colonel," Peter said, thinking the exact opposite.

"Good." Timothy Smithers stood up. "Now, settle into the Mess, take the rest of the day off and I'll see you this evening. Tomorrow we'll have a chat about those projects I mentioned."

Chapter Thirty

While unpacking in his room twenty minutes later, Peter Bennett wondered why he had acquiesced so easily to Smithers' decision. He didn't want to be treated normally; he wanted to get out of the Army, and being mollycoddled, even patronised, was not the answer. He was annoyed with himself and with Smithers.

As he walked out of the office he could hear the voices laughing at him.

He had thought twice about going to the dinner this evening, but then he decided that perhaps it would be the catalyst he needed; it would give him the opportunity to speed up his exit from the Army so that he could get on with what needed to be done.

Strolling into the bar in the Officers' Mess later that evening, the thirty or so people present fell silent and all eyes were on him. Internally Peter shrugged. What else did he or Smithers expect? The grapevine was better than any formal communication network. They would all know why he was sent here from *Wulfen*, but they certainly wouldn't know what else was going on.

Standing just inside the door, Peter surveyed the other faces. He hadn't realised that Smithers had followed him in until he was aware that somebody was at his elbow.

"Ladies and gentlemen," Timothy Smithers said, "may I introduce Captain Peter Bennett. He'll be with us for a short while so I would like to welcome him to the family and ask you to treat him as such." He looked at Peter and smiled. "What would you like to drink, Peter?"

"An orange squash, please, Colonel."

The woman who had accompanied Smithers took Peter's arm. "Come with me," she said, "and I'll introduce you to a few people. I'm Dee Smithers, by the way. The CO's wife."

She was a small attractive woman in her late thirties, with short brown hair and a slim figure. If her slightly muscular bare arms were anything to go by, she also kept herself very fit.

Dee Smithers guided him to a small group over at the window and did the introductions. The men in the group looked at Peter with guarded expressions whereas the women seemed a lot more interested. It was what he expected. The conversation was general and as it progressed Peter began to feel more and more out of place. Just before the bespectacled, grey haired German Mess Manager announced that dinner was about to be served, Peter almost turned on his heels and walked out. But he didn't.

In the dining room he was at a table with three other officers, two of whom were with their wives and the third officer was a young female lieutenant. He wondered whether the seating plan had been by design or just a coincidence.

Before moving into the dining room, Peter had taken more and more interest in Dee Smithers. There was something about her, something in her eyes that suggested his interest should be more than just passing curiosity. When dinner was announced a slim man with a German accent came up to the group, smiled, and asked whether he could escort Dee Smithers into the dining room. As Peter followed them down the short corridor between the bar and the dining room, he closed his eyes when the voice in his head said, “She will be number three.”

While eating, Peter watched Dee Smithers who was at a table next to his. The German was on her right, and another man in his mid-thirties was on her left. Peter asked the young female subaltern – Trixie Meadows – what the purpose of the dinner was.

“It's to welcome Manfred Dorf and his wife, Ursula, to the Mess,' Trixie said. “He's the Civil Labour Officer, a local term for the HR manager, and he's just been made an honorary member of the Mess.”

“And which one is his wife,” Peter asked.

“Ursula? She's the rather stunning woman sitting next to the CO. She's Russian, a white Russian if stories are to be believed, but with looks like that she has to be a spy.” Trixie laughed. “Seriously, she's a lovely woman. She works in the depot and she's got the entire workforce drooling over her. With boobs and a face like that, who can blame them?”

“And she's married to the man with Dee Smithers?” Peter asked.

“Yes,” Trixie said, solicitously, “can you believe it? I don't know the full story, but evidently before I arrived in the unit he disappeared off one weekend – people think it was to *Hanover* – and he came back with Ursula on his arm. They got married soon after she appeared on the scene.”

“You wouldn't put them together, would you?”

“That's what everybody says,” Trixie told him. “Either he's got hidden talents, or they've both got something to hide.”

As Peter looked at the woman he now knew was Ursula Dorf, she caught his eye and smiled, sending a shiver down his spine. No other female had ever looked at him like that and he wasn't sure why it had affected him this way.

“Do you have any hidden talents, Peter?” Trixie asked, as he felt her knee nudge his under the table.

July 1990

Chapter Thirty-One

By the time he was thirty-five, and after a number of failed relationships, Manfred Dorf decided that he would never get married. He enjoyed being a bachelor and the freedom that went with it, so nobody was going to interfere with his life and what he wanted out of it. More importantly, there were other things on which he needed to concentrate and the slightest slip could have disastrous results.

So women and relationships were not high on his list of priorities.

That was until the fateful night he walked into the *Kleine Stube* in *Hanover* three years ago. He was visiting his ageing parents and all he did was go out for some fresh air, a break from the smell that permeated through his parents' flat: a smell of decay, the odour of resignation, of giving up.

At the time, he was feeling pretty low.

It was a sultry evening.

All he wanted was a cold beer or two before he went back to the flat. He sat down in a corner booth he had always used in the past, having ordered a beer from a young but disinterested waitress he hadn't seen before.

He was more interested in looking out of the open door and watching the pedestrians passing by than what was going on in the bar. From what he saw when he walked in, there was nothing worth looking at anyway. He noticed a man on his own in one corner, a couple of teenagers in another, but there wasn't anybody that took his interest.

After a few minutes of disingenuous mind tricks, he sensed a presence at his elbow. He thought it was the waitress, so he turned to tell her that he wasn't ready for another beer yet. But it wasn't the waitress. He looked up into a young woman's face and saw a pair of the darkest eyes he had ever encountered staring down at him.

"I am sorry to interrupt you," the woman said, her accent vaguely East European, "but could you tell me where the railway station is?"

The incongruity of her question didn't hit him straight away; he was so mesmerised by those hypnotic eyes, it was as though they were boring into his very soul. "Yes, of course … I'm sorry, what was your question?"

"The station, the railway station … can you give me directions?"

"Yes, the railway station. It is … Oh, I'm sorry, I don't know."

He knew what would come next. "That is all right," she said, "I do not want the station but I would like a drink."

"A drink, of course, yes, a drink," he said, the exchange now complete and correct.

He signalled for the waitress. The woman slipped into the booth and sat down opposite him. She was young, very young, probably no more than twenty-two or three. With light tanned brown skin, high cheek bones, a straight nose and full lips, she was one of the most attractive females he had ever seen, let alone sitting only centimetres away from him. Manfred wanted to reach across the table and run his fingers through her lustrous dark brown hair.

He thought it was all over ... he had told them he was no longer part of the scheme.

The waitress brought the red wine the young woman had ordered.

She sipped her wine. "You must think this is rather strange," she said.

"Yes, of course … I mean, no … yes, I mean, yes."

She smiled, amused by Manfred's nervousness. "Can I give you my name and then perhaps we can start again?"

"Yes, your name." He couldn't take his eyes away from hers. Before she could say anything, he said, "My contact name was, I mean is, *Granatapfel*."

"Yes, I know," she said. "I also know your real name is Manfred Dorf. I know you are visiting your parents and I know that you live in a town called *Kaldenkirchen* near the German border with The Netherlands."

"How do you know?" She shouldn't have known anything about him other than his contact name. "How do you know these things? I don't know you, and the accent … where are you from?" The details she had given had never been released before.

"No, *Herr* Dorf, you do not know me. My name is Ursula Ivanovitch and I am Russian."

Leaning back against the rear of the booth, he closed his eyes and sighed. Nobody who looked like her would single him out for their attention unless they wanted something. He now knew what she wanted but it still didn't explain what she knew about him.

"I am sorry, *Fraulein* Ivanovitch, but I do not get involved with such things any more. I can guess who you have seen, but giving you my name and my parents' address, that should not have happened. I have finished with such things."

Ursula lowered her eyes, and let out a slow sigh of disappointment. "Yes, he said so but there was always hope, and it wasn't him who gave me your name ... well, not directly."

"I don't know what you mean by that and I don't want to know either, but there are others who can help you," Manfred said in an attempt to raise this beautiful young woman's spirits just a little.

"I know, but he said that you were the best."

Manfred looked around the bar to make sure nobody was within hearing distance. "Perhaps I was, but not anymore," he said. As she lifted her head, her eyes still penetrating his deepest thoughts, he added, "I have said too much already. Did the man give you a word to use when I asked you for it?"

His defences were down because her mere presence made him forget the procedures, not that they applied anymore. He had given it all up over a year ago.

"Yes," she said.

"And it was?"

"*Pumpernickel*," she said without hesitation and with the glimmer of hope Manfred did not want to see on her face.

He nodded, having heard the word so often before. "My contacts," he said, shaking his head now, "the routes, those in the right positions who would turn a blind eye for a few thousand Deutschmarks, they have all gone. The police, they were too good, arresting some of my contacts. I wait every day for them to come to my door and arrest me. No, I am sorry *Fraulein*, but there is nothing I can do for you."

"I will do anything," she said, her expression forlorn.

He looked at her.

She reached across the table and put her hand on his. "And I mean anything," she said.

"You are young, your German is not without an accent but you do speak my language very well and you are … you are very attractive. You should not have to be in the position where you need to say such things."

"*Herr* Dorf, I think I am what the authorities would call a displaced person. Although I hold a Russian passport, if I were to go back my arrest and imprisonment would automatically follow. I am twenty-five years old and until recently I was married." Ursula's eyes began to water. "My husband, Nikolai, was killed in an accident in Berlin three weeks ago. He was doing nothing more than crossing the road, but he died instantly. We were hiding in one of the safe houses run by the man I only know as *Avocado*. He was the one who told me about you."

Manfred nodded. He knew *Avocado* well, well enough to know his real name but he should not have revealed the details the girl now knew about him. Why had he done that? Was it so that she could apply more pressure on him?

"We had been in the safe house for nearly a month and Nikolai became very restless, he hated being cooped up. All he did was go for a walk. I –"

"Why did you leave Russia in the first place?" Although she had used the right password, had met with *Avocado* and seemed too nice not to be genuine, Manfred was still very suspicious … he had to be.

"Nikolai was a good man, *Herr* Dorf, but he got mixed up with the wrong people. The underworld in Moscow is worse than in any other city but foreigners outside Russia never get to hear about it. Nikolai needed money. We were getting married and he wanted the best start for us, but he couldn't get any work, not the sort that paid what he thought we needed.

"He was having a drink with some friends one evening when one of them suggested he might like to talk to a man who was looking for assistance with a project he had in mind – that is the way his friend described it to him. Nikolai was young and naïve, so he jumped at the opportunity but he didn't tell me what he was doing because he wanted the money to be a surprise. Before he knew what was happening, he was involved with drugs and gun running and it was too late. He tried to get out but they had him."

This young woman was using emotional blackmail and it was working, but Manfred was determined not to break the promise he had made to himself.

It was all over. He would not get involved again.

The illegal immigrants he had *helped* before were still out there somewhere and each of them could, if interrogated, lead the authorities back to him. This woman definitely could. Why? There was also the money. He had been very careful how and where he banked the money he was paid – nearly two million Deutschmarks – but if that were discovered, how would he explain having so much money?

No matter how this lovely young woman opposite him used her doleful eyes while telling him her sob story, he was not going to go back. She could try to manipulate him all she wanted but she was out of luck.

"When Nikolai and I got married, I had no idea what he was mixed up with. He provided us with a lovely flat, and we were living to a standard we had only dreamed about. But all the time I was still in ignorance of what he was doing. Then one night he came home and told me I had ten minutes to pack a case because we were leaving.

"Everything happened at such a speed I still don't really know how we finished up in Berlin. All I could do was trust Nikolai. I think he bribed some guards, but," she shook her head, "it was all too easy, remarkably easy.

"Eventually he told me what had happened. He told me about the drugs, the gunrunning and the intricate underground network that existed, which outsmarted the police time and time again or because some of the police were involved in the crimes in the first place. Nikolai's sister played a major part in us having to leave Moscow, leave Russia. She was nearly twelve years younger than him and he idolised everything about her. When Nikolai and I got married, he was twenty-six and Petri, his sister was only fourteen. She was a lovely girl."

Ursula finished her wine so Manfred ordered her another and a beer for himself. A few more customers had come into the bar, though fortunately nobody sat too close. Regardless of what he had promised, the process he knew so well had kicked in and an idea was forming in the back of his mind. But it would need more time, and time was something they would not have.

"When I say it was his sister, she had … why am I talking in the past? Petri is still very much alive. She has – that is better – she has no idea about the part she played. Once we were living in a nasty little room in *Kreuzberg* in Berlin, and Nikolai explained that as well as the drugs and gunrunning, there was also extortion and prostitution, and all the other criminal activities that most of us only read about in the papers and books. They say crime pays in Moscow and it certainly did for us. Would my ignorance have proven my innocence, *Herr* Dorf?"

Once again, she slipped her hand over Manfred's and stroked his skin. The silkiness of her touch was almost too much for him and he closed his eyes.

"It ... it doesn't work like that," he said after a few seconds.

"I know." Ursula shrugged. "I should have asked where the money was coming from, but we were so happy together …" Her voice trailed off, her hand still on his.

Without thinking, he took her hand in his and squeezed gently. "Go on," he said, "but I think I know what you're going to say."

She nodded. "It was when Nikolai discovered that young girls the same age as his sister, and even younger, were being smuggled in from Africa, from Malaya, Thailand, the Philippines, from all over, for prostitution, he knew he had to get out. He had tried before but without success. This time he had to find a way. Lured from their homes with promises of domestic cleaning work, waitressing and other innocent jobs that meant they could send money back to their families, most girls left freely. Of course, nothing like that ever happened. Nikolai said the girls were usually gang raped and beaten before they even left their own countries, and once they were smuggled into Russia – and Moscow – they were forced into prostitution. The network was incredibly complicated.

"There was never any money sent home. The girls were no more than slaves. If they became seriously ill or diseased, they were murdered and their young bodies reduced to nothing by putting them in acid, or they were incinerated." Ursula stopped again as tears rolled down her cheeks.

Manfred quickly put some money on the table, took her arm and ushered her out of the bar. They walked in silence to a small park not far away, and it was only then that Ursula resumed her story.

"Nikolai, poor, sweet, naïve Nikolai thought he could take on the criminal world single-handed. I don't know how he did it, or really what he did, but he gave as much information as he could to the police. There were raids and arrests, but it was too little too late. Within twenty-four hours of passing on the information to the police, he knew that he had to get out and very, very quickly. That's when he came home and told me to pack one case, and that we were leaving."

"It was probably the police," Manfred said.

"The police?"

"Who helped you leave Russia …"

"The police?"

"Stranger things have happened. You were lucky, very lucky. Did his family live in Moscow?"

"No, they lived to the west of Moscow in the *Smolensk* area, in a town called *Izdëshkovo*."

"Then maybe they are safe."

"You mean –?"

"I don't think I have to spell out what I mean."

"No, *Herr* Dorf, you don't. That is why I cannot go back."

"I understand. So how did you think I could help?"

Chapter Thirty-Two

In retrospect, Manfred could not believe that he added his own naïveté to that of Nikolai and Ursula's. After being part of another intricate network of deception and corruption, where the truth was hidden from some, but essential to others, and where trust was fundamental on both sides, he could not believe that in the space of a couple of hours he was taken in by simply the most beautiful eyes he had ever looked into. Her sheer allure and unspoken promises had trapped him into a decision that could be the biggest mistake of his life ... but he still went ahead.

After she accepted his offer to take her back to *Kaldenkirchen* straight away, he emphasised that it was a one-to-one offer and nothing to do with his past dealings. He was going to take no money and nobody in 'the system' would ever know. This was his decision, and his alone.

"I understand, *Herr* Dorf, and I am very grateful," she said.

"Call me Manfred," he said.

"Thank you, Manfred."

During the four-hour journey by car from *Hanover* in *Lower Saxony* to *Kaldenkirchen* in *Nordrhein-Westfalen*, Ursula did most of the talking. She told Manfred about her family, her love for her country, how she felt about leaving Nikolai behind and how she wished the world was a better place for all.

Manfred listened.

They stopped only once at the ***Autobahnraststätte*** near *Beckum*. While driving he did begin to feel more relaxed about the decision he had taken: what he was doing was very personal and only involved the two of them, but even so he still wondered if he had done the right thing.

However, any nagging doubts, any lingering concerns evaporated on their first night in his pristine bungalow. She had given herself to him in his immaculate bachelor bedroom. She had done things to him that he had never had done before. The moment she had touched him he started shaking, and he was still shaking when for the second time she took from him the remnants of his energy.

Manfred's two other sexual encounters were, in his opinion, disastrous for him and the result of his inexperience and lack of adventure. Afterwards he often wished that he could wake up one morning to discover he was a closeted homosexual; he was sure life would be easier. Instead, he ploughed all his energy into his work, both legal and illegal.

At one stage when Ursula was making unimaginable noises as she writhed beneath him, he did wonder how she could be so willing when only a matter of weeks previously she had lost the man she loved.

During that first night as Ursula fought her revulsion of what she felt she had to do, making the noises she knew he would want to hear and wishing she could be rid of him straight away, she wasn't thinking of Nikolai.

There was no Nikolai.

Everything she had told him was a lie.

The only honest words Ursula Ivanovitch had spoken to Manfred Dorf during their first meeting in the *Kleine Stube* in *Hanover* was that she was Russian.

She certainly was Russian.

She was also a Captain in Russia's Foreign Intelligence Service, the SVR (*Sluzhba Vneshnei Razvedki*).

Manfred Dorf was no more than a conduit through which she would pass and then embed herself in the British Army's biggest ammunition depot in Europe. If everything went to plan, she alone would be responsible for one of the biggest atrocities ever committed on a NATO base in Europe.

And the IRA would get the blame.

Manfred and Ursula were married three months after she moved into his house in *Kaldenkirchen*. The ceremony was legal, but attended by only a few witnesses. It was a marriage of convenience because it eventually gave Ursula German nationality.

Manfred remained oblivious to Ursula's true identity.

All he knew was that before leaving *Hanover* she had accepted his offer of temporary sanctuary in his house. He thought on that first night she was using her body to say thank you, no more, no less.

When Manfred first touched her, her skin crawled.

However, she had achieved her aim, their aim and her mother country's aim.

After accepting the assignment, she did not know the type of man with whom she would be sharing at least five years, if not more, of her life. She had seen photographs, and that was all she had seen. Her sense of duty was such that she was willing to give up everything if she were able to help with the security of her country. Her fanaticism knew no bounds.

Explanations contained the minimum of detail or lies.

It was all so simple.

Those who worked with Manfred found the lack of detail generated more questions than there were answers, and he certainly wasn't going give them any satisfaction.

He knew what others thought of him, so the fact that he married anyone was amazing enough, but getting married to a young, brown-eyed beauty only added to the mystery. The respect he commanded at work was one thing but his personal life was another, and that's the way it was going to stay … personal. Once they were married, Ursula made him very aware of what would happen if he ever told anyone about her background; she did not want anyone to know about the criminal activities in Moscow ... people were to be told they met in *Hanover* and it was 'love at first sight'.

Rumours abounded that there was more to him than met the eye, and he did nothing to dispel or confirm what others might want to think. He did not go overboard with the money he had made from his involvement in illegal immigration, but the car and his bungalow did not go with his salary.

They could think what they liked.

He could have inherited everything from a rich relative.

Ursula appearing on the scene added to the rumours. Conversation sometimes stopped when he walked into an office, so he guessed his marriage was intriguing everyone. They would be wondering whether it would last, and after a few months when Ursula didn't move on, there was an unsettled acceptance that Manfred must possess hidden talents.

With his help, Ursula got a job in a *Schnell-Imbiss* next to the Shell garage in the village of *Bracht*. After a short while her insistence that she would prefer to work in the depot forced Manfred to pull the necessary strings and arrange the appropriate clearances for her to work as a clerk in the explosives area of the depot.

When the Commanding Officer at the time, Lieutenant Colonel Martin Carruthers, found out that this new female working in his depot was Russian, he needed an explanation.

"Manfred, do not misunderstand me," he said, "I am delighted that you have found yourself a wife and such an attractive one as well, but I am none too happy about a Russian national working in my depot."

"Colonel, I can assure you that she has been thoroughly checked out by my people, and you have nothing to worry about," Manfred said. The strings he had pulled, and the favours owed to him, meant that all the right pieces of paper and reports were in the right files should anybody conduct a further check. "And we already have another Russian working here, Colonel."

"I do not doubt her legitimacy, Manfred," the CO said, trying to make light of what was, for him, a very serious situation, "but I suspect there aren't many British people, or Germans come to that, working in the Russian equivalent."

Manfred smiled nervously. "She is a white Russian, Colonel. Her now deceased parents escaped to the West many years ago. She has a German passport," – which was true but only because of their marriage – "so she is no different to the many Russian nationals who escaped to England during and after the war."

By the time Timothy Smithers took over command of the depot, Captain Ursula Ivanovitch of the SVR was a loyal, hard-working member of the civilian workforce. She was highly thought of and when the Commanding Officers changed over, she assumed she was a topic of conversation, but on this occasion it was probably because of her looks.

She was biding her time.

She was waiting for the right moment.

When the IRA started the bombings and shootings against the British Forces in Germany, her objective moved closer to becoming a reality.

August 1992

Chapter Thirty-Three

Ursula replaced the coffee cup in its saucer and looked across at Manfred, who was her husband now in name only. She hated the way his eyes were always on her, leering at her, the way he watched her wherever she was and whatever she was doing.

It was nearly two years since she allowed him to touch her, since she moved out of his bed into her own room. For outsiders, the pretence was always there. A smile in the right place, a touch, even a kiss on the cheek; she could manage those, but nothing else.

Rather like the previous evening when they had been welcomed to the Officers' Mess. She was being watched and assessed by the other wives, but just watched by their leering husbands. Why did men make it so obvious? Anyway, she was already an officer albeit in the SVR, so she was being welcomed into her rightful place. Her thoughts made her smile.

Ursula was a very physical woman: she needed a man in her life but not any man and certainly not Manfred – not any more. She only stayed under the same roof because it was a practical necessity, but she still needed a man. When Manfred had protested that she was no longer fulfilling her side of the bargain, she simply reminded him of what she knew and what would happen if she were to inform the authorities.

When he pointed out that she had as much to lose as him, Ursula would shrug and say, "I could leave you now if I wanted to. I could be absorbed into the German community without a problem and nobody would ask any questions. Do you want that, Manfred?" Then she would taunt him with, "Anyway, would you not prefer people to think you have such a beautiful wife? All the men will be wondering what we do together?"

There was one man who, if her assessment were correct, would be discovering what others only imagined. He like the others had stared at her, but she had already allowed her own imagination to take over.

It was going to be a dangerous game from the outset, but a game she was willing to play.

The by-products of the relationship, should she succeed, were justification alone for the affair to start and stay for as long as she was in control. But to find out if there was anything to be gained, she had to trap him physically first and then work on him.

So this was the notorious Captain Peter Bennett.

The stories and rumours arrived before he did. He was in trouble, deep trouble, and he was under investigation by the military authorities for something very serious. Having seen him last night, she didn't believe the affair she had been told about was anything to do with why he had been sent to this ammunition depot. Just looking at him told her that most women would fall at his feet and beg for just a few seconds of his attention. If he were in deep trouble then perhaps she could use the way he would be feeling to her advantage.

He had slipped away soon after they had left the table but she had also seen Lieutenant Trixie Meadows leave a few minutes later. Ursula hoped Trixie enjoyed what she was going to get from him, because it would be a short-lived affair once Ursula moved in.

The following morning it was easy to find an excuse to go to the headquarters building with some files that needed to be returned – files she didn't really need access to, but because she was now a trusted employee nobody asked any questions.

After giving the files to the Chief Clerk she went further down the corridor to see if she could find her mystery man. He was sitting in an office close to the reprographic room.

She stopped and looked in. He was as handsome and rugged looking in daylight as he was by candlelight, with brown curly hair and piercing grey-green eyes. She would admit that by candlelight he had a greater air of mystery about him.

He stopped what he was doing, his eyes slowly moving from her face to her feet and back again. There was a flicker of a smile, but nothing else. She liked that.

"Good morning," she said, deliberately exaggerating her Russian accent. Her English was by now probably better than her German.

He nodded.

She moved just inside the office. "You must be Peter Bennett."

He nodded again.

"My name is Ursula Dorf, I am married to the Civil Labour Officer."

He spoke for the first time. "I know. I saw you last night. Lucky Civil Labour Officer."

Ursula moved closer to the desk. She wanted to get a better look at this man. From his last remark he was going to be a lot easier than she first thought. "Welcome to the depot," she said, holding out her hand.

He rose from behind his desk and took her hand. "Under normal circumstances I would say thank you," he said, but did not volunteer any other information. His physical strength was evident although his handshake was gentle. She let her fingertips glide over his palm.

"I understand," she said.

"Do you? Why would you be able to do that?" He sat down again and she rested her thigh against his desk. His voice was deep and deliberate, which, when coupled with his penetrating eyes, made him an even greater challenge.

"I do not know the circumstances, no, but I think I am a reasonable judge of character," she said. She smoothed her skirt with her hand.

"In only a few seconds?" he asked.

"Yes, and watching you last night. That is sometimes all that is needed."

"And you want to know more?"

"Only if you want to tell me."

"I will think about it."

"When you have reached your decision, let me know," she said. "I work in the –"

"I know where you work and I will."

Ursula turned without another word and left the office.

Peter Bennett smiled.

If she was what he thought she might be, she was a dead woman walking. He had seen the way she conducted herself at the dinner the previous evening. Attentive, talkative and responsive to what Smithers was saying to her, but all the time she was watching, learning and storing away information. When their eyes met there was an exchange that nobody else will have seen. Two equals had met and communicated for the first time, but no words had passed their lips. It was a mutual understanding of equality.

The only problem was, if his suspicions were correct, that they would have been trained by opposite sides. But it wasn't really a problem, because the moment he saw her she became one of his victims, and that was before the voices were given the opportunity to pass comment. So, two of his potential victims were sitting at the table only a few feet from him.

They were such obvious choices.

He glanced across at Dee Smithers who was in conversation with Manfred Dorf and imagined what she would look like in death, then his gaze moved back to Ursula Dorf, but she was already looking at him with a slight smile on her lips ... it was almost as though she knew what he was thinking.

Seeing his second and third victims sitting so close together, Peter felt the sudden urge for release. Knowing that he was going to be responsible for the deaths of these two women made him feel excited, and when he was excited he had to do something about it.

Turning to Trixie Meadows he said, “You asked if I had any hidden talents.” He looked at her more closely. She had a pretty face covered in freckles and very communicative brown eyes which complemented a suggestive smile. Her hair was a reddish-brown and it hung over her right shoulder. She was showing quite a lot of cleavage but as she would be trussed up in a very unfeminine uniform for most of the day, Peter thought extremes might be her speciality. He had noticed the other two officers on the table looking and wishing ... and their wives’ disapproving expressions.

“I did, and ...?”

“I might have. And you?”

“If I do they will be in my room which is two doors down from yours.”

Trixie was a very willing and adventurous girl. The fact that she had a queen-sized bed in her room helped. Peter had heard her go down the corridor and into her room about ten minutes after he left the ante-room. Because of his relative notoriety he was sure his absence would be noticed, but it was his first night and he doubted if questions would be asked.

He didn't really care if anybody had seen Trixie leave.

Knocking on Trixie's door she replied with a soft, “Come in.” She was already in bed and her bare shoulders were just above the pink and blue duvet. “Close the door,” she said, “and lock it.”

As he looked down into her eyes thirty minutes later, Peter was pleased when he did not see death. Trixie Meadows was very much alive and that was the way she ought to stay. Giving him the release he needed was all he wanted from her.

He even said, “Thank you.”

Chapter Thirty-Four

Because she believed they both wanted the same thing it only took a week.

Ursula wanted him and once she had what she wanted she would begin to inveigle her way into his psyche. Her trips to the headquarters became more regular and each time his interest grew. She made sure others didn't suspect anything.

They arranged to meet at lunchtime and parked their cars by the *Am Weissen Stein* (White Stone): a secluded bar-restaurant at the end of the *Heidhausen* road through the forest right next to the Dutch-German border. The high perimeter fence and warning signs for the depot were clearly visible from the car park and the restaurant. She suggested they park either end of the car park so that, once again, nobody would connect them.

She felt excited, her frustration having built up and up since she first saw him at the dinner in the Mess. She didn't want to eat, she wasn't there to eat.

Ursula left her car first and wandered into the woods, knowing that Peter would follow a couple of minutes later. In her bag she had a bottle of red wine and two glasses, and he had a blanket ... that was all they needed.

Once inside the tree line he caught up with her and took her hand in his. It was the first time they had touched and she felt her arm tingle in anticipation.

"Over there," she said, "there is a hollow and we won't be seen."

Carrying the blanket he had taken from his room in the Officers' Mess, Peter followed Ursula. Before turning to face him she checked her choice of location, and pleased with it, she smiled.

For the next few minutes they were like the wild animals who might have been their only observers. As she lay naked in his arms after they had taken from each other what they so desperately needed, she accepted that it didn't matter now if he couldn't give her anything else. In a matter of minutes he had satisfied over a year's frustration. She had needed a man, a real man, and now she had found one.

Peter was also smiling.

She was good – very good – but eventually she would reveal what he really wanted to know. As she was gyrating on top of him, her hands on his chest, her eyes closed and whimpering noises coming from her parted lips, he decided that she could be of significant use to him before he killed her.

Having returned to his own bed after his brief encounter with Trixie Meadows, and after deciding for whatever reason that she wasn't going to be one of his victims, he began to mull over who the other two ought to be ... what criteria they needed to satisfy. Sandra Davies would be the first – she would be the test case. When he stared into her dead eyes he would know whether his choice had been the right one. Her death would also give that prat O'Connell something to think about. Dee Smithers represented authority and that smug bastard Smithers who thought his 'benefit of doubt' leadership style satisfied all circumstances ... he was a just a plonker and would pay for his stupidity.

The voices agreed.

Now, he believed Ursula Dorf or whatever her name might be, was different. She was a challenge. If what he thought about her were true she was going to give him the greatest satisfaction as he watched her life slip away.

The voices kept on telling him there had to be six. He had killed once, now he had identified three of his next victims, so two more and he would be free. All his victims would lose their lives in Germany. If the German police ever identified him he would be in England, identity changed and lost in the melee of Durham city and university life. He would become a mature student and get on with the rest of his life.

So who would be his final victims? So far the chosen ones were all guilty of something so perhaps innocence should play a role. Innocence, gullibility and naivety and perhaps he ought to add intelligence; she would need to be intelligent enough to realise towards the end that she was in a trap from which there was no escape. Where better to find somebody like that than at the finest of British universities. When he'd been at Cambridge there had been any number of parasitic spoilt brats whose street credibility was less than zero. Killing somebody who represented all his past hatred would be the ultimate sensation, the final thrill before he settled down to a normal life the voices had promised him.

His fourth victim would be a wild card. Somebody chosen completely at random, maybe a foreigner ... not German though. A dead German would give the local police greater enthusiasm to solve the murders committed on their soil. Would they apply the same passion if none of his victims were German? So maybe Dutch, French ... or Turkish. There were enough Turks in Germany to choose from.

When she presented herself he would know.

While he was waiting to find out how much longer he had to put up with the British stinking Army, he would enjoy himself. His plans were in place so perhaps he could relax. Ursula Dorf, the challenge, now took precedence.

To give him what he needed, Peter rented a small flat in *Frankenmühle*.

It was a small hamlet about five kilometres south of *Brüggen* but other than its residents very few people ever went to it, not even out of curiosity. There were no pubs or restaurants so no interest for outsiders. The flat was in the garret of an old farm, whose owner was more than happy to receive over the odds in rent to guarantee his silence.

Peter spoke German fluently so no questions were asked.

Chapter Thirty-Five

After Ursula and Peter had sex for the first time in the woods, some distance from the *Am Weissen Stein*, they met at his flat as often as possible.

She agreed that keeping his room in the Officers' Mess was necessary and if he slept there two or three nights a week it would allay suspicion. Asking for permission to live away from the Mess and especially for such a short time, would generate needless questions and, of course, permission could always be refused.

At every opportunity she was with Peter in the flat and more often than not they were in bed.

After their first encounter, they joked that it was the animal in them that steered them towards nature but now they had matured and were taking things a little more slowly. When he asked her who she really was and how she finished up working for the British Army, she became suspicious but only for a short while. She told him the same story she and Manfred had told everyone else, which she believed Peter accepted. She remembered one of her instructors telling her that if you look honest, trustworthy and sincere, and you are attractive, then most Western men would fall at your feet. She thought she had met her match with Peter Bennett, but he turned out to be no different from any of the others.

He loved her body and what she did with it – he was putty in her hands and eventually he would reveal more about himself than she was willing to tell him about herself.

"Have they set the date yet?" Ursula asked him one evening as they lay in bed.

She had learnt a lot about the British Army's way of doing things before she met Peter. Her training had been good but not always correct. She thought that there was too much emphasis placed on the supposed similarities between the British and American Armies. The more she worked among the British she realised they and the Americans couldn't be more different.

"No, not yet," Peter said.

"But I thought you said the CO had told you they had all the evidence they needed?"

“Having opinions and conclusions are not the same as having real evidence, and proving it is not going to be that easy, especially when there are so many people out there who want to see me totally humiliated.” He took hold of her hand, moving it down over his stomach. “The Army’s supposed lawyers are a load of crap, and everybody knows that without a water-tight case any civilian brief worth his salt will shoot holes in the evidence. Even if the evidence is irrefutable, the Army are so bloody useless the authorities will be scared they might lose.”

“So why are they going ahead with it? Surely what you’ve said will all go in your favour?” Ursula could still not come to terms with just how egalitarian the British military system was. If Peter had been in the mighty Russian Army he would have disappeared to the salt mines long ago.

“To make an example of me,” he said. “I am nothing more than a scapegoat, that’s why. We can’t have officers being let off, can we? Not good for the chaps to see, you know?”

“I think I understand,” she said innocently as she rolled towards him.

Peter wasn’t trying to be amusing, he was actually dead serious, but not even Ursula knew just how serious and why.

As her lips found his and his fingers gently ran down the length of her body, Peter Bennett was still planning. There were times when it was best to let a worthy opponent think they have won, and Ursula was certainly a worthy opponent. He was happy for her to manipulate him, to use her assets to think she was controlling him, but he had other plans and she was an unexpected bonus.

He was the one who was really in control.

After making love, Ursula snuggled back into the crook of Peter’s arm and fell asleep almost immediately. He put his other hand behind his head, stared at the ceiling and thought about what had started this comedy of errors that led to where he was now.

Yes, he was in trouble, but even that was working in his favour. If he hadn’t been moved to this God-forsaken place he wouldn’t have met Dee Smithers and Ursula Dorf.

As he thought his mother’s face automatically flashed into his mind.

A day rarely passed when he didn’t think of her; she was the only woman he really idolised.

He didn't care what happened to any of the others.

Just before sleep finally overtook him, he wished he could go back all those years and change the way he was.

He wished he was with his mother now, and it was she who was lying next to him, giving him her warmth.

September 1992

Chapter Thirty-Six

Peter couldn't believe his eyes.

Having gone into *Bracht* to get some more cash from the bank before it closed, he decided to walk some of the side streets and get a better feel for the town. He would have to extend his reconnaissance to the woods surrounding the ammunition depot because that was where at least two of his victims would lie in their last resting places, but as time was on his side, such detail could wait.

He was at the church end of *MarktStraße* when he saw her. Her hair was longer and darker, but there was no mistaking the profile. Before the abortive mission overlooking the farm in Carnagh, South Armagh, he and the others had been shown photographs of various members of the IRA they could maybe expect to see at the farm. Among the photographs were three females, none of whom materialised at the farm, but he was definitely looking at one of them now.

She was wandering down *MarktStraße* as though she was a tourist, but that would be the very last thing she was. She might be sightseeing but it would be to discover which pubs and restaurants were used by the soldiers from the depot, the nearby RAF base and probably the headquarters in *Rhinedahlen*. Whatever, she was doing she would be up to no good. He wasn't aware of any IRA activity in Germany this year, but that didn't mean to say there weren't any active cells operating in this area.

Sylvia Donnelly was known for her ruthlessness. In November the previous year, a British police officer was shot and injured in London when he confronted a man and a woman who the policeman believed were acting suspiciously. It was the woman who drew the pistol and shot the policeman before running off with the man. There was a follow-up search of the area and a truck-bomb was discovered and defused. If the bomb had gone off there would have been hundreds of casualties. When the injured officer was shown photographs of members of the IRA known to be operating in London, he had picked out the woman Peter was now looking at.

She was there alone. The rest of her cell were enjoying themselves in *Mönchengladbach* and under strict instructions that one of them would remain sober so that they could pull out if anybody started asking too many questions. The soldiers from the ammunition depot used the pubs in the village of *Bracht* for recreation and although the depot had been considered as a target and then dismissed, Sylvia wasn't convinced.

She was on one of her lone fact-finding missions.

After parking the hired car in the main square, or what she thought was the main square, and walking for a few minutes, she came to a narrow paved street called *MarktStraße*. It had a couple of small shops, a pizzeria, and two or three bars close together. She chose the one called Rosa's because of its name, and because from the outside it looked the sort of place 'squaddies' would frequent. She wasn't disappointed. It was early evening and only a few of the tables were in use, but the young men and women in there were obviously mainly British.

She did not feel the slightest bit concerned that she was a lone woman in a strange bar in a strange town; she frequently used the same tactic for her fact-finding missions in London and Belfast. Nobody ever knew what she really was but she always reminded herself of the close escape she had in London last year. She had shot to kill but had failed. She knew how important it was not to become complacent.

As it was a warm September evening, she was wearing a blue short-sleeved cotton dress which fell to just below her knees, tan sandals with heels that accentuated her calf muscles, no tights, and over her shoulder she carried a tan bag with a cotton sweater through the strap, just in case the temperature dropped. She didn't believe she could look more innocent or available.

As she approached the bar, she noticed some of the soldiers following her progress.

A large blonde woman detached herself from the far end of the bar, and without a smile came over to Sylvia.

"Can I help you?" she asked.

Sylvia smiled to herself. She got the same reaction from female bartenders wherever she went. A man would be asked what he would like to drink but because she was a woman it was 'Can I help you?'.

"A small beer, please," she said in German, holding the blonde woman's stare.

"A small beer," the woman repeated, reaching for a glass.

Sylvia felt in her shoulder bag for her cigarettes and lit one before looking round the bar. It was small L-shaped room with four or five tables tucked away round the corner.

"Sit down and I will bring it to you," the blonde woman told her.

Sylvia nodded before sauntering through to the alcove. Choosing a table that allowed her to see both sides of the bar, she sat down and waited, crossing her legs and making sure at least four inches of thigh were on display. A couple of minutes later, the blonde woman was at her elbow holding the glass of beer which she unceremoniously put on a beer mat that she marked with a pen. "Not many women come in here on their own," she said, "other than British soldiers that is, and I guess you are not a soldier."

Sylvia's German was very good but she still considered it a compliment that the blonde woman spoke to her in German. Although she was from Londonderry, she had significantly toned down the very strong Irish accent from her formative years, and then practiced and practiced to rid herself of the slightest sign of it. She now spoke English without any discernible accent and she hoped the same went for her German. She guessed the woman was in her mid-fifties and not, as she first thought, unattractive in a plump sort of way. Her floral skirt and green blouse were old-fashioned, but they went well with the ambiance of the bar. She wore too many bangles on both wrists, and lots of rings on her fingers, and she smelt of powder and perfume.

She was waiting for a reply.

Sylvia ignored the question but asked one herself. "Do you have a menu?"

"I don't need a menu. The list is very short. You have a choice between *bockwurst* and *kartofflen salat*, *bratwurst* and *pomfrites*, or *currywrurst* and *pomfrites*," she said brusquely.

"I'll have the *bockwurst*, please, and a glass of red wine."

The woman glared at her and then went back to the bar.

One of a group of three soldiers sitting at the nearest table to Sylvia got up and went to the bar. She couldn't hear what he was saying, but from the way he looked behind him towards her it was obvious she was being talked about. The woman screwed up her eyes and said something, but then the soldier smiled in Sylvia's direction before returning to the table where he and his friends went into deep conversation.

She wondered how they would react if they knew she had a loaded 9mm Beretta in her bag.

When she was half way through her meal and enjoying a surprisingly good red wine, a lone man walked into the bar. A few others had come in and one of the tables in her area was now occupied, but the bar was still not full. Something about the man who came in on his own intrigued her. He was probably six feet tall, with slightly unruly dark brown curly hair, a dark complexion, grey-green eyes, and dimples when he smiled. He was probably about her age – thirty.

After picking up his glass of beer, he made a beeline for Sylvia's table. The other soldiers and the woman behind the bar were watching him. He was wearing a short-sleeved light green Ralph Lauren polo shirt, a pullover round his shoulders, a pair of cream chinos and brown slip-on shoes. He walked as though he was determined not to make a sound.

She liked what she saw.

He stopped at her table. "Do you mind if I join you?" he asked in English, with a slight smile.

Sylvia lowered her fork onto the plate and looked up at him. "I'm sorry," she said in German, "what did you say?"

He rested his hand on the back of the chair. "I asked if could join you?"

Sylvia frowned, shaking her head slowly. "I'm sorry but I don't understand what you're saying."

The man pulled out a chair and sat down. "Rosa said that your German was very good but she would bet a thousand *Deutschmarks* that you were English."

"Perhaps I don't want company," she replied in English, aware that her face would suggest the opposite. Perhaps her German wasn't as good as she thought.

"A single female in a bar like this?' he said. "If you're not looking for company of that kind then you would be safer with a chaperone." The man pulled out a chair and sat down. "Now you have one."

"Perhaps …"

"Please, don't let me interrupt your meal," he said, indicating the plate in front of her.

"I've finished," she said, pushing the plate away.

"Another glass of wine?"

She hesitated just long enough to give the right impression and then accepted. "All right, thank you."

The man turned but didn't need to solicit Rosa's interest as almost everyone in the pub was watching them. He indicated Sylvia's glass and held up two fingers.

"So," he said, resting his elbows on the table, "what are you doing in here?"

"I wanted something to eat. I didn't realise I had to seek permission."

She lit a cigarette, trying to sum up the man in front of her. If he was a soldier he was a different kind of soldier. It was unlikely that he was an officer because officers wouldn't go into bars that their soldiers frequented.

"There are lots of places in Bracht to eat," he told her, "but this is somewhere you come if you want to do some serious drinking."

"Is that why you're here?"

"I haven't decided yet."

The blonde barmaid brought the wine to the table. She frowned at Sylvia, then picked up the empty plate and went back to the bar.

"That is Rosa, I presume. The one the bar's named after."

The man nodded. "Yes. Dear Rosa. You name it she's been there and done it, but she has a heart of gold. She looks after her customers very well, if you know what I mean."

"Is that why she was so suspicious of me?"

"You catch on very quickly," the man said patronisingly. "It's a bit early for the girls. They normally come in at about eight. Rosa thought you might be encroaching onto territory that she controls, and although some of the girls are your age and as pretty as you, Rosa wouldn't like it."

"Is that from experience or expectation?"

The man looked surprised. "You're pretty direct, aren't you?"

"I find it's the best way to be. It saves on misunderstandings."

"Okay, if we're being direct with each other then no, that's not why I'm here either. I've never needed to pay for it."

Sylvia feigned shock. "You said I was direct and if we're going to be so personal we ought to introduce ourselves. My name is Pamela Fellows, but Pam for short."

The man held out his hand. "Peter Bennett," he said, "Peter for short."

He shook her hand.

"All right, Peter, so what do you do, or should I guess?"

"Meeting somebody British in here, it's a pretty good bet what they do."

"I'm British and I'm not in the Army," she said.

"You're the exception."

"So you are in the Army?"

After stubbing out her cigarette she picked up her glass of wine. Gleaning information from this man, who said his name was Peter Bennett, wasn't going to be that easy, but it might prove interesting.

"For a little while longer," he said.

"You're leaving?"

"In a way."

His tone suggested that his reasons for leaving the Army might be worth returning to, but not yet. "I see," she said and paused for a few moments without breaking eye contact. "I'm a botanist," she added, "and I'm over here for the convention next week in *Mönchengladbach*."

She had seen the convention advertised in a local paper a few days before, and as she was on an unofficial reconnaissance it would be best to use an unofficial reason for explaining her presence in Germany.

"That doesn't explain why you are in Rosa's bar in *Bracht*," he said.

"Do I have to give an explanation?"

"It's a conversation piece."

"*Erica Polinaris*."

"I beg your pardon?"

"*Erica Polinaris*," she repeated.

"I thought that was what you said. Who is Erica Polinaris?"

"It's not a *who,* it's a *what*."

"All right, what is *Erica Polinaris*?"

"Heather."

"Who's Heather?"

"Not Heather – the plant that is called heather. Surely you've heard of heather."

She took a sip of her wine. She just might have struck gold with this mysterious man called Peter Bennett.

Peter smiled as much to himself as to anybody.

She was good, perhaps very good, but he had the advantage; he knew who she really was.

"All right, you're in *Bracht* because somewhere in the vicinity is a heather plant called *Erica Polinaris*?"

"Correct." She picked up her wine glass, her eyes still not leaving his. She probably thought he was playing games with her, and that she was better than he was. "I'm here to find and look at *Erica Polinaris,*" she said.

"A heather plant?"

"Yes." She frowned. "Does that not fit in with the image I present?"

He shrugged. "It takes all kinds. It's just that, well, I have this picture in my mind of what a botanist should look like and –"

"I don't fit that picture?"

"Sort of," he said.

"That's not an answer."

"Well, no you don't. You're wearing make-up, no glasses, you're dressed normally, you're pretty and from what I can see, you have a nice figure. That doesn't fit the image."

"That's your image of a botanist … glasses, no make-up, strange dress-sense, plain and no boobs?"

"All right, I admit it's what –"

"I'm sorry to disappoint you."

"Who said anything about being disappointed? So where is this *Erica Polinaris* stuff?" he said.

"Stuff? You don't call one of the rarest varieties of *Erica* … stuff." She lit another cigarette and exhaled towards the ceiling.

Peter held up his hands defensively. "Sorry, where is this rarest of heather plants called *Erica Polinaris*?"

"Behind a fence."
"A fence?"
"Yes."
"You are speaking English, aren't you?" He finished his wine and indicated to Rosa to bring another two glasses. She had poured them already, anticipating the probable way things were going. "So where's this fence?" he asked.
"All the way round an ammunition depot," Sylvia Donnelly said.
She had introduced her obvious intent very well. Using this heather plant was quite plausible but she really ought to have dressed the part.
"Something has just clicked," he said.
"Really, I didn't hear anything."
"This." Peter spread his arms. "This is why you are here in Rosa's."
Regardless of the circumstances, he liked her. She had a similar sense of humour to his, and on the surface she would have given the impression that she was good company. But he knew differently and what she really was. He would bide his time because things could get interesting before they got serious. Believing he had struck gold with Ursula Dorf, perhaps meeting Sylvia Donnelly was the equivalent of finding a large seam of platinum.
"In *Bracht*?" she asked.
"In Rosa's Bar," he said.
"Why?"
He looked over his shoulder. "It could be them,' he said, indicating the soldiers.
"And not you?"
"Me?"
"You're one of them, aren't you?"
"I hope I understood what you've just said."
"So do I. And?"
"And what?"
"Stop being so obtuse. Are you or aren't you?"
"Yes, I am, but as I said, not for much longer."
"I don't need very long so I'd better make use of whatever time you have left," she said.
"And what don't you need very long for?"
Sylvia moved the tip of her tongue over her lips. Tilting her head to one side, she said, "I want to get very close to *Erica Polinaris.* I want to touch it and take some photographs."
"There's an official way of doing such things, and there's the *Forstmeister* to think about. He's very protective."
"The official way takes too long, and who or what is a *Forstmeister*?"

"He's a local in the equivalent of our Forestry Commission," Peter said. "He looks after all the flora and fauna in the depot and the Germans take such things very, very seriously."

"Would he have to know?"

For a few seconds Peter played for time. "I don't suppose so."

"So you'll do it?"

"I might," he said.

"I would be very grateful," she said, pushing her knee against his under the table. She was clearly thinking that Peter Bennett might be an interesting sideline. "If you see what I mean," she added.

"Don't go making idle promises that you have no intention of keeping," he said.

"My promises are never idle, and I always keep them."

"We'll see."

"When?" she said.

"When what?"

"When will you take me into the depot?"

"Tomorrow."

"That's a date," Sylvia said, picking up her wine glass in a toast.

Peter toasted her in return.

He liked the name Pamela, it suited her more than Sylvia. He wasn't as sure about Fellows – Pamela Fellows aka Sylvia Donnelly. Pamela … masquerading as a botanist; Sylvia a fanatic or perhaps fantasist would be more appropriate.

Regardless, she had now joined his list. She would be his penultimate killing.

He just hoped she would still be operating in the area when it was her turn to die.

Chapter Thirty-Seven

Two weeks later Peter was summoned to the CO's office.

"Sit down, Peter," he said, coming out from behind his desk. "I won't offer you any coffee... or tea," he added, smiling. "Now, a decision has been made and I think it's one you might be quite pleased with and just a little relieved."

Peter nodded. "I thought that might be the reason you wanted to see me, Colonel," he said.

"For obvious reasons I still don't know what happened in Ireland, but I have my suspicions." He shrugged. "But what I know and don't know is actually irrelevant. Suffice to say, before you left *Wulfen*, you submitted your resignation, didn't you?"

"Yes, Colonel, that's correct," Peter said.

"Well, it's been accepted and as far as I am concerned you are free to hand in any kit that isn't yours, pack your bags and leave."

Peter was actually quite surprised. "What you mean that's it? There's not going to be —"

"Just accept what I have said please, Peter. No, there isn't going to be a court martial and all the charges with which you were threatened have been dropped."

This time Peter shook his head. "So my little diversion in *Wulfen* was unnecessary?"

Nodding, the CO allowed a smile to show. "I don't know what little diversion you are referring to, Peter."

"I presume this decision has been cleared to the highest level," Peter said, "and I mean the highest level."

"Your question is just a little impertinent." The smile disappeared. "Your resignation has been accepted and once the bureaucratic wheels have turned, in a matter of weeks you'll be a civilian again and you can do with the rest of your life whatever you wish. However, because of your background and what you know, the Official Secrets Act will continue to apply for the next five years."

"I suppose under the circumstances that's a small price to pay," Peter said.

"As I told you, I remain in ignorance, but what I will tell you is that your successes prior to whatever has now happened played a large part in the decision that has been taken. Those at the highest level, as you referred to them, decided you should go quietly. I think that is fair reward for your earlier achievements, don't you?"

Shrugging, Peter stood up. "Thank you, Colonel. I assume you played no small part in what was decided."

"I played a very small part, Peter. You, for obvious reasons, were the main player. The Brigadier is more than willing to see you before you head off back to England, or wherever you intend going but –"

"No. Seeing him now wouldn't achieve anything for anybody. As you suggested, I will just go quietly."

"What do you intend doing?"

"Reclaiming my life," Peter said.

Timothy Smithers also stood up and put out his hand. "I understand," he said, "and thank you for the work you've put in while you were in my depot. You will be a great loss to the Army, Peter, but this is for the best."

"I agree, Colonel." Peter turned to leave but then stopped. "But obviously that's a matter of opinion and we'll never know the truth, will we?"

When Peter left the CO's office his mind was working overtime. The news of his imminent departure was unexpected; he had prepared himself for a court martial and knew exactly what he was going to say and who he was going to take down with him. He wasn't sure that accepting his resignation was what he wanted – it was the easier option, but also a cop-out by the system. However, it did bring his plans forward by at least three months, which was no bad thing.

He needed to go to England and start his search as soon as possible; it would be ideal if his fifth and last victim could be chosen within twelve months. The timeframe didn't really matter, none of his victims were going anywhere, except maybe Sylvia Donnelly.

So before going to England he needed to see her. He had something rather dangerous to do but it was the only way he could be certain she might stay in Germany, or at least be in Germany when it was her turn. Ursula Dorf was different. He would continue to use his flat in *Frankenmühle* as his base in Germany; it was discrete and close enough for what he needed. He was due to meet Ursula there this evening. She wouldn't be happy that he was leaving for England tomorrow but he would be back every few weeks so she would have to get used to the change.

Peter rang the number Sylvia Donnelly had given him.

"Hello," a female voice said.

"Pamela, it's Peter, we need to meet."

"Of course, but you're lucky, I'm due to leave on Friday."

"I know and that's why I need to see you."

"Where and when?" she asked.

"Do you know the *Forsthotel* near the village of *Heidhausen*? It's tucked away in the woods."

"As a matter of fact I do. I came across it when I was following the perimeter fence of the ammunition depot, outside of course, when I was looking for *Erica Polinaris*," she said, and she laughed.

He wanted to tell her she could come up with a better story than that, but instead he said, "So you know you get to it by going via *Kaldenkirchen*?"

"Yes, I do."

"I'll meet you in the car park opposite the hotel at three this afternoon."

"Okay, this sounds intriguing."

Chapter Thirty-Eight

After parking her car, Sylvia had a good look through the trees at the hotel. Mainly a wooden two storey structure which she knew had a large terrace for *al fresco* dining, it had an eerie look but was still inviting. Nestled among the tall fir trees, it was very secluded and she assumed it was used for many illicit meetings. Was that why Peter had chosen it?

"So, what's this all about?" she asked as she climbed into Peter's car five minutes later. "I thought we'd agreed –"

"We did but ... close the door and I'll tell you."

She did as he asked, then looked at him quizzically. "We agreed that we ... well, as I said on the phone, I go back to England on Friday –"

"*Do* you? I show you the depot, you look at your *Erica Polinaris*, or you said you did – it looked like any other heather to me – and then you show me your gratitude by having sex –"

"Peter, what's going on? You know finishing up in bed together was a mutual ... it would have happened –"

"Would it? I know who and what you are," he said, his body tense as he followed her hand moving towards her bag. "Don't," he said. "Hear me out."

"What do you mean – you know who and what I am?" she said, her hand still near the top of her bag.

"Your name is Sylvia Donnelly, not Pamela Meadows. And you wouldn't know one type of heather from another, except by its colour." He reached across and pulled her hand away from her bag, and put his other hand on her shoulder.

She stared at him, her eyes darting from him to her bag. She tried to pull away but he closed his fingers round her neck. "Sylvia, I'm not what I seem either," he said slowly, "and I think we can work together."

"What ... what do you mean?" she said.

"I mean, regardless of our backgrounds, we might have more in common than you think." He pulled her bag towards him. Slipping his hand inside, he felt around, then removed the 9mm Beretta. "Do all botanists walk around with a loaded pistol in their bags?" He put the pistol in the glove compartment. "Now are you going to listen?"

She nodded, still confused.

"Just accept, Sylvia, that I am not what I seem and my sympathies lie with the Irish Republic and not with the British."

"What? You're undercover?"

"Something like that." he said.

During the one night they had previously spent together he had let her assume that the incident with Sandra Davies in *Wulfen* was his only misdemeanour and that was why he was being thrown out of the Army.

This time she listened, her unblinking eyes wide in surprise.

"Basically, Sylvia, I want what you want and I can see no better way of achieving what both of us want other than if we work together. Do you understand?" he said.

She nodded slowly. "I understand but why should I believe you?"

"Sylvia, we are sitting in the front of my car. Other than calling the police and having you arrested, I could just as easily kill you and dump your body in these woods. Who is going spend time looking for the executioner? According to the British you are an IRA terrorist. Nobody would shed a tear. Why would I suggest we work together if I'm not what I say I am."

"You haven't told me what you are and you might know who I am but you could just be using me to get to the rest of my cell, and then –"

"Look, what I will tell you ... have you heard of G2 in the Republic?"

"Yes, of course I have. It's the Directorate of Intelligence but –"

"It is, so just accept that G2 and I are connected."

"You could ... you could be making this up."

"That's a risk you will have to take, isn't it." Putting his hand on her leg he ran his fingers up her thigh. "And while we work together we can enjoy what we started the other night," he said, smiling. "Are you here because there's an ammunition depot over there, or are you more interested in the soldiers?"

"Both," she said.

"Well, perhaps we can help each other achieve both our aims with one of the biggest atrocities committed on German soil."

"What? A bomb?"

Peter nodded. "Yes, a bomb."

"But how –?"

"Detail is unnecessary at the moment, just believe me it can be done," he said.

Sylvia looked down at Peter's hand between her legs. "My bosses wouldn't allow this."

"Your bosses and mine need never know. When the shit hits the fan, you can claim total responsibility and I will disappear out of your life ... if that's what we both want."

“I don't know what I want.”

“How long will it be before you’re moved from this area?” Peter asked. “I know it won’t be in a couple of days time.”

Sylvia narrowed her eyes. “We’re here to gather intelligence,” she said. “I’m due to go to Belfast in a couple of months to tell my bosses what I've discovered.”

“And no action until after that?”

“No, unless we need to defend ourselves. Everything has to be coordinated. It could be the middle or even the end of next year before anything happens in this area.”

“Good, that gives me enough time.” He opened the glove compartment, retrieved the pistol and gave it to Sylvia, butt first. “There you are ... trust!”

Looking straight at him, Sylvia curled her index finger round the trigger and lifted the pistol. “I hope to God I’m doing the right thing,” she said, and put it back in her bag.

Peter smiled. “I think we ought to find out how comfortable the beds are in the *Forsthotel* as a way of celebration, don't you?”

The bomb was going to be his final calling card, and the type he would use and how he would get it inside the depot was already beyond the planning stage. He would do what was necessary in the UK; it was where his resources were and the people who could supply him with anything, though at a cost. It would be a simple car bomb; the explosive would be packed into places where it couldn't be detected and then it would be brought to Germany by his sixth and final victim.

Whoever it was would have no idea what she was doing and that she was driving a mobile bomb.

What could be more innocent than a young girl in a small car? Wherever she went nobody would ask any questions. He wondered where he would finally find such a girl, but he was sure he was going to enjoy the search.

She was out there somewhere.

Chapter Thirty-Nine

Gregor Crazkowski met Ursula Dorf in the departure lounge at Düsseldorf Airport.

She told him she had taken a day off on the pretext of needing to go shopping. The previous evening she had rung a Bonn number that was for use only in an emergency. She apologised but explained this was in her opinion an emergency but she had yet to convince her controller from Bonn.

"But he is a prime candidate for disaffection, Gregor," Ursula said. They had found a reasonably quiet spot but not so isolated that they would stand out. They spoke in English; not German which would be understood, nor Russian which might arouse suspicions.

"My dear," Gregor said, "I understand your conscientiousness and your eagerness to help the Motherland, but identifying a possible disaffected ex-British officer is one thing, succeeding in turning him is another. Besides you have not been trained to handle people like this. It is not as straight forward as you might think."

Gregor spoke to Ursula as though he was her well-respected and much loved uncle. He was certainly old enough to be her father. At fifty, Gregor Crazkowski hoped retirement was not too far away and as one of the many Press Attachés in the former Soviet and now Russian Embassy in Bonn he had been handling agents, German as well as Russian, for nearly five years. He hoped his retirement would happen before the upheaval of moving the embassy back to Berlin.

Inwardly he was very annoyed that Ursula had contacted him, but she had used *Code Red* on the phone, which told him it was critical that they should meet. Now that he had heard what she wanted there was nothing critical about it at all – just a young kid who had a good idea, or so she thought. He had come across such misguided enthusiasm in the past but he hoped he did not have to deal with such passion many more times before he retired.

Unfortunately, the forlorn expression on Ursula's face was hard to ignore.

"Ursula, you're perfect for what you were sent into Germany to do. You've done everything we asked of you …" He broke off as yet another flight departure was announced by a very metallic female voice. "You have infiltrated, you have become established, you are accepted, you are trusted, so what more can you do but wait?" By not saying anything, she accepted his question did not warrant answering. "You must wait, that is what you need to do. You knew that it could take a number of years before we could make use of you. Being a 'sleeper' can be frustrating, I know, but 'sleepers' do not try to turn likely disaffected British officers; there are other people who are specially trained for that type of mission.

"It could be that you are never 'woken-up', that you are never required. You could spend your entire service to the Motherland just waiting. A major catastrophe in a British Army barracks may not become necessary. However, we know you are there, that at any time you could be available if necessary. When this depot you are working in closes you will be even more established and trusted, so moving to Rhinedahlen on relocation and into the British joint headquarters will perhaps give us what we really need.

"It will be the first time we have infiltrated this headquarters, and it will be you who does it, my dear. Do we really want to upset these plans by going after someone who dislikes the way his country has treated him? If he has already left the British Army what use can he be? You have alerted me to him. That is good. But should he be of use later others will handle him." He paused, hoping that he had let one of his protégés down lightly.

Ursula looked over to the concourse where streams of people were milling about, staring at departure screens, drinking coffee, lugging heavy cases, while others just sat and looked bored. She was so sure that her controller would be pleased with her and agree.

"I've wasted your time, haven't I?" she said.

"I would not say wasted. I am an overweight, grey-haired, middle-aged man who is never happier than when he is in the company of beautiful young women. So time spent with you is certainly never wasted." Ursula smiled. "But you came to Germany for a purpose, my dear, and what you are suggesting wasn't the reason."

"I understand."

"This Peter Bennett – are you still seeing him and are you sleeping with him?" Gregor asked.

Ursula had anticipated the question. "Yes," she said.

"That is good but be very careful. If he was in trouble with his own people and you are seen with him they may look more closely at you. You must stay in the background," Gregor added, and she noticed his eyes straying to the top button of her shirt.

"Nobody knows," Ursula assured him. "We are being very discreet."

"As you and I are being. However, in speaking to you I am stepping outside my remit. I have a new tracking team assigned to me. They started last month, but they are not very good. I lost them before I left Bonn ... normally it takes a lot longer." Gregor's face lit up as he smiled, but then suddenly he was serious again. "As I said, you are beautiful, my dear. You receive a good allowance, you can do what you like and go where you like. If you want my advice, use this time while you have it. Millions of women in the Motherland would give anything to be where you are.

"We have seen many changes – the reunification of Germany and the breakup of the glorious Soviet Union to name but two. Who would have dared predict such things were going to happen? Espousing such theories only six years ago would have resulted in the traitor disappearing or sent to the salt mines, if he were lucky. But for us things are more dangerous now than they have ever been. What is happening in the former Yugoslavia is just the start, though it is a mere pimple on the backside of the earth. I lie in my bed at night and worry, my dear. You will see previous enemies joining forces to combat this new threat and you will see more changes that will amaze you. Can you imagine the West courting countries that used to be part of the USSR, even getting them to join the EEC and NATO?" Ursula shook her head in disbelief. "The Russian bear is watching and if threatened it will act. So you see, what you are doing now is more important than before. You are one of many special people who are here if we need them, so use the time, my dear. What may be waiting for us all could shatter our lives beyond recognition." Gregor paused before adding, "Now I must go."

Ursula put a hand on his arm. "Thank you, Gregor, and I'm sorry if I have inconvenienced you."

"Inconvenienced me? No, my dear, it has been a pleasure, especially to see you looking so well. The authorities frown upon any initiative emanating from our junior officers, but for me such ignorance could be the hallmark of our eventual failure if we ever have to go to war again. It is good to see that you are as the British say 'thinking on your feet', eh?" He covered her hand with his. "I will ensure that Moscow is made aware that this agent is thinking wisely, using her initiative – thinking on her feet as well as on her back, eh?"

Gregor Crazkowski smiled but didn't add that his report would also explain that Ursula Ivanovitch's initiative was misguided.

The fact that she had jeopardised her own identity by asking for the meeting, suggested that she was overstepping her remit. She was there to be his eyes and ears but he would only see and listen when he wanted to, not when she thought it was time.

She could not be withdrawn or just disappear, because either would arouse suspicion.

Regrettably, Gregor decided, as he felt the warmth of her hand in his, termination may be the only answer. She might have to meet with an accident which would be a pity. Not only did she show so much promise, albeit misguided, she was also so beautiful. It would be like plucking the most gorgeous rose from the bush simply because it was there.

She leant forward and kissed him on both cheeks, the aroma of her perfume lingering.

As he watched her walk away from him, his gaze following her swaying hips, he shook his head. "Why do these young people feel the need to use their initiative? Why could they not simply do as they are told?"

Chapter Forty

It was five o'clock in the afternoon and Sylvia Donnelly couldn't believe or understand what she had allowed to happen. Her clothes were on a chair, her bag was on the floor and in her bag was the loaded 9mm Beretta. Peter Bennett was in the bathroom, and she was lying naked on a hotel bed having been made to feel as though nothing else in the world mattered.

But what she had done did matter.

She wanted to believe what he'd said, and if it were the truth then together they could cause absolute mayhem. The seduction was to some extent neither here nor there; it was what went with it that scared her.

It was just her luck that he'd been sent to *Bracht* and she had been even more unlucky when he recognised her – she wondered whether G2 knew about every IRA operative. Nobody had ever told her of their involvement. He must have been undercover for years, but how better to glean intelligence than to be on the inside. As soon as he sat down at her table in Rosa's bar she should have been on her guard, but instead she had allowed her own arrogance to look upon him as a source of information.

He had been playing with her all the time.

Should she trust him and was he telling her the truth?

But now it was her turn to play with him. She quickly got off the bed, retrieved the Beretta from her bag, checked it was ready to fire, and put it under the pillow.

If he were for real then she was his to do with what she wanted; if he thought he was using her for whatever reason, then the reverse could apply ... she was sure of that.

The bathroom door opened. He was certainly her idea of what a man should look like. She didn't like men who were overly muscular; such ugliness suggested narcissism and she couldn't stand men who looked in the mirror more than any woman would. The discernible six-pack and his firm thigh muscles and biceps told her he was proud of his body.

"You're what every girl likes to see walking out of the bathroom," she said, sliding her hands over her ribcage towards her thighs.

"We need to talk," he said, with a hint of a smile on his lips.

"I know we do, but at the moment –"

“I can tell you're not convinced yet,” he said, sitting on the edge of the bed.

“By what?”

“What I am and why I'm here.”

She pulled up her knees and wrapped her arms round them, narrowing her eyes. “If I didn't think there was something in what you said, my pistol would now be under the pillow and not in my bag over there. But you have to accept that this is a pretty bizarre situation and if either of our bosses knew ... Do yours know?”

“No,' he said, “we’re both taking risks.”

“Me more than you.”

“That's as maybe, but ...” he shook his head. “So why are you and the others in this area.”

“I told you, assessing targets.”

“And how far are you away from doing something?”

She hesitated. “An ammunition depot is a prime target.”

“Only if the bomb is big enough and placed in the right place,” he said. “How do you intend doing that?”

“We're working on it.”

“I'm sure you are, and I've no doubt you'll come up with something,” he said, wrapping his fingers round her foot and massaging her toes. “What would you say if I told you I can take care of that side of things and at the same time you can concentrate on human targets?”

She looked down at his fingers. “And why would you do that? I still don't understand.”

He reached for her other foot. “I have my reasons,” he said.

“And they are not for me to know? Is that what you are saying?”

He nodded. “Something like that.”

“So,” she said, stretching her leg so that her foot was on his thigh, “what you’re suggesting is that I can trust you to put a car bomb in the depot, and at the same time we take out as many of the military as we can?”

“In a nutshell, yes, but I wouldn't become too adventurous. The CO and a couple of his officers would achieve the aim ... your aim.” He moved his hand up to her calf muscle.

“But why would you do this – risk you career with G2?”

“Just accept that it will happen,” he said, moving further onto the bed.

“Yes, I now believe it will,” Sylvia said, lying back and smiling.

Part Three

July 1994

Chapter Forty-One

Leah arrived at the Officers' Mess thirty minutes before *Herr* Dorf told her the meeting was due to start. She could not believe the coincidence of what Peter had asked her to do and the job that was allocated to her, especially when she remembered he had cross-examined her about her German: spoken, written and technical.

This morning and before the scheduled meeting, *Herr* Dorf explained further that the depot was regretfully earmarked for closure after nearly forty-five years and her first meeting as a translator was going to involve the Commanding Officer and Second-in-Command of the depot, the *Burgermeister* (Mayor) and the *Gemeindedirektor* (Area Political Representative) from *Brüggen*.

"Unfortunately," *Herr* Dorf had said, "neither of the officers I mentioned will be available to meet you before the meeting, but do not worry as they are both what the English call 'nice chaps'. The CO's name is Timothy Smithers and his Second-in-Command is a Major Clive Benton. Be watchful of him because he is a bit of a, again what the English call, 'ladies' man' – in other words he thinks a lot of himself."

"I can take care of myself," Leah said."What will I have to do?"

Herr Dorf shrugged. "Translate if and when necessary. The Colonel speaks some German but he tends towards literal translation, which on occasion can lead to misinterpretation and misunderstandings, and Major Benton speaks more German than he lets on. He thinks people will speak more freely in front of him because of his supposed ignorance of the language."

"What about the *Burgermeister* and *Gemeindedirektor*?"

"They both speak German very well," *Herr* Dorf said, his eyes twinkling, "but only *Herr* Dangers, the *Gemeindedirektor*, speaks a little English. *Herr* Mittelwalder, the *Burgermeister*? I don't think I have ever heard him use an English word other than 'computer'."

"And what is the meeting all about?" Leah asked, looking up from her note pad.

Herr Dorf settled back in his chair. "The old 3 Base Ammunition Depot was formed in a place called Bramley in the county of Hampshire in England in October 1939 after the start of the second-world war. The unit saw service in France, North Africa and then in Germany. In 1952 it moved to and established itself here in Bracht and has been the source of employment for many locals, as well as foreign workers ever since. The tight links it has developed with the towns of *Bracht* and *Brüggen* over the years, resulted in the unit being given the Freedom of *Brüggen* in 1979, a rare but great honour bestowed on only a few other British Army units elsewhere in Germany. There was another parade earlier this year to exercise this freedom." *Herr* Dorf spoke as though he was reading from a script. "However, only two months ago it was announced that as a result of the British Army's partial withdrawal from Germany, this depot was part of the closure programme. It is planned to close in September 1996."

"With the loss of many jobs," Leah volunteered.

"Not necessarily so. There will be a re-training programme for those who need it, but conveniently the date for closure is when many workers would be close to retirement anyway."

"I see, so this meeting is the first between the depot officers and the local authorities since the announcement?" she asked.

"It's the first formal meeting, yes."

"Will I have to take notes so that minutes can be written?"

"You need only record the major decisions, if there are any," he told her.

Leah took a deep breath as she raised her eyebrows. "I find it hard to believe that two days ago I was on a ferry crossing the Channel and here I am now – doing this."

Herr Dorf let a wry smile cross his lips. "You mean I am throwing you in at the deep end," he said in English.

"I will let you know after the meeting, but I am a good swimmer."

Leah was standing in the foyer of the Officers' Mess, wondering in which room the meeting was going to take place, when a tall man in his early sixties came through a swing door to her left. Once inside, the single storey building was deceptively large. The foyer was panelled from floor to ceiling in what appeared to be a light oak and as well as flower decorations on a couple of pedestals either side of the door, there were two tables: one had a visitors' book on it along with other military memorabilia. The walls contained two large prints of frantic looking men on horses – looking equally frantic – charging into battle.

The man stopped and looked at Leah, his eyes summing her up. "May I help you?" he asked in heavily accented English.

"Yes, please," Leah replied in German. "I am here for the meeting."

The man, who was smartly dressed in a white shirt, black bow tie, waistcoat, trousers and black shoes, suddenly beamed. "You must be *Fraulein* Carpenter."

"Yes, that's right. How –?"

"Do not worry *Fraulein*, *Herr* Dorf rang me and told me you would be coming." He held out his hand. "I am Fritz Breckmann, the Officers' Mess manager."

Leah took his hand, which was large but soft. "I am … but you already know who I am, *Herr* Breckmann."

"Yes, I do, but please call me Fritz. Everybody else does. You English are far less formal than we Germans."

Leah took to this lovely man straight away. "Yes, I suppose we are."

His silver grey hair was combed back from his forehead and he wore gold horn-rimmed glasses. His eyes told a thousand stories of his time serving the British Army.

"Follow me, *Fraulein*, and I will show you where to go. The ladies' toilet is just down that passage on the right. Would you like a cup of coffee or tea?" he asked showing her into what she thought would be the anteroom.

"Coffee please, and my name is Amy," Leah said, once again hating herself for having to lie.

The anteroom was no different from any other anteroom she had been in when her parents took her to Officers' Mess functions, but in this one, there was an exception. She took in the usual formal dark-brown leather chairs, low coffee tables and a further table with papers and magazines strewn over it; a maroon patterned wall-to-wall carpet and walls festooned with pictures of austere-looking Generals, battle scenes and the odd tasteful cartoon tucked away in one corner, plus, of course, the obligatory pictures of a very young looking Queen Elizabeth II and Prince Phillip. At the far end of the room, which was about the size of a tennis court, was a dining table with six chairs round it, and putting her bag on this table Leah looked up at the exception she had noticed straight away.

Taking up almost half the end wall was a relief map of what had to be the ammunition depot. Peter had told her that the depot covered an area equivalent to that occupied by Heathrow Airport but her mind had not let her visualise it. Now, she could. She walked over to the map and traced her finger to where she thought the Officers' Mess would be.

"Large, isn't it?" Fritz said behind her.

"Huge," she agreed, turning and accepting the cup of coffee. "It's massive."

Fritz moved to her side. "What you do not see, *Fraulein* –"

"I told you my name is Amy."

"The English might be informal but in here," he said, smiling, "I know my place."

Frowning, Leah thought this was rather a sad thing to say.

Fritz shrugged. "It does not worry me. I have been doing this job for over twenty years. What comes out of here," he said tapping his lips, "is not necessarily the same as what is being said up here." He tapped his head. "And words cost nothing." His gaze remained on Leah's face for a couple of seconds before he looked back at the map. "As I was saying, what you do not see is the way the high fence around the entire perimeter of the depot has preserved the beautiful wildlife – the trees, the insects and everything else – from being destroyed by human beings."

"Wildlife?" Leah asked, taking a sip of her coffee.

"As well as the normal foxes, rabbits and badgers there are also many species of deer and families of wild pig, eagles, buzzards and hawks. In one area there is some heather that only grows here, somewhere in Russia and in the north of Scotland. Naturists come from all over Europe to peer through the fence at this heather." Fritz pointed to a small area at one corner of the map. "But for me," he said, smiling, "it looks like all the other heathers I have ever seen. I …" Fritz stopped when he saw a large black Mercedes pulling up outside the Mess. "That is the *Gemeindedirektor* and the *Burgermeister*," he said, "so I must go and greet them." He placed his fingertips on Leah's forearm, and winked. "Do not worry," he said, "their self-importance will be melted by your beauty and your charm."

Looking at her reflection in one of the pictures on the wall, Leah tried to check her hair. She wished she had gone to the ladies' toilet as soon as she arrived. The door to the anteroom opened and two tall, bespectacled, dark-suited men walked in, both carrying small brown leather briefcases. They advanced across the room, the younger man scowling and the elder one smiling.

"This is *Fraulein* Amy Carpenter. She will be translating at the meeting today," Fritz Breckmann told them.

The grey-haired rosy-cheeked man bowed his head and proffered his hand, still smiling. "*Herr* Mittelwalder," he said.

"*Herr* Dangers," the dark-haired younger man said as he shook hands. Leah decided he was probably in his early forties but the clipped moustache, black-rimmed glasses made him look older. He was still scowling.

Leah thought it was rather rude that neither of the officers *Herr* Dorf had told her would be present had arrived early to greet the German officials. It was not something her father would have allowed to happen. Fritz withdrew to get the new arrivals some coffee. Going to the table *Herr* Dangers undid his briefcase and started taking out papers, but *Herr* Mittelwalder stayed at her side.

"You are new?" he asked in German.

"My first day," Leah told him.

"And you are English? I am sorry, I detect a slight accent."

"For my sins, yes I am, and please do not apologise."

Herr Mittelwalder frowned. "It is not normal for the translator to be English," he said before adding, "And where is *Frau* Weissmüller?"

"As I understand it, she's on maternity leave."

"So soon?"

Leah shrugged. "I wouldn't know."

"Your German is very good."

"Thank you."

The meeting got underway about twenty minutes later.

The British officers arrived ten minutes after the appointed start time, which annoyed Leah even further, and they didn't even have the courtesy to apologise. The Commanding Officer, who introduced himself as Colonel Smithers and not Timothy Smithers, was a tall balding man in his mid-forties with a very officious air about him. He sat at the head of the table and obviously wanted to get on with the business at hand straight away. He was wearing a grey slate coloured uniform, which was similar to one Leah had seen her father wear when he was stationed in Hong Kong. His Second-in-Command, Major Clive Benton, was not what Leah expected.

As they entered the anteroom, Timothy Smithers shook her hand almost dismissively, whereas Clive Benton held on to it for far too long, his fingers almost caressing her skin. As he looked her up and down, she could sense his eyes peeling away her clothing, layer by layer. He was handsome enough with floppy blond hair, deep blue eyes, a slight tan and broad shoulders, but rather than being pleased with his attention, Leah felt her skin begin to crawl.

Even now, sitting at the table, he was not concentrating on the discussion. He was sitting opposite Leah looking at her, his mouth and eyes giving away his thoughts. Leah, on the other hand, tried to concentrate.

The *Gemeindedirektor* did most of the talking on the German side. Leah quickly established that although *Herr* Mittelwalder, who was by far the nicer of the two German officials, was the senior by both age and position he was more like an English mayor, all pomp and circumstance but little authority, whereas *Herr* Dangers was speculative and challenging, looking to the future objectively. He was the one she was going to have to concentrate on, Leah decided. If Peter was going to get the information he wanted, Dangers was going to be the source ... among others.

"So, Colonel Smithers, may I ask why the change. A year ago we were being told that this depot had a future and that its workers were secure in their jobs until at least the end of the 1990s?"

Leah translated.

Timothy Smithers played with a pencil, not looking at *Herr* Dangers when he spoke. "Things change," he said. "My masters are constantly reviewing the situation in Europe and it has now been decided that we no longer need an ammunition depot in this area."

Leah translated.

"Rather like your Royal Air Force deciding that they no longer need three bases here either," *Herr* Dangers said. "*Wildenwrath* has closed, *Laarbruch* goes next, and then later *Brüggen* will go. Have you any idea the effect such closures have on the local economy? It is like closing three small towns of people overnight. The effect is economically devastating, not to mention all the job losses."

Herr Dangers sat back in his chair, his eyes narrowed and piercing. *Herr* Mittelwalder looked slightly embarrassed. Clive Benton was watching Leah as she translated and took notes. Timothy Smithers was still playing with a pencil.

"I am unable to comment on the closure of the RAF bases," Timothy Smithers said, "but I do appreciate the loss of so many people –"

"And jobs," *Herr* Dangers said in English.

"And jobs," the CO conceded. "And they will have a short-term effect on the local economy." Dangers tried to interrupt him again, but he carried on. "But in the case of this depot," he said, "the situation is not the same. The area we occupy," – bad choice of words, Leah thought – "is relatively unchanged from over forty years ago. I would have imagined you would welcome its return."

Herr Dangers looked sideways at the *Burgermeister* who, by raising his eyebrows, told his younger companion that he was on his own.

"Of course, to have returned so much land has to be to the benefit of the local people, but it is them I am really concerned about. This depot remains the largest employer within the *Gemeinde*."

The CO looked up as he slowly placed the pencil on the table.

"I acknowledge what you've just said. But surely in your position as the political leader of the *Gemeinde*, you can appreciate that decisions have to be taken that result in little short-term benefit for the people, but that in the long-term such decisions must be viewed differently. The fact is that two more RAF stations are closing along with the closure of this depot. In addition, there will be many other closures across the northern area of Germany. Surely this must indicate that we and the rest of Europe feel that since the re-unification of Germany and the demise of the USSR, Europe is now more stable than it has ever been and there is no longer a need for the same level of British representation on your soil."

"And what is happening in the former Yugoslavia is an example of your more stable Europe, is it, Colonel?" *Herr* Dangers said.

With the pencil back in his fingers, Timothy Smithers looked distinctly uncomfortable.

Herr Dangers smiled for the first time.

"I think –" the CO started to say.

"I am being a little unfair, Colonel," *Herr* Dangers said. "You are a soldier first and you do as you are told. I am a politician who under the right circumstances can do the telling. My area of influence is small, but your depot takes up a good proportion of it. I accept the decision to close the depot, but what I think you and I must do is ensure the retraining of your workers if necessary, and the sourcing of alternative employment. We have just over two years, and in the months remaining to us I think we have plenty of time to come up with a phased programme that will benefit both you and my people. Do you agree?"

Timothy Smithers looked both embarrassed and relieved. "Of course I agree, *Herr* Dangers, as that was always my intention."

Clive Benton spoke for the first time but without diverting his attention from Leah. "Have you any idea what you will do with the land, *Herr* Dangers?" he said.

Both the *Burgermeister* and the *Gemeindedirektor* looked straight at the Second-in-Command.

It was *Herr* Mittelwalder who spoke. "It is early days, Major, very early days."

Chapter Forty-Two

When Leah arrived in *Brüggen* the previous Sunday she had felt apprehensive and very lonely. On the Monday morning as she drove to the depot, even greater uneasiness and then foreboding had joined her apprehension. However, as she left the Officers' Mess after the meeting on her second day at work, her confidence was back.

While driving down to the other end of the administrative area, she asked herself why her feelings had changed so drastically.

From her perspective, the meeting went well. There was nothing at all difficult in the translation, especially as there were times when she caught *Herr* Dangers – she still didn't know his first name – nodding his approval. She concluded that he spoke better English than he let on. He and Clive Benton were from the same mould. Half way through the meeting *Herr* Karl-Heinz Mittelwalder passed her a piece of paper to tell her he ran a restaurant in *Brüggen* and if she ever wanted to sample his wife's cooking she only needed to turn up. Having read the note Leah decided he was the perfect gentleman.

The CO, Timothy Smithers, continued to do his best to ignore her, and at the end of the meeting he merely collected his papers together, said his farewells to the two Germans and then left. Clive Benton on the other hand played the host. He suggested that they withdraw to the bar for a drink but *Herr* Dangers had an immediate excuse and as Karl-Heinz Mittelwalder was travelling in the same car, he too had to decline but with an affectionate smile.

After some not so subtle persuasion, Leah agreed to have a drink.

The bar, at the other end of the Officers' Mess beyond the dining room, was quite an informal room with the ubiquitous military prints on the walls and above the bar at least fifty Regimental plaques, some of which Leah recognised.

As Leah and Clive Benton entered the bar, one man was sitting in a corner, leaning on the bar with a glass of beer in front of him. He looked over the top of his paper and nodded.

"Hello, Bill," Clive said. "You're a bit early today."

"It's been one of those mornings," the man said, looking at Leah with interest.

“This is Amy Carpenter,” Clive said “Amy, this is Major Bill Streets, the Quartermaster.”

Bill Streets jumped off the stool and held out his hand. “Amy,” he said.

“Major Streets,” she replied, shaking his hand.

“Bill,” he said before resuming his seat and going back to his paper.

Fritz came in behind the bar and poured their drinks, a *Bitburger Bier* for Clive and a diet Coke for Leah.

“Will you be having some lunch, *Fraulein* Carpenter?” he asked, his eyes telling her that she must understand the formality.

“No, no thank you Fritz.”

“You can if you want,” Clive suggested hopefully, picking up their drinks before heading for a corner table.

“No, seriously, I very rarely eat lunch, thank you.”

Leah, with a backwards glance at Fritz, reluctantly followed Clive towards the table.

“So,” Clive said, sipping his lager, “where have you hailed from?”

Leah slipped automatically into her story, wondering why, having taken such an instant dislike to him, she was now sharing a lunchtime drink with Major Clive Benton.

From behind his desk in his wood-panelled office, Timothy Smithers looked up at Manfred Dorf. “Manfred, I’m well aware that Madeleine Weissmuller is on maternity leave,” he said, pushing to one side a plate of sandwiches brought in by his PA, “but I don’t expect you to spring a surprise on me like that again. And why couldn’t you have translated at the meeting?” he added.

“Colonel, I am sorry.” *Herr* Dorf stood in front of the desk, his hands behind his back. Inwardly he was gritting his teeth, objecting to this officer speaking to him as though he was no more than a common soldier. As the Civil Labour Officer and the principal yard foreman, he was after all the senior civilian working in the depot. “But it seemed like too good an opportunity to miss. I had a works council meeting to attend this morning and *Fraulein* Carpenter just appeared in my office yesterday.”

“Just appeared? So you decided that this stranger could turn up to my meeting without clearing it with me?” To add insult to injury, the CO started eating a sandwich.

“Her German is excellent and a lot better than *Frau* Weissmuller’s English,” *Herr* Dorf said.

“That’s not the point, is it? That meeting was particularly sensitive and the vital link between the two sides was a complete outsider to us all.”

“But she is English. I checked her passport.”

"Manfred, a passport does not make its holder bona fide." The CO selected another sandwich.

"Accepted, Colonel, but I only took her on as a casual labourer. There was no need for a full –"

"Don't you dare tell me there was no need for a full security check. Casual labourers are allowed nowhere near the security areas or any other restricted area. You know that."

"She was in the Officers' Mess, Colonel, I –"

"Manfred, that was the first official meeting with the German authorities since the closure was officially announced. Don't you think its content might have been slightly confidential and just a little sensitive? I felt completely inhibited by her presence."

"Then you should have –" *Herr* Dorf stopped before he overstepped the mark.

"I should have what, Manfred?"

"Nothing, Colonel, and I am sorry. I should have realised."

"Yes, you're dead right you should have realised. We've known each other for a long time, Manfred, and I've never known you do anything as misguided as this before."

"Colonel, I said I am sorry. It will not happen again."

He turned to leave the office, screwed up his eyes and wished he had the courage to say what he really thought. He had merely done what Ursula had asked him to do and he certainly could not see there was any harm in employing a young, pretty girl who had an English passport.

Timothy Smithers let him get as far as the open door before he said, "Oh, and Manfred, she was actually very good and a darn sight more pleasant to look at than Madeleine Weissmuller. Check her out, but you can keep her on in the meantime."

Herr Dorf turned round and said, "Yes, Colonel, thank you, Colonel."

Timothy Smithers smiled. "I like your taste, Manfred, but I would have thought Ursula was quite enough for you to cope with."

Chapter Forty-Three

Clive Benton's imagination was working overtime.

The word had obviously got round that the Second-in-Command was sitting in the Officers' Mess bar with some dolly-bird, and more people than normal popped in for a look before going home for lunch. Out of politeness, he introduced everybody to Amy and it was obvious from their reactions that she had lived up to rumour control. His thoughts though didn't waver much from what had crossed his mind the first moment he saw her.

He had already decided that Amy Carpenter was going to be his next conquest. She might not realise she was close to having the experience of her life, which was now maybe only a matter of a few days away.

To the outside world and within his mind, Clive Benton was single, but in military parlance this was not strictly true.

He was divorced.

His ex-wife, Charlotte, fed up with his philandering, walked out on him over two years ago, and the divorce was finalised shortly before his posting to Germany. His previous CO had given him an ultimatum: he had to sort himself out or do the honourable thing and resign his commission.

At the time, Clive wondered what all the fuss was about; he had never been accused of messing around with anybody else's wife, although that was only because he was never caught and there were no complaints from the benefactors of his obvious charms. His marriage, as far as he was concerned, had been on the rocks for years.

Anyway, he didn't like the way the Army interfered with people's private lives. He would probably resign his commission in any case, but it would be when he wanted to, not when the Army thought he ought to. However, that was in the future; the present was sitting across the table from him drinking the last of her diet Coke.

"Are you sure you don't want anything to eat?" he asked, trying to see beyond her formal suit jacket and white blouse underneath.

"No, I really don't," she said, looking at her watch, "and I really must be going. *Herr* Dorf wants the key points from this morning's meeting written up before the end of the day."

"That bloody slave-driver. He thinks he's in charge of the place."

"I think he's rather nice in an innocent sort of way," Amy said.

"Wait until you've been here a few weeks. You will be here that long, won't you?" Her answer would determine how soon he would have to make his move.

"I hope so. *Herr* Dorf said that *Frau* Weissmuller would be off for at least three months."

Three months was longer than he expected and perhaps long enough for him to build a rapport with this new challenge. He would see what she was like the first time and then decide whether it was worth the effort. Anyway, by this time next week Amy would be wondering why so far she had been wasting her life with amateurs.

"I look forward to seeing you again then," he said.

Not if she could help it, Leah wanted to say. Handsome and single he might be – having ensured during their conversation to slip in the fact that he had no ties – but he could forget any plans he might have for her. She had standards and his type came well below even the lowest of them.

"Yes, I understand your office in the headquarters is just down the corridor from mine," she said.

"It certainly is," Clive said, his lascivious leer giving away his full intentions.

Leah felt herself shiver.

Once back in her office – a small narrow room with a desk, chair, coffee table with two easy chairs, and three ugly floral prints on the magnolia walls – somebody had left a file on her desk entitled 'Unit Brief – Real Estate'. Leah sat down, flipped open the cover and began reading.

'The Headquarters is a single storey building and is one of three in the Administrative Area, or what is locally known as the bottom camp. The top camp, Wortham Barracks, contains the Quartermaster's offices and stores' – the boss of which was Bill Streets whom Leah met at lunchtime – 'the single soldiers' accommodation, the NAAFI club and shop, Officers' and Sergeants' Messes, a families' centre, a small church and the gymnasium.

Opposite Wortham Barracks, with a public road dividing the two, is Roberts Barracks where many of the foreign – and some of the German – depot workers live in single storey accommodation buildings. They have individual rooms and pay very much reduced food and accommodation charges compared with what they would pay elsewhere.

Turning right out of Wortham Barracks or left out of Roberts Barracks, the public road leads to the remainder of the depot. However, it remains a public right of way because there are many tracks leading off this road into the woods that border it to the left all the way to the main depot: roughly half way down this road there is a left turning that leads to a working quarry. To the right of the road, a fence runs down from Wortham Barracks to the bottom camp (Administrative Area) and behind this fence there is a single rugby pitch, and two football pitches. There is a cricket square between one of the football pitches and the rugby pitch. There is also a small assault course nestled into some trees behind the gymnasium.

Closer to the bottom camp and to the left, there is a fenced area with another barrier that leads to the Motor Transport Section, the Fire Brigade buildings and all the technical stores buildings. The Technical Quartermaster heads this organisation. He is responsible to the Commanding Officer for supporting all activities that go on in the main ammunition depot. Just after the Fire Brigade on the left, is the main gate, a large wrought-iron sliding barrier which stops anybody from entering the Restricted Area where the Headquarters is located. Leading from the Restricted Area and through yet another barrier is the Explosives Area, a large 4500 acre plot of land where over 25000 tons of ammunition is stored.'

After looking at the map attached to the unit brief, Leah closed the file and put it to one side. She felt the brief lacked imagination and could be a lot more colourful and descriptive, but at least she could now relate the large relief map she saw in the anteroom in the Officers' Mess to what was actually there.

If she were to get Peter the information he needed, she guessed the future of the explosives area was critical to any plans. From the translator's office window, she could see the vehicles passing through the final barrier into this area. She could also see the guard in his little cubicle checking every vehicle and the special passes needed to gain entry, which Clive Benton had described to her.

Turning back to her desk and ready to start typing up her report, she stopped when she saw Timothy Smithers standing at the door of her office, watching her.

"We got off to a bad start," he said moving into the office. "Shall we try again?" He went over to her desk and held out his hand.

"*Herr* Dorf did explain that he ought to have introduced us before this morning's meeting," Leah said, thinking the CO had particularly large hands, "but I understand you were away somewhere with Major Benton."

Timothy Smithers perched on the arm of an easy chair in the corner of the office.

She had watched the CO closely at the meeting, as she had watched everybody. There was more to translation than just listening to the words, because an individual's body language quite often said a lot more. Timothy Smither's body language was now very different: he appeared relaxed and he was smiling.

"Yes," he said, "Clive and I had to go to another meeting in Rhinedahlen that unfortunately finished late which meant we got back here late. I'm sorry about that. It was probably not what you expected from the supposedly efficient military. Do you have any military connections?"

"No," Leah said without hesitation. "What's in Rhinedahlen?" she asked although she knew the answer to her question.

It was seven years since her father had been there but she doubted whether it had changed very much, although she had. She had been a flat-chested fourteen-year old schoolgirl in those days. The photograph on the dependant's pass issued during her father's final tour in Herford four years ago and now secreted in her handbag, looked something like her but …

Herford was over one hundred miles east of where she was now sitting.

"It's the Joint Headquarters, colloquially known as JHQ that houses those who are supposed to run all the British Forces in Germany."

"You sound as though you're not convinced," Leah said.

"Oh, it's nothing. I just feel that on occasions certain individuals who are in the headquarters like to assume a level of knowledge they previously were incapable of taking on board. They lose touch with the coal face."

"Was the meeting to do with the closure of this place?" Leah kept her eyes fixed on Timothy Smithers. It was his confidence she had to win as well as *Herr* Dangers'.

The CO looked out of the window as he spoke. "Yes. There was an official press release last week but inevitably the *Rheinischer Post* got hold of the story before anybody else and by the time we announced the closure officially, everybody knew about it anyway. The Brigadier in Rhinedahlen wanted to know who had said what and to whom. He didn't like it when I suggested it would be easier to find a needle in a haystack."

Leah smiled. "And did it really matter?" she said.

"Exactly," Timothy Smithers said with enthusiasm. "It didn't make the slightest bit of difference. Rumours were rife anyway." He stood up. "Anyway, I must get back behind my desk and do a bit of work. I'll send Sam Cox down to see you. She's my PA and is probably the best one to show you the ropes. Welcome aboard again, and I'm sorry if we got off to a bad start. We must have a longer chat soon so that you can tell me all about yourself. I understand you'll be with us until Madeleine Weissmuller's return?"

"Yes, if I get through the first week that is," Leah said, grinning.

"If this morning is anything to go by, Madeleine had better look to her laurels, especially as it was only your second day," he said, but then held up his hand. "Only joking, but you were excellent and if you don't mind me saying so, you added a certain … no, I'd better not say what I was going to say."

He blushed.

To cover his embarrassment, Leah asked, "What do I call you? At the meeting the Germans called you Colonel, as did Major Benton. Is that what everyone calls you?"

"It's what most people seem comfortable with. You'll find some of the Army traditions rather strange. The officers and civilians call me, Colonel, but the RSM has decreed that he and all those below him on the military side will call me, Sir."

"The RSM?"

"Oh, you won't have met RSM Tucker yet, he's on leave. He's the Regimental Sergeant Major and when he returns from leave you'll probably hear him before you see him. He thinks he runs this place, and by coincidence Manfred Dorf thinks he's in charge as well. I don't disillusion either of them. By thinking they are in charge I get the best out of both of them."

With a smile and a wave of his hand, Timothy Smithers left Leah's office.

She stared at the empty space by the door. She always considered herself a good judge of character but on this occasion her earlier judgement was completely wrong.

She rather liked Colonel Timothy Smithers.

Chapter Forty-Four

Standing in the shower and letting the jets of hot water soothe her body, Leah tried to come to terms with the last forty-eight hours of her life. After leaving work at just after five-thirty, she felt very tired but extraordinarily happy.

And it wasn't just because Peter's plan had come together.

Just before five, Sam Cox walked into her office and introduced herself.

"Sorry, I couldn't get down earlier but the Colonel had a lot of interviews to do and reports he needed typing," she said.

Sam Fox was an efficient looking brunette in her mid-thirties. She was the same height as Leah, and a similar build, but she was devoid of make-up and her thick black hair was in a ponytail and held in place by a pink band. Other than a wedding ring, she wore no other jewellery. Her large dark brown eyes made her look quite formidable and probably ideally suited to be the CO's PA.

She was carrying two mugs of coffee.

"Black, no sugar," she said, passing one of the mugs to Leah.

"How did you guess?"

There was no suggestion of shaking hands.

"The Colonel described you to me and you sounded like a 'black no sugar' sort of person."

"The Colonel is very astute," Leah said.

"And very descriptive," Sam Cox added, perching on the same arm of the chair Timothy Smithers had sat on earlier. "So what brings you to Germany?"

Leah once again reeled off the story she had told Clive Benton earlier. Sam Cox listened, peering at Leah as she sipped her coffee. She was wearing a simple green blouse, with just one button undone, a full-length cotton summer skirt and brown sandals but no tights. As would be expected with her black hair and brown eyes, she had a dark complexion.

"It was pure luck that *Herr* Dorf was looking for a temporary translator," Leah said.

"But why on earth did you choose *Bracht*? You won't get much excitement round here."

"It's not excitement I'm looking for and *Herr* Dorf asked the same question. My father isn't too well so I wanted to be somewhere to practice my German but also be within easy reach of the Channel ports," Leah said.

Sam seemed to accept the explanation. "The Colonel was very impressed with you this morning."

"Yes, he implied as much. That was very kind of him, especially as it was my second day and my first meeting."

They chatted for another twenty minutes or so before Sam explained she had to get home to give the two children their supper – Sarah, aged ten and Patrick, who was eight. Their father was a Warrant Officer who worked in JHQ Rhinedahlen, but they lived in army quarters in *Bracht* village.

Leah liked Sam Cox immediately, which only added to her increased confidence.

After rinsing her hair and drying herself, she padded naked into the living room, plonked herself down in one of the chairs to think about what she was going to eat. She was exhausted and must have dozed off because the shrill ringing of the phone suddenly woke her.

"Hello," she said cautiously into the receiver.

"Leah, it's Peter."

She almost dropped the receiver. "Peter! I thought we weren't –"

"A slight change of plan but before going into that how did your job-finding go?"

"Well," she said slowly, "it … where are you?"

"It doesn't matter where I am. Did you have any success?"

Leah, shaken by his tone said, "Remarkably well." She told him just how well the interview with *Herr* Dorf had gone and then the success of the meeting she attended this morning.

"That's excellent," he said with a little more enthusiasm. "We couldn't have asked for anything better."

"Peter, I –"

"Listen, my bosses are getting a little impatient. They have the option of some land just over the Dutch border near *Maastrict* but they don't want to start any negotiations until they have some idea whether the *Bracht* depot is going to be an option. We need to speed things up a bit."

"Peter, I've been in the job for two days, I can't work miracles. I –"

"I'm not suggesting you can but because things have worked out so well, you may find that you have access to information that you would otherwise have had to go digging for. The meeting this morning for example – was anything said there about what the Germans intend doing?"

"The Second-in-Command, a Major Clive Benton, asked about their plans and was told that it was early days. The closure isn't due for quite a while, over two years. They weren't being cagey, just honest."

"All right, but I need something to tell my bosses in two weeks' time."

"Two weeks? I thought I wasn't going to see you again for months."

"That's what I meant by a change of plan. I'll be coming to Germany the weekend after next. Once I'm there I'll ring you with a place and time to meet."

"But –"

"No buts, Leah, because it's vital I have something to pass on. You do want to help, don't you?"

"Of course I do, but –"

"Then keep listening and asking. Get into the ammunition depot and speak to some of the locals. Rumours can quite often prove to be very accurate."

"I'll try, but –"

"Leah, please. The possibility of closure has been on the cards for some time. I don't believe that plans aren't already being discussed."

"Peter ..."

She was talking to the dialling tone. Why was he insisting on calling her Leah when he was the one who had changed her name to Amy?

She stared at the receiver yet again.

What was happening?

Why was Peter so cold and calculating?

Peter was in bed, his hands behind his head, a cynical smile on his lips.

"Silly gullible little bitch," he muttered. He would never have believed it was going to be so easy. She was besotted with him: if he told her to jump from the tallest building in town she would do exactly that, believing he would be there to catch her. In reality, he would be right behind her to give her a nudge in case she hesitated.

"Well?" Ursula asked, her body languid after their recent exertions.

"I'm not sure who is more naïve – young, innocent Amy Carpenter or your husband."

Reaching for her cigarettes Ursula lit one, and he wished she hadn't. "He's just a fool," she said.

He had never told her that Amy Carpenter was really Leah Carmichael; nobody else would need to know until the time came.

"Manfred just thinks he's doing a favour for a friend of a friend."

"And what will he think when the balloon goes up?"

"He'll have met with an accident long before that happens," Ursula said, drawing deeply on her cigarette and exhaling towards the ceiling as though she was firing a rocket. "He won't be around to think anything."

Peter ran his right hand over her stomach onto the top of her thigh. "You're an ice-maiden, aren't you?"

"Not when you do that," she said, leaning over his body to stub out the half-smoked cigarette.

Feeling himself reacting to the softness of her touch, Peter at least acknowledged that killing Ursula was not going to be the easiest of tasks because she was by far the best of them all. As far as sex was concerned, she took from him more than he did from her. He liked that ... and she was quite capable of taking care of herself.

But killing her was a little way off yet, so until then he would enjoy what she had to offer.

Ultimately though, watching her die would be the final thrill he would ever share with her.

Chapter Forty-Five

Leah felt so tired. She was in the bedroom and just about to get dressed, when the phone rang again. She had decided she could not be bothered to cook and was going to pop across to Da Marcello's again. Their pasta dishes were very good.

"Hello," she said. It wouldn't be Peter this time.

"Amy?" a man's voice said.

"Yes."

"It's Clive, Clive Benton."

She closed her eyes. She had known he would make a move at some stage but not this quickly. "What can I do for you, Clive?" she asked, suddenly irritated.

"It's what I can do for you," he said.

"And what can you do for me?"

"Buy you dinner?" he suggested.

She was just about to say she had already eaten when she realised that after Peter's phone call, Clive Benton might be of more use than she originally thought. As Second-in-Command, he would have access to every aspect and area of the depot. Peter said she needed to get into the depot and speak to the locals, so Clive Benton might be of use after all.

"And why and where were you thinking of buying me dinner, Clive?"

"The why is easy. I enjoyed your company today and I'd like to get to know you better. And the where … well, that depends on what you like to eat."

He sounded quite proud of his minor triumph. "I might have very expensive tastes," she said. It would be fun to play him along for a while.

"And I might have the means to pay for those tastes."

"All right," she said, "surprise me. I'll be ready at eight o'clock."

"I'll be there."

"I haven't told you where I live."

"You don't have to. *Frau* Spinks can be quite free with her information if you flatter her. How do you think I got your telephone number?"

"I did wonder."

"I'll see you at eight o'clock then."

"All right." Leah put down the receiver and smiled.

Major Clive Benton was in for a bit of a shock.

If she had been asked what sort of car he might drive, she would have said it would be something flashy, and she was not wrong. As he held the door open for her, the smell of leather wafted into her nostrils. It was a grey metallic Mercedes sports car and she had to admit it was rather nice.

Inside it was spotless and very, very comfortable.

"So where are we going?" she asked as he lowered himself into the driver's seat.

"You told me to surprise you, so you'll have to wait and see," he said.

He was wearing a yellow Ralph-Lauren long sleeved shirt with an obviously expensive silk tie, cream slacks and brown brogues. It was a warm sultry evening, so Leah had opted for a loose silk white dress that she had gathered at the waist with a simple red belt. She deliberately left her legs bare and wore a pair of tan, open-toed sandals.

As Clive selected reverse from the automatic box and expertly manoeuvred the Mercedes out of the small, tight car-park a few yards from Leah's flat, she felt that this was yet another occurrence she could not have imagined a few days ago. She had not known Clive Benton existed then, but the fact that it was happening with anybody was a surprise.

Clive drove slowly, staying well within the speed limit.

"So, Miss Carpenter," he said whimsically as they drove out of *Brüggen*, "what is the real reason for you coming to this area?"

His question took her by surprise. "I told you at lunchtime," she said, on her guard, "I wanted to come to Germany to practice the language but be close enough to the UK so that I could get home quickly if I needed to."

"Oh, yes, your ailing father. I remember."

There had been no sarcasm in the way he spoke but something in his tone kept Leah on her guard. "Why, what's wrong with that?" she asked.

He shook his head. "Nothing, but I don't believe it," he said.

"What don't you believe? That I want to speak German or that I have a sick father."

She hated lying about her father. Peter had insisted it was a perfectly plausible explanation for choosing the area, but she wasn't so sure and now Clive Benton was proving her point. But why?

Clive smiled, his eyes remaining fixed on the road. "Don't misunderstand me because I'm not calling you a liar, I –"

"I should hope not," she said indignantly.

"Well, I'm not. It's the *Brüggen – Bracht* bit I don't understand."

"What do you mean?" Despite the air-conditioning in the car, Leah felt a bead of perspiration run down between her shoulder blades.

Clive took his eyes off the road and glanced at her. "You've caused a bit of a sensation, a bit of a stir," he said.

"That doesn't answer my question, and what do you mean – a sensation?"

He took his hand from the steering wheel and ran the backs of his fingers gently against her thigh.

Leah flinched.

"It's not every day someone as gorgeous as you comes into our rather drab lives," he said.

Leah realised she was on the receiving end of what Clive Benton thought was a subtle chat-up line, and relaxed.

He took his hand from her thigh. "You're the talk of the town. You have been described to everyone in the NAAFI and the Sergeants' Mess, and as you saw at lunchtime, the Officers' Mess came out in force to have a look at you. *Herr* Dorf is all aquiver and Sam Cox insanely jealous. As I said, you've made quite an impact."

"Don't talk such rubbish," Leah said.

"Rubbish? You wait and see. You'll have every man in the depot coming to your office with something that needs translating."

They were driving through some woods when Clive slowed down and turned into a side road that soon led to a very opulent looking building. He parked in a slot as close to the main door as possible. The ornate sign above the main door told her the restaurant's name was the *Wald-Buhne,* and Leah wondered if she was going to be under-dressed.

"Is this it?" she asked.

"It is."

"It's rather grand."

"You said you had expensive tastes."

"I know but …"

"The food is superb."

"I'm sure it is. There might not be a table."

"There will be."

"Did you book?"

"I did."

"When?"

"This afternoon."

"You're pretty sure of yourself, aren't you?"

"Yes, I am."

The meal was as delicious as it was expensive. Clive refused Leah's insistence that she should pay half, and settled back with a large brandy in front of him.

"So, are you going to answer the question I asked about three hours ago?"

It was approaching eleven o'clock and Leah could not remember the last time she had enjoyed herself so much. She felt guilty about having such a good time with another man, but why shouldn't she? Peter had been horrid to her on the phone when she had really deserved a bit of attention. Clive Benton had certainly given her all the attention she needed. His manners were impeccable and his conversation both informative and amusing, and the informative bits were justification for her being there in the first place.

Clive told her about his marriage, quite open about why it had failed, and that before, during and since his divorce he had really enjoyed himself with a string of women. All the obvious warning signs were there but Leah felt in control, although she did understand how his harem had fallen for his charms. A combination of the wine and his amusing anecdotes made her feel very relaxed, the tiredness she had felt earlier no longer there.

She had been wrong about Timothy Smithers, and now she realised she was wrong about Clive Benton as well. He was rather obvious but fun to be with, although if he tried it on with her, he was in for a bit of a shock … but maybe she would have a bit of fun first.

"Because I knew you were going to be here," she said at last, fluttering her eyes at him.

"I do the chat-up lines," he said.

"All right, let me think. I have a thing about men in uniform ... how about that?"

"I haven't got mine with me, in the car that is."

"That's a pity," she said. "What about the simple fact that I lacked confidence? I thought that if I got a job with the British Army, it would be like being at home – almost?"

"That'll do."

"So what happens next?" she asked.

"What do you mean?"

"Do I invite you back for coffee where you will misinterpret what I meant and I will have to fight you off – or do we part as friends with a promise that we must do this again, but it will be on me if we do?"

For the first time since they met, Clive Benton seemed slightly flustered. He raised his eyebrows. "You're quite a girl aren't you?"

"Play your cards right and you might find out … one day."

"Arc you coming on to me?"

"Surely that's a whole new experience for you, isn't it?"

"I really don't know how to take you," he said.

"That too will have to wait …"

"Amy, please."

"What?"

Clive shook his head, but at the same time he smiled. "You're playing me at my own game aren't you?" he said.

"I'm not sure what you mean but I'm not going to go to bed with you, not tonight anyway. If you're a good boy then perhaps, just perhaps, I may decide you warrant further investigation … but thank you for a lovely evening. You've been a perfect host and gentleman and if your talents are as good in other departments, then we both have something to look forward to, don't we?"

As they left the *Wald-Buhne* restaurant Leah knew she had gone too far. You don't love somebody the way she loved Peter and then say what she had just said. She had almost promised to go to bed with Clive Benton, and maybe she would have to, to get the information she wanted. Regardless, she knew she would regret her behaviour when she woke up with one hell of a hangover in the morning.

Chapter Forty-Six

Over the next two weeks, Leah became more and more confident and content in her job.

Clive had been right; there was a steady procession of people who had been told about 'the new translator' and wanted a look. However, as she became accepted and less of a novelty, the flow dropped off … a little. She began to feel quite guilty about deceiving people; after the first week she wished she had come to Germany using her own identity. Unfortunately, there was not a lot she could do about it. She lay in bed on her second Saturday morning in *Brüggen* and imagined the situation:

'Oh, good morning, *Herr* Dorf, and how are you? I thought it best if I came to tell you that my name is not Amy Carpenter because it's actually Leah Carmichael.'

'Good morning, Miss Carpenter … I mean Miss Carmichael. No problem, I will get *Frau* Spinks to change your documents, and the guardroom to change your car and personal pass details. Don't worry. This sort of thing happens all the time. We don't need an explanation, but thank you for letting me know."

She smiled but questioned again why she had to be somebody she wasn't. If anything, having a father who had been in the army would have been a help towards getting a job … and if they had needed to do a thorough security check on her then there certainly would not have been a problem. It was something that was constantly in the back of her mind: what if they did conduct a thorough check and discovered that ... no, it was too late and too horrible to think about what might happen.

She had never really appreciated what it was like to be part of an Army unit, albeit in a civilian capacity. It was not a unit in the true sense of the word because it was more like a community, a small village, where everybody knew everybody else's business. They had four pubs (Officers' and Sergeants' Messes, the Junior Ranks Club and the NAAFI), a good well-stocked shop (The NAAFI) and their own church. The gymnasium was their fitness club and the playing fields a bonus. People worked together, socialised together, played sport together and lived together: it was all a bit incestuous really. When her father was in the Army, she had been on the periphery, a child, a dependant and a visiting teenage schoolgirl. She remembered hearing her mother and father talking about things in a way that, at times, was completely alien to her.

Now she understood.

Regardless of what Clive Benton had implied about her insane jealousy, Sam Cox and Leah became good friends quite quickly. They began taking their breaks together, although Sam wasn't always free because Timothy Smithers quite often worked through his lunch hour, expecting her to do the same and she didn't mind. There were other days, though, when he was away at a meeting and she was able to make up for lost time.

Because her husband was a Warrant Officer, Sam was able to use the Sergeants' Mess, so they went there for their coffee breaks and sometimes for lunch.

They took their coffees into a quiet corner and chatted. Because an awful lot of what Leah was able to tell people was true, she had no difficulty in sharing experiences. Apart from saying her father had been a diplomat rather than in the army, and she had been to Bristol University rather than Durham, and a few other minor things, a lot of life's happenings were the same.

Leah met Sam's husband when she was invited round to their house for supper on Tuesday of her second week, and it was the first time she felt unsettled. He was a gentle giant of a man, who obviously worshipped the ground that Sam walked on. Probably because of his background, he asked Leah some rather searching questions. Not that he was trying to catch her out, but they were nevertheless searching and over curious. At one stage, Leah felt as though her cover story was going to be exposed.

It was a warm evening so Leah wore the same dress she had worn when she went to the *Wald-Buhne* with Clive. The more difficult questions started once they had finished eating and were sitting out on the patio with their coffees.

"So, Amy what brings you to this part of Germany?" Frank asked.

Once again Leah gave the same explanation she had given to Clive and everyone else. As it was at least the tenth time she had told the story she was beginning to feel quite confident with her answer.

When she finished Frank said, "I would have thought the JHQ in Rhinedahlen would have been a better bet than an ammunition depot. I know as things turned out you did the right thing, but did Rhinedahlen ever cross your mind?"

"I didn't know that JHQ existed until I got here," she told him, once again hating the fact that she was lying.

"And yet you knew that there was an ammunition depot tucked away in the woods in the middle of nowhere. That's strange," he said as he looked at her and smiled.

She shrugged, but her mind was racing as she tried to appear relaxed. "It was a friend at university – her father had served in the Army and in the depot some years ago and she told me what a great place it was. She knew I wanted to be as close to the Dutch border as possible with easy access to a motorway and an airport, just in case."

"You've just described what JHQ could have provided, or even one of the RAF stations at *Laarbruch* or *Brüggen*. Sorry, I'm not quizzing you but it just seems a little strange, that's all."

"But, as I said, this friend at university told me about it and where it was. I accept what you are saying, and yes, that's where I might have finished up if there hadn't been this job in the depot." Amy picked up her coffee cup and prayed that she could think of some way of changing the subject.

"You were fortunate to get accommodation where you did as well. It's at a bit of a premium in this area," Frank said.

"Yes, I was very lucky. I went through an agent in Bristol."

"Oh, which one, I know Bristol quite well. I –"

"Stop interrogating the poor girl," Sam said. "She came round here for supper, not to be given the third degree."

Frank smiled that smile again. "Sorry, Amy, but it goes with the job. Sorry if I was asking too many questions."

"No, that's all right. I accept everything you say. They say life is full of coincidences and I agree that perhaps the last couple of weeks have produced quite a few for me. I guess I just got lucky."

After Amy left, Frank and Sam were in the kitchen washing up.

"There's more to Amy Carpenter than meets the eye," Frank said as he wiped a plate.

"What do you mean?" Sam asked, wondering why she always did the washing up and Frank the drying.

"Something's not quite right about her, that's all."

"Sorry, Frank, but you've lost me." She scrubbed away at the roasting tin she had used for the leg of lamb, swearing that she would buy that bloody dishwasher whether he agreed or not.

"Her answers to my questions. They were too contrived."

"I'm going to stop asking people round here. They all get the third degree."

"No they don't, but Amy … I don't know. She's a lovely looking girl –"

"I noticed that you noticed. Why do men's eyes have to wander all over a woman's body rather than making eye contact when they're talking to them? Is it because men's brains aren't in their heads most of the time?"

Frank ignored her. "As I said she's a lovely looking girl and very young too, but it simply doesn't add up."

"You just can't leave your work at work, that's your problem." Sam put the tin in the drying rack and wiped her hands on the tea towel Frank was using. "Right," she said, "I'm going to bed and when you've finished drying up you can forget about Amy Carpenter and turn your mind to the fact that we're trying for another child. It's the right time of the month and I can't get pregnant on my own." When Sam got to the kitchen door she stopped and looked back at her husband. "On second thoughts, perhaps you ought to carry on thinking about Amy Carpenter. It might increase your sperm count."

"Yes, dear," Frank said, obviously not having heard one word his wife had said.

Sam shook her head and smiled.

Chapter Forty-Seven

The next day Leah was summoned to an emergency meeting attended by Timothy Smithers, Clive Benton – she had already detected that the CO didn't move without his Second-in-Command by his side – the *Gemeindedirektor*, *Herr* Dangers, the local Police Chief, *Hauptmann* Pieter Goldschmidt and the Head of the Depot Fire Service, Superintendent Klaus Braun. Leah had heard the news and wasn't surprised that the meeting was called.

Over the previous two days, three incidents, two in Germany and one in the UK, generated the need for a review of security arrangements. In the UK there had been an IRA mortar attack on Heathrow airport, and although nobody was killed or injured and collateral damage was minimal, it tended to concentrate the minds of those present. In Germany, the situation was a lot more serious. A bomb detonated in the early hours of the morning by the the perimeter fence of Barker Barracks in Paderborn: once again and fortuitously, there were no injuries, but the blast damaged a building that housed the pumping station for the barracks. The second occurrence was as serious as it was tragic. Somebody shot at a car leaving the NAAFI shopping complex in *Hanover* in the middle of the afternoon, and its occupant, an army Major's wife, was killed.

The IRA claimed responsibility for both attacks in Germany.

Timothy Smithers gave an outline of what had happened and Leah translated. He then went on to explain that Intelligence suggested there was at least one IRA cell operating close to the Dutch border. At the end of the meeting that lasted for nearly three hours, Leah checked her scribbles to ensure she had noted the action points that would form the basis for revised procedures throughout the depot and the way in which its soldiers and their dependants went about their everyday lives. Afterwards, in the CO's office, she went through the points again with him and Clive Benton.

"Thank you, Amy," Timothy Smithers said. "Could you write a letter for my signature to go to the police and the *Gemeindedirektor* covering those points? You'd better discuss with Manfred Dorf what should go on the Civilian Orders. Anyone who works in this depot is as vulnerable as the rest of us." His expression told her exactly how grave the situation was.

"Of course, Colonel," Leah said.

She had read about the IRA, and there were times when she remembered overhearing her mother and father discussing the ongoing crisis, but they – whoever *they* were – had never touched her life so in essence she was a mere bystander. Now she was in the thick of it and acting as some form of liaison between the military and the local authorities.

"There is a limit to what we can do. The bottom line is that people must be vigilant and not adopt observable routines." The CO turned to Clive Benton. "Clive, you're on the security meeting at JHQ this afternoon. If there are any other points discussed that we haven't covered, let Amy know."

"Yes, Colonel."

"God, what a mess – as if we haven't got enough on our plates."

"It's been with us for quite a while, Colonel," Clive said and looked at Leah to give her a smile of reassurance.

"I'm well aware of that, Clive, but they've never been this audacious before. Murdering a dependant moves the threat into a whole new dimension."

"They were probably targeting her husband, Colonel."

"Where did you get that from?"

"A chum of mine up country rang me last night."

"What else do you know?"

Clive looked at Leah again, raising his eyebrows. Leah saw that the exchange was not lost on Timothy Smithers. "Not a lot other than they reckon the weapon used was a high-powered rifle, probably a sniper's rifle. The car she was in wasn't hers. Well, when I say it wasn't hers, it was the one her husband usually used for work but hers was in for a service."

"Why didn't you mention this at the meeting?"

"It's uncorroborated, Colonel. As I said, it's just the rumour that's going round."

"Anything further on the Paderborn incident?"

"No, nothing there.'

"Keep me in the picture, Clive. There's a good chap."

Leah felt slightly embarrassed by the exchange between the two officers, so she made her excuses and left.

Ursula Dorf read the relevant articles in the *Rheinischer Post* to Peter.

"They made a mess of all three attacks," she said.

"It's not so much the success of the attacks, it's more to do with the threat. The attacks were successful because once again they made the authorities realise how vulnerable they are." Peter drained his coffee cup. "I must leave."

"When will you be back?"
"On Saturday."
"Will delaying your return to England cause any problems back there?"
"No."
"Peter, you seem …"
"What?"
"Nothing."
Peter collected his bag and went down to the car. Ursula shivered as she watched him from the window. It was as though somebody had walked over her grave. He had changed. He used to be so warm and caring, now he was cold and dispassionate. They used to make love but now he simply used her for sex … and she used him.

Seeing the brake lights flicker on when he reached the junction, she longed for the old days, their first encounter … but that was all in the past. The time for action was approaching and they must concentrate on the task.

Their affair was a by-product, an unnecessary but pleasurable complication.

As soon as Leah reached her apartment she phoned her parents on the pretext that she was just checking in, but they too were well aware from news broadcasts what had happened and the implications.

"Look, Mummy, I'm perfectly safe. I'm a civilian."

"So was the woman who was killed," her mother said.

Leah very nearly repeated what Clive Benton had told them but thought better of it.

"Mummy, I'll look after myself, I promise," she said before going on to tell her mother how happy she was with the job.

After putting down the receiver she thought about Peter Bennett.

He said he would be back the following weekend and she had still done nothing about getting the information he needed. She wondered whether the increased security would prevent her from going into the Explosives Area.

Maybe not now that she was well known.

Chapter Forty-Eight

Leah smiled as Clive stirred beside her, the movement breaking into her thoughts.

He was still asleep, facing her with the quilt only covering the lower half of his body. She closed her eyes wondering if she was doing the right thing. It was only a couple of weeks since they first went out together and now here he was sharing her bed. She admitted, though, he had lived up to expectations. She thought Peter was attentive to her needs but Clive managed to move sex into a different dimension for her ... not better but certainly different.

He had been incredibly gentle and thoughtful.

It hadn't happened that first night after dinner at the *Wald-Buhne*, and she wouldn't have let it get that far anyway, but she thought her forwardness had stumped him … just a little. His parting comment as he prepared to drive away after dropping her off, confirmed what she thought.

He lowered the window and leaned across the passenger seat. "You don't strike me as a first night sort of girl and I respect that," he said, "but next time you might just have to fight me off."

She smiled now, thinking back to her 'first night' with Peter and the way she had broken her own principles by going to bed with him that first night.

"We will see," she said, her thoughts returning to her 'first night' with Clive. "But thank you for your respect and also for a lovely evening."

Clive had then been away quite a lot during the next week and she hadn't had the opportunity to ask him about going into the depot, but she still thought he could be the main source of information. After he had returned from a trip to *Bielefeld* the previous day, she went to his office to tell him that if he were free, then she was more than willing to buy him the return meal that evening. He jumped at the opportunity but agreed that he should choose where they went because Amy still didn't know the area too well. They also agreed that as their possible relationship was in its infancy, they should go to a restaurant where it was unlikely they would see anybody from the depot. A small Indian restaurant they found tucked away in a side street in *Venlo* just over the border in Holland proved to be perfect.

Once again, the evening was thoroughly enjoyable – their laughter causing some derisory looks from other customers – but Leah made sure she did not drink as much as before. She thought it was because he made her laugh so much that she decided she wanted to see what he was really like.

When they got back to *Brüggen* and Clive parked his car, she said, "So are you going to come in for a coffee?"

He hesitated. "Is the offer open to misinterpretation?" he asked.

"Possibly," she said.

"Then I don't know."

"What sort of answer is that?"

"You frighten me."

"*I* frighten *you*? What has happened to the confident womaniser you were telling me about? Where is the man who had sex with another man's wife while her husband was in the next room? I'm offering you a cup of coffee, not asking you to marry me."

"I know but …"

"Look, come in for a coffee and if in half an hour's time you get back in this car to drive to camp then it'll be because we both wanted it that way, all right?"

"I'm just not used to not being in control," he said.

"I'm glad I'm not an English language teacher. I think I could shoot holes in your grammar."

"You see, you're at it again."

"At what?"

"Deflating my ego."

"All right, Major Benton, have it your own way," Leah said, reaching for the door handle. "Thank you for a lovely evening. We'll probably meet in the corridors of power next week sometime."

"All right."

She turned back to him. "All right what?" she said.

"All right, I'll come and have a cup of coffee."

They didn't manage the coffee.

As soon as they were inside the flat it was as though their very lives depended on who could get the other's clothes off first. 'Total abandonment' were the words that came into Leah's mind when nearly an hour later they both collapsed, gasping for air.

What she couldn't understand was that Peter did not cross her mind once, well not until it was over. As she straddled Clive, her hands on his chest, gently rocking forwards and backwards, the only person that flashed through her mind was … her mother, and it wasn't because she thought she would disapprove.

When Leah turned seventeen, her mother had started dropping hints that there were a lot of young unattached subalterns in the Officers' Mess who would be delighted to take her out. When she showed little interest, her mother had been unable to hide her disappointment.

She looked down into Clive's face, his eyes closed as he strained to delay what he did not want to happen too quickly, and she wondered whether this was what her mother had meant. She was naked on top of a major ten years older than she was, not a pimply, inexperienced subaltern.

And she loved the power she had over him.

Clive understandably felt he was the one being seduced.

He could not believe that within a couple of weeks of deciding that Amy Carpenter was his next conquest, she was the one who was looking down at him so triumphantly – not vice versa. It was not his victory ... it was hers. Other than his feeling of guilt, she was everything he had expected. She probably had the loveliest body he had ever touched or had the opportunity to look up at, and she knew how to use it.

She was breathtakingly lovely.

Her body wasn't flawless; whose was? But thank God he had agreed to have that cup of coffee.

Yes, the seducer had definitely become the seduced.

"I thought you wanted a cup of coffee," Leah said eventually. She was lying in the crook of his arm, her fingers playing with the hairs on his chest.

"I did."

"So what happened?"

"You didn't put the kettle on."

Leah slipped out of bed, went to the loo and then padded into the kitchen. By the time she was making a drink and buttering a couple of slices of toast, Clive was awake.

"Here's the coffee you wanted last night," she said as she handed him a mug.

He looked like a schoolboy virgin who was now just a schoolboy. The quilt still covered him so only his hairy chest was visible.

Sitting on the side of the bed, Leah placed the plate of toast between them. After putting on her cotton dressing gown she had deliberately made sure it was only loosely fastened. She felt totally wanton but loved every minute of what she was doing. She wanted information and she didn't really care what she had to do … or had already done … to get it.

While in the kitchen she concluded that she didn't love Peter after all. It was nothing more than infatuation. He had been an obsession. She had been going through a phase where she craved attention and he had arrived on his white charger and given her exactly that. In return, she had felt she needed to love him … but even if she had, she didn’t love him now and she would tell him so when he came the following weekend.

Anyway, he was being horrid.

Chapter Forty-Nine

"Are you up to your tricks again?" Timothy Smithers asked Clive Benton.

They were in the CO's office, behind a closed door.

"What do you mean, Colonel?"

"You know exactly what I mean, Clive, so don't be coy with me." Timothy steepled his fingers and looked sternly at his Second-in-Command. "I can ill-afford, under the circumstances, to worry about what you are up to when you should be concentrating on the security of this depot."

"Sorry, Colonel, but I really don't understand what you're talking about." Clive did know what he was being accused of but he wanted the CO to spell it out.

"Amy Carpenter, that's who I'm talking about."

"What about Amy Carpenter?"

"You think you're such a hotshot, don't you? I accepted you into my unit because we were old friends. I thought you still had something to offer regardless of your past. I was willing to give you a chance, and this is how you repay me."

"Are you saying you're not happy with my work, Colonel?"

"No, that's not what I'm saying at all and you know it. There are standards and by doing what you're doing you are letting me, this unit, and yourself down."

"What exactly am I doing?" Clive asked.

Timothy Smithers voice was suddenly raised. "For Christ's sake," he almost shouted, "the girl's been here for just two weeks and you've already found your way into her knickers."

Clive looked genuinely shocked. "Are you accusing me of knocking-off Amy Carpenter?"

"If you're not then I can see no other reason for you to have left her flat at six o'clock this morning," Smithers said with some satisfaction.

Clive had made sure he left at that time so nobody *would* see him. "Who was it?" he asked, resigned now to the fact his CO really did know.

"It doesn't matter who it was."

"All right, how did whoever it was, know that it was Amy's flat I was leaving?"

"That doesn't matter either. Are you denying that you are sleeping with her?"

Timothy Smithers did his best to calm down.

He wasn't sure who he was more disappointed with, Clive or Amy. He liked Clive, and he was an excellent Second-in-Command who had an innate ability to see the bigger picture. There had been times over the last six months when by virtue of his lateral thinking, Clive had prejudged a situation so well that Timothy had managed to outwit his own bosses. What Timothy lacked in wisdom he more than compensated for in subtlety. He reckoned that he certainly gained a few bonus points because of Clive, and therefore his career and chances of further promotion were on course. No, he liked and respected Clive but his womanising could quite easily upset the applecart.

Amy, on the other hand, was an unknown quantity, but she certainly had not seemed the sort of girl who would get caught in Clive Benton's womanising net so easily. Timothy had to admit to himself that she was a lovely looking girl, which only added to his confusion. When you look like that you can have whoever you want, so why had she, in just a couple of weeks, become so taken in by smooth-talking Benton? Well, okay, he was still only in his early thirties, he was tallish, good-looking and an absolute charmer – Timothy's wife, Dee, had told him often enough just how charismatic Clive was.

"I don't think that is any of your business, Colonel. Who I associate with in my own time is my business and nobody else's."

"Everything that happens in this unit is my business, everything. You're one of my officers and I have standards," Timothy said.

Clive looked at him quizzically. "That could be taken in any number of ways. If I *am* sleeping with Amy, you're implying that either she is not good enough for me or I'm not good enough for her."

"Don't be flippant with me, Clive."

"Colonel, I am not being flippant. I am single, she is single and we like each other. Is that really a good enough reason to call me in here and give me a bollocking?"

"I'm … I'm not bollocking you, I just don't want you –"

"Do I note a modicum of jealously, Colonel?"

"How dare you? For Christ's sake, she's someone's daughter!" Timothy Smithers was trying to keep his voice down, although he knew Sam Cox would be able to hear every word.

Clive threw his head back and laughed. "God, if that were a good enough reason none of us would be here. The human race wouldn't exist."

"Anyway, you're almost old enough to be her father."

"In that case, you're almost old enough to be mine. So is this a father to son chat, or officer to officer."

"Now you're being insolent."

"No, Colonel, not insolent. I'm trying to be adult about it. All right, I admit that I have slept with her, and will, if I'm lucky enough continue to do so, with or without your approval. But just to put the record straight, it wasn't me who talked my way into her knickers, as you so quaintly put it, it was she who took them off and invited me in ..."

"There's no need to –"

"There's every need, Colonel. She might give the impression that butter wouldn't melt in her pretty little mouth, but Miss Amy Carpenter is a bit of a goer, and I defy any man, including you, to refuse the offer if it were made."

"I suggest you leave," Timothy said between clenched teeth.

Chapter Fifty

Leah nestled into Clive's shoulder, her body still tingling from their recent lovemaking. Closing her eyes, she wondered once again what her mother would think if she could see her now. She was twenty-two years old, in a foreign country, lying naked in bed on a Sunday morning next to a divorced but very handsome man who was almost old enough to be her father. Well, maybe he wasn't that old.

Would her mother have kittens?

Possibly.

Why was she thinking about her mother?

Perhaps she ought to be wondering about her father's opinion instead.

As she was growing up, Leah had been aware of her father looking at her, but in many ways that was only natural; didn't parents always watch their offspring going through dramatic changes? As she'd begun to develop physically, she had been very conscious about covering up. At the age of fourteen when her breasts began to grow and when her periods started, her hormones played havoc with her mental state. Although she always felt relaxed at home, she thought everybody was looking at her. Later she realised they were, but not for the reasons she had thought at the time.

She wasn't a freak after all, because she was blossoming into a beautiful young woman. As a child she always loved the story about the ugly duckling – especially the ending:

'We're swans like you!' they said, warmly. 'Where have you been hiding?'

'It's a long story,' replied the young swan, still astounded. Now, he swam majestically with his fellow swans. One day he heard children on the river bank exclaim: 'Look at that young swan! He's the finest of them all!"

And he almost burst with happiness.

Of course, Leah always substituted *he* for *she*.

After what seemed like ages, which in reality was only a year, she came to terms with the changes. Of course she talked to the other girls about what had happened to them, and about the boys who had started to take an interest. Although she was aware that some of the other girls experimented with sex, Leah thought it wrong at such a young age. Her mother had talked to her about what was happening to her as well, so before she was sixteen her own experience with boys was very limited ... a fumbling kiss, nothing else.

However, she would never forget the morning after her sixteenth birthday. Her father had paid for Leah and a few of her friends to have a day out at Alton Towers, and Leah had lain in bed the following morning with a hangover. Having promised her father that none of them would drink, a couple of the other girls were rather persuasive especially when they produced a bottle of vodka and cans of Coke from their rucksacks. When Leah got home, she was able to tell from the way her mother and father looked at her that they knew exactly what she had been doing.

It was so many years later but she could still see the look on her mother's face because it was the first time she felt she had let her parents down. The following morning she opened her eyes slowly and her head was thumping. The sunlight was glaring through the curtain, and normally she would have smiled but on this particular morning, she shut her eyes quickly and groaned. It was then she became aware that she wasn't alone and also that during the night the bedclothes had slipped onto the floor.

Leah had squeezed her eyes even tighter, not knowing whether to look over her shoulder, grab for the bedclothes on the floor, or to stay as she was. She was lying on her front, one leg over the side of the bed. She felt the hairs on the back of her neck begin to prickle, but then she heard the door click closed.

She was alone again.

After showering, she dressed and went down to the kitchen. Her mother was preparing vegetables for lunch, and her father was reading the newspaper, a steaming mug of coffee in front of him.

"Hello, dear," her mother said quietly as she turned to peer at her over her glasses. "Did you sleep well?" Nothing was said about the state she had been in the previous evening.

"Yes, thanks Mummy." Leah bent down and kissed the top of her father's head. "Morning, Daddy."

"Morning," he mumbled, reaching for his coffee. Normally he would have hugged her, but not on the morning after her sixteenth birthday. Leah knew who had been in her room this morning.

She blushed at the thought that her father would have seen her in all her glory, spread-eagled on the bed. He had been into her room many times before, sitting on her bed and holding her hand when she was upset about something, and laughing with her when she was happy. He even cried with her when she was sad. However, the thought that he had seen her naked filled her with horror. She cringed. It wasn't his fault. He would have gone to her room just to check that she was all right.

A lot of the close hugging, sitting on his lap, and other little father-daughter intimacies, stopped from that day.

She guessed that he was as embarrassed as she was.

Leah felt Clive take a deep breath, and sigh.

"It wasn't that bad, was it?" she asked him, the tips of her fingers running across his stomach.

"Far from it," he told her, "it gets better every time."

"So why the big sigh?"

"I was just thinking," he said.

"What about?"

"Something the CO said this week."

She looked at him. "I beg your pardon. We have just made love and all you can do is think about something the CO said."

He smiled, brushing his hand down the side of her face. "It was us he was talking about."

"Us?" Leah asked, just a little surprised.

"He asked me if I was sleeping with you."

Leah's eyes opened even wider. "He what?"

"Evidently I was seen leaving here after that first time, and he got to hear about it."

"But … but what's it got to do with him?"

Clive shrugged. "There are those who believe that officers in the British Army aren't part of the human race."

Leah screwed up her eyes. "What do you mean?"

"We must always act with the utmost decorum. We must never misbehave, or do anything that might bring the Services into disrepute," he said.

"And sleeping with me is classed as misbehaving, is it?"

"He seems to think so."

"And what is he going to do about it?" Leah asked.

"There's nothing he can do. He probably gets his kicks from imagining us together."

"What, doing it you mean?"

Clive smiled. "I can think of worse things to imagine."

"Is it because I am, well, a low paid civilian?"

He shrugged again. "No, no, nothing like that. It's you he was protecting, not me. He thinks I'm too old and not the right type for you."

"What right has he …? No, I'd have thought he'd have been pleased that one of his officers was screwing a Brigadier's daughter."

It was Clive's turn to look astonished. "A what? A Brigadier's daughter? You never told me … You said he was a diplomat."

Leah swore under her breath. "Yes, I did, didn't I?" She had thought she'd been doing so well, and yet one little slip like this could ruin it all. Leah Carmichael was back in the UK, she was in Germany and her name was Amy Carpenter. Her father wasn't retired Brigadier Bartie Carmichael CBE. She'd been doing so well, but now she'd made her first mistake. "I ... I didn't want people to know he was in the Army because I thought they might not treat me as I wanted them to, being a diplomat –"

"So, daddy's a Brigadier, is he?" Clive remarked, his eyes giving away his amusement. He ran his finger down between Leah's breasts. "That's more than interesting."

"Why should it be?" Leah asked, chastising him and slapping his hand away. "I don't know what your father is or was. Why should what our fathers do or did make any difference? Anyway, my father's retired ... from the army that is."

"It doesn't make any difference at all but it was you who introduced the subject, not me."

"Well, you know now. Can we get back to what the CO was saying to you?"

"Yes, Ma'am," Clive said jokingly. "That's what Brigadiers' daughters are called, isn't it? Anyway, I don't know any Brigadier Carpenters."

"Stop it," Leah said, hitting him playfully. "I should never have mentioned it. What did he say?"

"As I said, he was more concerned about you."

"And what did you say?" she persevered.

"I told him to mind his own business, and I should have told him that if he wanted something to worry about he should look closer to home."

"Why?"

"His wife Dee – she's been, and probably still is, playing away from home," Clive said with satisfaction.

"She's not ..." Leah said, genuinely surprised.

"Yes, she is."

"Who with?"

"Some guy in *Rhinedahlen*."

"How intriguing."

"In fairness," Clive said, "Timothy Smithers has good reason to keep some of his officers in check."

"Why?" Leah asked, lifting herself up so that she could kneel on the bed. Clive was bound to want to know more about her father, but at least she had gained time to think about what she should say.

"Last year there was a spate of courts-martial and I think the Brigadier in JHQ told him to get his act together. A senior NCO was done for sexual assault, another for fiddling the books, and an officer was almost court-martialled for conduct unbecoming ... among other things."

Leah frowned. "I thought that sort of thing went out ages ago," she said.

"Well to be truthful, with the officer it never reached court-martial. The officer concerned was told that he would be court-martialled if he didn't just go quietly. He'd resigned anyway."

"I've heard nothing about anything like that since I've been here."

"It's a while ago and we've moved on. His name was Peter Bennett, and –" Clive stopped when he saw the expression on Leah's face. "What's the matter?"

With her mouth open, Leah just stared at Clive. It was too much of a coincidence; it had to be the same Peter Bennett. "I think …" she started to say but then stopped. "What did he do?"

"Do you know him?" Clive asked.

"No, no! I once knew a Peter Bennett but that was ages ago and he had nothing to do with the Army." Leah tried to regain her composure. "What did he do?" she asked again.

"Screwed just about everything in sight, including a corporal's wife up in *Wulfen*."

"I've heard of *Wulfen*, isn't that the other ammunition depot near *Münster*?" Leah knew it was a strange question to ask under the circumstances, but her head was spinning.

Clive nodded. "An officer screwing a corporal's wife is unbelievably moronic."

"Which bit is important, the fact that she was somebody's wife, or the fact that her husband was a corporal."

"Both, the whole is greater than its parts though, if you'll excuse the expression. She's gone now, but a young female officer called Trixie Meadows let everybody know once Peter Bennett had left, that she went to bed with him on his very first night in the place."

"I see," Leah said. "But is that all he did? Screwing everything in sight?" She was almost in tears.

"He was sent to *Bracht* from *Wulfen* to await his fate. When I say he screwed everything in sight, there was never any proof but have you met Ursula Dorf, Manfred Dorf's wife?"

"I've seen her, but I haven't met her. She's Russian isn't she?"

"Yes, and a bit of all right actually. How Manfred ever trapped her nobody knows. But –"

"And this Peter Bennett was having an affair with her?"

"There was never any proof but it was the duty rumour at the time." Clive stretched. "I'm famished. Do you mind if we have some breakfast?"

“Of course.” Leah swung her legs off the bed. “But only if you carry only telling me about this Peter Bennett.”

“Why are you so interested in him?” Clive asked, padding towards the bathroom.

“It sounds a fascinating story, that’s all.”

“So what happened?” Leah asked as she munched on a piece of cold toast.

“Not a lot really. As I said, many rumours went unproven. He did go quietly and that was the last we saw of him. He’d already resigned before he came to us but the affair put that on hold, though not for long.”

“Well, that’s a bit of a let-down. I thought there was going to be more to it than that.” Leah licked her fingers, trying to be as nonchalant as possible. “Tell me about the rumours that weren’t proven.”

Clive sipped his tea. “You really want to know about him, don’t you?” Leah broke eye contact and nodded. “He was a strange character. Before he shat on his own doorstep he had a very bright career ahead of him. He was earmarked to go to the very top.”

“And he ruined it all with this corporal’s wife?” she asked.

“That’s what we were all told but there had to be more to it. While he was with us he kept himself to himself, but he was always there, if you see what I mean.”

“No, I don’t.”

“He was one of us but then again he wasn’t.”

“I still don’t understand.”

“It was almost as though he was there to spy on us, when in fact he was so deep in the crap he was lucky to be given any freedom at all.” Clive shook his head. “Something happened before he went to *Wulfen*. What he did there just compounded whatever the previous felony might have been.”

“And you’ve no idea what it was?” Leah asked.

“Sword of Honour winner from the military academy, Queen’s Gallantry Medal from Northern Ireland and then Special Forces … he was riding high one minute, the next he was in Germany with his tail between his legs. More than that, I don’t think even the CO knows what really went on.”

“When you say Special Forces, you mean the SAS?” Leah asked, not wanting to show too much knowledge. “Daddy sometimes talked about them.”

“Yes, he was 22SAS. It was unusual for a Corps man to be accepted into the SAS.”

“Corps man?” Leah asked.

“He was the same cap badge as me. He joined the RAOC.”

"I think I understand. So he resigned and that's the last anybody saw of him?"

A rueful smile crossed Clive's lips. "That's what he'd have everyone believe. He's been back in this area because he's been seen. Well, somebody thought they saw him, and although there's no proof, I wouldn't be surprised if he wasn't still shagging *Frau* Ursula Dorf."

Leah made a mental note that she was going to meet Ursula Dorf, but that wasn't for Clive to know. "Who's seen him?"

"Probably the same nosey person who saw me leaving here. It's just another rumour."

Leah had so many questions she needed to ask but she didn't want Clive to think she was overly interested … he was already suspicious. She closed her eyes momentarily as she tried to come up with an explanation of why Peter didn't tell her he'd been in the Army and at *Bracht*. If he was who he said he was, why couldn't he have revealed that he'd been in the Army, stationed in the very place he'd asked her to get a job? If he simply wanted to know what was going to happen to the depot, surely he'd made enough inside contacts to answer all his questions – Ursula Dorf for a start, and then her husband? Why had he needed to go to Durham of all places looking for somebody who was a total stranger?

"What are you thinking?" Clive asked her. "You look miles away."

"Oh, nothing," she said, shaking her head. "It takes all kinds to make a world, doesn't it?"

Clive grinned. "That's a strange thing to say." He put his mug on the table. "So, young lady, what plans have we for today? The weather looks settled."

Leah moistened her lips with the tip of her tongue. "Would you take me into the depot?"

"Would I *what*?"

"Take me into the depot proper." Leah shrugged. "It's just that I've been here nearly three weeks and I've never been in there yet. I don't know what ammunition looks like other than the pictures I've seen."

"Why on earth would you –?"

"Humour me, Clive, please. I've heard so many people say how beautiful it is, so cut off from everything. And there's the wildlife." She put her fingers on the back of his hand and pouted. "Go on, please."

"All right, but don't raise your hopes too much. God knows who told you it was beautiful."

Leah tried to smile, but she was actually wondering what the hell she had got herself into.

Part Four

Chapter Fifty-One

Sandra Davies crossed the main road in *Wulfen* village having just been to the baker's to get some fresh *brötchen* for breakfast. Even the continuing strained marital relationship with Trevor hadn't stopped this Davies family routine ... fresh rolls on a Sunday morning. Actually, she was thinking that it was a great surprise to everybody when she and Trevor stayed together. Once knowledge of her short affair with Captain Peter Bennett had become public almost a year ago, everybody thought he would throw her out but if anything, the reverse had happened. Trevor had really tried. He lost over a stone in weight, smartened himself up and started buying her presents. From his point of view things had improved, but for Sandra all the presents in the world weren't going to make her fancy him again – ever. She didn't know why, but it was something she always thought about on Sunday mornings when she went for the fresh rolls.

Somebody else would come along soon and then she really could kiss Trevor and the bloody Army good-bye. She couldn't wait. The fact that she was sacked from her job in the Officers' Mess after what she'd been doing became public, didn't matter because the Civil Labour Officer relocated her to a job in the depot itself. It never ceased to amaze her how men could be so gullible – the hint of a promise that something might happen and when accompanied by the right suggestive smile, worked wonders.

Having parked the car behind the *Sparkasse* bank, she was absentmindedly searching for the keys in her bag when she had a funny feeling that somebody was watching her. She had seen a few people at the baker's shop but her car was the only one in the car park, which wasn't overlooked by any buildings other than the bank, and its window and door shutters were lowered for the weekend.

Shrugging away the sensation, she found the keys, pointed the fob at the car and pressed it.

The sensors flashed and there was a beep.

"Hello Sandra," a voice said from behind her.

She let out a little cry of surprise, turning round as she did so. "Peter!" she exclaimed. "What on earth …? I was just thinking –"

Peter Bennett leant forward, cutting off her words as he kissed her. Sandra almost dropped the bag of rolls as she automatically put one hand on his shoulder. She hadn't felt those lips on hers for so long and yet it seemed like only yesterday. She hoped her breath was all right, she hated bad breath.

"Just thought I'd pop by and say hello," he said, his hands now resting on her hips as he pushed his body against hers.

"But … but, it's been ages and what are you doing here?" she asked, glancing up at the windows of the bank to make sure they really were alone. She felt her skin begin to tingle as the memories of what they had done together flooded back. Wow! This was something she hadn't foreseen – could Peter Bennett really be that somebody?

"As I said, I was passing so I thought I'd say hello." His voice was low and sultry.

"How did you know where I was?"

"You told me once about your Sunday morning routine ... coming to get the rolls at exactly nine o'clock."

"But that was ages ago."

"So?"

"Well, what are you –?"

"Shall we leave the questions until we have a little more privacy?" Peter took the keys out of Sandra's hand and smiled.

"What are you doing?"

"Just thought we'd go for a little drive, and get reacquainted." He opened the driver's door. "You go round the other side. I'll drive."

"Peter, I can't. Trevor will be expecting me home and –"

"Trevor can wait half an hour can't he?"

"Well, I suppose ..." The temptation was too much for Sandra. Peter looked even better than she remembered him. He was more tanned, probably a little leaner, his hair was longer and she really liked the designer stubble. What harm would thirty minutes do? "All right, but we mustn't be any longer."

"We won't be," he said.

Peter drove out of the village on Route B58 towards *Wesel* but then took the first right turning towards *Lembeck.* Soon after the turning, he left the road and took a track that led deep into a wood that he had reconnoitred earlier that morning. He had done quite a lot that morning but the evidence of his hard work was well off the track on which he now stopped the car.

"What are we –?"

"If we've only got half an hour we haven't got time to talk," Peter said, cutting her off, leaning across and kissing her once again. He slipped his hand under her top.

"Peter, I –" Sandra shivered as his lips pressed hard against hers.

He reached across and opened the passenger door. "Come with me," he said.

Sandra swung her legs out of the car and waited for him to join her.

They walked off the track and into the wood. When they reached a slight gully, Peter stopped and turned to face her. She lifted her arms as he pulled her top over her head.

"Peter, this really –"

"I told you we haven't time to talk," he said before removing the rest of her clothing. Her body shuddered with obvious excitement and expectation as the breeze wafted across it. She looked around apprehensively but she wouldn't see anybody – he had chosen the spot well. As he looked at her he felt his own excitement and anticipation building.

"Aren't you going to … you know? I'm beginning to feel a little silly standing here with nothing on."

Stepping towards her he put one hand behind her back and pulled her towards him so her eyes were only inches from his, searching for an explanation.

His lips stifled her muffled cry as he pushed the razor sharp blade between her ribs and into her heart. He felt her warm blood on his hand. Twisting the blade slightly, he watched her eyes turn from surprise to terror and then to the glazed stare of death. He lowered her body onto the leaf strewn ground.

After withdrawing the blade slowly, he put a piece of cloth over the wound to prevent her blood from soiling his clothing. He wiped the blade on her stomach before putting the knife back in the sheath attached to his belt behind his back.

Dragging her lifeless body a few yards, he rolled it into the shallow grave he had dug earlier that morning. He straightened her legs, crossed her arms over her chest and put her hands together, then bent down and kissed her dead lips and closed her eyes. He quickly covered the body with loose earth and leaves. There had been no point in digging the hole any deeper; even if it were discovered today, he would already be miles away.

Retracing his steps back to the car, he made sure he left no signs that anybody had been to the spot. Stripping off his shirt, he rolled it into a ball. He would burn it later. He smiled when he saw there were no blood stains on the t-shirt he was wearing underneath. After placing Sandra's clothes on the passenger's seat, he started the engine and drove down the track until he reached the main road.

He parked the car in the same spot behind the bank and then placed the bread rolls on top of Sandra's neatly folded clothes, wiped the steering wheel and door handles, left the keys in the ignition and walked away.

There was nobody about and even if there were …

As he walked, he smiled. She had given him exactly what he wanted ... the exhilaration, the excitement and the satisfaction. The others would be easy now.

One down, four to go … the elation of the kill still consuming him.

The voices told him they were pleased.

It had started.

Chapter Fifty-Two

From outside the perimeter fence, Sylvia Donnelly and Pat O'Reilly had been watching movement in the depot for the last few hours and were just about to leave their observation post when the sound of an approaching vehicle caught their attention.

The noise materialised into a civilian car – a grey Mercedes sports car.

Sylvia had chosen a Sunday because it was the quietest time to observe, though possibly it might not give them the movement detail they needed. After having been shown the depot by Peter Bennett nearly a year ago – a minor detail she had kept from the remainder of her cell – she had been ready to go a matter of weeks later, but hadn't received the support she expected. After reporting that the depot was a soft target, she was summoned back to Northern Ireland to face an inquiry into why she assumed she was suddenly able to make her own decisions about what was deemed a target and what wasn't.

"But it's so vulnerable," she repeated for the umpteenth time. "It would be so bloody easy to get in there, plant a bomb and be across the border before it went off." She wanted to add that it would be especially easy when she had someone to do the planting for her.

"And, tell me, what would that achieve?" John Flatterly, Chief of Staff for overseas operations asked.

It was Flatterly's responsibility to select and allocate targets to the operational sections located wherever the British Armed Forces were based. He relied on his heads of section giving him reliable feedback so that he could formulate plans. He had said he admired initiative, but Sylvia felt she was over-stepping the mark.

"Look, Sylvia, we've reconnoitred that bloody depot on any number of occasions, but regardless of its vulnerability I can't see what would be gained. Have you any idea what would happen if you did put a device near one of those sheds?" John Flatterly said.

"It would create a very big bang, an even bigger hole, and a lorry load of kudos for us," Sylvia said.

"Would it now? Is that what you think? It's a bloody lorry load of explosives you'd need, not bloody kudos. And in the first place, how do you intend getting that amount of explosive into the depot?"

“It could be done,” she said, smiling.

“It's not bloody funny, Sylvia. Saying it could be done and doing it are two totally different things.”

“I’ve been in there so I know what it’s like,” she said.

“And that’s another thing ... did you give any thought to what you were doing when you went off gallivanting without asking me? Bloody *Erica Polaris* … you must have had a mental aberration, so you must.”

“*Erica Polinaris*,” Sylvia corrected him, “and anyway it was an impulse opportunity, there wasn’t time.” She thought that telling him she had managed to talk her way into getting access to the depot would add credence to her – and Peter Bennett's – plan, but it seemed to do the opposite.

John Flatterly slammed his fists into the arms of the chair. “No fucking time?” he screamed. “You know that direct contact with the enemy is forbidden for everyone except those who are specially trained. If caught you would have compromised our whole operation in Germany, so you would. You could have undone years of planning and just because of what you so lightly call an impulse opportunity. I told you it could be over a year before you became active, and here you are not only trying to bring forward an operation but change its direction. You're there to select human targets, not to do the impossible.”

Sylvia stiffened.

They were sitting in a safe house in the middle of the Shanklin Road. She knew there were observers – body-guards – on every street corner in the vicinity, so the time she had to convince the Chief of Staff was limited. John Flatterly was the highest-ranking officer she had ever met and he necessarily kept on the move, never staying in the same place for more than a couple of nights. His reputation for dealing with miscreant operators was well known, and kneecapping wasn’t just reserved for informers and men. He exacted discipline by the most effective means possible and his punishments were not restricted to kneecapping. Being female, Sylvia Donnelly knew exactly what her punishment would be before she disappeared ... for good.

She saw the tension leave his fists. “Look, Sylvia,” he said more calmly, “I appreciate what you were trying to do, but you must understand that you were out of order, so you were. We haven’t yet reached the stage where we have to resort to suicide bombings, not that there wouldn’t be volunteers, but that’s what it would take. It would be suicide. We go for soft targets, targets we can hit and then run. Putting a car bomb in the middle of a group of Army quarters is far preferable, and easier, than trying to blow up an ammunition depot. Surely you can see that?”

Sylvia nodded, her eyes never leaving his. She was scared, but she was determined not to show it. "I understand what you're saying, but –"

"There are no buts, Sylvia. If you had come to me with the idea before you did anything, I would still have said no. You knew that anyway. Before you went to Germany you were told what sort of targets we were looking for and ammunition depots weren't on the list."

"I know, but –"

"No fucking buts, Sylvia. If you want to make an impression then do what you were sent there to do. I want to know movements, routines, who, where and what. The quarters there are what are vulnerable, not the depot. *Bracht* village is the home for at least five different groups of quarters. Even the Commanding Officer's house is right in the middle of the village. There are so many soft targets. Why are you wasting time on the depot?"

"I just thought –"

"I do the thinking and you do the doing. Understand?"

"Yes."

"Right, I'm glad we're in agreement. Now, when you go back I want you to concentrate on the village. I want an assassination … preferably the Commanding Officer and his wife if necessary, and I now want it soon rather than later. You've got a safe house in Holland, haven't you?"

"Yes, we've rented a flat in *Eindhoven*. We'll be moving there from *Mönchengladbach* as soon as targets are found and agreed."

"Good. Can you not see why *Bracht* was my choice? You can be over the border and into Holland before anybody realises what has happened. Do what has to be done and then get the hell out, lie low for a couple of months and then contact me again and I will tell you whether it's safe to go back in."

"Yes."

Sylvia realised the meeting was over.

Chapter Fifty-Three

"It's a civvy car," Pat told Sylvia as he trained his binoculars on the vehicle that was topping the hill about half a mile away.

"Passengers?"

"Driver plus one. Male and female, I think."

The car being observed stopped almost directly opposite where Sylvia and Pat were hiding. Initially the couple just sat and talked but then the doors opened and they got out.

Pat whispered beside her, "I wouldn't mind –"

"I'm well aware of what you wouldn't mind doing, Patrick, so just keep your eyes on the job and not –"

"That's what I'm doing, so it is."

Sylvia ignored him. The man in the car was probably in his early thirties and wasn't unlike Peter Bennett from a distance, but the young woman, certainly no more than twenty five, was, she had to agree, rather stunning. They were both casually dressed in jeans: he was wearing an England rugby shirt, and she a pink short-sleeved t-shirt. Sylvia was surprised that they held hands when they started walking away from the car; she thought it a little incongruous for some reason.

"Are they of interest?" Pat asked.

"We shouldn't move until they've gone," Sylvia commented as she watched the couple disappear round a bend in the track.

"What do you think they're up to?"

Sylvia glanced sideways at Pat. "Just let your vivid imagination run away with you," she said.

"I will," Pat retorted with a wicked smile.

Corporal Trevor Davies made himself a second cup of coffee.

In the last thirty minutes he had constantly glanced at his watch and the clock on the kitchen wall. "Where the hell is she?" he asked out loud.

Sunday was their day. It was sacrosanct. In all the time they had been married, and even when she was off having yet another affair, she had always reserved Sundays for them. When they had an argument, she would tell him it was her day of rest, her day off. On other occasions, she just said that if they were going to work things out they needed some time together.

Trevor looked forward to Sundays, not just because Sandra was with him for most of the day, but because he did regard it as a day of rest – a day to forget their differences, a time to reflect and a time to plan. For the past few months he no longer appeared the laughing stock because his antagonists had moved on to another unsuspecting source of ridicule. Trevor was proud that he had weathered the storm and he even believed that he and Sandra were now getting on a lot better, which gave him hope.

After an hour, he went to find Sandra.

Their Army flat, which was on the top floor of a four-storey block, was only five minutes' walk from the centre of *Wulfen*. He could never fathom why Sandra always took the car, especially when she liked to keep herself so fit.

As with most Sundays, *Wulfen* was like a ghost town. Other than the church bells ringing and the odd car going slowly along the main road, there wasn't a sound. He didn't see anybody he knew, in fact he hardly saw anybody at all. He knew where Sandra always parked their car, so he headed straight for the *Sparkasse* Bank.

It was just after eleven in the morning as he turned the corner and saw the car. There were two other cars in the car park but nobody was about. For some reason he had imagined their blue Ford Escort wouldn't be there, so he was quite surprised to see it. She may have bumped into one of her friends and was having a coffee somewhere.

He reached the car and tried the door handle. Again, he was surprised when it opened. He saw the bag containing the rolls, then froze when he realised what was underneath it. Climbing into the driver's seat, he moved the bag of rolls to one side and lifted Sandra's pale green top which he recognised immediately. Her neatly folded jeans, bra and pants were underneath and her sandals were in the well, side by side.

Shaking his head, Trevor closed his eyes.

What the hell was going on?

Where was she and, more importantly, what was she wearing? She wasn't up to her old tricks again, was she? Had she taken other clothes with her to change into?

It was Sunday and it was their day.

Trevor leaned across to open the glove box and the ignition keys rattled against his knee. He hadn't noticed the keys were there. Why would she leave the car unlocked and the keys in it? An opportunist thief would have had a field day. Still looking at Sandra's clothes he got out of the car and lit a cigarette. If she had gone off with someone and walked out on him, would she have left her clothes? She may have left the car, and the keys, so that he could take it home … but her clothes?

Why leave her clothes?

Was she trying to tell him something?

As he drove the car back to the flat, he began to cry. After breaking the rolls into little bits for the birds, he threw the crumbs onto the grassed area in front of the flats, the tears still streaming down his face. He was still crying when he put her clothes and shoes away, then automatically reached for the whisky bottle. "I love you, Sandra," he said through his tears. "Why did you leave without telling me you were going? Especially on a Sunday."

Sunday was their day … wasn't it?

Chapter Fifty-Four

"I still don't know why you wanted to come and look at this God-forsaken place," Clive muttered as they approached one of the ammunition storage bunkers. They had seen a few deer and he had pointed out the damage the wild pigs did to the traverses that surrounded all the bunkers.

"I told you, I've been here weeks and I still haven't seen what it's all about," Leah said.

"Well, there you are," he told her, pointing at the building. "That's what it's all about."

"It looks as though it'll fall down any moment."

"Built in the 1950s, that's over forty years ago and it's still here. I'm sure it and all the others like it will last another couple of years."

"Can we go inside?" she asked.

"No, not today, I don't have the keys. But if sometime next week you'd like to take a closer look I'll give you another guided tour."

They walked through the gap between the traverses that surrounded this particular building. "It's a massive area, isn't it?"

"It's the biggest military logistic depot in North West Europe, in terms of area that is," Clive told her.

"And the Army is giving it all up?"

"No further need for it," he said, shrugging. "The Army in Germany is less than half the size it was a few years ago. There's the other depot I told you about, up at *Wulfen* between *Wesel* and *Münster*, and what they can't provide can be shipped from the UK on an 'as required' basis. I think it's called progress."

"You don't sound convinced."

Clive shrugged. "I don't have feelings one way or the other. I'll be leaving in eighteen months so it doesn't make any difference to me." He sat down on the grass opposite one of the main doors into the bunker.

"What will it be used for?" Leah asked, sitting down next to him.

"There are lots of rumours, but we've got to empty it and make it safe before anything can be done."

Leah thought for a moment. "Somebody told me they might put a leisure park here. You know, a sort of Centre Parcs or something."

"I've heard that too, but I don't think it'll ever come to that."

"Why not?"

"The Greens," Clive said.

"The Greens?"

"The Green Party … this place has stood still in time for nearly fifty years. You've seen the trees and some of the wild life. I think there'll be so much opposition to development that you'll be able to come back in ten or fifteen years and it'll still be the same."

Leah lay back, putting her hands behind her head. The high banks made the area into a suntrap. "It's warm, isn't it?"

"Very." Clive smiled down at her as he rested his fingers on her bare midriff.

"How well did you know this Peter Bennett you mentioned earlier?" she asked. Because of what Clive had already told her, she now had no doubt about what she'd been asked to do, but she wondered if Peter's involvement was different from what he had told her.

"Why does he suddenly come into your mind?" Clive moved his hand so that his fingers were under her top.

"I just wondered," she said. "And you can stop that," she added, but made no attempt to brush his hand away.

Clive twisted his body so that he faced Leah and pressed his lips against hers.

"Somebody might see us," she said, trying to pull her head away.

"There's nobody to see us. Just lie back and think of England… and satisfy one of my fantasies."

"I'm bloody starving, so I am," Pat grumbled.

Sylvia admitted that it was hot and that she could do with a drink. Expecting to be here for only a couple of hours they had only brought a small water bottle with them, and that was finished well over an hour ago.

"We'll just wait for them to come back and then we'll go."

"But why?" Pat asked.

"I didn't get a good look at them when they first arrived. He looked old enough to be important … You never know – he might be an appropriate target."

"You never did say what went on when you were back to see God all-mighty."

"He just wanted an update, that's all," Sylvia said, not willing to reveal too much.

"An update, was it? Does that mean we're going to hit this place, or is this where we're going to do the shooting?"

"Probably the shooting," she said.

"I could take those two out with a pistol from here."

"I'm sure you could."
"Wouldn't want to shoot her, though," he said.
"She's as much of a target as anybody else."
"She might be German."
"So?"
"I thought …"
"Just wait."
"And the rest of it?"
"The depot you mean?"
"Yes."
"The depot remains a possibility," Sylvia said, and that was all she wanted to say.
"And how do you intend doing that?"
"I'm not a hundred percent sure yet. We'll see what the others have to say."
"They'll be back by now, stuffing their faces."
"I'm sure they will."
When the two people they had watched still hadn't returned to their car after another hour, Sylvia reluctantly agreed that they should leave. She was in a very pensive mood when they reached their own vehicle parked with many others at the *Am Weissen Stein*, and set off to meet up with the other half of their cell.

Chapter Fifty-Five

Ursula Dorf was waiting for Peter Bennett's return.

As usual they had agreed to meet at his garret flat in *Frankenmühle*. During a flaming row she had with Manfred just over an hour ago, she was so annoyed that to spite him she'd been on the point of telling him who she really was, and how was he going to explain that he was married to a Russian spy and had been for over three years? The cause of the row was no different from many of the previous causes – sex. She could always tell when he was frustrated: he would follow her around the house waiting and hoping that she would feel sorry for him and give in. He was too weak to start anything himself; if he had, she might – but only might – have given in.

Such occurrences were rare and afterwards she always felt disgusted with herself. There was a brothel not one hundred metres from where she first worked in *Bracht* – why couldn't he go there?

Lying on the bed in the flat, she didn't feel any pity for Manfred ... she actually thought that giving in every now and again made matters worse. Perhaps she ought to stop altogether, then he would know exactly where he stood.

Moving her thoughts away from Manfred, she was a lot more interested in what Peter had to tell her. She couldn't believe he'd been so easy to seduce into doing what she wanted. He was still livid with the way the British Army had treated him and what he wouldn't do to get his revenge was beyond most people's imagination, but not hers.

For Ursula it was music to her ears.

She remembered how angry Gregor Crazkowski was when she met him at Düsseldorf airport. By going ahead with her plans she was ignoring his anger and advice, but she was also convinced that in the end he and his superiors would thank her for sticking with what she believed in.

She and Peter were already lovers by the time she suggested he could use her to get the revenge he so badly wanted. His anger had been extreme, even to the point when he scared her because of what she sensed lay hidden beneath the surface of a man who appeared to the outside world to be almost normal and in control. She saw from the look in his eyes, that the sheer contempt and hatred he felt for anybody or anything that represented the organisation he had once loved, was enough on occasions to drive him to the point of insanity.

"Can't they begin to understand what they've done?" he asked her a few weeks after he was no longer in the Army.

Never having seen such bitterness, not even in the regime she was used to, it was initially difficult for her to understand.

"I was destined to reach the top," he said. "And just because I made a split-second decision to rid the world of a bunch of animals, they used their own cowardice to make an example of me. Me, for fucks sake! I was – and still am – better than all of them put together."

He told her all about what had happened on that fateful day in South Armagh. He described in detail how he'd felt when he was about to witness the execution of a tortured and pathetic female – and that was why he became the executioner. As he pulled the trigger he hadn't shot a human being, he'd executed an animal, but even *animal* was too good a word to describe the despicable lump of flesh and bone that was magnified in his telescopic sights. He'd enjoyed the feeling when he saw her head disintegrate from the power of the bullet passing through her brain. His only regret was that she didn't suffer and he wished he could have looked into her eyes as she died.

Ursula didn't flinch when he described his feelings during the incident because she had experienced executions that made his appear gratuitous. She had seen death under the most gruesome of circumstances, witnessed torture and seen human beings, both male and female, suffer slow and painful deaths at the hands of the most sadistic men and women. A bullet through the brain was an immediate and painless end.

Peter had been humane and not inhuman.

There were occasions when he cried.

His emotions took him through anger to total desolation when he realised that no amount of verbal rage, or even physical rage, was going to claw back what he had lost. It was this anger that Ursula played on. She listened and waited, waited and listened. Slowly she reeled him in so that he told her more and more, and with each revelation, with each confession, she wrapped her net around him. She didn't feel threatened because he had never laid a finger on her other than from tenderness and understanding. If anything, she was fighting her own emotions. This man, whom she regarded, not unlike Manfred, as an opportunity, was slowly moving from her head to her heart. He treated her like no other man had ever treated her before. He was affectionate and considerate and wanted to please her as much as he thought she wanted to please him.

She controlled the conflict between her heart and her head, allowing each to take precedence when the time was right.

That was why, when she heard footsteps on the stairs leading up to the flat, she felt a twinge of excitement. She wanted to see him, she wanted him to touch her and she wanted to touch him. Her resolve wasn't weakening, but she had needs like any other woman.

And for the time being, this man could satisfy them.

"Hello, Peter," she said, turning to face him. "You look exhausted."

Sitting on the bed, he put his arms round her and they kissed.

"So, was it a successful trip?" she asked him. Something had happened, she could tell, but he would enlighten her when he was ready.

"It was as I expected," he said.

Chapter Fifty-Six

The four of them were squeezed into the small single bedroom at the back of a downmarket hotel in *Mönchengladbach.*

Seamus and Robert had been back for some time, eaten and if their breath was anything to go by, they had already made full use of the small bar just inside the main entrance to the hotel.

They weren't all staying in the same hotel. Three men and one woman – a couple with strong Irish accents – in one location within close proximity of the British Army would have roused the suspicions of even the dimmest of hotel staff … and police.

Of the three men in her cell, Sylvia preferred Seamus. Robert Shaughnessy was a lot like Pat: although they pretended to do everything for the good of the bigger picture, they couldn't fool her. They were in it for the money and the sheer satisfaction of causing havoc among groups of people who just wanted to go about their everyday lives in peace and quiet. There were prices on both their heads, and rightly so. They had been responsible for the deaths of any number of innocents in Northern Ireland, but they simply didn't care. They were ruthless, scheming and untrustworthy, but somebody believed in them and that was why they were part of her cell.

On the other hand, Seamus Docherty was totally dedicated to the *Cause*. At thirty-five he was only a couple of years older than Sylvia. He could pass as an executive in any environment and like Sylvia, he spoke without a trace of an Irish accent. He had an MSc in electronic engineering, and could quite easily have led a perfectly normal life, but he chose the *Cause* instead. He was Sylvia's Adjutant, her Second-in-Command, her guiding hand, her shoulder to lean against and to cry on if the time ever came.

She wouldn't mind if he was her lover too, but ...

None of the men seemed to mind that a woman was leading them. They all knew Sylvia's reputation, although Robert and Pat often discussed, and in front of her, how somebody like her, young and pretty as she was, could have so little respect for human life. Seamus always defended her because he understood. She had lost one grandfather, her father and one brother in the *Troubles*, as her mother called them, and Sylvia was determined to get her revenge. Seamus had told her that he knew she was working to her own agenda and he admired her for that. There was nothing wrong with somebody using their initiative as long it didn't disrupt the primary objective.

However, Seamus was different in another way and Sylvia, regardless of her own ruthlessness, respected the fact that he didn't enjoy killing in the same way as the others did, although he did accept that death was necessary and it was inevitable. When he had to kill, Seamus preferred it to be at close quarters not with a bomb, or a sniper's rifle. He had told her that he needed to know the person he was killing to be sure he or she was the actual target and not some innocent who happened to be passing by.

"So," Sylvia said quietly, "what did you two glean from today's observations."

Seamus spoke because Robert rarely said anything. "Not a lot," he said. "We saw the odd vehicle or two, and a few totally disinterested dog-handlers with dogs that were probably the more alert."

Sylvia let a smile cross her lips. "What about the wire?"

"That was …" Pat started to say, but Sylvia held up her hand to shut him up.

"The dannert wire on top and on the ground on the inside of the fence looks worse than it is," Seamus said. "The fence isn't electrified for obvious reasons, and there are no alarm wires either."

"How long?"

"To get through?"

"Yes."

"Ten minutes, no more … probably less."

Pat narrowed his eyes. "Inside, is it? I thought we were here to do a bit of shooting, not going for nature walks in an ammunition depot. You said –"

Sylvia glared at him. "You'll get your bit of shooting, but I've waited long enough to do something spectacular. It's an ideal opportunity, and it'll be so easy."

"And precisely what are you going to do?" Pat looked sideways at Robert for support, but he was inspecting his nails. "Blow up the whole depot, is that right?"

"You know damn well what we're going to do, so stop trying to impress the others." Sylvia turned to Seamus. "Once inside the wire we'd need to cover one hundred yards or so, before we were close enough to anything worth placing a bomb next to. What do you think?"

Seamus shook his head. "The buildings might be thin-skinned but the packaging the ammunition comes in isn't. We might be able to carry enough explosive but it would be better if we could use a car or a van."

"You're going to cut the wire and then drive a van through it, are you?"

Sylvia glared at Pat again. "If you can't be more constructive then keep quiet."

She hadn't told them about her somewhat risky relationship with the man she'd met in Rosa's Bar in *Bracht* village. Neither had she told them she and her lover had formed more than just a physical alliance ... she was still not convinced about his connection with G2 in the Republic but it was a risk she was willing to take. It had been on his suggestion that he had gone to the UK to talk some naïve female into coming to Germany to do their dirty work for them. It was a masterful plan. When it all happened and the IRA claimed responsibility, Sylvia would have had her revenge, her moment of glory. Perhaps her masters would have more faith in her afterwards. That was why she was trying to convince the others that the ammunition depot should be one of their targets. Even they wouldn't know, when it happened, that it had all been down to her. On this occasion, revenge would be very personal.

When Peter Bennett told Sylvia who he had selected and that she was an ex-Brigadier's daughter, the final outcome would be even better. The irony of who it was became the icing on the cake. They would trace the car of course, and they would trace it back to Leah Carmichael. It was another masterful stroke – on her suggestion this time – to get him to persuade poor, naïve Leah Carmichael to come to Germany under a false name. What bedlam there would be when the authorities realised that the person responsible for blowing up a British Army ammunition depot was an ex-Brigadier's daughter – who had been deliberately travelling under a false name – and she had to be in league with the IRA. Of course there wouldn't be anything left of Miss Leah Carmichael a.k.a. Amy Carpenter: as the bomb detonated she would be blown into little pieces.

The car, packed with explosives before it left the UK, was probably sitting outside the depot headquarters as she spoke – further irony. Sylvia had to admit that preparing the bomb in the UK had been her idea as well. If the authorities had ever weighed the little Peugeot they would have discovered that it was at least two hundred pounds heavier than it should have been – odourless PE4 moulded into the tightest of corners made it into a mobile bomb. Even the remote firing device was already in place, tucked behind the fire extinguisher in the boot. Miss Leah Carmichael had no idea that she had driven an enormous bomb from the UK to Germany and that each time she got into the car she was sitting on what would be the cause of her own death as well as blasting the biggest political hole in the British Army's arrogance.

And if she were discovered to be driving a mobile bomb in the UK or on the Continent, the same traces and connections would be made.

Regardless of her protestations, who would believe she didn't know she was sitting on a two hundred pound bomb?

Whichever way it went it would be a tremendous coup.

Chapter Fifty-Seven

Dee Smithers really enjoyed her game of squash, but she enjoyed what happened afterwards even more, even though she knew the affair would have to end, and soon.

Not wanting a scandal and to ensure that his standing as Commanding Officer in the depot wasn't harmed, her husband might overlook her behaviour if he were to find out, but she didn't want to take that risk. He couldn't sit in judgement of others if his wife was not squeaky clean. It was a callous way of looking at it but under the circumstances, necessary. She wasn't looking for a replacement; she loved her husband in her own way, but she was a very physical woman and needed more attention than he was able to give her.

Of course she was flattered when Mark Armstrong, the leisure centre manager, had begun to flirt with her. He was at least eight or nine years younger than she was, had an excellent physique and a very cheeky but rugged face. She was intrigued when he suggested that perhaps they ought to go for a drink after one of her fitness and squash sessions. Her intrigue became an obsession when he took her back to his small flat in *Lüttelforst*, a small hamlet that nestled in the woods just outside the main *Rhinedahlen* complex, and made her feel like a young woman again.

They met twice a week, Dee's squash and aerobic classes a prelude to something far more physical and enjoyable. Mark dismissed Dee's suggestions that she was nothing more than a cheap thrill by telling her that he preferred his women to be mature and experienced. She in turn had accepted the comment about her maturity but rejected the observation that she was experienced, even though Mark taught her things about herself that previously had lain dormant.

However, she regretfully knew that it must all end. Lying in Mark's bed this evening after he had once again made her feel totally fulfilled, Dee decided it was time to finish their relationship.

Mark was smoking a cigarette and looking very pleased with himself when she said, "I think my husband knows about us." She didn't like lying but she had to find a way out. It was marvellous while it lasted but now the guilt was beginning to set in.

Mark didn't respond immediately but after a few seconds he said, "Do you mean he knows about me or that he thinks you are simply seeing somebody else?"

"There's nothing simple about it," Dee said.

"No, I'm sorry I didn't choose my words very well. What makes you think he knows?" Mark stubbed out his cigarette and picked up Dee's hand.

"I was sitting at the dressing table a couple of weeks ago and he commented that I had some bruises on my bottom."

"And what did you say?"

Dee shrugged. "I told him I'd been hit a couple of times playing squash that evening."

"And?"

"He didn't say anything."

"How long ago was this?" Mark asked.

"About two weeks."

"Two weeks? So why are you telling me now?"

"He's changed," Dee said.

"You told me he was impotent."

"No, I don't mean in that way. I've caught him looking at me."

"You're worth looking at …" He moved his fingers up her thigh.

"I'm being serious, Mark."

"I know."

"I think …"

"What?"

"I think we ought to cool things down a bit." Dee closed her eyes as she spoke. It was the last thing she really wanted to say.

"You mean end our relationship?"

"Yes."

Mark rolled over onto his front so that he could see her. "We agreed at the outset that if either of us wanted out then the other promised to understand."

"You mean …?"

"I mean," he said, resting two fingers against her lips, "that if it's what you want then it's what will happen. It has been great while it lasted, better than either of us could have hoped for, but if you are worried then I'll know and things won't be the same."

"You're not going to try to persuade me to change my mind?"

"There would be no point. If you ever do change your mind, you know where I live, you have my phone number and you know everything about me. All you'll need to do is ring or call."

"But …"

“Dee, you’ve been on edge ever since we got back to the flat. I knew something was wrong.”

“I’m sorry.”

He lowered his lips onto hers. “Don’t be, we both knew it would end one day.”

Twenty minutes later, Dee drove away from *Lüttelforst* on her way back to *Bracht*, but her mind wasn’t on her driving. Half of her felt relieved to have ended the affair but the other half was already regretting her decision. She would miss Mark and what he had done for her, but her future was with Timothy and although he was ignoring her infidelity now, there would come a time when he would start asking questions.

She would have time to think of the right answers so that her expectations were secure.

Her thoughts were broken into when she noticed the headlights in her rear-view mirror were flashing. The car behind moved out a little, and the headlights flashed again. This time she saw the lights in her door mirror. It was still daylight, so whoever was driving the car must be trying to tell her something.

She was suddenly alert.

She didn't recognise the car or its driver as he – if it were a he – was just a blur behind the windscreen. It was a narrow road, so she slowed a little pulling over to the edge thinking that the other car wanted to pass. The car did go past but then swerved sharply in front of her and braked. She had no choice but to brake also.

The other car stopped, not leaving enough room on the narrow, quiet country road for her to get past. The driver got out of his car and for Dee there was an immediate sense of recognition, although the man’s name wouldn’t come to her. Because she recognised him, she didn’t feel so frightened, just a little surprised.

The man walked back to her car.

Lowering her window a little she peered at the man, but then there was full recognition so she lowered it further and smiled. “Peter, what on earth …?”

“Sorry, Dee,” Peter Bennett said, bending down. “But I noticed your offside rear tyre. I think you may have a puncture.”

“Puncture? But …”

“You must have run over some glass or something.”

“Yes, I suppose I must. But I didn’t feel ...”

“I’ll take a closer look. Stay there. I won’t be a sec.”

She watched in her door mirror as he went to the back of her car. He bent down and punched the tyre a couple of times. Shaking his head he shouted back to her, “Yes, I’m sorry. In fact, both rear tyres are well down.

Look, why don't I park your car up that track over there, and then I'll run you back to *Bracht*. You can get the car recovered tomorrow."

"But …"

"If you drive on those you'll damage the rims and you've only got one spare," he said.

"I suppose … but what are you doing here? You left months ago, no it must be nearly a year."

"Yes, it's almost a year," Peter said, opening her door.

Dee reached onto the back seat, picked up her sports bag then followed Peter towards his car. "This is very kind of you," she told him climbing into the passenger seat, "and such a coincidence. We all thought we'd seen the last of you." Dee became a little flustered. "No, that's not what I meant to say, it was just that –"

"You thought I'd never show my face in the area again?"

"Well … yes."

He smiled. "I'll just move your car off the road so that it doesn't cause an obstruction. Can I have the keys?"

Dee handed him the keys. "We'll start this conversation again when you've done that."

Chapter Fifty-Eight

Peter reversed up the track into a small wood making sure the car was out of sight of the road.

Like everything else, he had planned this particular encounter down to the last detail. The track led about fifty yards into the woods, and then stopped. There were signs that it had gone further but the rest of the track had become overgrown. When he reached the road on foot, he looked back and was happy. Even if found quickly, there was nothing in the car or near it that would lead anybody to where Dee Smithers would be.

Unlike Sandra Davies, Dee had become one of his victims the moment he met her and her haughty attitude only added to her eventual demise. For her age, she was attractive enough, but she seemed to think that her husband's position determined her right to be superior. She represented authority and how better to express his hatred for the system than by killing the Commanding Officer's wife.

The cat would be well and truly among the pigeons.

He had followed her to *Rhinedahlen* and waited while she played squash. He wasn't surprised when he saw her leave the sports centre with a younger man. She was cheating on her husband but still felt she could criticise others … such bloody arrogance. Well, she wouldn't be doing that for much longer. A little annoyed at having to wait outside the flat in *Lüttelforst*, his flexibility and patience cut in but regardless, the outcome would be the same. While he waited he saw one of the other occupants in the block of flats put some rubbish in the containers at the side of the building, and smiled when an idea came to him.

"So, let's start again." Dee suggested as Peter got back into the car and turned the key in the ignition. "Why –?"

"I'm in Germany visiting a few friends," he informed her, pre-empting her question.

"Did you know it was me when you saw the car?" Dee asked, secretly smiling to herself.

She had never been this close to Peter Bennett before, and if she were being truthful, he had always fascinated her. There was something about him, something mysterious and beguiling. He was the silent, secretive type.

When he was in her husband's unit, he was never there and yet he was always there. There were functions in the Mess and it was the officers' duty to attend. Once, just when she thought Peter Bennett was deliberately challenging the system by not attending the function, she spotted him across the other side of the room. She also caught him watching her. There was that look in his eye that suggested he was as interested in her as she was in him … but she must not show it.

She remembered that very first evening when they had welcomed Manfred Dorf and his wife into the Mess, and she had seen him for the first time. His sensuality had hit her straight away. And when she saw him going off with that young Trixie Meadows she wished she could have taken Trixie's place.

She had asked her husband about him but other than discovering he was in a lot of trouble because of an indiscreet affair and could be court-martialled, Timothy kept whatever he knew about Peter Bennett to himself. If anything, the intrigue made Peter Bennett more fascinating but then quite suddenly he was gone and even afterwards she didn't discover anything further. It was as though he never existed.

Now that she was sitting closer to him than she'd ever been before, she sensed the sexual tension in him, and wondered if he was as nervous as she was. Having had sex with Mark over an hour ago, she let her imagination take over and wondered what it would be like with Peter Bennett.

"No," he said, his eyes on the road. "Not until I saw you. My mind was on other things until I just happened to glance down at your rear wheels. I hope I didn't startle you when I flashed the lights."

"I have to admit I was a little worried, but there's so much of it about these days …"

"It?"

"Well, you know, you don't know who you can trust and who you can't."

"And which category do you put me into?" Peter asked.

"Now I know it was you … well, it's obvious, isn't it."

Peter smiled. "That's good to know." He slowed at the junction, turning right for *Waldniel.*

After a few seconds silence Dee relaxed even further. "So, do you miss the Army?" she asked.

"In a way," he said. "I miss the comradeship, the feeling of being part of something that mattered."

"What are you doing now?"

"I'm a scout."

"A scout?"

"Of sorts … I'm sussing out possible locations for theme parks."

"Theme parks? You do surprise me," she said.

Peter smiled again but didn't turn to look at her. "It's a reasonable job that allows me to travel. That's another reason why I'm over here."

Dee screwed up her eyes. "*Bracht* ... is that why you're here?"

This time he did look at her. "Very astute," he said, nodding. "Yes, I'm here to assess the opposition."

Having gone under the A52 Autobahn, he turned left at the next roundabout for *Linde* and *Amern.*

"Do any of the others know you're here?" Dee asked, sensing that Peter was going to confide in her.

"The others?"

"Well, Timothy, or Clive Benton?"

He shrugged. "I doubt it. I think your husband was rather glad to see me go, and Clive, well he and I never really saw eye to eye."

"Tim very rarely discusses work, but you were an exception. He said on more than one occasion that you were a great loss." It wasn't exactly a lie because her husband had suggested that if circumstances had been different, having Peter Bennett in his unit would have been to his and Peter's advantage.

"It's a pity the rest of the army didn't agree," Peter said.

"You were a bit naughty."

"I don't know what you know."

"Not a lot other than you … how can I put it … you acted a little injudiciously when you were at *Wulfen.*"

"Injudiciously? That's a very nice way of putting it. I fucked a corporal's wife."

Dee didn't want to appear shocked by his candour, because that's probably exactly why he said it. "I didn't want to –"

"I know." Peter looked at his watch. "You don't have time for a drink, do you?"

"A drink?" This time she couldn't hide her surprise. "Well, yes, I suppose … what time is it?"

"Just after six."

"I am earlier than normal. I suppose another thirty minutes or so wouldn't make any difference. Why?"

Peter slowed the car as he drove into the outskirts of *Amern.* "It's just that … it's just that I've never had the opportunity to explain, to really explain what happened."

"And you want to talk to me about it?"

"I know it's a bit of a cheek …"

Dee looked out of the side window so he wouldn't see the smile that had come to her lips. "I understand. Yes, I'll go for a drink with you but I'm not really dressed for –"

"Don't worry about that. I know this place in the woods beyond *Bracht*. Nobody you know will see you."

As Peter had expected, there were only a few other cars in the car park. It was too early for diners and the serious drinkers. He'd chosen the same place he'd been to with Sylvia because of its proximity to the forest.

"I've never been here before," Dee said as he parked at the far end of the car park. "In fact I don't think I even knew this place existed."

"It's a bit remote I must admit. Would you like to go for a short walk before we have a drink?" Peter opened his door. "I can talk more privately if we're out of earshot of anybody else."

Dee hesitated for a moment. "Sounds intriguing so why not? I'm more suitably dressed for walking."

Peter steered her towards the track which led away from the hotel and car park. After fifty or so yards the track became no more than a footpath but wide enough for two people to walk side by side. The sun, now low in the sky, was glinting through the trees, a slight breeze ruffled the leaves and the birds were still singing.

A few minutes later Peter left the main footpath and Dee followed. They came to a small clearing, and in the far corner and just discernible in the fading light was a pile of earth.

"What's that?" Dee said. "It looks as if an animal has been scraping at the earth. It's too big for rabbits, maybe a fox or a badger did it."

Peter dropped behind her and watched as Dee Smithers became more inquisitive. She wandered over to the mound and looked down into the dark hole.

"Good Lord," she said, "it looks just like a grave."

When her comment was greeted with silence she turned round slowly.

Stepping to one side, Peter slipped a piece of nylon cord round her neck and tightened it. The look in her eyes was the same as Sandra Davies – disbelief.

Peter smiled. She must know what was happening.

Her fingers went to the cord as she began to struggle but it was too late.

After only a few seconds, her body went limp.

He quickly and methodically stripped off all her clothes. After laying her in the grave he crossed her arms over her chest, put her hands together and closed her staring eyes. Except for the blue tinge on her face, she looked at peace. Her figure was athletic, strong thighs and calf muscles, her hips narrow, and no sign of excess fat. Many women half her age would have been pleased with a body like hers. Retrieving the small spade from where he had left it behind a tree, he covered her body with loose earth before moving leaves and undergrowth over the disturbed area.

Stepping back, he was happy that she would be found but not for a while.

He picked up her clothes and headed back to the car. "Two down, three to go," he muttered to himself as he joined the main track to *Lüttelforst,* smiling.

"Two down, three to go," the voices chanted in his head.

He smiled, feeling the exhilaration hitting every nerve in his body.

Chapter Fifty-Nine

The local police did not take long to identify the nationality of the victim. The most obvious clue was the wedding and engagement rings, which she wore on her left hand rather than the right, as was the custom in Germany. The second clue was the small tattoo on her right hip which said 'Trev' surrounded by a heart.

The nearest and most logical source of the British victim was the military camp on the other side *Wulfen*. Two days after the discovery of the body, the local *Polizeihauptkommissar* telephoned Lieutenant Colonel Mark O'Connell, the Commanding Officer at the ammunition depot, and asked for an immediate appointment. The Commanding Officer agreed to see Detective Inspector Wilhelm Gauler an hour after he took the call.

Accepting Mark O'Connell's offer of a cup of coffee, Willy Gauler sat down next to the small table in the corner of the office. He had never been that keen on the presence of British soldiers on his patch, but he had to admit that over the years they hadn't been too much trouble. There had been the odd scuffle with the local German youths but they were normally as much at fault as the British soldiers. Willy had also been invited on an annual basis to the Officers' Mess cocktail party, occasions he had initially loathed but when he'd seen who else was invited he was quite happy to rub shoulders with such dignitaries. Then soon after Mark O'Connell had taken over command, Willy and his wife Suzanne received an invitation to what the British called a ladies' dinner night. They had been two of only six guests, and they had gone home feeling that perhaps they were rather special.

He watched Mark O'Connell close the door before sitting opposite him. "So, Willy, this sounds as though it could be serious."

Willy's English was much improved and he now prided himself on his ability to speak the language. "It is not a question of it could be serious, Mark, it already is."

Mark O'Connell smiled ruefully. "Maybe for you, but allow me to be the judge of whether it is for me."

Willy glared at his host, wondering why the British thought the Germans were arrogant. "Mark," he said in a controlled voice, "there has been a murder and we think the victim may be one of yours." He felt uncomfortable using the Colonel's first name but he had reluctantly accepted the informalities practised by the British. "An old man out walking his dog discovered the body, and when he looked down at what used to be a human being he said he was physically sick. He described the scene as unbelievably ghastly but as hard as he tried, he could not drag his eyes away from the corpse. The head and part of one shoulder had been uncovered and there were signs that an animal, a badger or fox maybe, had eaten some of her flesh. The old man said he was crying as he left the wood to telephone the police."

Willy saw the colour drain from Mark O'Connell's face. "You said the victim could be one … one of mine? A British soldier you mean."

"That is a possibility, but we think she was more likely to be the wife of one of your soldiers."

"She was female?"

"Most definitely."

"And why do you think she's from here?" Mark O'Connell moved the mug of coffee nervously between his fingers.

"There's evidence to suggest she was not German, and not from Continental Europe either. Have any of your soldiers reported anybody missing?" Willy Gauler lifted his mug of coffee to his lips, wishing he could have a cigarette.

Mark O'Connell shook his head, "No, I'm not aware of anybody, and I would know."

"I am sure you would." Willy replaced the mug carefully on the table. "The victim had a tattoo on her right hip, a small heart that contained the letters T, R, E and V. Do the letters mean anything to you?"

"T, R, E and V," Mark repeated slowly. "Trev … it sounds as though they might be an abbreviation for a name, and the only one I can think of is Trevor. May I ask where she was found?"

"Later, Mark. I will be able to give you more details later. It is not unusual for Germans to have non-German first names but Trevor is not one I am familiar with. Are any of your soldiers called by this name?"

Mark O'Connell shook his head slowly, "No, not that … no, wait a minute, there is one I know of, he's a Corporal, Corporal Trevor Davies, but he hasn't reported –"

"Just one soldier?" Willy asked.

"I tend not to know their first names. Would you like me to call the Adjutant in and ask her?"

Willy Gauler held up his hand, "No, not at this stage. The fewer people who know why I am here the better, don't you think?"

"Of course, of course." Mark O'Connell stood up. "Bear with me for a second, I've got a complete list in my desk, soldiers' first names and their wives' details if they're married." He went over to his desk and after extracting the list from the right hand drawer, he ran his finger down each of the pages. "No, Corporal Davies is the only Trevor we have, but that doesn't mean to say ..."

"You were going to tell me that maybe the tattoo is an old one that refers to a previous relationship ...?"

"Well, yes."

Willy Gauler nodded. "That is a possibility and one we will investigate if necessary. Is this Corporal Davies here on your camp at the moment?"

"He should be, I don't know."

"May I see him?"

"Erm, there are certain procedures we must go through ..."

"Yes, Mark, I am aware, but this is just a preliminary enquiry."

"I appreciate that, but –"

"If we are able to establish that his wife ... is he married?"

Mark O'Connell looked at the sheaf of paper again, "Erm, yes."

"I just need to ask whether his wife is here with him."

"Well, yes, I can't see any harm with that. Perhaps I could get the Adjutant to ask him," Mark O'Connell said. "Can the German police interview a British soldier without a solicitor being present? Then again, perhaps because it's only a preliminary enquiry, a unit representative would be sufficient."

"If you don't mind, Mark, I would like to see him alone. I can assure you everything will be done correctly."

"Alone? I'm not sure ..."

"If his wife is here and I can see her, we will then be able to move on. Surely we do not need to go to a lot of bother for just that."

"No, I suppose not," Mark said.

Chapter Sixty

Fifteen minutes later Willy Gauler interviewed Corporal Trevor Davies in the works council office in the headquarters building. As well as the Inspector, Sergeant Dieter Muller was also in the office, having waited patiently in the police car while his boss was with Mark O'Connell.

Willy Gauler smiled at the obviously nervous corporal sitting opposite him. "I am sorry I had to ask you to come and see me, Corporal Davies, but we hoped you might be able to help us."

"I will –" Trevor Davies started to say, his expression not giving anything away. "Is it to do with the traffic accident I witnessed?"

"No, it is not but yes, I am sure you will be able to help. I am *Polizeihauptkommissar* Wilhelm Gauler, and this," he said indicating the man next to him, "is *Polizeihauptmeister* Dieter Muller. Do you speak German?"

Trevor Davies shook his head. "No,' he said.

"In that case I will speak in English. Sergeant Muller also speaks a little English but I may have to translate some of what we say."

"I understand."

"Thank you, Corporal Davies."

Inspector Gauler picked up the glass of water in front of him and took a tentative sip, his eyes never leaving Trevor Davies. His right earlobe was itching: whenever his earlobe itched, he knew he was on to something. He refrained from scratching it. "Are you married?"

Trevor Davies looked up quickly, and Willy Gauler knew his intuition had been right. "Yes."

"And your wife's name?"

"Sandra." Beads of perspiration broke out on the corporal's forehead.

Willy Gauler glanced sideways at his sergeant, a knowing look passing between them. "Is your wife at home now or does she work?"

"Erm, she's at home, well she would be at home if she wasn't away, if you see what I mean."

Willy Gauler shook his head. "No, I am afraid I do not see what you mean. Either she is at home or she is not. Which is it?"

"Erm, she's away. She's visiting friends in the UK," the corporal said.

"And how long ago did she go away?"

"Two weeks, well just over two weeks, two weeks yesterday."

"So fifteen days ago?" Willy Gauler said.

"Yes."

"And where is she in the UK visiting these friends?"

"Erm, all over, she's gone to see quite a few friends."

"I see. Are they her friends only or do you know any of them?"

"I've met some of them," Trevor said nervously.

Willy Gauler nodded, stealing another look at Dieter Muller. It was something he did deliberately; it was supposed to be unnerving … and more often than not it worked. "Have you spoken to her since she went to the UK?"

"Yes, of course, three or four times." Trevor Davies said. His eyes darting from one policeman to the other, telling them he was lying.

"When was she the last time you spoke to her?"

"She …" Trevor Davies stopped. "What's she done?"

"Done, Corporal Davies, why do you ask what she has done?"

"You wouldn't be here if she hadn't done something," he said.

"Not necessarily. Maybe she has had something done to her."

"What do you mean?"

Willy Gauler ignored the question. "Corporal Davies, let us go back to the beginning. When did you last see your wife?"

"I told you, just over two weeks ago."

"And where was that? Where was she when you last saw her?"

"I … I drove her to the ferry. She went over to the UK on the ferry."

"The ferry? Where from?" Willy Gauler asked.

"Calais. I took her to Calais and she went over as a foot passenger."

"All right, so on that Sunday you drove your wife to Calais so that she could go to the UK on a ferry?"

"Yes."

"And then in the UK she was going to visit all these friends of hers without a car?"

"She was going to hire a car."

"Hire a car, I see. Why didn't she take your car in the first place? I would have –"

"I needed the car for work."

Willy Gauler raised his eyebrows. "For work? Your wife goes to England for an extended stay where she will be travelling 'all over' I think you said, and you keep the car here to travel less than a kilometre into work."

"Yes."

"Corporal Davies, if I send my sergeant to your house and he asks your neighbours when they last saw your wife, they will be able to corroborate your story that she is in England, will they?"

"Yes, well …"

"Corporal Davies, when did you last see your wife?"

"I've told you …"

"No, I think what you have told me is, how do you say it in English? Yes, a pack of lies," Willy Gauler said, hunching forward. "I would suggest that you tell me the truth now before we go any further."

Lowering his head, Corporal Davies sighed deeply. "I'm sorry," he muttered.

"I did not hear you."

"I said I'm sorry."

"Your wife is not in England, is she?" Willy Gauler said.

"I don't know where she is."

"When did you last see her?"

"I told you the truth about that, it was on the Sunday two weeks ago."

Inspector Gauler nodded. The timeframe and the decomposition of Corporal Davies' wife's body fitted with the timeframe. "And where was she when you last saw her?"

"She went out to buy some rolls for breakfast. It was something one of us did, but it was usually her, every Sunday morning. On that particular Sunday, she went."

"Into *Wulfen* you mean? She went to get the rolls in *Wulfen*."

"Yes, to the bakers."

"She went to buy some bread rolls and you have not seen her since, is that what you are saying?"

Trevor Davies could only nod. "Has –?"

"Corporal Davies, does your wife have a tattoo on her right hip?"

"Yes … but how do you know that?"

"This tattoo, does it spell your name, or a shorter version of your name?"

"Yes … yes, and it spells 'Trev' and I have one here,' he said pointing at his upper arm, "that says 'Sandi'."

"Corporal Davies, are you sure there is nothing else you would like to tell us at this stage?"

Trevor Davies moved his head slowly from side to side. "No," he whispered. "She went out to get the rolls and didn't come back."

"That was fifteen days ago. Can you tell me why you have not reported her as missing?"

Inspector Gauler and his sergeant took just two more days to piece together enough evidence to arrest and charge Trevor Davies with his wife's murder. Sandra's infidelity and Trevor's belief that she had run off with one of her lovers, was used against him.

Detective Inspector Gauler quickly established the type of relationship Trevor had with his wife, and her betrayal was just the motive he needed to persuade his superiors that an arrest was the only way forward.

Although arresting a British soldier for such an offence could be political dynamite, Willy Gauler's immediate superior agreed with what he wanted to do.

There was no chance of him getting bail so Corporal Trevor Davies was locked up in a cell under the police station in *Münster* to await his fate.

Chapter Sixty-One

After what Clive had told her, Leah felt her apprehension was justified.

She was an hour away from seeing Peter Bennett for the first time since she arrived in Germany and she was worried. Originally he told her it would be months before they met again, but she hadn't believed him. On the grounds that Clive might become suspicious, Leah hadn't pushed for more details about Peter Bennett and his time in the depot, but she had posed a few not so obvious questions to others in the unit, which were met with mixed reactions. All those she asked remembered Peter Bennett. Some opinions were derisive but others suggested he was a sort of local hero: he took on the system and although he lost, he made his presence felt in no uncertain terms. A couple of the women Leah spoke to had simply swooned at the mention of Peter's name. So she concluded there was good reason to be slightly nervous.

Nobody mentioned he had any association with Ursula Dorf.

Sitting in her office and pondering what she was going to say to Peter, wondering whether she should tell him what she had discovered, she became aware that people were scurrying up and down the corridor. Something else was going on and she wanted to find out what it was.

When she had arrived at work this morning there was a military police car parked outside the headquarters building, and rumour had it that its occupants were in the CO's office. Nobody knew anything but as the morning progressed the grapevine suggested that the police were there to investigate the loss of some money from one of the unit's accounts.

Going into the corridor Leah immediately bumped in to Sam Cox, the CO's PA, who looked as though she had been crying. Leah asked her what was wrong but Sam shook her head and said she couldn't say, but then she ushered Leah out of the building and into the car park where Sam suddenly blurted out, "It's Dee, the CO's wife, she's missing."

They stopped at Leah's car. "Missing? What do you mean by missing?"

"She didn't go home last night and the CO doesn't know where she is," Sam told Leah with tears in her eyes.

"Are you saying that something might have happened to her?" Leah unlocked the Peugeot and threw her bag onto the front seat. She may as well leave now to meet Peter, as she needed to pick up a few things first.

"I don't know. The wall between my office and the CO's is thin, but I didn't catch everything."

"So what you're telling me is something you overheard, not something you were told," Leah said.

"Yes, is that awful of me?" Sam was by all accounts a good PA. She protected the CO very well, and was highly efficient, but she was prone to being a bit of a gossip. As the CO's PA, she knew a lot more than anybody else did. Sam was never malicious, just a little free with what she had heard or read. Leah wondered if Sam had overheard the CO speaking to Clive about his relationship with her. She had never said anything, so Leah hadn't told her about it either, but she still wondered if Sam knew.

"No, but you seem very upset."

"Did you know her?"

"I've met her once or twice but I can't say I know her," Leah said. "Why are you talking in the past tense?"

"Something awful has happened, I can just feel it. I've never seen the CO in such a state so I suppose I am upset for him. She was such a lovely woman, and they were so devoted to each other."

Leah didn't think repeating what she'd heard from Clive Benton was the right thing to do. "Yes, so I understand. Anyway, I'm sure she'll turn up."

"Yes, but that's not everything," Sam said solicitously.

"Everything? Why what else is there?"

"The CO had a telephone call yesterday from Colonel O'Connell, the CO at *Wulfen*." Sam looked around her to make sure there was nobody else within hearing distance. "Evidently, one of the wives there has been murdered."

Leah felt her body stiffen. "Murdered?" She realised she repeated the word rather loudly so she laid her hand on Sam's arm and said, "Sorry."

"Yes, a woman called Sandra Davies. She was married to a corporal there, and he's been arrested and charged with her murder."

"You're joking?"

"Not about something as serious as that."

"And you think there may be a connection?" Leah asked.

"No," Sam said, shaking her head vigorously, "not at all, but it's a bit of a coincidence that less than a few days later Dee Smithers goes missing."

"Well let's hope –" Leah stopped as she saw a group of soldiers approaching, and looked away when she received the inevitable smiles and comments. She wondered why soldiers had to make their feelings so obvious. When they had passed, she looked at Sam. "I'm sure that's all it is, a coincidence. However, what happened in *Wulfen* is awful. Does anybody else know?"

"They're not supposed to but you know what things are like. If it's not already all round the unit, it will be within a few hours. The soldiers and families at *Wulfen* will know, and," she shrugged, "they won't be able to keep it quiet."

"And this Corporal Davies has been charged?"

"Yes. His wife was a bit of a, how can I put it? Let's say she enjoyed male company, a lot of male company. It seems the police found her body on Monday and had charged her husband by the Wednesday evening."

"God that was quick." Leah hadn't the faintest idea why she thought it was quick because she had no experience of such matters.

"Exactly."

"They must have had proof."

"One would hope so."

"Well, I'm sure it's just a coincidence."

Sam nodded. "I hope you're right. Look I've got to go. You won't tell anybody what I've told you, will you?"

"Of course not," Leah said.

Chapter Sixty-Two

Meeting Peter in the centre of *Roermond* was understandable because he wouldn't want to be seen in the area around *Brüggen* and *Bracht*.

Why had he lied to her?

Leah had been to *Roermond*, a town just over the border in Holland, a couple of times before so she had no trouble in parking and finding the town square. She remembered it was the scene of an IRA atrocity a few years earlier. She couldn't remember exactly what had happened or if anybody had been killed.

Although *Roermond* was not new to her, *La Cascade* restaurant was.

She was due to meet Peter at seven o'clock but she arrived ten minutes early. His phone call had not been unexpected, although once she started seeing and then sleeping with Clive, she wished she was in Germany for completely different reasons.

After hearing what Clive Benton and the others had told her about Peter Bennett, Leah had decided she would tell him this evening that she didn't want to continue with their agreement. He had lied to her and she didn't like that. She knew it would mean her moving out of the flat and probably having to pay back the money she had already spent, but it didn't amount to much because she'd been quite prudent. The money she spent on herself was her own, either what she brought with her or what she was paid. But she would have to pay back the rent. Maybe she wouldn't have to move out of the flat – maybe she could just take over the contract. She hoped so because she liked the flat and its location.

She wouldn't tell Peter about Clive.

Neither he nor Clive must know about the other.

She hoped Peter wouldn't be difficult.

Although Leah's decision meant her relationship with Peter was at an end – he had said she could pull out at any stage – this evening she had made a special effort for him. She caught sight of herself in a mirror as she went into the restaurant and was pleased with what she saw. She had chosen 'the little black number' she'd bought only a week ago to please Clive, and it hadn't been worn before. The dress showed off her shoulders, clung to her figure, and finished just above her knees. She had chosen high-heeled black shoes, a silver necklace and matching dangle earrings and had to admit she felt sexy. Her hair was a lot longer now and she wore it so that it hung over her right shoulder.

Yes, she felt good.

Stopping at the lectern that held the bookings for this evening, a formally attired young woman looked enquiringly at her.

“Hello,” Leah said, smiling. “I think there’s a table booked in the name of Bennett for seven o’clock. I’m sorry I’m a little early.”

“Not at all, Madam,” the woman said, also smiling. She looked down at the booking sheet. “Yes, Madam, there is a table in that name but your host has not yet arrived.”

“Do you have a bar I can wait in?”

“Yes, Madam,” the woman said indicating an alcove beyond the main dining area. “You can wait there or I can show you to your table.”

“No, the bar, please.” Leah was going to add that she needed some Dutch courage but wondered if it would be appropriate. The woman spoke perfect English but she might not understand what was meant by 'Dutch' courage.

“Yes, Madam, follow me please.”

Leah followed her to the bar, ordered a gin and tonic, then perched on one of the stools and crossed her legs. The barman was very attentive, but his English was limited and Leah didn’t want to embarrass him ... or herself.

Chapter Sixty-Three

"Hello, Leah."

Peter was suddenly there, standing right next to her. She was lost in her thoughts and hadn't seen him come into the bar. He bent forward, put a hand under her chin and kissed her gently on the lips. Leah remembered the soft but intimate kiss from their early relationship.

"Hello, Peter," she said, still feeling his lips on hers. "It's good to see you after so long." He was looking as smart as ever, in a lightweight beige suit, yellow shirt and red tie.

Peter smiled then turned his attention to the barman. "A whisky soda," he said. "Leah?"

"No, thanks." She shook her head. "This will do me for the time being."

Peter smiled. "You're looking an absolute picture."

"Thank you, you don't look too bad yourself."

He inclined his head slightly and she saw his eyes drift down her throat to her cleavage. "You've put on a bit of weight and it suits you."

"Not exactly what a girl wants to be told," Leah said, but she returned his smile.

"I meant it as a compliment."

"I know you did, thank you. You're right though, I have put on a few pounds."

Peter looked round the bar. "So how are things?" he asked.

"Do you mean me personally, or what you want from me?"

"What I want from you can wait," he said. "No – you, how are you?"

"I'm fine thanks. The job is going well and it's turning out to be very interesting."

"That's not what I asked."

Leah put her glass on the bar. "I told you I'm fine."

"I can see that, but what about the inner you, how is she?"

A waitress came up to them and indicated their table was ready.

"The inner me? I'm not sure I know what …" she started to ask as she was ushered towards the dining room.

"How have you managed without me?"

"I'm sorry?"

Once seated, and after they each had ordered a chicken salad, Peter stroked his fingers down the side of her face. "You're a very physical girl, Leah, you have your needs."

"Are you asking what I think you're asking?"

Peter shrugged. "I've missed you. I suppose I'm asking if you have missed me."

"Of course I've missed you, but –"

"You feel I'm using you?"

Leah realised that was exactly how she felt but she wasn't very happy with the way the conversation was going; she wanted to be in control this time. She put her hand on Peter's. "Yes, that is the way I feel."

To her surprise, Peter smiled. "I'm sorry. I've been giving the way I've treated you a lot of thought and you have every reason to think that way. Yes, I did go looking for you … for someone, and after we met and you told me all about yourself, a relationship was necessary although it wasn't obligatory because of what I wanted from you. Part of my not seeing you for so long after you came over here was because I felt that we were getting too close. I was beginning to feel guilty. My feelings for you and what I was asking you to do simply didn't go together, so something had to give."

"Peter – you're not making sense. What was – or is – that something?"

"That's up to you," he said.

"What do you mean?"

"If you feel used then what I've asked you to do doesn't matter anymore. I've discovered that there are other ways I can find out what I need to know. I –"

"I was going to say that … that you'll have to find another way," she said. "I've not been able to find out very much anyway."

Peter smiled again. "I'm not surprised. My other contacts, ones that I haven't told you about for obvious reasons, tell me that the Germans are playing things very close to their chests."

"So what are you saying?"

"I suppose I'm saying that you're relieved of your duties."

She ignored him. "And what about us?"

"That's the bit that is up to you."

Leah knew what she wanted to say, but she didn't know how to say it.

"It's time I let you get on with your life," he added, after sitting back as the salads were brought to the table.

Leah frowned. "There's more to that statement than you're saying." She was annoyed because she wanted to tell him his future, but he had now done it for her. Picking up her knife and fork she began to eat.

Peter put his hand on hers, breaking eye contact. "The last few months have given me time to do a lot of thinking about what needs to happen."

"Are you telling me that I'm dumped?"

Peter smiled, regret in his eyes. "Dumped isn't the word I would use. As I said, I've had time to think and I …"

Leah narrowed her eyes. "Let me get this straight. You pick me up in Durham nearly a year ago, you wine me and dine me, we go to bed and we go on holiday together and then you tell me what you really want from me." Leah paused for effect, trying desperately to make her eyes water, "besides the obvious that is." Peter was watching her, his face emotionless. "And, after weeks of not seeing you, you turn up and tell me I'm dumped without any real explanation."

"It's what you want as well," Peter said, almost in a monotone.

The first tear ran down Leah's cheek. She was no longer hungry so she placed her cutlery back on her plate. Peter's statement threw her and she decided to change tack. "What ... what about the flat and the money you put in the bank? The car? Everything?"

"The lease on the flat runs out in January. It'll be up to you whether you renew it or not. The money is yours, as is the car."

The waiter was hovering and asked if everything was all right, indicating Leah's half-eaten meal.

"Everything is fine," Peter told him. "We have both suddenly lost our appetites." He ordered coffees without asking Leah if she wanted anything else.

"And me? What about me?" The tears were there, and Peter was just a blur.

"You?" Peter shrugged. "That's entirely up to you, isn't it? You can stay or go. You have a job, you have somewhere to live for the immediate future, what else …?"

"I'm talking about me? I've been Amy Carpenter for the last two months because of you." She sniffed. "I can't just start telling people that I'm really Leah Carmichael."

Peter picked up her hand, holding her fingers gently in his and kissed them. She wanted to snatch her hand away but didn't. "Leah, you're one of the prettiest girls I've ever met. In every respect what you've done for me is fantastic and under different circumstances we may have had a future together, but …" He hesitated, looking down at her hand. "I haven't been strictly honest with you." He drained his coffee cup. "Look, Leah, can we go somewhere a little quieter. I've got some explaining to do. I can't tell you everything, but I think you warrant some of the truth."

Leah wiped away a tear. He was going to make it easy for her, but even so she believed she might miss him. She nodded. "All right, and I've got some questions for you including why you never told me you'd been in the Army." There was no reaction. "Where do you want to go?"

He picked up one of the napkins and dabbed her eyes. "It's a nice evening. We could go for a walk by the river, and yes, I've got some explaining to do ... including about my time in the Army."

"A walk? In these shoes?"

"We'll drive to the river, and then we don't have to walk far."

She was pleased she remembered to bring the jacket that went with her dress. "All right," she said, "but I must go to the bathroom first."

Chapter Sixty-Four

Fifteen minutes later they were strolling along the path that ran parallel to the River *Maas*. Although it was a warm evening not many people were out walking.

Peter was just about to start his story when Leah said, "What a beautiful sunset. It's a rather fitting background if our relationship is to end too."

"Ever the romantic," Peter said as he guided her towards a lone tree and an empty bench. They both sat down.

"I'm not what or who you think I am," he said quietly.

"You're not who you told me you were, you mean," she said, taking a packet of cigarettes from her bag.

"For once I'm going to ask you to listen without interrupting me. I'll tell you as much as I can, hopefully enough for you to understand."

"It sounds fascinating, I –"

"Please, Leah, just listen." He waited a few seconds before saying anything further. "I'm nothing to do with adventure parks, or anything else to do with the leisure industry. What I do couldn't be further away from leisure or anything remotely associated with being pleasant." Peter gazed towards the opposite bank but he knew Leah's eyes were on him, and only him. "Until just over a year ago I was in the SAS ... you know what the SAS is, don't you?"

"Special Forces, isn't it? Daddy was in the Army, remember."

"Of course, sorry." Peter paused. "To all intents and purposes I'm still on their books, still part of their set-up. I still carry an Army identity card and the Army still pays me. A couple of months before I met you, I was seconded to an organisation that must remain secret. For the last few months you've been my eyes and ears in an area where I would have been too obvious."

"But you –"

"Please, Leah I won't be able to answer any of your questions. I've cleared what I'm going to tell you at the highest level, but it has to be on the understanding that you must know nothing more." He moved his hand a little further up Leah's thigh until it was resting against her hip. "You've discovered that I was in the Army and that I went to *Bracht* under a cloud, but it was all a cover for what I was really sent there to do. I came to

Germany to await my fate. I was attached to the other ammunition depot at *Wulfen* for a short period, to come to *Bracht* straight away would have been rather obvious, so *Wulfen* was the first place I went to but then this incident was arranged so that I would have to be transferred from there. I –"

"Can you tell me what the incident was?" Leah asked.

"That's one question I can answer, because it's general knowledge. I deliberately had a very brief affair with a married woman but made sure the authorities knew about it. No name, I'm afraid, but she was suited to what I needed to do."

"Did you know there's been a murder at *Wulfen*?" Leah asked.

Peter feigned surprise. "No, who was it?"

"I don't know … well, if what I've been told is true, it was a corporal's wife and he's been charged with her murder ... wait, I do know her name, it was somebody called Sandra Davies."

"Sounds fascinating," he said, pleased that his ruse had worked.

"I wouldn't say fascinating, it's all a bit gruesome. And that's not the only thing –"

"Let me finish what I was telling you, Leah."

"Sorry."

"In *Bracht* I had to keep myself to myself, and once the novelty of having a black sheep in their midst wore off, my job was made that much easier. However, what I hadn't been told was that the person I'd been put into *Bracht* to watch was a little more astute than the authorities had realised. She –"

"She?"

"Leah."

"Sorry."

"I understand where you're coming from but you must understand that I'm almost reading from a script. Everything I'm saying has been agreed." He took his hand from her thigh and ran his fingers down her cheek, and then round the back of her neck. Pulling her head towards him, he kissed her gently on the lips. "You weren't quite what I was looking for," he said, "but there was something about you when I saw you sitting by that tree concentrating so deeply and oblivious to what was going on around you. You were too young and too pretty, but you were also a challenge for other reasons. It had been a long time and I thought you were going to be no more than a –"

"A challenge?"

"Not how I ought to put it, but you were." He kissed her again, and she didn't resist him. "As we got to know each other better it became rather apparent that you were what I was looking for in more ways than one.

Your knowledge of the Army because of your father, the fact that you could speak German – it all fell into place. Once I'd cleared your involvement, the rest followed and to a great extent you are aware of what happened from then on."

"That's rubbish, Peter," Leah said. "So far you've told me nothing I didn't already know ... except for what you've said about the Special Forces. Who is this woman I was supposed to watch?"

"You weren't supposed to be watching her," he said.

"Then what was I supposed to be doing?"

"You were my eyes and my ears."

"For what? You're not telling me … how could I be your eyes and ears when I didn't know what I was supposed to be watching and hearing?"

"You've got to swear that nothing I'm about to tell you will ever be repeated to anyone."

"Peter, for God's sake, I've no idea what you're going to say but … but if it helps, I swear I will not tell anybody anything."

"All right. It's Manfred Dorf's wife, Ursula."

"Ursula Dorf, she's lovely. What on earth …?"

"What do you know about her?"

Leah shrugged. "Not a lot actually, other than she's married to *Herr* Dorf, well supposedly …"

"Supposedly?"

Leah hesitated. "It's just that … well, some people think that the marriage is in name only."

"And?"

"And what?"

"What conclusions do you draw from that?"

"I don't know … it's a marriage of convenience?"

"Convenient to whom?"

"Well, Ursula, I suppose," Leah said.

"And why would being married to Manfred Dorf be convenient?"

"I thought you said there were to be no questions."

"This one is from me to you," Peter said.

Leah thought for a moment, and Peter watched her intently. "Well, she's Russian …"

"Exactly. Her maiden name is Ivanovitch, and you're quite right, she is Russian but more importantly she is what is known as a *sleeper*."

"A *sleeper*? What –?"

"Ursula Ivanovitch is a Captain in the Russian security services, what you will remember being called the KGB. The most villainous, murderous and nefarious security organisation in the world. And what makes them even more dangerous is that over two billion pounds sterling is allocated to them on an annual basis. There are tens of thousands of them, and their support staff is staggeringly large. They are a machine, and one that generally works like clockwork, both internally within Russia and externally, all over the world."

Leah's mouth was open and her eyes unblinking. "I … I don't believe it. She … she's such an ordinary woman, very attractive, but ordinary in every other way."

"That's what makes her so dangerous. She is a killer, Leah. She would feel just as at home slitting your throat as saying good morning."

"I really …" Leah shook her head. "I really don't know what to say. How … how did you know about her?"

Peter looked deliberately smug. "There are thousands of them here in Germany, and we know about ninety per cent of the ones who have infiltrated into our military. She made it all rather obvious. From the moment Manfred Dorf brought her back with him we were on to her, and we've been watching her ever since."

"But there's been nothing that would have alerted me or anybody else if it comes to that. Does Timothy Smithers know about her?"

Peter shook his head, letting a wry smile cross his lips. "No, nobody knows about her. As far as they are concerned, she's a white Russian immigrant who escaped the might of the Soviet system years ago. She's regarded with sympathy. She's been cleared by the authorities, so in theory she doesn't present a threat. Of course, her clearances were manufactured. She's like a coiled python, waiting to strike."

"And what am I supposed to do with what you've told me?"

"Absolutely nothing," he said. "You must treat her as though this conversation hasn't taken place."

"But ... but that's going to be –"

"Just behave as though nothing has changed."

Leah stood up and walked to the water's edge before turning to face Peter. "An awful lot has changed, Peter, an awful lot. So you were put into *Bracht* to watch her?"

Peter nodded. "Yes."

"And you couldn't stay there because she suspected you were on to her?"

"Yes."

"There's a rumour that you and she were ... you know, having an affair," Leah said.

Peter smiled. She really had discovered more than he thought she would. Still, it didn't matter now. "People have vivid imaginations," he said.

"So it didn't happen."

"No, it didn't happen."

"And all this business about you being threatened with a court martial, and then being told to resign your commission, was to throw her off the scent?"

"I didn't know you knew about that, but how you know doesn't matter. However, the answer to your question is, yes, but they didn't tell me to resign, I had already resigned before I went to *Bracht*. I needed to do that for show."

Leah's eyes opened wide again. "Wow!" she said, "this is the sort of thing you read about. It doesn't happen in the real world." She walked back over to Peter and knelt in front of him. "So where did I come into all this? How could I, regardless of my father and my ability to speak German, how could I help? What gave you the right to involve me in something like this without telling me what it was? You lied to me. You made it out to be nothing more than … well, you know what you told me."

Peter reached forward and took her hands in his. "Leah, I'm sorry, but there are times when the security of the Nation must come before personal resentment. I did what I did because I had no other choice. You were perfect."

"You keep on saying I was perfect, but you still haven't told me what for."

He looked down at her hands in his. They were so delicate, and almost flawless. Once dead and at rest she would look the best of them all. "It was more to do with me than the Ivanovitch woman."

"Sorry?"

"I needed to know what was being said. I needed to know if I might have been seen."

"You're losing me again."

The sun was already below the horizon and its warmth had disappeared with it. Leah shivered.

"As I told you, everybody had to believe I was in real trouble. They all, the CO, everybody, had to think I had resigned and left under a big black cloud. After I left, and when I wasn't with you, I was over here, watching Ursula Ivanovitch. Regardless of how good I am at what I do, there's always a chance that there might have been an opportune sighting of me, somebody who might have seen me at a distance and maybe just thought it was me. I also needed to know what people knew, if you heard anything from anybody about me. I needed to know what they were saying and why?" Leah shivered again. "You're cold, shall we go back?"

"In a minute, I'm all right for a minute." Leah looked at the ground. "I'm so confused, and my confusion generates so many questions, but you said –"

"You've been told that I was in *Bracht*, haven't you?"

"Well, yes … I –"

"And you weren't going to tell me, were you?"

"Er … no, not directly but I did want to know why you'd lied to me."

"That's why I'm telling you about Ursula Ivanovitch."

"But I still –"

"I can answer your questions about your involvement," he said, making his voice sound as sympathetic as he could.

"All right, what about the period between you leaving *Bracht* and me coming here – who was your eyes and ears then?"

"I was particularly careful. It was the early stages, and my visits weren't so frequent."

"Do you mean that since I've been over you here, you were here as well?"

"Yes."

Leah closed her eyes, shaking her head. "Peter, I really don't know whether I'm coming or going. Is it common practice that whatever organisation you're working for uses civilians like me and without them knowing, to watch their agents' backs?"

"No, not always, but when there are special circumstances, it is an option."

"But I didn't know why I was really here. Why were you so sure that I would tell you if anybody had said anything?

"You would have told me," he said.

"Why are you so sure?"

"I just know."

"But I didn't even know that you'd been in the Army," Leah said, "let alone that you were in *Bracht.*"

"Exactly."

"Exactly! What does that mean?"

"If you'd known, you might have inadvertently given the game away. By not knowing, you couldn't let anything slip. You couldn't ask questions. If for example you had asked Ursula about me, she would have guessed what you were doing straight away, and then … then, you may have met with an unfortunate accident."

Leah stood up quickly. "Jesus, Peter," she shouted at him. "I feel totally used. Are you telling me now you put my life in danger?" She turned her back on him and started to walk along the path but stopped. "I want out," she said, "but most of all I want to be away from you."

"I understand the way you feel."

"So why? Why tell me a pack of lies one minute and then some of the truth the next?" She started walking away again, in tears. "And on top of all that, you ... you take what you want and then dump me. You're a bastard Peter Bennett, or whoever you are."

Peter caught up with her and held her arm. Leah tried to shake him off but he turned her round, putting his hands on her shoulders. "Leah, listen to me. If I'd played this by the book you wouldn't even know the little I have told you. It's because of the way I feel about you that I had to tell you. Can't you see that? In a couple of weeks you would have been free of me anyway, it would all have been over. You could have stayed in *Bracht*, gone back to the UK, whatever, and you would have been none the wiser."

"So ... so why have things changed? And don't tell me it's because of how you feel. If you'd felt anything for me at all you wouldn't have involved me in the first place."

He moved his hands closer to her neck. "I think Ursula Ivanovitch is planning to assassinate the General in *Rhinedahlen*."

"What? What the bloody hell are you on about now?"

"I can't tell you any more than that, but if my information is correct then she'll do it within the next week or so."

Leah stared at Peter. "No, I've heard enough to know that my involvement with you is at an end." She spoke calmly. "Whatever else you thought you were going to get me to do, you can forget it. If you think an attempt is going to be made on the General's life I would suggest that you tell whoever needs to be told so that he can be protected, but you can count me out of anything you have planned."

"I can't," he said, his thumbs now at the base of her throat.

Leah gripped Peter's wrists and tried to pull them away. "Peter, I don't want to know any more. This conversation is at an end. You've scared me to death, and if that isn't enough you want me to accept everything you've said and risk even more. I'm sorry, but you chose the wrong person, you got it wrong. None of what you've said makes any sense to me. You've lied to me from the day we met. You're a lying bastard, Peter Bennett, and I want nothing more to do with you ... and ... and take your fucking hands off me."

The voices were urging him on, telling him to kill her now. He looked beyond Leah and to his right but couldn't see anybody. 'Now,' the voices were saying, 'do it now.'

Increasing the pressure on Leah's throat, he moved his thumbs so that they were against her windpipe. He saw the expression on her face change to one of terror.

The grip on his wrists tightened as she tried to pull his hands away. Her unblinking eyes were staring at him, her mouth open as she gasped for air.

"I know an apology means nothing to you now, but I really am sorry. I'm sorry for what I've done and I'm sorry for what I must do now."

He bent down and kissed her.

Chapter Sixty-Five

A crowd of students appeared out of no-where. Peter saw their heads first in the dip to his left – about ten of them and it was obvious that a few of them were very drunk. Two of the girls in the group were being supported by young men on either side.

He released the pressure on Leah's throat. She gasped for air. Quickly he put his arms round her, pulled her to one side and kissed her. As her death had not been planned for this evening, he hadn't prepared a grave for her, but if it had been her day to die, a watery grave had awaited … the River Maas. The river's current was strong and it would have taken her body many miles downstream. Although her discovery was inevitable, it was a risk he would have been willing to take. There was nothing to link him to her. The staff in the restaurant might remember them, but nobody else was aware that they even knew each other let alone that they had been lovers. Ursula knew of Leah's existence but she wouldn't give evidence … dead people can't talk.

The voices had gone silent.

Leah Carmichael was going to die, that was a certainty, but not yet.

As the students passed they made what were obviously vulgar comments, but as they were in Dutch Peter didn't understand them, although one of the girl's did shout in faltering English, "When you have finished with her, I will be next." He wondered why she had spoken in English.

All the students laughed before carrying on unsteadily along the path.

He took his lips from Leah's. "Are you all right?" he said.

Expecting her to struggle, Peter kept his arms round her. She was looking up at him, her eyes still unblinking, her mouth open as though she wanted to speak but couldn't.

"I'm going to take you back to your car," he said, "and once there I will explain a few home truths to you. Do you understand?" He looked down at her. "Nod if you understand."

With her mouth and eyes still wide open, Leah nodded.

The silence as they walked back to Peter's car continued during the short drive to the car park where Leah had left her car. "So," Peter said as they stopped at her car ten minutes later, "I suppose this is the end of an unusual relationship.

She was numb with shock.

Her throat hurt, but the pain was nothing compared to the sheer terror she felt. She daren't even look at him; she knew that if she tried to run she wouldn't get away. If she screamed he would kill her.

Once in the car park she stayed where she was until he opened the passenger door, grabbed her arm and pulled her out. He pushed her roughly towards her car and then spun her round so that her back was against the driver's door.

He moved a little closer. "You need a lesson or two," he said, running his fingers down the side of her face.

She could do nothing but stare at him.

"Don't ... don't do that," she managed to say.

He smiled, his hand dropping to her shoulder and then onto her breast under her jacket. "I thought you liked to be stroked."

She tried to knock his hand away with her forearm, but any resistance was useless.

He was going to kill her and there was nothing she could do about it.

His finger was under her chin. As she turned her head to face him a tear ran down her cheek.

She didn't want to die.

Brushing his thumb against her lips he bent down and kissed her, at the same forcing his body against hers.

She had parked her car in the corner furthest from the pedestrian exit, which meant she and Peter were also on the blind side of the car. The only other people about were too far away to take any notice of them.

He was going to kill her.

Bringing her knee up she tried to force him away. "Peter ... Peter don't, please. If you ever thought anything for me … I'll do anything –"

"You have no idea how I felt about you," he said, pinning her against the side of the car, holding her wrists with one hand and looking down at her.

"Stop –"

"I want you to listen and listen very carefully." His voice was metallic, her nipple was between his fingers and he was squeezing.

"Peter, you're hurting me."

"Shut up and listen. What I did to you down by the river was a warning. You are mine to do with whatever I want." He took his hand away.

"Peter, why –?"

"Shut up," he said as he forced himself against her so that she couldn't move. Lifting up the hem of her dress he hooked his fingers into her pants and pulled them down, ripping both sides. “Now,” he said with his teeth bared, “I think you need to be made aware of a fact or two.” She could feel his fingers moving. “The authorities might be interested in finding out who you really are. Did you know it’s illegal in Germany to give a false name when renting property? I would guess it’s illegal everywhere, but especially in Germany. I’m going to let go of your wrists now but if you struggle I might be forced to hit you.” He looked down into her face as tears streamed silently down her cheeks.

“Why are you crying, we’ve done this so many times before. You normally can’t get enough.”

He let go of her wrists and Leah dropped her arms to her sides. She knew there was no point in struggling or screaming; this stranger was going to rape her and then kill her. “Peter, please …” she sobbed.

“Come, come, Leah, where’s your sense of adventure?” She closed her eyes, clamping her lips together in an attempt to stifle an instinctive scream. “Did you also know that it’s illegal to drive a car with false insurance, a false driving licence, and false identification?”

She could feel him against her and she saw through her tears the eyes of a madman, the sneer on his lips as he forced himself into her. She ignored the pain, the feeling of total revulsion. She ignored the need to scream and never to stop screaming.

“I wonder what the British authorities would do to you if they found out you were not who you said you were. I wonder what they do to people who work in sensitive jobs when they discover they have been deceived. I wonder …”

Then it was over.

As he stepped away from her, pulling up the zip on his trousers, a smile replaced the sneer. Leah slumped down to her knees. He bent down, took hold of her arms and lifted her upright.

“Your papers may have been produced by the very authorities I refer to, but they would deny any involvement because the people concerned were paid handsomely to do what they did and to keep their mouths shut. Did you hear what I said to you?”

All she could do was nod. Her eyes were closed and now she wanted to die.

“Good. I’m actually sorry I had to resort to threats to get you to do what I needed, but you gave me little choice. I can assure you that if the German and British authorities do find out that you’re here using a false identity you will be in a lot of trouble. Do you understand that?”

She nodded again.

“Then you understand that you are still mine to do with you whatever I want?”

Another nod.

"Excellent. You're in no fit state to take in the detail so I'll be in touch very shortly." He began to walk away, but then stopped. "Oh, and Leah, if you even think about going to the authorities yourself, or telling somebody about what has just happened, you will be dead before you're able to talk to anybody. You'll not only be dead but you'll also be in so many little pieces, it'll be like a jigsaw puzzle to put your chopped up body back together again. Do you understand?"

"Yes," Leah whispered, her whole body shaking.

"I'm sorry I didn't hear you."

"Yes," she said a bit louder.

"Splendid. Now tidy yourself up. You look such a mess. Get in your car and go home to your darling Clive. Oh yes, I know about you and Clive Benton. I'll be in touch very shortly."

Leah slumped down at the side of her car, her entire body convulsing with disgust, fear and ... relief.

Chapter Sixty-Six

"Amy, you've got to talk," Clive Benton said through the bathroom door. "Something has happened, I know it."

"Leave me alone."

"Amy, at least let me in."

"The door's not locked," she said.

Clive went into the bathroom. Leah was sitting in the bath, the suds covering most of her body. Facing away from him, she was resting her head on her knees and her hair was wet.

He'd been sitting in the bar in the Mess having a beer with the Quartermaster, Bill Streets, discussing Dee Smithers disappearance and the murder up in *Wulfen*. As he was on duty, Clive had expected more activity under the circumstances.

"Do you think I ought to go round to the Colonel's quarter," he asked Bill. "He'll be worried sick."

"It might help," Bill said, "but then again it might do the reverse."

"Are you staying in the Mess tonight?"

"Yes, Liz has gone to the UK for a few days. Her mother's not well. I hate cooking for myself, so I'm staying in Mess while she's away."

"Look, would you mind standing in for me while I go round to see the Colonel?"

Bill Streets shrugged. "Makes no difference to me," he said. "Happy to do the whole duty for you if you want, then you can go and snuggle up to young Amy after you've been to see the Colonel. I find the very thought quite appealing – snuggling up to Amy that is, lucky bugger," Bill added, smiling.

Clive did go and see the CO, but it was obvious that Timothy Smithers didn't want to discuss what might or might not be, so Clive left him to it and went straight to Amy's flat. He was surprised she wasn't in, but she had been out a few times with Sam Cox, so he guessed that's where she was now.

When Amy returned about an hour later, Clive was sprawled on the sofa watching a video. He only needed one glance at her to realise all was not right. She had obviously been crying, she looked dishevelled and she didn't make eye contact with him.

"What on earth has happened?" He went across the room to her, but when he tried to put his hands either side of her face, she moved away, turning her back on him. "Amy, please, what is it? What has happened?"

She pushed past him. "Nothing … leave me alone." She went into the bedroom and locked the door.

Clive spent a long five minutes standing at the door trying to coax her out so that they could talk. In his mind, the state she was in meant one thing and he didn't know how to handle the situation. If Amy had been with Sam Cox, what could have happened? His mind was working overtime and imagining many previously unimaginable scenes.

Amy remained silent but shortly after he moved away from the door, she came out wearing her dressing gown. She looked at him fleetingly before scurrying into the bathroom. He crossed the room, put his ear to the door before going into the bedroom.

The black dress and jacket were on the floor – she normally took so much care with her clothes – her shoes were over by the wall, and her bra was hanging half out of the washing basket in the corner. Clive picked up the dress and inspected it. There was nothing. He took it and the jacket over to the wardrobe and hung them up. He went back to the washing basket … something was not right. Other than her discarded bra, the basket was empty. Her evening bag was on the bed so he picked it up and opened it. Her pants were the first thing he saw. Pulling the pants from the bag he noticed they were torn on both sides.

Clive sat down on the bed, still clutching the pants. "You poor, poor girl," he whispered. "What bastard did this to you?"

With a heavy heart he walked slowly to the bathroom, knocked softly on the door and when she told him it wasn't locked, he went in and sat down on the stool next to the bath. He couldn't see any bruising, but he could only see her shoulders, arms and knees. As he put his hand on her wet shoulder, she flinched.

"Amy, I don't know what to say or do," he said with a catch in his voice.

She said nothing and didn't move her head.

He stroked her wet hair. "I want to help, but I don't know how I can. I want to be here for you, but … but unless you tell me what has happened …"

He didn't want to say any more.

She had been raped.

It was the only conclusion he could draw.

Leah stared at the white tiles. She couldn’t face him.

She mustn’t let him see the marks on her throat; she would have to think of an explanation, but what?

She wanted to tell him everything, but she couldn’t.

She hadn't expected him to be here when she got home, but now she wished he was a thousand miles away. Being alone would allow her to cope in her own way and not have to think of him, or anybody else.

She could still feel Peter Bennett's fingers pressing against her throat, could still feel the horror as he raped her, but now she was scared witless by the threats he had made. He was an animal. They had made love so often and he’d always been so gentle, so caring, but the man who almost killed her and then raped her wasn’t him – he was a stranger, a sadistic monster.

He said he knew about Clive. Was that the reason why he had changed?

If she did report what had happened her background would be investigated and she would be found out, and then what? It wasn’t only her life and body that had been violated, it was also her mind, her very existence … but she couldn’t tell anyone, not even Clive.

“I found your pants,” Clive said. “Amy please tell me what has happened. I can’t help unless I know.”

Leah closed her eyes. When she had felt able to get into her car and drive, she had instinctively picked up her pants and stuffed them into her bag.

Why?

She should have left them where they were or thrown them in a bin. How stupid. God, what was she going to do? She didn’t have to tell him … clearly he already knew.

Turning her head away from the bathroom wall, she looked at him. “Will … will you get me a drink?” she whispered.

“Of course,” he said.

Chapter Sixty-Seven

Clive watched as she fell into a troubled sleep.

It was a mixture of alcohol and sheer exhaustion. After the first whisky she had another and then another. She said very little and Clive hadn't probed any further. He believed he knew what had happened and when she was ready to tell him, he hoped that would be precisely what she would do.

She was in shock and needed understanding not cross-examining.

Once she was asleep, he went into the living room and drank the remaining whisky. If he'd been asked the previous evening how he felt about Amy, he would have hesitated. She was the most gorgeous looking female he had ever been associated with, but the age gap was more of a problem for him than it appeared to be for her.

So he would have hesitated more from her perspective than his.

As he consumed his third glass of whisky, he asked himself whether he loved her. His heart had gone out to her when he saw her come back into the flat so utterly distraught. The fact that she had been violated, raped, abused, whatever anybody wanted to call it, didn't make one iota of difference. Nor did it make any difference after a considerable amount of whisky and it wouldn't make any difference in the cold light of day. None of his previous conquests had been hurt the way Amy was hurting. He didn't feel revulsion nor let his imagination work overtime. All he felt was that he had let her down. He should have been there to protect her.

God knows where she had been and with whom.

When he felt his eyes closing, he forced himself to wakefulness, then went back into the bedroom to check on Amy. The duvet had fallen on the floor, revealing her young body: its sheen, its softness and its sheer innocence. There was no bruising that he could see, although there were a few marks on her throat that hadn't been there before. How could anybody violate something so beautiful? Somebody had scarred her for life and when he found out who it was he would make sure they were equally scarred, equally violated.

He covered Amy with the duvet and went back into the living room to spend an uncomfortable night on the sofa. As he drifted off into a drink-induced sleep, he wondered again whether what he felt for Amy was love.

If love meant that he was willing to put everything on the line for her, even his life, he decided that he was in love after all.

At just after six o'clock in the morning he stirred. His mouth was dry, his head ached, and his back felt as though somebody had jumped all over it. As he tried to turn over, he groaned with the sheer effort.

"Would you like some coffee?"

His eyes shot open. He was facing the back of the sofa.

"Would you like some coffee, Clive?"

He looked over his shoulder. She was sitting in a chair, one towel round her head, another round her body, and a mug of steaming coffee in her hands. Her face was devoid of make-up but he could see nothing in her demeanour to suggest the previous evening had happened. The marks on her neck had disappeared.

"Am I dreaming?" he asked. The dryness in his mouth made speaking awkward.

"Dreaming? Why would you be dreaming?"

He swung his legs off the sofa and rubbed his eyes. "This," he said, indicating the sofa, "and the state you were in last night."

"Yes, I'm sorry about that. I never did like whisky so why I drank so much I don't know. Coffee?" she asked again, holding out her mug.

Clive screwed up his face and wondered whether he was seeing and hearing things. "Yes, coffee. Yes, I would like some coffee, please."

Amy bounced towards the kitchen, and after a few seconds, Clive followed her.

"I hope you didn't have a too uncomfortable a night," she said without turning round. "Was I snoring? I always snore when I drink too much alcohol."

Clive leaned against the worktop next to her. "Amy, what's going on? You know very well why I slept on the sofa last night."

When she turned round to give him his coffee, there was a look in her eyes that Clive had never seen before. He couldn't describe it but its message shrieked out at him. She was in total denial; she had put what had happened into her subconscious, locked it away and now, whatever it was had never taken place.

She was clearly not going to share her ordeal with him ... not yet.

"Of course I do, silly, although I missed you." She looked at him appraisingly. "You could do with a long hot bath, a shave and whatever else men do in the bathroom. Take your coffee with you and when you're comfortable I'll come and wash your back."

He took the mug of coffee and moved towards the kitchen door.

"Oh, and Clive," she added, "You must let me deal with this in my own way. All right? It did happen but I'm not even going to tell you what *it* was. All you need to know is that I love you more today than I did yesterday."

Clive put his coffee down and they met in the centre of the kitchen.

Their embrace was totally different from anything either of them had experienced before.

It was as though their very lives depended on the existence of the other.

Chapter Sixty-Eight

By a process of elimination and from information given, the search for Dee Smithers led the civil and military police to *Lüttelforst*. It hadn't yet been decided who would assume primacy over the investigation because it wasn't known whether a crime had actually been committed. After finding the abandoned car, tracing it to Dee Smithers took a matter of minutes, but nothing in the car or near it gave any further information as to where she might be.

The fact that the car was abandoned was worrying but the place in which it was found was testament enough that something very serious had happened.

Because the civil police had a more sophisticated and modern analysis system, the military authorities were happy for the car to be taken to the police headquarters in *Mönchengladbach* for forensic testing.

Sergeant Kevin Masters from the RMP and *Polizeihauptkommissar* Jurgen Hausmann from the *Kriminal Polizei* were in Mark Armstrong's flat, his identity having been discovered because his card had been found in the glove compartment of Dee Smithers' car.

"So, Mr Armstrong, you admit that you knew Mrs Dee Smithers?" Sergeant Masters was conducting the interview having ascertained that although Jurgen Hausmann's English was reasonable, he was happy to stay in the background for the time being.

Mark Armstrong appeared flustered and Jurgen Hausmann guessed his and the RMP's presence were part of the cause, but maybe if they had drawn the right conclusions, Armstrong was more worried about his affair with Dee Smithers becoming public. If proven, he would almost certainly lose his job.

"Of course I knew Mrs Smithers. She was one of my students, and we played the odd game of squash together," Mark said, sitting back in his chair.

"And how often did you see her?"

Mark shrugged. "It varied. Sometimes she would come to the centre twice or three times a week, sometimes only once."

"How long has she been attending your sessions?" Kevin Masters asked.

"For about a year."

"How old are you, Mr Armstrong?"

"What's that got … erm, thirty-five, why?"

"And were you in the Army?"

Jurgen Hausmann nodded. Kevin Masters had told him he had done a background check, so he knew quite a lot about Armstrong already.

"I was, yes. I left three years ago," Mark volunteered.

"Why did you leave?"

"I'm sorry, but I don't see the relevance of what you're asking."

"Relevant to what, Mr Armstrong," Kevin Masters asked. "What should my questions be relevant to?"

Jurgen Hausmann smiled to himself this time. He'd never had much confidence in the British military police, but he had to admit that this Sergeant Masters was good.

"I've no idea. You haven't told me why you are here. All I know is that you're making enquiries about Mrs Smithers – is she missing or something?"

"Should she be?"

"How would I bloody know?"

"When did you last see her?"

"A couple of days ago, she came down for one of her normal sessions."

"And what sort of sessions are those?"

The front doorbell rang and because the door was next to where Jurgen Hausmann was sitting, he opened it.

"*Herr* Hausmann," Detective Helmut Schenke said. "*Ich denke, daß Sie kommen sollten, zu haben einen Blick an, was wir gefunden haben*."

Jurgen Hausmann looked across at Kevin Masters. "I will go, Sergeant," he said. "Detective Schenke says he has found something."

Jurgen Hausmann followed the detective, leaving the door slightly ajar.

Turning back to Mark Armstrong, Kevin Masters said, "I'm sorry, Mr Armstrong, you were about to tell me about the session Mrs Smithers last attended."

"Well, erm, it was aerobics … aerobics and then a game of squash on Tuesdays and Thursdays," he said, his eyes darting from the door to Sergeant Masters and back again.

"I asked you earlier why you left the Army, Mr Armstrong. Would you care to enlighten me?"

"I don't see –"

"Mr Armstrong," Kevin Masters said patiently, "I have your details. It would only take me a couple of phone calls to find out the answer to my question. Do you not think it would be better if it came from you?"

Mark Armstrong bowed his head. “There was an accusation.”
“What sort of accusation?”
Mark looked up, his expression now defiant. “I was accused of rape.”
Kevin Masters nodded. “And?”
“It never got to court because the girl withdrew the accusation.”
“So why did you leave?”
“You bloody know why, you know how the bloody Army works. Courts are irrelevant. If the Army decides you are bloody guilty regardless of the circumstances, you can kiss your career on the arse. They forced me out. They did me on an admin discharge and I got nothing. After fourteen years’ service, I got fucking nothing.”
Kevin Masters didn’t want to let him off the hook. “How old was the girl who made the accusation of rape?”
“What’s that –”
“Mr Armstrong, you know from your military experience that I can find out every detail if I want to. How old was she?”
“Fifteen.”
“You were accused of raping a fifteen-year old girl, is that right?”
“Yes, but I told you she withdrew the accusation. It never got anywhere.”
“And what about Mrs Smithers? Could she accuse you of anything?”
“What are you fucking getting at? I’m not sure you have any right to be asking me these questions anyway, not on your own. Where’s the other bloke?”
“There were three implied questions there, Mr Armstrong. Let me take each in turn,” Kevin Masters said smoothly. “I’m not getting at anything. All I’m attempting to do is establish your relationship with Mrs Smithers. Secondly, I have every right to ask you these questions because as you work for NAAFI in Germany, you come under military law and I am a representative of that law. As to where the other bloke is, Detective Inspector Hausmann has popped out for a minute or two and will be back shortly. Now, back to Mrs Smithers and your relationship with her, we found a card from you ...”
The door opened further and Inspector Hausmann looked at Kevin Masters. “Can you step outside, Sergeant Masters, please?”
“I won’t be a second,” Kevin Masters told Mark Armstrong, who was sitting forward in his chair, looking extremely worried.
“Yes, Inspector,” he said, once outside.
“They’ve found some clothes in the rubbish skip at the entrance. There’s a jogging suit and women’s underwear, and somebody has made an attempt to burn them.”

"I see. Is there sufficient material left for them to be recognised?" Kevin Masters asked.

"Yes."

"What a bloody fool. You'd have thought he'd have got rid of them rather than leave them there, wouldn't you?"

Inspector Hausmann smiled. "I do not think we are dealing with an immense brain in *Herr* Armstrong. He is an over-confident, arrogant man who knows more than he is telling you. He thinks he is smart, but I think we now know what he is *not* telling you."

"I'm inclined to agree with you, but we must establish whose clothing this is before we –"

"Of course, Sergeant, but can I suggest that our men stay here while we go and see Colonel Smithers?"

"Exactly what I was going to suggest," Kevin Masters said.

Chapter Sixty-Nine

"Colonel Smithers, we're sorry to disturb you at this time of the evening," Sergeant Masters said.

As agreed, Mark Armstrong had been left under the watchful eyes of their subordinates. It was just after six o'clock and a very strained looking Timothy Smithers had opened the front door to them.

"Not at all," the colonel informed them, "you know that you can call at any time of the day or night, I just want my wife back safe and sound. Come in."

The sergeant and inspector exchanged looks as they went into the living room. It was a spacious room: the front windows overlooked the main road running through *Bracht* village, and on the opposite side of the room French widows opened onto a large and well stocked garden.

Sergeant Masters took the exhibit bag from the Inspector. "There are a few items of clothing to look at to see if you can identify them," he said.

Timothy Smithers sat down, glancing from one policeman to the other. He had lost any remaining colour from his face. "My God," he said. "They're Dee's, aren't they?"

"We don't know, Sir, that's why we need you to look at them." After putting on a pair of latex gloves Sergeant Masters opened the bag. "I can't let you touch them, Sir, we may need to conduct tests later and the least number of people who have handled them the better." He extracted the burnt joggers first. "Do you recognise these, Sir?"

Timothy Smithers just stared at what he was being shown, then closed his eyes and nodded. "They're Dee's or very much like the ones she wears."

"And these, Sir?" Kevin Masters showed him a pair of pants and a bra.

"Yes, I … I think so. Where did you find them?"

"I am afraid we cannot say at this stage," Inspector Hausmann said. "But there is no doubt in your mind that they belong to your wife?"

"I cannot say for sure but certainly Dee has joggers, pants and a bra like these. They are nothing special, just something she wears for her trips down to *Rhinedahlen*."

"Thank you, Sir." Masters looked at the Inspector, who nodded. Turning back to Timothy Smithers he asked, "Sir, does the name Mark Armstrong mean anything to you?"

Timothy either didn't hear or ignored his question. "She's dead isn't she?"

Inspector Hausmann spoke again. "There is no way of knowing one way or the other at the moment, Colonel. However, I must advise you that if these items are definitely your wife's then, yes, there is a possibility that she may have come to some harm, or she is being held somewhere against her will."

"But why, why would anybody want to harm her?" There were tears in Timothy Smithers eyes as he spoke.

"Sir, do you have a hair brush or comb belonging to your wife that we could take with us for DNA testing?"

"Yes, of course." Timothy Smithers began to get up, but sat down again. "If you find her you will tell me straight away, won't you? It's the children you see, they don't know their mother is missing yet and if the worst becomes reality, I must be the one to tell them."

"We understand, Sir, and you have our assurance."

Timothy left the room returning after a few minutes with a hairbrush.

"Thank you, Sir." Sergeant Masters dropped the brush into another bag. "We'll keep you informed, but as the inspector suggested, we do think you should prepare yourself for the worst."

"Yes, I suppose I must."

"Is there anybody you would like to be with you, Sir?" Kevin Masters asked as they moved towards the front door.

"No, it's all right, I mean, I'll be all right, but thank you for asking."

"Are you sure, Sir?"

"Yes, yes," Timothy replied almost impatiently, "if I need anybody I'll … well, I think I may prefer to be on my own anyway."

"Very well, Sir. We'll keep you informed."

The two detectives were half way down the path when Inspector Hausmann stopped and went back to Timothy Smithers. "Colonel, I am not suggesting there is a connection but were you aware that a corporal's wife was recently found murdered not far from the British ammunition depot in *Wulfen*."

"Yes, Inspector, I'm only too aware of what happened there. I speak with the CO at *Wulfen* nearly every day and we share confidences. It was an awful occurrence. You say you're not suggesting a connection. I thought the woman's husband had been arrested and charged with the murder, so why do you ask?"

"We go for years without there being any serious civil crimes committed by members of the British forces, and then in the space of only a few weeks, and without including the IRA atrocities, we have a woman murdered in *Wulfen* and now your wife is missing – and I am afraid we must assume the worst. I do not always believe in coincidences, Colonel. Do you?"

"Inspector, under the circumstances I find your questions a little insensitive. Although I will assume the worst as you advise, I will pray that my wife is still alive. Only if she is found dead will I draw any conclusions with regard to coincidences."

"Thank you, Colonel. I am sorry if I appeared inconsiderate but all avenues must be explored."

"I understand," Colonel Smithers said before closing the door.

"What do you think, Inspector?" Sergeant Masters asked as they turned left onto the main road and headed back towards *Lüttelforst*.

"You know my suspicions, I –"

"No, I mean about Colonel Smithers, do you think he could have had anything to do with her disappearance?"

"No, Sergeant, I do not. I have been a detective for more years than I care to remember, but in that time I have learnt an awful lot about the human race. His concern was too genuine. I think we can strike the good colonel from our list of suspects. I also believe that he was very much in love with his wife, but all was not right with their relationship. I could see it in his eyes."

"What could you see?"

"Guilt, but not of the kind we are looking for," the inspector said.

"And do you think there's a connection between the *Wulfen* murder and this one?"

"If it is murder we are investigating, then yes, Sergeant, it is certainly an option I think we will need to explore further."

"And what about Mark Armstrong? Do we have enough to arrest him?"

"That is a matter of opinion, Sergeant, but first we must establish jurisdiction. I am going to recommend that we are given primacy in this case. Do you have any objections?"

"Not at all, Inspector, but I would like to continue to work with you if you are happy?"

"My dear Sergeant," Inspector Hausmann said, "I would not want it any other way."

Chapter Seventy

Sylvia Donnelly had been waiting in her car for more than thirty minutes.

It wasn't like him to be late.

Something must have happened.

Their meetings had been infrequent, but each time they met they always had sex before discussing their next move. They needed each other in more ways than one. Once he had officially left Germany and the Army, they had always met at the *Forsthotel*. She accepted that after their first meeting in Rosa's Bar, and once they formed a working as well as a physical relationship, discretion was paramount. This agreement suited her down to the ground. Flatterly believed that her aberration had run its course. He believed Peter Bennett was no longer involved, and she may have incurred a black mark against her, but what was going to happen would put her well and truly back in credit. The unknowing owner of the car bomb had access to the depot so it would be so easy.

No wires to cut, no risks to take.

But what about Peter Bennett?

She would continue to enjoy him for a little longer but then he would be told his fortune – he might be with G2 but that didn't mean the relationship needed to continue afterwards. Perhaps it would be necessary to dispose of him: she could always say he was a legitimate target. One of the others would do that because she wouldn't be able to do it herself. It would be bad enough being told that he had been taken care of, but having his blood on her hands was one thing she was willing to live with as long as she didn't do it herself. Anyway, she wasn't equipped to kill a man with his expert training. He would have to be disposed of from a distance. When the time came, she would set up a meeting, somewhere remote. In fact where she was now would be perfect.

For once she would not be early.

It would be better if she were not present. His appointment would be with a bullet in the back, fired by Pat. Pat would enjoy killing him especially when she told him she had discovered that he was a bomb disposal expert. She'd be sorry to lose Peter Bennett but he would have served his purpose in more ways than one.

Sylvia was jolted back to the present as the passenger door opened and Peter Bennett slipped into the seat next to her.

"Sorry I'm late," he said. "There was an unexpected complication."

Sylvia put a hand on his thigh and turning her head, expected to be kissed. When he didn't oblige she said, "Not anything to worry about, I hope."

"No, not at all, just the need for a little gentle persuasion."

"Do you want to tell me about it?"

"Nothing to tell, really."

Peter Bennett smiled to himself as Sylvia glanced out of the side window into blackness.

Ironically, the cars were parked only a hundred yards from where the still undiscovered body of Dee Smithers lay and it would be Ursula Dorf's last resting place as well.

Leah had really annoyed him. She had upset both his plans and his control. When they were at the riverside, she had been seconds away from losing consciousness, but it was good that he'd stopped, regardless of what the voices were saying to him. Driving back from *Roermond* to meet Sylvia, he decided that perhaps Leah deserved a different sort of death. Yes, he wanted to look into her eyes as she breathed her final breath and to be the last person she saw before passing into oblivion, but he also wanted her to see, to acknowledge, that the control had always been his. She would do what he wanted without question, then she, out of his five chosen victims, would suffer the most.

Her death would be slow and he would be with her every step of the way.

"What happened doesn't upset our plans does it?" Sylvia said, breaking into his thoughts and taking her hand from his thigh. She will have sensed something was wrong. A few words of greeting followed by sex were the norm.

"No, it will happen as we discussed," he said in a monotone.

"I want to talk about that further when you're ready."

He stared through the windscreen. There wasn't a sound: even the usual night noises were masked by the confines of the car. In a matter of days he will have achieved what he had set out to do. His conscience would be clear.

The need for revenge, and the voices would be satisfied and afterwards they would leave him alone. They had promised.

The woman sitting next to him would be next. Then Ursula. And finally – Leah.

He had taken the lives of two women already … it had been so easy, so incredibly easy.

And so satisfying ... exhilarating. Although he hadn't killed Leah, the look in her eyes as his fingers pressed on her windpipe was enough to make him need her.

With Sylvia Donnelly and Ursula Ivanovitch, he would be liquidating enemies, not only his enemies but enemies of the state. They were both intent in their own way of bringing harm to a system of which he used to be a part. A system that had kicked him in the teeth, but it was still his system. He was the only one who had the right to do it damage.

Sylvia Donnelly was scum.

Somebody who killed innocent people and children indiscriminately deserved to die.

Ursula Ivanovitch was different. Her motives were far more serious. She represented another system, a system that was so hypocritical that anybody associated with it deserved to die. As she died, part of her system would die with her.

Discovering Sylvia Donnelly's identity from intelligence files while in Northern Ireland was fortunate and not just a coincidence. She was supposed to be at the farm, but she hadn't been there, now he knew why. His photographic memory had logged all the details and her image was engraved on his mind. And the rest was history. He still had contacts who had given him the extra information he needed.

Ursula Ivanovitch was different again. She was an incredible but fortuitous coincidence. He hadn't known anything about her until he'd gone to *Bracht* but from the moment he saw her she became so bloody obvious. You only had to look at Manfred Dorf and then at her to realise what was going on.

But Ursula wasn't scum.

Ursula was probably as good as he was, but in a different way. That is why he had to seduce her, although she had to believe she had seduced him. He fed her the right lines, told her what she wanted to hear so she believed he was ripe for picking. Unusual as it was, he knew she had been in contact with her *minder* and he guessed being told to back off hadn't pleased her. But like Sylvia Donnelly, when a woman believes she is right then no man will ever understand what the word *obdurate* really means.

Little Leah Carmichael was the catalyst … the link.

Sylvia Donnelly believed that Leah's recruitment was for her own purposes, as did Ursula Ivanovitch. It had been marvellous to watch. An IRA killer, a Russian assassin – and little innocent Leah Carmichael: it had turned out better than he could have prayed for.

Dee Smithers?

Well, she had just got up his nose. If it hadn't been her, somebody else would have come along.

His revenge was almost complete; he was reaching the climax. And then?

Then he would just disappear.

Nobody would ever connect him to the murders of either Sandra Davies or Dee Smithers. Sylvia Donnelly and Ursula Ivanovitch were the really masterful strokes. If found and their deaths investigated, the authorities would clamp down on anything being made public – embarrassment was something a government could do without. Being taken out by undercover assassins working for the British or German Government, which wouldn't be too far from the truth, would guarantee files would be buried or destroyed altogether.

Both Governments would deny their involvement. That was a matter of routine. Denial was a politician's right, wasn't it? But he wished he could be there when they had their internal enquiries.

Who had sanctioned the killings?

Who had authorised them in the first place?

What a coup!

Leah?

Little innocent Leah?

He could hear them now.

Subversives at university would get the blame for turning the innocent Leah Carmichael — aka Amy Carpenter — into a terrorist car-bomber. Unbelievable? She was recruited, brainwashed, radicalised, had her identity changed and sent to Germany. The blonde hair, the chocolate-box face, the trim figure and the butter-wouldn't-melt-in-her-mouth attitude: who would believe that subversives could turn somebody so incredibly innocent and attractive? But she was, wasn't she? She was the one who drove a car bomb from the UK to Germany and then when the right day arrived, parked it in the middle of a British Army ammunition depot. Perhaps we ought to learn a lesson or two from that one?

Peter smiled a smug smile and shook his head slowly at the wonderment of it all.

It had all come together so very easily, and he had coped with minor upsets – like this evening – without a problem. If Leah hadn't been around to plant the bomb, Sylvia or Ursula would have stepped into her shoes ... but that wouldn't be necessary now.

It was a pity he'd had to rape her but she had needed to have things spelled out ... and he needed the release. He had never raped a woman before, never wanted to or needed to, although there was some satisfaction in seeing her sheer terror and pain. If she had stayed compliant it would never have happened. She deserved to be punished and she was now back under his control – probably more so than before, because now she was too scared to do anything about it. It was a risk, but one that had been necessary and therefore worth taking.

Sylvia was next.

Then Ursula.

He would get particular satisfaction from watching Ursula die because he wanted to see her face when she realised she had been the one taken in, not him.

It would be wonderful.

Chapter Seventy-One

It was beginning to drizzle.

Sylvia glanced sideways … his eyes had glazed over, but she had learned to be patient. He had often gone into suspended animation, deep in thought. She always wanted to know what he was thinking about but after her first attempt to get him to talk, and the look she got, she backed off. He would talk when he was ready.

He was nearly ready now. He was blinking more frequently, and his eyes were less glazed. He was nearly back with her. Should she pre-empt his complete return? She decided to take the risk. Putting her hand back on his thigh, she moved it up his leg until her fingers touched the front of his trousers. She watched him carefully. His lips parted, but he continued to stare through the windscreen. She felt for the zip, pulling it down slowly. Her fingers slipped inside.

"Don't," he said, grasping her wrist and pulling her hand away.

"But, we always –"

"Not this time." There must be no evidence, nothing that would connect him to his victims.

"Why? You know we both need each other." Sylvia was worried. He'd changed. Previously he was always willing, but now he was different and today he was acting even more strangely than before.

Peter moved his head slightly, and for the first time in a very long time, Sylvia Donnelly felt genuinely frightened. He was glaring at her. There wasn't a flicker of emotion on his face and even in the dim light she could see that his eyes were not part of him. There was something going on behind those eyes and she needed to know what it was.

"You said you wanted to talk," he said, his voice still a monotone.

Sylvia moved away from him. Something was very wrong. What had happened? Why had he been late? Why wouldn't he tell her? "It can wait," she said.

"No. If you've got something on your mind then I want to hear about it now."

The drizzle turned to rain. The drops plopping on the roof of the car were like a clock clicking out of control. "I don't think you're in the right frame of mind."

"You have no idea what frame of mind I'm in." He was still glaring at her, his hands still resting on his thighs.

"I ... I wanted to suggest a change of plan," she began. She could feel the 9mm Beretta against her back, tucked into the waistband of her jeans. She always carried a pistol when she was out on her own; it was her insurance, and it was worth the risk. Trying to steady her voice, she said, "I've been taking a closer look at the ammunition depot, and I think maybe it would better if we changed where we put the car bomb."

"I showed you the depot a year ago and we chose the location then."

"Yes, I know," Sylvia said, "but that was before you recruited this Carpenter woman."

"What's she got to do with it? She'll do as she's told," he said angrily.

"I know, but trying to get the car inside a building containing ammunition worries me. Even she might question what she's being asked to do. Why else would she be told to park her car in the depot ... and leave it?"

"I know what I'm doing – but what are you suggesting?"

"The open sites, where the RAF bombs are stored. Wouldn't one of those be better?"

Peter was silent for a few seconds. "It's a possibility," he said. "We would have to position the car very carefully because it would need to be in line of sight and no more than two hundred yards from whoever is controlling the remote. The car would have to be right next to the bombs, otherwise we wouldn't achieve sympathetic detonation. We would just scatter them about a bit … in other words have little effect."

"Leave the remote to me," she said. "It will be done. I've looked at the depot from every angle, and the conditions you want are there. But only in the open sites."

"I know the inside of the depot well enough to know that it's not only getting the position of the car right for detonation, but also making sure it's next to something that will have the desired effect. Munitions near the car would need to be thin skinned. It would be a futile exercise if we just caused a firework display. Do something like you're suggesting and it would have to be catastrophic. There's little point otherwise."

Sylvia relaxed a little. She sensed that he was returning to normal – well, as normal as he ever was, and he was paying attention to what she was saying. "The two hundred yards you mentioned – what if the remote is operated inside the depot rather than from outside the perimeter fence, which is what I think you were suggesting?"

Peter shrugged. “Then it could be anywhere.”

“The fence is easy to cut. The dogs and their handlers are so laid back and don’t patrol as conscientiously as they ought to. It would be very easy to get somebody in, detonate the bomb, and get them out without being detected.”

“And who would that be?”

“I’ve got the ideal person.”

“I thought you might have,” he said.

“But the problem for us would have been getting a big enough bomb into the depot in the first place. Because of you, and what we planned together, that problem has never existed, but the person I’m thinking of doesn’t know that yet.”

“So what you’re suggesting is that Amy Carpenter drives her car into the depot, leaves it in an open site close to the RAF bombs and then walks out, leaving her car there.”

“Yes.”

Sylvia Donnelly was now relaxed. Amy Carpenter wouldn’t be blown to pieces as the bomb exploded after all but Pat would get the opportunity to put a bullet into her brain instead. He would like that.

Peter shrugged. “All right,” he said. “I agree.”

Chapter Seventy-Two

As Peter Bennett drove back to *Frankenmühle* and to Ursula Dorf, he was considering a third change of plan. All this talk of remotes, line of sight and proximity was necessary to keep Sylvia happy, but it would never happen. He admired his own flexibility, especially the way in which he allowed alternative doors to open as others closed.

The voices agreed.

"Ursula Ivanovitch will now have the grave I've dug for Sylvia Donnelly," he said to himself as he parked the car round the back of the barn. "She's become an unnecessary complication now and I need Sylvia a little longer."

Climbing the stairs to the top floor garret flat, he smiled in anticipation of the fun he was about to have. The excitement sent his blood coursing through his veins.

"You're late," Ursula said as he let himself into the flat. Curled up in an easy chair, she had a book on her lap and it looked as though she had recently showered. She was wearing a white towelling dressing gown, and there was a small towel wrapped round her wet hair.

"I told you I was going to be late," he said, throwing his jacket onto the back of a chair.

"Yes, but you did not say how late."

Regardless of his intentions, Peter had always found Ursula's Russian accent appealing – the almost childlike over-emphasis on the preciseness of each English syllable – but now that it was her turn to die the intonations were beginning to grate.

After pouring himself a whisky, he leant against the cupboard. "Well I'm back now."

She put the book down and looked at him. "Do I detect a problem?" she asked, uncurling her legs.

He took a large gulp of whisky. "The little bitch decided that she no longer wanted to be part of what she referred to as *my little game*. She needed to be taught a lesson."

"And that is what you did, is it?" Ursula said sarcastically. "You taught her a lesson so that she is now obedient again."

"Something like that."

"And what sort of lesson did you teach her?"

"She needed a few things explaining to her," he said.

"Will you get me one of those," she said, indicating the whisky, "because it sounds as though I will need it."

Peter poured three-fingers of whisky into a glass. Breathing in the aroma of her scent as he handed the drink to her, he felt himself becoming aroused again, not because he intended having sex with her but because he knew that within a very short space of time she would be dead.

"Did you take time off as we discussed?" he asked.

"Of course. That is what we agreed. I am now on holiday for the next two weeks so that I am free to do what needs to be done."

"And where does he think you are?"

"By *he* I presume you mean Manfred? He thinks I am visiting friends down near *Koblenz.*"

"What friends?"

"That he does not need to know."

"What if you're seen in this area?"

"I did not say I would be down there for all my holiday. Anyway, the same applies to you. There are some people here who will remember you," she said.

"I've told you before – I can take care of myself."

"Then grant me the same respect. I want to know more about what happened with Amy Carpenter."

Peter smiled for the first time since returning to the flat. "It would be best if I showed you."

"Showed me? Why? What have you done to her?" Ursula leant forward in the chair, her dressing gown falling slightly open.

"Get dressed, and I'll show you."

"But it's approaching midnight."

"It's better if we go when there's nobody else about, especially on a night like this."

"Peter, what have you done? We needed her?"

"You will see," he said.

Half an hour later Peter parked his car in the same place from which he had taken Dee Smithers to her death. It was also where he had recently been with Sylvia Donnelly, but he wasn't worried about being seen: it was well after midnight and there was nobody about.

Ursula had put on a pair of jeans, running shoes, a loose top, and a waterproof.

As she got out of the car she said, "I hope this is worth it, Peter."

He closed the door behind her. "In a few minutes you'll see why I had to bring you here."

It was still raining, although not quite so heavily, and the trees were dripping water on them as they walked. The path was muddy but leading the way with his powerful flashlight Peter made sure he kept to the harder grassed area.

Getting to within twenty yards of where he buried Dee Smithers, he switched direction down another narrow overgrown track.

"If you have done what I believe you have done, Peter, I think you have been very, very stupid." Ursula looked up and when raindrops fell into her eyes she pulled the hood further over her head. "I cannot understand why you had to do this. You said she needed to be taught a lesson, so why here?"

Peter said nothing.

They were nearly there.

He shone the light to his left, and through some small fir trees he could see what he was looking for.

Ursula followed him.

He shone the torch into the hole he had dug.

"But it is empty," Ursula said.

Peter stepped to one side as he withdrew the knife from its scabbard.

"For the moment," he said as he moved behind her.

As he expected, she suddenly sensed that she was in danger. As her training took over she lunged to one side, rolling over as she did and coming up in a crouch as she tried to see where Peter might be. He knew she was unarmed and that the realisation she was in danger would be generating the adrenalin she needed. She would be confident that she was a match for any man.

Having deliberately shone the torch in her eyes seconds earlier, it was obvious that in the resulting gloom she didn't know where he was. Her breathing steadied as she listened for any sound that would give his position away. Once she could see as well as he could, they would be on equal terms. Her mind would be racing, wondering why and how she had got it so wrong. They had been together for a long time and not once would she have detected anything that would have raised her suspicions. She had believed he was now as devoted to what needed to be done as she was, but for different reasons. He needed revenge against a system that had ruined him.

He smiled.

She felt his breath first and then his arm as it went round the front of her neck. A classic error she thought as she dropped to one knee, twisting her body so that she could throw him over her shoulder.

Nothing happened.

She took a deep breath, dropped further forward and tried again. It was like trying to lift a ton of concrete.

As his arm tightened about her throat she felt a sharp jab just above her right hip.

She felt no pain.

His mouth was next to her ear.

"Do you know what that is?" he whispered, pushing the thin blade further into her body.

He released her and she fell forward onto the soaking wet ground. Yes, she knew what it was, but why hadn't he killed her? She felt the blade as he withdrew it, but still there was no pain, but that would come in a matter of seconds.

He rolled her over onto her back. She could just make out his shape as he knelt above her. Her laboured breathing suggested he had punctured a lung.

Taking a deep rasping breath she tried bringing her knee up as hard as she could towards the shape in front of her. He was too quick. His foot was on her leg, forcing it back to the ground.

"Don't be silly. Just accept the fact that you are already dying. It won't be long, just long enough for us to have a little chat."

Her right arm was pinned underneath her: he had his knee on the other. What had he done to her legs? She couldn't move them.

He reached over for the flashlight, switched it on and placed it on the ground so that she could see him. "There," he said, "it's so rude talking to somebody if you can't see them."

He unzipped her waterproof, then with the razor sharp knife he sliced through her cotton top, exposing her upper body. Her skin glistened as raindrops fell on it.

Her breathing was getting harder. Now she knew why he hadn't killed her. He wanted to watch; he wanted to see her die slowly.

Why?

The tip of the knife was against her nipple.

"Have you nothing to say? I'm the last face you'll ever see, and yet you have nothing to say. Surely you want to call me names. Let's hear a few Russian profanities. What is *you fucking bastard* in Russian, something like *blya ublyudok*, isn't it? Come on, Ursula, where's that fighting spirit you tried to show a few moments ago?"

She closed her eyes. She tried to speak. Her voice was a groan. The pain had hit her and was becoming more intense. She knew she was bleeding to death.

"Why?" she asked, her voice a whisper.

"Why?" he repeated. "Why have I killed you? I would have thought that was obvious. Because you are the enemy, that's why. Of course, being female is an absolute bonus, and if you'll excuse the pun, it kills two birds with one stone. Your death will rid the earth of another enemy of the State, and there will be one less scheming female on this earth. It's as simple as that, you see – two birds with one stone."

"Why …?" she closed her eyes again. The pain was becoming unbearable. "Why … why have you waited … so long?"

"Just because everyone else walks round with their eyes closed doesn't mean to say I had to. If your controllers put you into Germany as a representative of their elite agents, then I feel sorry for the rest. Ursula, you were so obvious. The moment I set eyes on you I knew what you were."

When he saw her eyes begin to flicker, he moved the point of the blade to her throat. "Come on Ursula Ivanovitch, it's very rude to ask a man a question and then die on him before he can give his answer."

Her eyes closed completely.

"Ah, well, I will just have to assume you can still hear me. You asked why I waited so long. That's a fair question and one that I'll attempt to answer in just a few words so that you don't have to hang around for too long. There had to be five of you. You were going to be the fourth, but as I explained I had a bit of bother tonight and I had to bring you up the order. You've got good company here. You will have heard that 'God Almighty's' – that's Lieutenant Colonel Timothy Smithers to you – you will have heard his wife is missing. She's lying about twenty yards from here, at peace as you soon will be. Then there's Sandra Davies, a slut of the highest order. I added her to the list to make it up to five. She could have been anyone, but she was a scheming little bitch. She died because it was convenient that she should die. The police have arrested her husband, exactly as I planned. He had every reason to kill her. I suppose if the truth be known, I did him a favour."

Peter put his fingers against Ursula's neck.

"Still a slight pulse," he said, "but it's very weak. It won't be long now, Ursula. Anyway, I've nearly finished." He paused, lifting his head to let the raindrops run down his face. "Revenge, my dear Ursula, is a human failing. I am human, I couldn't do what I've done if I wasn't, could I? Only we humans kill for pleasure." He placed the point of the commando knife just under her left breast, broke the surface of the skin, then pushed the blade into her heart.

"And it's been a pleasure killing you, Captain Ursula Ivanovitch," he whispered.

Chapter Seventy-Three

"*Polizeihauptkommissar* Wilhelm Gauler," he said into the mouthpiece, twisting his watch so that he could see the time.

It was just after seven-thirty on Monday morning, and other than the duty staff, he was the first one in. He was in early because he had a backlog of paperwork to get through. Leaving his wife sleeping wasn't easy but he loved his job as well.

In a job where you can be, and invariably were, called out all hours of the day or night, going into work early and voluntarily didn't go down too well but she wouldn't know until she woke up. He had left her a note to say he loved her.

"My name is Jurgen Hausmann," his caller said. "I'm your opposite number in *Mönchengladbach.* I don't think we have ever met, have we?"

"Jurgen Hausmann, did you say? No, I know a Jurgen Hausmann but he's not a police inspector. How can I help you?"

"Firstly, I apologise for calling you so early but it is necessary, Inspector."

"I understand, although you're lucky to find me in this early, but it has been a relatively quiet weekend."

"Lucky for some I suppose," Jurgen said. "Inspector, I am ringing about a murder that happened on your patch a few weeks ago. I saw the brief details on the usual reports we exchange."

"In the last few weeks you say. Well, there have been three. Which one are you interested in?"

"It was a British woman, a *Frau* Sandra Davies."

"Oh yes, the British woman. A nasty business," Willy said.

"Your report said that you had arrested her husband, Corporal Trevor Davies."

"Not only arrested, but he was charged and he is being held in *Münster.* Bail was refused."

"Has he admitted to killing his wife?" Jurgen asked.

"No, no, not at all. He has not changed his initial story. Everything he says is the same as before. He's either telling the truth or he is fooling us all and lying about what really happened."

"I think he may be innocent," Jurgen told his opposite number.

Wilhelm Gauler sat forward in his chair, suddenly very interested. “What makes you say that?”

“Before I answer your question, may I ask how she died? It said in the report that she was stabbed.”

“There are stabbings and stabbings. This one was unusual in that a very thin blade or a similarly pointed object was used.”

“Have you found the weapon?”

“No,” Willy said. “The area round where she was found was clean, as was the flat she shared with her husband.”

“Was there anything strange about where or how she was found – I mean anything out of the ordinary?”

“I suppose the fact that a very thin blade was used was unusual. It's normally a carving knife taken out of a kitchen drawer. The pathologist said this one was uniform in shape. The blade was razor sharp on both sides and it could have been a military issue knife. It was a very professional job, in between the second and third ribs and straight into the heart. She would have felt very little before she died.”

“Was there anything else?”

“She was found in a shallow grave. She was naked, her arms had been crossed over her chest and her eyes were closed.”

“Was there any evidence of a sexual attack?” Jurgen asked.

“No, none but she’d had sexual intercourse about three hours before she died, but that was with her husband, the man who has been charged. He said it was their ritual, sex before breakfast on a Sunday. There was no bruising or scratches on her body, nothing under her fingernails. If it wasn’t such an open and shut case, we may have had difficulty in catching whoever it was.”

“Why is it such and open and shut case?”

“Ah,” Willy said. “This goes back to your point that he may not have done it. Well, I am sorry to disappoint you, Inspector, but her husband had every reason to want her dead. She was what the British amusingly refer to as ‘the local bike’. Evidently she liked being ridden by more than just her husband, in fact, without exaggerating too much, it was more difficult to find someone who hadn’t been to bed with her rather than someone who had … no that’s an exaggeration, but I’m sure you know what I mean … hence the colloquialism I used. No, Corporal Davies had every reason – if she’d been my wife I may have felt the same.”

“Is there any evidence other than conjecture?” Jurgen asked. “Sorry, I didn’t mean that the way it sounded, but there are many husbands and wives out there who have just cause to want their opposite number dead, but, fortunately for us, very few go through with it.”

"I understand what you are saying and no offence taken, but yes, there is some pretty damning evidence. She had gone out to get some bread rolls on the Sunday morning after having sex as was their custom. The man in the bread shop remembered the time she arrived and the time she left almost to the exact minute. It seems that he looked forward to her visit every week, always very disappointed when her husband went instead. He had a thing about her. He not only remembered the time she was in his shop but also what she was wearing. We found the exact same clothes neatly folded away in the main bedroom in the flat. Someone saw her parking her car behind the *Sparkässe* Bank in the village, but nobody saw her leave, although the same person did see a man, Corporal Davies as it turns out, collecting the car later. After the discovery of her body, Corporal Davies initially tried to tell us that she was in the UK visiting friends and relatives when in fact he said later, when he changed his story, he didn't know where she was. He swears he did not murder her, but I'm afraid the evidence suggests otherwise."

"Bear with me a little longer, Inspector," Jurgen said, "then I will get to the point of my phone call."

"Certainly."

"When did you last investigate a case where a husband stabbed his wife to death, stripped her and then buried her, before taking her blood spattered clothes home and putting them away?"

"Ah, you raise another matter," Willy said. "We believe she may have been naked when she was killed. There was no evidence on the clothing we found – the clothing we know she was wearing when she went to the bread shop."

"He may have washed them," Jurgen suggested.

"No, analysis suggested they hadn't been washed recently."

"Don't you think that strange?" Jurgen asked.

"Now, you mention it, maybe, yes. However, back to your question, I must say in the twenty or so cases with which I have been involved, I cannot remember another case where a knife like the one they think was used was the murder weapon. It's usually a beating, or strangulation or a carving knife, and sometimes poison, but never ... you have a point, if you'll excuse my choice of words."

Jurgen Hausmann sniggered. "I have kept you waiting long enough, but one more question. When did you last investigate the murder of a British serviceman's wife?"

"About five years ago. She was out jogging in the woods south of *Münster* ... raped and then bludgeoned to death. The usual, you know."

"So the motive was rape?"

"That is what the court decided, yes," Willy said.

"Thank you, Inspector, you have been most helpful and very patient. I will get to the point now. A British officer's wife, in fact he is the Commanding Officer of the ammunition depot in *Bracht*, went missing last Tuesday. We have not found her yet, but we have found her clothing. Other than a few mud stains, there was nothing on the clothing that was of help. We found the partially burnt clothing in a rubbish bin behind a flat complex in *Lüttelforst*, a village a few kilometres from the Joint Headquarters in *Rhinedahlen*. She had been to a keep-fit and squash class at the leisure centre the day she went missing, and the manager from the leisure centre lives in one of the flats in *Lüttelforst*. We have established that he and the missing woman were having an affair."

"Then I think he must know where she is," Inspector Gauler said.

Jurgen nodded. "Yes. That is the logical conclusion. But like your Corporal Davies, the man concerned – a man called Mark Armstrong – is adamant that he knew nothing of her disappearance. He admits he was having an affair with the missing woman – her name is Dee Smithers – and that they had slept together the afternoon she went missing. He even admits she wanted to end the affair the same day and he wasn't happy, but he swears he doesn't know where she might be or how her clothing got into the rubbish bin he uses. It might surprise you, Inspector, but I am inclined to believe him."

"I see," Willy said. "You are suggesting that there may be a connection between your missing British wife and my murdered British wife?"

"Exactly!"

"And what would you like me to do?"

"It's a long shot, but now that I know this Sandra Davies was having affairs, maybe you could get a list of those you can find out about, and if I do the same this end, perhaps, you never know, we may discover something."

"I will gladly do that," Willy said, "and I know precisely where I will start – Corporal Davies himself, but as I suggested it might be a longish list. He has been very open with the fact that he knew what his wife was up to, but to date he was unwilling to name names. If, though, he thinks it will help his cause, he may choose to be a little more forthcoming."

"Thank you," Jurgen said, "I will ring you again in a few days. If anything comes up this end, I will also let you know. I'm afraid we are more than likely dealing with murder here as well."

"I'm sorry to hear that."

"One final thing and it's only just come to me regardless of it being so obvious," Jurgen said. "As well as the probability that we will find another British soldier's wife dead only a couple of weeks after Sandra Davies' body was discovered, there is also the connection that both women were married to men who worked in British ammunition depots. I appreciate the connection is somewhat tenuous, but it is a connection."

"You're right. It is obvious … a coincidence, maybe, but one that is worth bearing in mind."

"I have discovered too often and sometimes to my cost, that the obvious is often overlooked."

"I am the same," Willy said. "Tell me, do you have primacy over the British military police?"

"They have agreed in principle, and I've made formal application, but I probably won't hear until later today. Although I would stake a year's salary on it being murder, there is yet to be proof that a crime has been committed."

"I understand."

"I will call in a couple of days."

"Yes, and thank you for calling this time," Willy said. "You have sown seeds of doubt in my mind and you may have prevented an embarrassing situation occurring."

"I think, and it is just a thought at this stage, that the person who murdered your Sandra Davies, has also murdered Dee Smithers. We may be dealing with a serial killer."

Chapter Seventy-Four

Inspector Jurgen Hausmann intensified the search for Mrs Dee Smithers.

He was absolutely convinced that when they found her body the tenuous connections he had discussed with Inspector Gauler would strengthen. He was also convinced that other women's lives might be at risk.

As he sat at his desk pondering his discussion with Inspector Gauler, he wrote down what he had gleaned from their conversation:

British – English?

Married to British servicemen – Davies (Corporal) Smithers (Lieutenant Colonel)

Davies – type of knife used (professional killing?)

Smithers – not yet known.

Davies – found stabbed and naked but no sexual attack

Smithers – not yet known

Davies – shallow grave close to where she lived (3 kms?)

Smithers – not yet known

Davies – unwashed (?) clothes found in flat (too obvious)

Smithers – half-burned clothes found in dustbin outside lover's flat (too obvious)

Davies – car driven home by husband (too obvious)

Smithers – car found 3 kms from lover's flat (too obvious)

Both husbands work in British ammunition depots

Both women known to have had extra-marital affairs

Gap between murder (Davies) and disappearance (Smithers) – 2 weeks

Conclusion – (tenuous but all I have to go on) – Smithers in shallow grave somewhere but where? Near Lüttelforst? Near Bracht? 3km radius? 5 km radius?

Which?

He reached for the phone. "Ah, Grossfeld, dig out a 1:50,000 map of the *Bracht* area and bring it in, will you?"

Jurgen Hausmann sat back in his chair tapping a pen against his teeth. At forty-five and after over twenty years as a detective, he had investigated any number of serious cases, which included over forty murders. Although he was offered promotion on numerous occasions, he always turned it down. He was happier working at the coalface rather than sitting in some ivory tower giving orders.

He had been married to Krista for twenty years, and they had twin nineteen year-old girls, both of whom were at university in Bonn. He loved his wife, but he often wondered how she had put up with him over the years. She never really complained, but each time the phone rang at some ridiculous time in the early hours of the morning, he knew what she was thinking. But whenever it happened, and it was often, she always got up as he was dressing and made him a cup of coffee, then kissed him at the front door of their flat before he left.

He was overweight, looked older than his age, took next to no care of himself, but he was dedicated. For him, solving crimes was an obsession, and he was very good at it.

That's why he had stayed an inspector.

With the murders he had investigated, he had solved over sixty per cent of them by looking for the obvious. There were some very clever criminal minds out there, but people who committed murder weren't always that clever. If their compulsion to take life was premeditated then it was more difficult, but even so, mistakes happened, and he needed to find those mistakes. If he found just one mistake he was confident he would find the murderer.

This case was no different.

There was a knock on his office door. "Come in."

Jurgen Hausmann looked up as *Polizeihauptmeister* Grossfeld walked into his office. As was the norm, he was dressed impeccably. A product of the Police Academy in Dusseldorf, which meant he was going places, Sergeant Grossfeld certainly wouldn't choose to stop at inspector as he had done. He was destined for the most senior position possible. Hausmann knew it and Grossfeld knew it. Hausmann also knew that at some stage, and probably within the next two or three years, he could be working for Grossfeld. However, giving credit where it was due, Grossfeld always treated Hausmann with the utmost respect.

"The map you asked for, Inspector."

"Thank you." Jurgen Hausmann spread the map on his desk and put his finger on *Bracht*.

"Can I ask what you are looking for?"

"A grave," Inspector Hausmann said.

"A grave," Grossfeld repeated with a slight smile on his face.

"Yes, a grave. I'm looking for a grave in a wood. It will be off the beaten track, but within three to five kilometres of the British ammunition depot." His finger was tracing over the area.

Grossfeld went round behind his boss. "There are a lot of woods in the area. In fact it is one big wood."

"Yes, but somewhere in that big wood there is a grave." Jurgen picked up a pencil from the tray in front of him and circled three areas.

"Is this the Smithers' case?"

"Yes."

"I thought we were concentrating on the *Lüttelforst* and the *Rhinedahlen* areas."

"We were, but I want to switch to *Bracht*," Jurgen Hausmann said.

"Resources?"

"Switch all of them."

"What about the British?"

"They will agree primacy but I would like them to stay working with us. It's one of theirs we're looking for so they will want to help."

"We haven't got authorisation yet," Grossfeld said.

"If we wait for authorisation there could be another murder. We will assume the authorisation is on its way. The British will understand."

"When do we switch."

"Now! I am going to *Bracht* to see the Commanding Officer and I want you to come with me."

When Jurgen Hausmann and Günther Grossfeld drove down *St Barbara Straße* towards the depot headquarters, they came up behind a small red Peugeot driven by what appeared to be a young blonde-haired woman. They followed her all the way down the road, past Wortham Barracks to the main depot entrance. After negotiating four speed ramps as they approached the barrier, Grossfeld was watching the car in front very closely. He prided himself on being a bit of an expert on cars. His wife, Kathcrine, often complained that their car sat outside in all weathers, while his pride and joy, a self-built 1.8 litre DVD Magnum, lived in the garage.

"That car either needs its suspension checked or its driver is grossly overweight," he observed.

"I'm more concerned about the acres of forest we're passing," Jurgen Hausmann said, "but what do you mean?" he asked, switching his attention to the car ahead.

"It's a bit low on its suspension anyway, but when it went over those speed bumps its shock absorbers were working overtime."

"I wouldn't know. If something goes wrong with my car it goes in to the nearest garage."

Grossfeld watched as the Peugeot and its driver were checked at the main barrier and then allowed to proceed to the car park opposite the single storey headquarters building. The police car Grossfeld was driving was waved through without being checked and he parked near the Peugeot. Glancing towards the other car he saw its strikingly attractive driver and decided he would take his observation a little further. His English was good, as was his French, Italian and Spanish.

"Excuse me a moment, Inspector."

"Leave the poor girl alone, Grossfeld. She doesn't need you breathing down her neck on a Monday morning."

"It's not her neck I'd like to breathe down," he said smiling as he opened the door.

"I thought your brain was supposed to be in your head."

"It is, but it slips every now and again."

Leah spotted the police car in her rear-view mirror as soon as it came up behind her. Police cars always made her nervous but especially so in Germany. On this occasion she felt she had ample reason to be nervous. Her naivety had allowed her to dismiss as incidental the fact that she was in Germany under a false identity, but now that Peter Bennett had threatened to expose her she felt very vulnerable, and very scared.

Only she could deal with the fact she was almost killed and then raped.

She couldn't report what had happened ... she was alive and would deal with it.

At the edge of her vision she saw the police car pull into the headquarters car park a few spaces from her, so she opened the glove compartment and began rummaging for something … anything that would make things look normal.

When one of the men from the car tapped on her window, she went rigid but managed to lower the window while at the same time trying her best to smile.

"Good morning, *Fraulein*," the man said, looking concerned. "I am presuming you are British?" he said in English.

"Yes," Leah said.

"Ah good, excuse my English but I will do my best," he said.

"That's all right. If you would prefer German please go ahead," Leah replied in German.

"Ah," the man said looking very surprised this time. "You speak my language better than I speak yours," he persisted in English.

"Whatever," Leah said, her mind working overtime. "How can I help you?"

"Yes, I am sorry, I did not introduce myself. I am *Polizeihauptmeister* Günther Grossfeld of the *Kriminal Polizei* based in *Mönchengladbach*."

"Oh, this sounds serious," Leah said, the false smile now firmly on her lips. The dull ache she had felt between her thighs since being raped intensified. The foundation she had used on her throat had worked because Clive hadn't said anything. She had expected there to be internal bruising, but swallowing was normal.

"Why we are here is serious but for you, not at all, *Fraulein* eh, *Fraulein…*?"

"Carpenter, my name is Amy Carpenter."

"It is good to meet you *Fraulein* Carpenter." He reached through the open window and shook her hand. Behind him, and still in the police car, Leah could see the other man becoming increasingly impatient.

"You too, Sergeant."

"Would you mind stepping out of your car for a moment? There is something I would like to show you?"

"Oh, all right," Leah said hesitantly.

Grossfeld stepped back to allow her to open the door. Leah was wearing a skirt so she kept her knees together and swung her legs as modestly as she could out of the car. She saw the policeman's eyes follow the movement.

"Your car is very low on its suspension," he told her, "and I think it should be checked. Look, let me show you." He went to the rear of the car and pushed down hard on the bodywork. "Oh, that is not what I expected. Your shock absorbers are not as bad as I thought."

"My what?"

"Your shock absorbers. They keep the car steady, otherwise it would always be bouncing up and down."

"I see."

"Yes, *Fraulein* … is everything all right?" the Sergeant asked, "you look as though you have been crying."

"Do I? Yes, I'm sorry but … but I had some bad news earlier."

Grossfeld frowned. "I presume it is nothing I can help you with … no, that is silly of me, we have only just met … but it is not a police matter?"

"No, no, Sergeant, it's very personal."

"Then I am sorry for asking … it was just that –"

"Please, don't apologise," Leah said, wishing she could tell him everything.

Sergeant Grossfeld coughed, still looking slightly embarrassed. "Are you carrying anything in your boot that is very heavy?"

"No, the usual rubbish that everyone carries. Oh, and an accident warning triangle, a first-aid box, and a 5-litre petrol can."

“*Fraulein*, I am not testing you, but in that case, may I suggest you have your suspension checked at the earliest opportunity?”

“So you are saying it could be my shock absorbers?”

“Yes, your shock absorbers could be at fault.”

“Then I’ll have them checked,” Leah said.

“Come on, Grossfeld,” the other man shouted from the police car, “We have work to do.”

“Take my advice,” Sergeant Grossfeld said.

“Thank you, Sergeant,” Leah said, smiling at him.

Sergeant Grossfeld smiled back and then joined the other man at the entrance to headquarters.

As Leah got into her car tears sprang to her eyes.

In just twenty-four hours her life had gone from a light-hearted dream to an absolute nightmare and she wasn’t sure she was going to be able to cope.

Chapter Seventy-Five

"Colonel, it is good of you to see us without an appointment," Inspector Jurgen Hausmann said as he sat down. "We expected to find you at your house." He indicated the chair next to Timothy Smithers for Sergeant Grossfeld.

"Not at all. I told you the other day that under the circumstances I would be available any time of the day or night, and sitting in the house worrying wouldn't achieve anything."

The CO sat down in one of the other chairs that were round the small table in his office. "Sam will bring us some coffee shortly. Do I take it you have some news for me?"

"No, nothing really new, I am afraid, Colonel. I have come to ask for your assistance."

"Anything, you know that."

There was a knock on the door and Sam Cox brought in the coffee, and helped each of the men to milk and sugar. As she poured a little milk into Timothy's cup their eyes met and she gave him an understanding smile.

"I must be a little insensitive when I ask you this favour, Colonel," Jurgen Hausmann said after Sam had left the office.

"There is no room for sensitivity, Inspector," the CO said. "You know I have assumed the worst, and you have done the same – you said as much the last time we met. So what can I do for you?"

Jurgen Hausmann outlined the discussion he'd had with his counterpart Willy Gauler in *Münster*. "So you see, the connections are tenuous, but the coincidences are there."

"Are you saying you want to search the depot?"

"No, not yet. I don't think it will come to that. Initially I would like to concentrate on an area two or three kilometres around the depot, but we haven't liaised with the Netherlands police yet, so it will be mainly on the north-east side. If you are happy with my suggestion, Sergeant Grossfeld here will be co-ordinating the search."

"It's a vast area. How on earth are you going to cover every possibility," Timothy asked.

"Methodically," Jurgen Hausmann said. "I have already selected three areas which I have prioritised and each should take perhaps six to eight hours to search if I have the right number of men."

"Are the British military police helping?"

"Sergeant Grossfeld spoke to them on the way here. They will meet us at the first rendezvous in about," he checked his watch, "an hour. They have managed to get thirty or so military policemen together, but even with the same sort of number coming from the local police and elsewhere, there are still not enough."

"You would like some of my men, is that it?"

"If you can spare any, then yes, they could be of great assistance."

"Spare any?" Timothy said. "I will close the depot. The powers that be will understand."

Sergeant Grossfeld glanced at the inspector. "How quickly can they be released, Colonel?"

"I'll call the RSM and he will have them paraded within thirty minutes."

"That is excellent. May I ask what you will tell them?" Jurgen Hausmann asked.

"The truth. They all know my wife is missing. There are no secrets in a place like this. About thirty women soldiers will join the men so that will make one hundred altogether. I will have to leave the officers and senior ranks on duty to supervise the civilians, but the rest you can have for as long as you need them." Timothy Smithers thought for a moment. "But what about the civilians? There are nearly a thousand working here, I'm sure some of them would be willing to help."

"In a situation like this," Jurgen Hausmann suggested, "there can be too few and then too many. If there are too many the searches will be difficult to co-ordinate. The hundred you are offering plus the others I mentioned should be enough. If Sergeant Grossfeld needs more we will let you know."

Timothy Smithers reached for the phone on his desk. "Sam, can you get the RSM for me please? No, not on the phone, in my office. Thank you."

Two minutes later the RSM joined the group. He was the epitome of everyone's idea of a British Army Regimental Sergeant Major: tall, heavyset, with very short dark brown hair and the inevitable neatly trimmed moustache. He was carrying his pace-stick, and the peak of his hat almost touched his nose.

The RSM stamped his feet, saluted and said, "Sir!" quite loudly. Timothy saw the police officers react.

"RSM," he said, "this is Detective Inspector Hausmann and Detective Sergeant Grossfeld of the German police. I think you can guess why they're here. This, gentlemen, is RSM Tucker."

"Yes, Sir," the RSM said a little more quietly, shaking hands with the police officers. "May I ask if there is any news, Sir?"

"No, none yet," the CO said before outlining what he wanted done.

"Very good, Sir. They will be on parade in twenty minutes at the outside. I'll get on with that now, Sir."

"RSM Tucker," Inspector Hausmann said, "with the colonel's permission, would you be willing to work alongside Sergeant Grossfeld here? I think it would be best if there was a military person to help manage the search. I am sure the British military police will have –"

"In a situation like this, the RMP will do as they are told, Sir, by me that is. Permission to carry on, Sir?" he said, turning to face his CO.

"Yes, thank you RSM. They'll need transport of course."

"Of course, Sir." He saluted then turned to the two police officers. "Gentlemen," he said, nodded and then left the office.

"Are all British RSMs like him, Colonel?" Sergeant Grossfeld said.

"Most of the ones I've met, Sergeant, are exactly like him."

"He is quite …" he hesitated, wanting to use the right word, "scary, don't you think?"

"On most days he is, but on a day like today he is worth double his weight in gold. You will not have any problems with my soldiers or the RMP. Not while the RSM is around."

"I thought not," Sergeant Grossfeld said.

Chapter Seventy-Six

After ten minutes Leah followed the police officers into the headquarters building, going straight to her office. She inspected her face in the small mirror on the wall by her desk and was reasonably satisfied. The German police officer had commented but … anyway, she didn't look too bad now. Although she was over an hour late getting to work, nobody seemed to have noticed. Her job took her all over the administrative area and to meetings elsewhere, so when she wasn't in her office it was accepted that she was somewhere doing what she was paid to do.

She was taking her jacket off when the phone rang. "Hello," she said, apprehensively.

"Amy it's Clive. Are you all right?"

"If you call a brush with the police an everyday occurrence, then yes, I'm all right."

"The police?" He sounded very worried.

"I'm winding you up. Two German policemen have gone in to see the CO, and one of them said my car could do with having its suspension looked at."

"Why on earth …?"

"I don't know, I'll tell you about it this evening."

"Don't you think you ought to –?"

"Clive, please don't interfere. It's for me to deal with, please ..."

"Okay, but ... there doesn't seem to be anything new on Dee."

"I haven't spoken to anybody yet, but no doubt Sam Cox will be down when the police have gone. She tells me she doesn't gossip but she does need to take somebody into her confidence. Evidently I can be trusted." She moved round her desk and sat down.

"You sound perfectly normal, almost as though –"

"Almost as though nothing happened, Clive? Is that what you were going to say? I told you I will deal with it in my own way, but that doesn't imply I didn't mean what I said this morning. I do love you, please believe me."

"Would it sound rather vain if I said of course I believe you?" he said.

"Not at all, I want you to believe me."

"And do you accept that I feel the same about you?"

"Yes," Leah said, although a little reluctantly.

"Then we both know where we stand, don't we?"

"I'll see you this evening," she said.

"That sounds like a good idea."

"And … Clive?"

"Yes."

"Be patient with me ... please."

She put the receiver down, fighting back the tears that tried suddenly to rush into her eyes. He was going to have to be very patient. It was going to be a while before she ever let anyone touch her again, even Clive. If he did really love her, then his love was going to be tested … if it hadn't been already.

She looked at the documents in her tray and groaned, but she still reached for the top file which necessitated her leaving the headquarters and going to the civil labour office.

"Good morning, *Frau* Spinks," Leah said, walking into the outer office.

Frau Spinks looked up from her typewriter. "Good morning *Fraulein* Carpenter. If you have come to see *Herr* Dorf, he's not in this morning. He phoned in sick earlier."

"No, I've brought these documents he wanted translated." She put the letters in the tray nearest to her. "I tried to get hold of *Frau* Dorf, but she's not in either."

"No, she has taken some holiday owed to her. She said she was going to see some friends in Koblenz."

"Do you think *Herr* Dorf has gone as well?" Leah asked.

"No, he sounded genuinely unwell, I told him to go and see the doctor."

Leah was just about to leave when she heard the RSM shouting orders almost outside the window.

"What's going on," *Frau* Spinks asked, getting up from behind her desk.

"No idea," Leah said peering out of the window.

The main square was just beyond the civil labour office and they could see soldiers lining up in their squadron formations.

"Something must be happening," *Frau* Spinks said. "They will already have had one parade this morning up in Wortham Barracks."

"I know who will know," Leah said. "Can I use your phone?"

"Of course."

Leah tapped in the extension she wanted. "Sam, it's Amy. What's going on? Why are all the soldiers on parade?"

"I can tell *you*, Amy. In fact I've just been down to your office but you weren't there."

"No, I'm in the civil labour office."

“Oh, I see,” Sam said. “Nobody else can hear, can they?”

“I’m not alone but it’s okay to talk,” Leah said glancing at *Frau* Spinks who was still looking out of the window. Amy had never established just how much English *Frau* Spinks spoke or understood.

“Well,” Sam said, “the police came to the Colonel’s office about forty-five minutes ago …”

“I know I saw them.”

“Well, promise not to tell anyone else?”

“Of course, but won’t the soldiers be told why they are there?”

“Yes, I suppose they will, I hadn’t thought of that. It’ll be all right to tell you then.”

“You were going to tell me anyway.”

“Oh yes, so I was. Well, they’re going to form part of a search party … they’re going to look for Mrs Smithers’ body.”

“Her body? What do you mean?” Leah said, stealing another look at *Frau* Spinks.

“The police think she’s been murdered and that she’s been buried somewhere near here.”

“Oh, God … how awful.”

“Look, I’ve got to go. If I hear anything else I’ll let you know,” Sam said.

“Thank you.”

Accepting that why and what they were searching for wouldn’t be kept from the soldiers, Leah told *Frau* Spinks what was going on, and she immediately burst into tears.

After consoling *Frau* Spinks for a few minutes, Leah returned to her office.

If anything, Leah felt the rather macabre news put her own situation into perspective and she felt her spirits lift a little.

Chapter Seventy-Seven

"I am impressed, Colonel," Jurgen Hausmann told Timothy Smithers as he watched the soldiers forming up on the parade square. Sergeant Grossfeld had already left the office to go and organise the rendezvous point.

"Thank you. I would normally have gone and briefed them myself but under the circumstances I don't think it would be right, do you?"

Hausmann turned from the window. "You are being very brave about all this. I cannot put myself in your place, but I know how I would feel if it was my wife they were going to look for."

"More coffee?" Timothy asked and Hausmann nodded. "It's not a question of being brave. It's more about hanging onto the remnants of hope. I know it looks as though I must now face the worst outcome, but until she is found there is always hope."

"I understand, and of course there is always hope." Hausmann sat down and picked up the coffee cup in both hands.

"Colonel …"

"Look, I know it will break with protocol and all that, but do you think we could dispense with the formalities. My name is Timothy, Tim, for short. I would much prefer it to being called 'Colonel' all the time, especially when it's my wife you are trying find."

"Of course, Timothy," Jurgen Hausmann said, lifting his hand. "My name is Jurgen, but it isn't shortened to anything. I could tell you what my wife calls me …" He saw the look in Timothy's eyes and stopped. "I'm sorry – that was insensitive."

"If we're going to sort this one out we must be free to say what we feel to each other. We have a saying in England about 'walking on eggshells', or 'pussyfooting around'. What needs to be said has to be said. There will be plenty of time for other things later, plenty of time."

"In that case, Timothy, I am going to be rather direct."

"That's the only way."

"Did you know your wife was having an affair?"

Timothy Smithers stood up and went straight to the window, mainly to hide the tears that had immediately sprung to his eyes. He clasped his hands behind his back, and rocked slowly on his feet. "I ... I had my suspicions, Jurgen," he admitted after a while, "but it's not the sort of thing … in my position ... well, I'm sure you understand."

"Yes, I do understand."

"And you think there might be a connection?"

"Yes," Jurgen said. "The last time we met I couldn't tell you where we found your wife's clothes, but now I think it would be appropriate. We found them in a rubbish bin close to a block of flats in *Lüttelforst*."

"And this man she was having an affair with lives there, does he?"

"Yes," Jurgen said.

"Is there something else you're not telling me, Jurgen?"

"In what way?"

"I presume you've arrested whoever it is. I must also presume that he has admitted to killing my wife and he has told you where she is."

"No, Timothy, he has not been arrested because I do not believe that he did kill your wife." Then he added quickly, "If that is what has happened. If he had and he had told us where she is I wouldn't have organised the search. We would have gone straight there."

"Yes, sorry, that was silly of me. Why are you so sure this man hasn't harmed her in any way?"

"Experience, Timothy, that is all … just experience. Do you want to know who he is?"

Timothy Smithers turned round. "No, not at the moment but if you change your mind about him then I might have to know."

"I have to say you are very understanding."

"Am I? I love my wife, Jurgen, I love the ground she walks on. She is a very physical woman, her needs are – how can I put it? What every other husband could possibly want in his wife, if you see what I mean. But I chose to ignore my suspicions thinking I might lose her."

Jurgen Hausmann appeared embarrassed by Timothy's candour. "Thank you for telling me, Timothy. Do you think this man –?"

"Was the only affair she was having? Is that what you were going to ask?"

Jurgen nodded.

"Even I have my limits, Jurgen. Yes, as far as I know she is not, or was not seeing anybody else, nor had she seen anyone before. Although she tried to be discreet, I believe the affair was not only known about by me. I was expecting a phone call any day to tell me that unless she stopped what she was doing I would have to vacate this post, but I want her back under any circumstances."

Jurgen nodded. "I understand," he said.

Chapter Seventy-Eight

"So you've decided," Seamus Docherty said as they joined the autobahn and headed north.

"It'll be spectacular, Seamus," Sylvia said.

"I'm sure it will, but I'm not so sure that 'he that has to be obeyed' will be of the same opinion."

"You wait and see. Trust me."

Seamus pulled out to overtake a couple of articulated lorries. "I trust you more than you'll ever realise." He sensed rather than saw her looking at him, so he said hurriedly, "And the other two are to be left out of it, is that right?"

"Too many cooks etcetera, etcetera."

"I'm not sure they fully understood the significance of where you sent them."

"I just needed them out of the way for a few days," Sylvia said.

"It'll be more than a couple of days. It's a long drive to Bavaria."

Sylvia shrugged. "No matter. They knew we were going to have to do it at some stage so why not now?"

"Will they know what they're looking for?" Seamus asked.

"You were there when I told them. Would you?"

"Oh yes, I would know, but I have a few brain cells. I sometimes wonder about them."

"They're good at what they do," Sylvia said.

"I'll give you that … nothing better than professional killers without any feelings whatsoever."

"We are no different."

"I think we are," he said.

"Anyway, I feel a lot happier with them looking at British Army adventure training lodges in Bavaria than being with us."

"I suppose I should take that as a compliment."

"You know what I think of you."

"Do I?"

"Are you winding me up?"

"With your reputation, Miss Donnelly, I wouldn't dare."

She nudged his leg with her hand. "I'm not that bad, am I?"

“What’s that female spider that eats its mate after they’ve made love?”
“Seamus! That’s an awful thing to say.”
“Just being honest,” he said.
“We’ve never done anything like that anyway.”
“Not for the want of thinking about it.”
“Are you saying what I think you’re saying? But you’ve never …”
“You’re the boss, and regardless of whether I fancy you or not, the two wouldn’t mix.”
“How would you know if you don’t try?”
Seamus’ foot slipped off the accelerator. “Are you being serious?”
“I might be. I did say the others would be away for a few days. So …”
“Right then, that’s really given me something to think about.”
“Play you cards right and your thoughts might become reality.”
“And how am I going to concentrate on what’s ahead of us today?”
“Be the professional we both know you are,” she said, “and that starts from now. We need to find somewhere to have an uninterrupted planning session. It’ll need to be within walking distance of the depot perimeter and well off the beaten track ... and I know just the place.”
“How?” Seamus asked.
“That would be telling.”

The Army lorries pulled up at the *Am Weissen Stein* and disgorged the soldiers.
RSM Tucker immediately got the soldiers to form three ranks, stood them at ease and when he was happy he called the RMP Staff Sergeant over and suggested his men and women joined his parade at the far end. The Staff Sergeant began to protest but one look from the RSM told him that his reaction was very unwise.
The few people that were about, some on bikes, some out for a walk, all stopped and gawked at the gathering. The five German police cars and three minibuses would have attracted anybody’s attention.
RSM Tucker went towards the police seeking out Sergeant Grossfeld. He located him talking to a small group of police officers. The RSM waited on the periphery until Grossfeld saw him.
“RSM Tucker, is that what I should call you?”
“RSM will do nicely, Sir.”
“Sergeant will do nicely, RSM, not Sir.”
“Sergeant,” RSM Tucker said.
“Thank you for being so … you British have a saying for it … thank you for being so … welcome?”
“I think you mean ‘Wilko’, Sergeant.”

"Yes, that's it, 'Wilko'. May I ask how many soldiers you have brought with you?"

"There are one hundred and two from the depot, and twenty-eight Military Police, that's one hundred and thirty altogether."

"Excellent, RSM … the area we are going to be moving through is to the north east." Grossfeld spread his arms to indicate the area he meant. "I would guess there is some rough going, but I am sure your soldiers will cope. I am more worried about my police officers."

"Sergeant, have you done one of these sweeps before?"

"Sweeps?" Grossfeld said, frowning.

"Erm, searches."

"Searches, ah yes, but not on this sort of scale."

"May I make a suggestion?"

"Suggest anything you like, RSM."

"There are about thirty of you, nearly thirty military police and a hundred of mine. Can I suggest that they move in extended groups of five: one of yours, one military police and three of mine. And each man should be able to touch the hand of the man next to him at all times, except when going round trees and things."

"And there are lots of those, RSM."

"What's that, Sergeant?"

"Trees, RSM. There are lots of trees in the forest?"

"Wouldn't be a forest if there weren't," the RSM suggested, giving him a funny look.

"And you English say we Germans do not have a sense of humour," Grossfeld said, smiling. "Your idea is good, RSM. Can I leave you to organise it? I will tell my men what is happening and then they will join you."

"What exactly are we looking for? I need to tell my people."

"A grave, RSM … freshly disturbed earth, anything that may suggest a hole has been dug. And of course pieces of clothing, shoes, anything that may be of help."

"Have you heard of the expression 'needle in a haystack', Sergeant?"

"I have and in German it is, *eine Nadel in einem Heuschober* and this *Heuschober* is exceptionally big and the *Nadel* very, very small."

"You never know," RSM Tucker said.

"No, RSM, you never know."

Chapter Seventy-Nine

Peter Bennett packed the few items of clothing that Ursula Dorf had kept at the flat into a holdall, and put his own things into a suitcase. He put tins of food, packets and anything else he could find into a cardboard box before going in search of his landlord.

He found him in one of the barns.

"Ah, there you are *Herr* Schmidt."

The old man stopped what he was doing. "*Herr* Weiss, it is good to see you." He rubbed the stubble on his chin and crossed the few yards to the barn door. "What can I do for you this fine morning?"

"It is a nice morning," Peter Bennett agreed. "My, erm, girlfriend and I have to move on I'm afraid."

"Oh, that is a pity, but –"

"Yes, I know I agreed that I would give you at least a week's notice but I'm sure if I give you an extra month's rent you will understand."

"A month's rent you say."

"That plus a bonus for being such an excellent landlord," Peter Bennett said.

"A bonus you say."

"I calculate it to come to exactly five thousand Deutschmarks."

"Five thousand you say."

"If that is acceptable."

"Yes, *Herr* Weiss, that is most acceptable." The old man rubbed his chin again. "The young lady, she has already gone?"

"Yes, she has gone to stay with friends near Koblenz."

"Koblenz you say."

"I've packed everything up and there are a couple of boxes of provisions in the kitchen you might like to make use of, or throw away … whatever."

"Throw away? I throw nothing away, what I don't eat the goats will have."

"Right then." Peter reached for his wallet and counted out ten five hundred Deutschmark notes. "Cash all right?" he asked, noting the gleam in *Herr* Schmidt's eyes.

"Cash you say. Yes, cash will be fine, just like today."

"Just like today, *Herr* Schmidt." Peter handed over the notes.

After loading the single case into his car, he headed for the room he had booked in the *Zum Treffpunct* Hotel in *Kaldenkirchen*.

The town was a stone's throw from the Dutch border, and his escape route.

"And how did you say you found this place?" Seamus asked Sylvia as she parked the car.

"I didn't," she replied, smiling. "I discovered it months ago but have never had reason to come here before."

"The *Forsthotel*," he read from the sign outside the building in front of her. "Looks like a very good place for secret meetings."

"That's why I chose it," Sylvia said, retrieving her coat from the back seat. "Come on, a drink and a bit of planning." She opened the door and got out.

Seamus watched her set off towards the hotel. He hadn't the faintest idea how he had managed to get this far. To infiltrate the IRA was one thing but to be Second-in-Command of a cell in Germany was another. Every day, every hour and every minute, he expected his cover to be blown. He thought that when she sent Pat and Robert off to Bavaria, he was about to be uncovered. He thought she would take him to a welcoming party in some back of beyond location where he would receive a bullet in the back of his head if he were lucky; if not, the alternative wasn't worth contemplating.

Seamus Docherty a.k.a. Captain Roland Fallon, Irish Guards, shook his head in wonderment as he watched Sylvia Donnelly wiggle her way along the path towards the hotel. Yes, she had got rid of the other two because she had other plans, and yes, her other plans were to do with him, but … and what a bloody but … it was because she fancied him.

"Roland, you sod, you're about to have it off with a notorious IRA killer," he said to himself. "How does that grab you?"

He acknowledged Sylvia Donnelly's beckoning finger with a wave of his hand and as he got out of the car he said, "All in the line of duty, me old son, all in the line of duty."

Sitting outside with a couple of beers in front of them, Seamus thought they looked like any other couple.

Sylvia had gone to the ladies straight away, and when she returned he smelt something he'd never associated her with before – perfume and a good quality one at that. She was attractive enough – at times she appeared bloody gorgeous – but he had almost decided that if she had a sex life it might not be with a man. Did he go around with his eyes closed? His bosses in HQ Northern Ireland, and even more so in Whitehall, would have an apoplexy if they knew what he was contemplating.

"Seamus, I have a confession to make," Sylvia said, the tall beer glass an inch from her lips.

"Another one?"

"And what do you mean by that, may I ask?" She allowed her usually hidden Irish accent to come out for the first time in his company.

"I mean, so I do, that you're full of surprises today, so you are," he said, mimicking her.

"Your accent is even worse than mine … so it is!" Her eyes were shining and her smile alluring. "No, seriously, I do want to tell you something but it's literally for your ears only. If you ever tell another soul I'll cut your balls off and have them sliced and grilled on a piece of toast. That's after I've finished with their other use."

"You have a way with words," he said.

"Look, I want to be serious for a moment." She took a sip of her beer. "If I told you that there's a ready-made car bomb with two hundred pounds of PE4 waiting to be used, would you believe me?"

"I have no reason to doubt you, but go on," he said, suddenly very alert.

"It's not only ready-made but it could be positioned anywhere in that ammunition depot some of us have spent hours observing, without us having to lift a finger."

"You had my interest but you now have my full attention. How on earth …?"

"It's in a car. Brought over from the UK. And the car's driver works in the depot. She –"

"She?"

"Why are men so surprised when the word *she* is mentioned? I'm a *she*, aren't I?"

"I'll confirm that later – one way or the other. All right, I accept it's a *she* without further question, but how –?"

"Just accept that what I've told you is the truth, he –"

"It's a *he* now is it? What –?"

"Yes, I've had help but it's from somebody I trust. Why do you think we've been here this long without anything happening? I've been waiting for everything to be in place. And now it is."

"What? The bomb is already in the depot?" Seamus asked. He needed to know more. This disclosure was very serious and any information gleaned from Sylvia would have to be passed on without him breaking cover.

"No, not yet, but it can be as soon as I give the word."

"But you're not going to tell me who it is?"

"No, I can't."

"It sounds as though you're dealing with a rogue bull elephant, the most dangerous of animals on this planet."

"Seamus, my dear friend, I've been close enough to him on any number of occasions. When is a man at his most vulnerable?" she asked.

"You're going to tell me you've slept with him, aren't you?"

"Yes, and on each occasion it would have been so easy to put a knife in his back, or anywhere else if it came to that. Did you see the film *Fatal Attraction*?"

"I did, but what happens on the big screen and what happens in reality are poles apart. Surely what you've experienced over the last fifteen years tells you that."

"If Sharon Stone can do it on a film set, Sylvia Donnelly can do it for real," she said.

"You're mad."

"Probably, but it's going to happen, and soon."

Until this point they had been the only ones on the terrace, but two other couples drifted in and they also sat outside – one couple occupying the table next to Seamus and Sylvia.

"We had better move inside."

"It'll be less private in there. Perhaps under the circumstances we ought to leave."

Sylvia took a key from her pocket. "It can be as private as we want it to be," she said, smiling.

"When did you get that?"

"When I went to the loo and it's ours until ten o'clock tomorrow morning."

"As I said, you're full of surprises."

"Shall we go and find out?"

Chapter Eighty

The extended line of soldiers and police moved very slowly.

Spread over nearly three hundred yards and regardless of the speed the line moved at, RSM Tucker and Sergeant Grossfeld were finding it difficult to control movement. The radios helped, but each time somebody found something of interest, the whole line had to stop. After an hour they had covered less than five hundred yards. Adding to the problem was the variable ground cover. Those moving through open areas had to move at the same speed as those in thick undergrowth. Heading northwest towards *Kaldenkirchen,* and passing *Heidhausen* to their right, the six hours that Inspector Jurgen Hausmann had estimated looked ominously optimistic.

RSM Tucker and Sergeant Grossfeld took half the extended line each, and by midday they decided it was time to have a proper break.

"Right, stop where you are," RSM Tucker shouted. "Fifteen minutes break, but stay in line." Some sat down, others leaned against trees, some had a cigarette, and others took out the water bottles they had the forethought to bring. RSM Tucker was pleased when he saw some of his soldiers sharing both cigarettes and water with the German police.

Tucker and Grossfeld met up in the centre of the line. Grossfeld offered RSM Tucker a cigarette.

"No thanks, I don't,' RSM said.

"What were you saying about a needle in a haystack, RSM?" Grossfeld asked.

"I know. They're doing their best but somebody could have buried an army in these woods and we wouldn't find them. How do you expect to find a single grave? If what your boss thinks may have happened, did happen, then whoever did it won't have left any signposts. He'll have made sure the body was well covered and left no signs of his having been here."

"You're right, but what's the alternative?"

"Are your boss's hunches normally pretty good?" RSM Tucker asked.

"I am sorry. I do not know the word 'hunches'."

"Erm, instincts, gut feelings, you know."

"I understand instincts." Grossfeld took a deep lungful of smoke and shrugged. "He's been a detective for a lot of years and he's one of our best. The fact that our superiors agreed to this search, and to allocate so many resources, that must say something about what they think of his hunches." They both smiled at his choice of word. "Normally we would have carried on with the search near where Mrs Smithers' car was found, but after he'd spoken to Inspector Gauler in *Münster*, he suddenly changed his mind."

"That was to do with the Davies woman's murder, was it?" RSM Tucker said.

"Yes. They talked for a very long time early this morning, and here we are five hours later searching this area."

"I spoke to my opposite number at *Wulfen* and he said you'd arrested her husband, and that he'd been charged with his wife's murder"

"Not me, RSM, the *Münster* police."

"That's what I meant, sorry."

"Yes, what you were told is right, but Inspector Hausmann is convinced that he did not do it. He thinks whoever murdered Sandra Davies may have also killed Mrs Smithers."

"I see." The RSM looked towards the area they had yet to cover. "This wood is massive so we'll have to do at least another three or four sweeps to cover the area as best we can." He checked the map he was carrying. "The vehicles will be at the *Forsthotel*, that's about another five hundred yards from here. They'll have brought some refreshments. We'd better get started again."

"You think of everything, RSM," Sergeant Grossfeld said, smiling.

"If only that were true." The RSM put his hat back on. "Right, you lot, let's get started again."

The noise of the Army lorries arriving at the *Forsthotel* car park made Sylvia Donnelly and Seamus Docherty stop what they were doing.

"What's that?" Sylvia asked, lifting her head.

"Sounds like heavy vehicles."

"Yes, but what would they be doing this far off a main road?" She threw back the duvet and padded naked to the window. Moving the curtain to one side, she peered out. She could just see the car park through the trees. "I can see two of them, but there are more. They look like British Army lorries. What ... hang on a minute ... there are German police and British military police vehicles as well. Seamus," she said turning towards the bed, "I think we're in trouble."

Seamus got off the bed and joined her at the window. A British military police Land Rover went past the entrance to the hotel. "There's definitely something going on, but I don't think it's anything to do with you and me."

"What makes you so sure?" Sylvia asked.

"Why would the Army be here? If it is us they are after it would just be the civilian police. Look, you wait here and I'll go and find out."

"What? Go and ask?" she said.

"What could be more innocent? A British tourist asking stupid questions, it happens all the time." He went over to the chair where he had thrown his clothes.

Sylvia went up behind him and wrapped her arms round his chest. "Thank you for the last hour or so, it was you who was full of surprises."

Seamus turned and kissed her. "You had a few of your own."

"When and if we get the opportunity, you'll have to tell me what they were."

Seamus walked out of the hotel and then sauntered towards the car park, surprised by just how many vehicles there were. He passed a couple of the staff he recognised from the hotel. One of them was next to a police car talking to a German police officer.

The Army drivers were out of their vehicles and in a group, talking and smoking – two young women, and three older men.

"Hello there," Seamus said, smiling. "What's going on here?"

The group looked at him and then at each other. "You English?" the girl nearest to him asked.

"Yes, I'm visiting the area. I didn't expect to see all this in the middle of the woods."

The girl looked at her friends again and shrugged. "There's a search on."

"A search? What sort of search?" he asked.

A military police corporal detached himself from his own group and came over. "May I ask who you are, Sir?"

"I was just saying, I'm a tourist visiting the area and I didn't expect to see the British Army out here in the middle of nowhere."

"No, Sir, I'm sure you didn't," the corporal said. "I'm afraid we can't discuss with civilians what we're doing."

"Oh, right, but this young lady said there was some sort of search going on, is there any way my wife and I can help?"

"No, Sir, there are plenty of people already out there."

"May I ask what you are searching for?"

"You can ask, Sir, but I can't tell you."

The corporal was only doing his job, and he was doing it well, but Seamus was reasonably satisfied that he and Sylvia Donnelly were not what or who they were searching for, and if it was anything to do with what Sylvia had told him earlier, they would be searching inside the depot. "Well, thank you, if you change your mind, my wife and I will be in the hotel."

"Right, Sir, and thank you for your interest."

Seamus headed back up the path to the hotel. As he got to the entrance gate he stopped and turned round.

His sixth sense told him somebody was watching him, and no, it wasn't somebody he had already seen or spoken to. Although still alert he carried on down the path but somebody ran up behind him and touched his sleeve.

"'Scuse me," one of the female soldiers said. "Do you think they'd mind me using their toilet? I'm bloody bursting."

"No, I'm sure they wouldn't," Seamus said. "I'll show you where it is."

He led the girl into the hotel, smiled at the only person behind the bar before showing the girl where the women's toilet was.

"Thanks," she said, and scuttled off.

Seamus was just about to go up the stairs and back to the room, when he had an idea. He waited at the bottom of the stairs until the girl came out. "Excuse me, Miss," he said solicitously, "but I wonder if you could just tell me a little bit more about what's going on?"

"Well, I –" she started to say.

"Look," he said, taking her arm and guiding her towards a corner. "It just so happens that I'm on a sort of busman's holiday."

"A what?"

"Oh, it doesn't matter, but I'm a reporter with one of the national papers back home. If there's some sort of story going on you'd be doing me one hell of a favour if I got in there first."

"A reporter, I don't think I –"

"No, you don't understand. I wouldn't mention your name or anything, but if the story developed you could be paid on the quiet for giving me the information."

"Paid? No, I don't think … how much?" She was a pretty little thing, no more than nineteen-years old, and pint sized, and Seamus wondered how she managed to drive an army lorry. She couldn't be more than five feet tall.

"Well, that depends. But it could be as much as five hundred."

"What? Pounds?" Seamus nodded. "Bloody hell, but, no, I would get into a lot of trouble."

"As I said, nobody would ever know, it would just be between you and me."

"Well, I suppose … look, I'll tell you what I know, and that isn't very much."

"That's fine," Seamus said.

"Well, the CO's wife went missing about three or four days ago. They think she's been murdered and all them others are out there looking for her."

"The CO being the Commanding Officer," Seamus suggested.

"Yeh."

"Of which unit?"

"Where I am, 3 BAD."

"The ammunition depot?"

"Yeh, how'd you know that?"

Seamus ignored her. "What's his name?"

The girl hesitated. "Smithers, I don't know his first name but she's called Dee. Ever such a nice lady."

"So this Mrs Dee Smithers is Colonel Smithers' wife, right?"

"He's what's called an 'alf colonel, always makes me laugh 'cos he's quite tall."

Seamus smiled at the girl's comment. "All right, the wife of Lieutenant Colonel Smithers, Commanding Officer of 3 BAD, went missing three or four days ago, they think she's been murdered, and there are soldiers and police out in these woods looking for her body. Is that right?"

"Yeh, that's all I know."

"You've been very helpful," Seamus said. "Now your name. I know where you're working, but if you give me your name, and anything does come of it, I'll send you the money."

"It's Dawn, Dawn Martin, Private Dawn Martin," she said, looking about.

"Private Dawn Martin, you've been most helpful. Thank you." He held out his hand. She took is tentatively, looked very deeply into his eyes, smiled and then ran from the restaurant.

As Seamus went up the stairs he made a mental note to send Dawn Martin a few quid when he was next in the UK – courtesy of MI6.

Chapter Eighty-One

After Peter Bennett had offloaded his things into his room at the hotel in *Kaldenkirchen*, he decided to drive through to *Brüggen* and search Leah's flat. He wanted to find and remove the personal documents he had given her. He appreciated that there was every chance she would have kept them in the car, but that didn't worry him. As well as having keys to her flat he also had keys to her car. He wanted to be rid of everything that would even slightly connect her to him.

She wouldn't need any identity papers where she was going.

Approaching the turning to *Heidhausen* he saw two military vehicles turning out from the village and heading the way he had come. Following close behind were further military and civilian police vehicles. He slowed down and stopped just past the turning. It was too much of a coincidence. Discovery of one or even both bodies was a possibility, or maybe there was just a search going on. He turned his car round, increasing his speed so that he caught up with the last vehicle, a green and cream German police Audi.

He followed the convoy into *Kaldenkirchen* and it then took the left turning down *Grenwald Straße*. His suspicions were confirmed: the vehicles could only be going to one place, therefore he wasn't surprised when after a few kilometres they turned left again, down the forest track towards the *Forsthotel.*

Knowing the vehicles couldn't get beyond the hotel car park he slowed and turned down a track about two hundred yards from the hotel. After parking his car out of sight of the main track, he set out on foot towards the hotel, keeping inside the tree line. The small play park almost opposite the parking area gave him the vantage point he wanted, at the same time ensuring he couldn't be seen.

The drivers of the vehicles got out and drifted into small groups, lighting cigarettes and talking. He had already noted when he first saw the vehicles that in each vehicle the only soldier was the driver. It was obvious they were going to the *Forsthotel* to collect their passengers. He moved slightly to get a better view of the hotel as well as the car park.

And then he saw Roland Fallon.

"Well, bugger me," he said softly to himself, "what the fuck are you doing here?"

The man he had spotted was the same age as Peter, and had been at the military academy at the same time as he was. Peter had joined the Royal Army Ordnance Corps and Roland the Irish Guards. Their choices of regiment meant they had very little contact with each other while at the academy, but because they were in different colleges – Peter in New College and Roland Old College – all they were aware of was that the other existed. They met more formally at the pre-selection board for the SAS. They both passed but due to availability they attended different selection courses. They met up again in Hereford but then went their different ways, both to Northern Ireland but for different reasons. Peter never really discovered where Fallon went but he had his suspicions – under-cover – but his suspicions were yet to be confirmed.

When they did meet during pre-selection they had not got on. Peter guessed that for others it would appear strange: they were a similar build and height and despite their choices of regiment, either would have suited the other's choice. They also had similar interests. Bystanders put the obvious friction down to these similarities and the resultant competition.

Peter Bennett watched as Roland joined the group of military drivers. It was clear from the way they reacted that they didn't know who or what he was, and even if they did he certainly didn't look the part – well, perhaps he did. His hair was longish and the stubble was obvious even from where Peter lay hidden. The walking boots, scruffy jeans, T-shirt and lightweight anorak made him look as much like an army officer as any other society dropout.

Peter's mind worked overtime. The coincidence was too much. He watched as an RMP corporal wandered over to the group, and a minute or so later Roland Fallon walked back towards the hotel.

Peter was just about to change his position again when he saw one of the female drivers detach herself from the group and follow Roland down the path.

They exchanged a few words before they disappeared through the front doors of the hotel.

Chapter Eighty-Two

Seamus Docherty went back into the room to find Sylvia Donnelly sitting on the bed, fully clothed, cleaning her 9mm Beretta.

"You won't be needing that, and I could have been anybody," he said, going across to the window.

"I heard your footsteps," she said. "Did you find out anything?"

Seamus pulled the curtain back slightly. "It appears there's been a murder and you'll never guess who it is."

"I'm not in the mood for games." Sylvia put the magazine back in the pistol.

Seamus looked over his shoulder. "All right, how about Mrs Dee Smithers."

"What? Not –"

"Exactly. It looks as though somebody is doing our job for us."

"It was her husband who was the main target, not her," Sylvia reminded him.

"I know, but it's a bit of a coincidence, isn't it?" He let the curtain fall but quickly opened it again as he saw soldiers and German police officers begin to arrive in the car park. "And it looks as though the cavalry is just coming in."

Sylvia crossed the room to peer out of the window. "So what are they doing? Searching for the body?"

"That's what I was told, yes."

"We'd better leave. I feel a bit uneasy with so many police so close." Sylvia headed for the bathroom.

"If I may be so bold, I disagree. It looks as though they're just having a break or something. Can I suggest we sit it out? It would be a pity to waste such a nice room."

She hesitated at the bathroom door. "I'm not staying here one minute longer than we have to."

"That's up to you, you're the boss. But now isn't the right time to show our faces. Wouldn't you agree?"

"I suppose so, what …?"

Seamus went over to her. "We could use the time to our advantage." He pulled her T-shirt out of her jeans then ran his hands round her back to remove the Beretta from her belt. He placed it on the chair next to them.

She smiled. "This isn't very professional."

"It's as good as you're going to get."

"Thirty minute break," the RSM shouted. "Put all litter back on the trucks, pick up your dog ends, and if you need a pee go into the hotel – it's been arranged."

"It is good of you to share your food with us," Sergeant Grossfeld said as he and the RSM moved to one side.

"I told the cookhouse to prepare enough. It's a bit basic, I'm afraid. They didn't have a lot of time."

Grossfeld looked across at the intermingling that was going on. "They all seem to be getting on well enough."

"Give a diverse group of people a common cause and they soon overcome their prejudices," the RSM said, biting into a cheese and pickle sandwich.

"You are a bit of a psychologist, RSM."

"No, not at all, to me it's all common sense." He looked over the area to his right. "I suppose we ought to start from here again, spread out both ways, head to the edge of the wood and then sweep back down the far side."

"Yes, I think that would be wise."

"It's just after one o'clock now so we may get two more sweeps in before dark."

Sam Cox wasn't in her office so Clive Benton knocked on the CO's door.

"Come in … oh, hello Clive, I thought you were from the Mess. I've ordered some sandwiches for me and Jurgen. You haven't met have you, Detective Inspector Jurgen Hausmann, this is Major Clive Benton, my Second-in-Command." The two men shook hands.

"If it's not convenient, Colonel, I can come back."

"No, that's all right, Clive. You need to know what's going on anyway. I'm sorry to bring the depot to a grinding halt, especially on a Monday morning."

"Colonel," Clive said, sitting down next to Jurgen Hausmann, "I think that what's happening is a little more important, don't you? There's plenty the civvies can be getting on with and I've told headquarters what's going on and the Brigadier said he wants to be kept informed."

"Thank you, Clive."

"Do I take from what's happening that …" He looked at the German police officer "… that you have something to go on."

"Not as such, Major Benton," Jurgen Hausmann said. "As the colonel and I have discussed, it is just a possibility at this stage."

"I see." Clive's mind raced back to the picture of Amy walking into the flat the night before. There was little point in saying anything, mainly because he didn't really have any facts to relate, but also he didn't want to detract from the importance of the search.

"It'll take the rest of the day, probably tomorrow and possibly the day after, Clive," Timothy Smithers said. "Can you plan accordingly?"

"Of course, Colonel."

There was another knock on the door and a very solemn looking Fritz Breckmann, the Officers' Mess Manager, came into the office carrying a tray of sandwiches.

"Thank you, Fritz."

Fritz Breckmann nodded at the Inspector and put the sandwiches on the coffee table. "If there is anything else, Sir, you will call me?"

"Of course, Fritz, thank you again."

"May I say how sorry I am, and I bring you the thoughts of all the Mess staff as well."

"Thank you."

Fritz Breckmann bowed and withdrew.

"You'll stay and have some lunch with us, Clive?"

"If you would like me to, Colonel."

"I would."

Chapter Eighty-Three

The extended line moved off slowly.

Peter Bennett didn't like the direction they were moving in, but his confidence hadn't waned. Even if they did find something – but they wouldn't – there was nothing to link what they might find back to him.

He would have to bring his plans forward.

At least while the depot was empty of soldiers, getting the car into place was going to be a lot easier. Actually, a large explosion in the depot with the appropriate fallout would create absolute havoc if none of the soldiers was there. Perhaps they had played into his hands.

He liked Sylvia Donnelly's idea. He hadn't arranged to meet her again until the following day, and there was no way of contacting her, but there wasn't any reason why he couldn't bring his plans forward. All he needed to do was get in touch with Leah Carmichael and she would do as she was told.

Seeing Fallon was one hell of a shock, but it wasn't going to change anything.

He waited until the line had moved out of sight, and then doubled back to his car because he needed to find a telephone box. His instinct told him to follow the search line, but that was too risky; there were too many pairs of eyes and he would be spotted.

The voices agreed.

Sylvia Donnelly looked down at Seamus. "God, that was good," she said, still breathing heavily. "It must have been having the police so close that generated an extra thrill."

"Do you have to analyse everything?" Seamus asked her. She had wanted to dominate so he let her and she certainly seemed to get as much out of it as he did. "I suppose we are a little vulnerable at the moment." He needed more information but he had to get his timing right.

"My Beretta is under the pillow," she said.

"Tell me about it."

She ran her fingernails over his chest. "So what do we do now?"

“At this precise moment I am quite happy with things as they are.” Sylvia rotated her hips and smiled. “See what I mean?” he said.

“Was I ever one of your fantasies?” she asked, not believing that she and Peter Bennett had shared the same bed. It was quite a thrill, especially after a lengthy period of abstinence. A couple of the staff had recognised her from when she had been there with Peter, but what did it matter?

“All the time,’” he said.

“We’ve done everything I imagined us doing,” she said.

Seamus let his fingers drift up her thighs. “So, let me ask you the same question – what next?”

“We need to have another look at the depot. I want to decide on an entrance and exit point.”

“At the moment I would have said both were rather obvious,” Seamus said.

“I’m being serious.” She leaned forward and put her lips on his. “But I suppose even freedom fighters have their needs, and you certainly came up to expectations.”

“Are you sure this idea of yours is for the best?” he asked, his hands on her hips. “I just wouldn’t want an excellent career so far to come to a rather inauspicious end.”

“Let me worry about that. Once it’s done they will see the wisdom of it.”

“I hope you’re right, but are you really sure that what you think is going to happen … will happen?”

“It will happen, Seamus. You have my word. Now, the pleasure must end and work needs to begin.” She put her hands on his chest, kissed him again, and then lifted herself off. She went over to the window. “It looks as though they have started the search again. A quick shower and then you and I, Seamus Docherty, are going in the opposite direction.”

Leah was in the Chief Clerk’s office when she heard her phone ring. She had seen Clive going into the CO’s office about half an hour ago, but they were still behind closed doors. She hoped he would call in to see her before he left.

“Hello. Amy Carpenter,” she said into the receiver.

“You know who this is –”

“I …” she began, recognising Peter Bennett’s voice.

“No, you have nothing to say, just listen. Meet me in the café beside the Go-Kart *Bahn* over the Dutch border on the Roermond road. Just say ‘yes’ if you know where I mean.”

“Yes.”

“Be there in thirty minutes.”

“I can’t just –”
“You can and you will. Thirty minutes.”

Chapter Eighty-Four

"Shit," Lance Corporal Steve Jones shouted, tripping over a tree root and throwing his hands out in front of him.

"Clumsy fucking git," Private Annabelle Pritchard, who was on his right, said to him.

"What a plonker," Corporal Stuart Crossier said on his left.

Steve put his hands down in front of him to lever himself up and felt something sticky on his fingers. Sitting back on his haunches, he looked at the gooey, reddish mud. "Fuckin' 'ell," he said. "Shit! Is this what I think it is?"

The others had moved on, but Annabelle Pritchard went back to see what the fuss was about. She knelt down in front of him. "That's blood," she said.

"You're dead fuckin' right it's blood," Steve said, wiping his fingers on his camouflage trousers.

"Over here!" Annabelle shouted.

"Stop!" the RSM bellowed from forty yards away.

A chorus of "Stops!" rang out down the extended line in both directions.

The RSM went over to the two soldiers who were still on their knees. "What's it this time?" he asked impatiently.

When they first got under way the line had stopped and started so many times that they had made insignificant progress. But once Sergeant Grossfeld had gone up and down the line, explaining once again what they were looking for, movement improved.

"I think it's blood, Sir," Annabelle said, holding out Steve Jones' hand.

"Whose?" the RSM asked.

"Don't know, Sir," Steve said. "It was here on the ground."

Grossfeld came up behind the RSM. "What is it, RSM?"

"They've found some blood."

Grossfeld looked at Steve's fingers. "Where was it?"

"I put my hand here and it –' He moved a few leaves to one side, revealing quite a large patch on the ground.

Putting his index finger on the patch, Grossfeld looked downwards. "It certainly looks like blood. It is congealed but …" He looked up at the

RSM. "Can you get everybody to pull back about twenty or thirty metres. I will get my men to have a closer search of this area."

"Pull back, you lot," the RSM shouted. "Stay in line but go back twenty paces."

After five minutes the search started.

All the German police officers went down on their hands and knees in a line and began clearing every inch of the ground. They found another patch of blood, and then another. After only ten minutes, and after uncovering an area of undergrowth, one of the police officers called Sergeant Grossfeld over.

Having looked at what his officers had discovered, he went across to the RSM.

"I think we've found what we were looking for, RSM. Can you get your people to mark the area where they are now? We will then know where we need to start again if it's necessary. When they've done that, please send them back to the car park. We must not disturb this area any further. It might take forty or fifty minutes for the forensic people to get here."

"Wilko!" the RSM said but without an accompanying smile.

One of the German police officers started taping off an area around the find.

When the soldiers ambled back into the car park, a buzz of excitement evident, Sylvia Donnelly and Seamus Docherty were about to get into their car.

"Uh-oh, they're back," he said as he opened the door, but then spotted Dawn Martin, the girl he'd met earlier, walking in a small group towards the army lorries.

Without checking with Sylvia, Seamus ambled over to the group and drew Dawn to one side. "Why are you all back so quickly?"

Dawn shook her head. "I can't."

"Shake your head again then you can say you didn't tell me anything, but in just a couple of words, what is it?"

Dawn hesitated. "Blood," she whispered. "They've found some blood."

"Nothing else?"

"No, not yet."

"Thanks, you've probably just added another fifty quid to your bonus."

Dawn Martin smiled and rejoined her group.

The RSM used his radio to contact Timothy Smithers. "Sir, I don't want to suggest that it's anything to do with your good wife, but I thought you ought to know we have found something. I didn't want you to hear it from anybody else."

"Thank you, Mr Tucker, but Sergeant Grossfeld has already spoken to Inspector Hausmann. He's on his way out to the scene."

"Oh, I'm sorry I didn't get through sooner," the RSM said.

"Don't worry, RSM, at least I know."

"Yes, Sir."

"What are you all doing?"

"We're going to wait here at the hotel just in case we resume the search," the RSM told him. "There's still time for another sweep or two."

"Do you think I should come out?"

"No, Sir. Not at this stage. It's in the hands of the police now. I'll ring you if there's anything else."

"Thank you."

The RSM ended the call and then looked towards one of the groups of soldiers. "Private Martin, get your backside over here."

Private Dawn Martin doubled over to the RSM. "Sir!" she said, standing to attention in front of him.

"Who was that you were talking to, young lady?"

"Where, Sir?"

"Don't 'where Sir' me. You know exactly who I'm talking about."

"Erm, he was a civvy, Sir. I don't know his name."

"What did he want?"

"He asked me what was going on." Dawn Martin let her gaze drop to the ground between them.

"He spoke in English, did he?"

"He was English, Sir. Well … British."

"So what did you tell him?"

"Nothing, Sir. I told him it was none of his business."

"Why did he single you out?" the RSM asked.

"Don't know, Sir."

"All right, but none of what's going on can be told to anybody, understand?"

"Yes, Sir."

"Go on, get back to the others," the RSM said.

"Thank you, Sir."

"Oh, and Private Martin."

She stopped and turned round. "Sir?"

"If I find out you've just lied to me, your feet won't touch the ground. Do you understand?"

"Sir, I promise, I didn't –"

"I hope not, young lady."

Five minutes later Inspector Hausmann arrived and he, the RSM and a uniformed German police officer went back to the area being searched.

Chapter Eighty-Five

Peter Bennett watched from his own car as Leah parked hers and walked slowly towards the entrance to the Go-Kart *Bahn,* an indoor track with a large café and bar just inside the doors. When Leah disappeared through the doors into the building, he gave her five minutes and then followed.

She was sitting in the far corner. Not wanting their presence to arouse any suspicions for whatever reason, he went to the bar and bought a couple of Cokes.

He put one of the Cokes in front of Leah. "You see," he said sitting down so that he could see the rest of the room. "It wasn't that difficult, was it?"

"What do you want?" Leah asked. "I … I can't believe I'm sitting here – after what you did to me. I hate you and I want you out of my life."

He smiled. "Leah, my love, we only did what we have done so many times before. Why are you being so hostile?"

"Peter, just … just tell me what you want then you can fuck off out of my life … forever."

"That's not very polite, especially from somebody ..." He paused and took a deep breath. "I hold all the cards, Leah. I hold your future in the palm of my hand, don't I? So, I suggest you should be a little more civil."

He looked at her, imagining how it would be within the next forty-eight hours. That pretty almost unblemished face, with those pouting lips that she knew how to use, and the beseeching blue eyes … all would be lifeless … those unblinking, staring and lifeless eyes would say it all. You are going to die very soon, Leah Carmichael. You are going to be number five and the last … but not the least.

But there were things to do before he used his knife for the final time.

"For a start I want to know what's going on at the *Forsthotel*, the other side of *Heidhausen*."

"How … how do you know about –?"

"It's of no concern of yours how I know. Just tell me what you know." He slipped his hand under the table, put it on her knee and squeezed. Leah winced. "Just do as you're told and there won't be any more of that. Understand?"

"Yes … yes, I understand, but you're still a bastard."

"That's as maybe. So what is going on?"

Leah reached for the Coke. "The… the CO's wife is missing and they are searching for her."

"Are they now? And why are they looking in that area?"

"I don't know. Two German police officers came to see the CO this morning, then … then all the soldiers were on parade and they went off in lorries. I didn't know where they'd gone until you mentioned the *Forsthotel* just now. How do you –?"

"I told you it's none of your concern."

"But …"

"You're here to do as you're told, Leah, not question. Now …" Peter Bennett went on to describe to her in great detail precisely what she was to do that afternoon. He did allow her to ask questions because her understanding was critical to what he had in mind. However, he did not reveal at any stage the real reason behind what he was telling her to do.

"Do you fully understand?" he asked finally.

"Yes, but … but I'm scared."

"There's nothing to be scared of. If you do exactly what I've told you, I'll be out of your life by Wednesday evening. What you do then is up to you. However, it might be best if you disappear, and become Leah Carmichael again. You know, that name really doesn't suit you, I much prefer the one I chose for you."

"I … I can't just disappear like that," she said.

"Oh yes you can, Leah. I'm certain of that."

Chapter Eighty-Six

RSM Tucker watched the activity with solemn interest.

Screens had been erected and Sergeant Grossfeld had told him that his officers were clearing the area carefully, leaf-by-leaf and twig-by-twig. Men and women wearing white suits and masks came and went, some carrying bags which were labelled and numbered.

With the RSM now were Inspector Hausmann and Sergeant Grossfeld. No talking, just watching. And other than the breeze in the branches, little noise. It was almost as though the birds were also looking down and waiting in silence out of respect. Maybe they already knew the answer; maybe they had witnessed whatever happened.

Then one of the white-suited men came out from behind the screen, looked towards the RSM and the others and came over to them.

"*Es gibt eine Menge …*" he started to say.

"Do you speak English?" the inspector asked.

The man nodded. "Yes," he said looking at the RSM. "There is a body. It is female and she has not been dead for a long time. It is my belief it could be as little as twenty-four hours since she died."

"Are there any obvious signs of how she died?" the inspector asked.

"It would be good if you come and look for yourself, Inspector."

Jurgen Hausmann turned to the RSM and said, "What I am going to ask is most unusual, but would you mind if I called you over shortly to see if you can identify whoever the dead woman might be?"

"Of course, Sir," the RSM said.

He watched the police officers and the other man disappear behind the screens.

About two minutes later Sergeant Grossfeld appeared and beckoned the RSM, who took a deep breath before crossing the short distance to the screens.

His thoughts were darting all over the place. Very shortly after joining the Army he was involved in the Falklands conflict, and then only a few years ago he was a Company Sergeant Major in the Gulf War. He had seen his share of dead bodies, some mutilated and others just silent in death. However, he had never seen a dead woman before. When his mother died just before he went to the Gulf, he was unable to see her in the chapel of rest. His two sisters had paid their respects but he just wanted to remember her as she had been.

What greeted him behind the white screens was not what he expected.

Lying in the shallow grave was the naked body of a woman but it was almost as though she was asleep rather than dead. Even lying in these surreal surroundings she looked at peace. With her arms crossed over her chest, her hands clasped as though in prayer, she looked so peaceful: her legs and ankles were together and her eyes closed. Even her hair was tidy. Her white body was clear of any earth, although there was a smudge of mud on her stomach and thighs. No tell-tale tan-lines obtained that summer or during previous summers were evident. But just below the forearm that was covering her left breast, vivid on the whiteness of her skin, was a red stain surrounding an obvious entry wound.

The RSM was aware that the others were watching him. He lifted his head slowly and looked at Inspector Hausmann. "It isn't Mrs Dee Smithers, Sir," he said slowly, "but I can tell you who she is. It is Ursula Dorf and she is married to the Civil Labour Officer at the depot – Manfred Dorf."

"You are sure?" Inspector Hausmann said.

"I am certain, Sir."

"Thank you, RSM." He looked down at the body. "I am afraid this means that the search must continue. I am sorry."

"There is no need to apologise. If we had found Mrs Smithers, then this poor woman might not have been found."

"My thoughts exactly, RSM. Sergeant Grossfeld will go with you. I would suggest we concentrate on this immediate area."

The RSM hesitated before slowly retracing his steps back to the hotel.

His mind was playing tricks ... he didn't understand what he had just seen.

Chapter Eighty-Seven

Although she had been into the main ammunition depot on any number of occasions since her first visit with Clive Benton – and she now wished she had said 'no' because she was sure they were being watched – Leah had only visited the squadron offices and not the many and varied ammunition storage buildings. There were two squadrons based in the explosive area: 'A' Squadron that looked after all the technical aspects of the ammunition, and 'B' Squadron that was responsible for the storage of ammunition. Each of the two squadrons had a major in charge and comprised thirty or so soldiers, and a couple of hundred civilian workers.

Leah already knew that most of the soldiers were out with the search party.

After driving to the 'B' Squadron offices, she parked her car and looked at the map of the depot and the piece of paper on which Peter Bennett had written a location number. She was very nervous and was sure it wasn't going to work, and even if it did there were too many opportunities to make a mess of things later. When entering the controlled area of the depot the civilian in the security hut had given her a small disc which would have to be handed in when she left … this system ensured no unauthorised vehicles remained in the depot overnight.

On leaving the car, she entered the 'B' Squadron's headquarter building, went straight to the civilian supervisor's office and knocked on the door.

Herr Johann Kruger looked up. "*Fraulein* Carpenter," he said in German, which pleased her because it would help reduce any misunderstandings. "You do not grace us with your presence often enough." He smiled, and indicated the upright chair next to his desk. "This is a bad day for all of us but at least you have brought a little light into an otherwise black picture."

Johann Kruger was nearly fifty. His grey hair was receding, his complexion looked dry and blotchy – probably from too many *Schnapps* and cigarettes – and his short frame was overweight, but he still thought he was every woman's dream ... so Leah had been told.

"It is a sad day, *Herr* Kruger,' Leah said, 'but let us hope that the search proves fruitless and Mrs Smithers returns safely."

Johann Kruger frowned. “From what I have heard that is unlikely, *Fraulein*.”

“I think so too.”

“So, what can I do for you?”

Leah tried to remember exactly what Peter Bennett had told her to say. “It is more of a courtesy call. I’m preparing the revised ‘Memorandum of Understanding’ between the British Army and the Royal Air Force on the storage of their aircraft bombs in this depot. As you know, a copy of any such agreement has to go to the *Gemeindedirektor*, *Herr* Dangers. I don’t like translating such documents without knowing something about what I’m reading and translating. I’m here to let you know that I am going to drive to the open storage sites in Roads E and G to see whether I can relate what has been written to what is actually on the ground.”

Johann Kruger put his hands together and smiled. “My dear *Fraulein*, I wish your predecessor and her predecessor had been so conscientious. I would like to escort you to these places, but with Major Harrison in the UK and all the military either in the depot or out on the search I must be here to answer the phone.”

“Thank you for the offer, *Herr* Kruger, but I can find my way. I understand why you must stay here.” Leah tried not to show her relief too much.

“Do you have time for a cup of coffee before you go?” he asked.

“Maybe another time, *Herr* Kruger.”

His disappointment showed in his face. “Yes, another time.” His gaze moved to her knees and it took all of Leah’s strength not to pull down the hem of her skirt. Peter Bennett had told her to use her innocence and femininity whenever necessary. Johann Kruger went to the door with her and gave her general directions to the roads she wanted.

Once back in the car, Leah checked the small map against the directions given by *Herr* Kruger. As she drove out of the car park she thought about what Peter Bennett had told her to do.

She made a number of wrong turnings before she found the right road. Not having seen any other people about helped her confidence slightly, but as she moved slowly down the narrow track that ran parallel to the high grass banks she again questioned what she was doing, but no answers came.

The gap in the grass bank Peter Bennett told her about was easy to find, so she drove off the road onto the pierced steel planking that covered the entire site and saw the bombs for the first time.

There were literally hundreds of them, about six to a pallet. She drove the car carefully between the rows of pallets until she was in the centre of the open storage area.

The bombs looked sinister.

They were big symmetrically shaped blobs of dark green and grey metal, but she now knew each one contained enough explosive to devastate an area the size of four football pitches. The high grass banks were on all four sides, making her feel as though they were moving in on her, just as she knew the authorities would do before long.

"Are you going to tell me why I have to do such a stupid thing?" she had said. "What if I'm stopped and asked?"

"You won't be and no, I'm telling you nothing more. Just do as you're told. If you don't then you know what'll happen."

She manoeuvred the car back and forth a couple of times until she was happy. Opening the glove compartment she reached for the car documents but they were not there. She frowned. She didn't remember taking them out. Why would she have removed them? Shaking her head she got out of the car stealthily, locked it and then started the half-mile walk to the A Squadron offices.

Arriving at the offices thirty minutes later, she walked in through the back door of the single storey block and went straight to the technical documents office.

"Hello Petra," she said, doing her best to bounce into the office. "Sorry I didn't let you know I was coming."

Petra Kristal, a twenty-two year old university graduate, was filling in time and banking a little money before she went off round the world with three of her friends. She had been working in A Squadron offices for three months. Her father worked in the depot and her grandfather had retired three years earlier having worked in the storage area since the early 1950s. Leah always felt sorry for Petra. She was large, dark, wore glasses and was spotty, but she was also one of the nicest people she had ever met.

"Hello Amy," she replied, looking at her over her glasses. "As gorgeous as ever, I see."

"I've brought you those documents you wanted translated," Leah said ignoring the compliment and reaching into her shoulder bag.

"Oh, I wasn't expecting them until next week."

"Yes, I know. I managed to finish them early." She passed the documents over. "I got a lift into the depot so that I could bring them to you."

"A lift?"

Leah took a deep breath and said, "Yes, my car had to go into the garage," repeating the lie Peter Bennett had told her to use.

"Not a big problem, I hope?"

"No, I'm just having the suspension checked." She had told Peter Bennett about her exchange with the police officer. "Actually, are you going out of the depot shortly, I haven't got a lift back?"

Petra looked at her watch. "In about ten minutes."

"Could you give me a lift?"

"Of course but how are you getting home?"

"*Frau* Spinks said she would take me."

Back in her office, Leah packed into a small grip the few belongings she kept there. Going back to the flat with an extra bag wouldn't generate any interest because she often took work home. At just before five-thirty she looked around her office, made sure she hadn't left anything behind and locked her door before putting the key back in the key press in the Chief Clerk's office. Under normal circumstances she would have been sad to leave. However, now she was just wishing time away so that she could get back to England and be Leah … be herself again. Peter Bennett had at least said that he would give her a lift to *Düsseldorf* airport. She had already secreted her real passport and other documents in her bag. She would fly as Leah Carmichael, land at Heathrow as Leah Carmichael and go home to her mother and father as their daughter. They would be surprised to see her, but she had been able to tell from the frequent phone calls from her mother that they really missed her, and she admitted, she missed them just as much. She would simply disappear from *Bracht* and *Brüggen* and re-emerge in the UK as though she had never been anywhere near Germany, let alone the ammunition depot.

There was a good chance she would get away with it all and never have to answer any searching questions.

Clive Benton watched from the CO's office window as Amy walked from the headquarters to the civil labour office. He liked to see her walking. The swing of her hips made him realise just how lucky he was. They would get through whatever had happened to her … they had to. After all, she was doing her best to overcome it herself. Together they would get through it and then … then perhaps they could start thinking about their future together.

She disappeared into the civil labour office but only moments later she came out again with *Frau* Spinks. They went across the car park and got into *Frau* Spinks' car.

"That's strange," Clive said to himself. "I wonder where her car is."

Timothy Smithers put down the phone and Clive sat down again, still wondering why Amy had gone off with *Frau* Spinks.

Timothy was looking very solemn. He closed his eyes as he spoke. “They’ve found a body but it’s not …”

“I’m so sorry.”

“But it’s not Dee,” Timothy said.

“It’s not …? Do they know who it is?” Clive asked.

“Yes. Ursula Dorf.”

“What? Ursula Dorf?” Clive repeated incredulously. “They’ve found Ursula Dorf dead?”

“Yes.”

“I can’t believe it. Isn’t she supposed to be down south somewhere visiting friends?”

Timothy shrugged. “I didn’t even know she was on leave. There’s no reason why I would know.”

“No, of course not, but they have found her body? I’m sorry, but I really can’t believe it.”

“Well, I can assure you it’s the truth, Clive. The RSM has positively identified her. Manfred Dorf is off sick, isn’t he? I do know that much. Inspector Hausmann is arranging for him to be told.”

“God, this really is unbelievable,” Clive said.

“No matter how many times you say it’s unbelievable, Clive, it’s not going to make it any less real.”

“Yes … I mean, no. I’m sorry, Colonel, but *here!* In *Bracht!*”

“You seem to be forgetting that my wife is still missing. That has happened here in *Bracht*.”

Clive shook his head. “Yes, I’m sorry again, that was uncalled for. I presume –”

“No, they have found nothing but they are carrying on searching the immediate area. They’ll go on until just before nightfall and that’s not for at least another couple of hours. Can I ask you to ring the cookhouse and let Sergeant Copeland know he’ll need to delay the evening meal, and that he can expect more than the usual quota … we’ll feed the RMP and the German police.”

“Yes, of course. I’ll do the same for the Messes.”

At that moment he heard a knock and Sam Cox poked her head around the door. “I’ll be going now, Colonel, if that’s all right.”

“Yes, of course it is, Sam.”

“Are you sure there’s nothing I can do?” she asked, looking from the CO to Clive Benton.

“No,” Timothy Smithers said. “Major Benton will be staying on but there’s no need for anyone else to stay behind.”

“There’s nothing yet then, Colonel?”

“No, nothing yet, Sam,” he said quietly.

Clive guessed that the news of Ursula Dorf's body being found would get round quickly enough without the CO starting the ball rolling. He had enough to worry about.

"All right, you have my home number if I can do anything."

"Yes, Sam. I have your home number."

Chapter Eighty-Eight

Lying in the undergrowth forty yards from the perimeter fence of the depot, Sylvia felt very different from how she had felt this morning. She would not have believed that just a few hours with somebody she thought she knew could change her so completely. What she and Seamus had done together was so against the rules that she could think of nothing else that would compare.

Why had it happened?

Why when she was so committed to being in Germany and what was expected of her, had she, in such a short space of time, done something that turned that and everything else on its head? She was no longer in control. When he had spoken, she had listened. When he had tried to remind her that she was the boss, she didn't want to know. All she wanted was to know what he thought, what he suggested they should do. She was now the leader being led, and she was more than willing to be told what to do and when to do it. It was so alien to what she believed in and yet so much what she wanted.

She had even told him that her contact was an undercover agent with the Republic's G2 Department. But regardless of how she now felt, she wouldn't give a name or any further detail.

She moved her arm so that her hand was inches from him, then when his hand covered hers she felt complete. Such a small but significant contact was all she wanted, all she needed. Why had it taken so long? Why when they had been operating together for so long had they not realised what was happening? So many questions, yet so few answers. She wanted to go back to the *Forsthotel* and forget what had gone before. She wanted what they had for just a few hours, to go on forever. It was crazy, utterly unrelated to the way she knew she should feel but it didn't seem to matter. Nothing mattered anymore. Could she really forsake the reason she existed because of the way she felt now?

She had never felt like this before about anybody, so how on earth could she know the answer to her question? Could it just be sex? That had happened often enough and with Peter Bennett: she took what she wanted, gave a little in return and then moved on. But with Seamus it had been very different. It was the way he touched her, looked at her, waited for her and … loved her.

In the space of a few unbelievable hours, her life had changed.

Forever?

She hoped so.

Seamus enjoyed the warmth of her hand under his. It had been automatic. Her hand was there and it needed to be held. There was nothing calculated, nothing premeditated and nothing deliberate about what he had done. He had just wanted to feel her skin against his.

This was crazy … it wasn't supposed to be happening. She was the enemy. If he had received the order to dispose of her before getting the hell out, he would have done – and by whatever means it took.

But not now.

What the bloody hell happened? He went to bed with her; that was supposed to be just a bonus, or so he thought. She instigated what happened between them; he merely followed her lead. It had been necessary, no more than a bodily function to keep at bay any suspicions she may have had. So why was he feeling this way? Why did he suddenly care what happened to the woman lying next to him when just twelve hours ago he would have quite easily slit her throat or put a bullet in her brain?

Seamus tightened his fingers about hers and looked at her as she slowly turned her head towards him. Their eyes said everything, asked everything as they also searched for the answers. Without any hesitation he leaned towards her so that their lips could touch.

"What's happened?" she asked huskily as their lips eventually parted.

"I've just been asking myself that very same question," he replied, but not understanding or wanting to understand what he was saying.

"It was sex, just sex, wasn't it?"

"Is that what you wanted it to be?" he said.

"If I'd wanted just sex then it wouldn't have been with you," she said.

"So why was I there?"

"Because."

"Because … what?"

"Because I wanted you to be."

"Did you plan it?"

"No, and yes."

"What sort of answer is that?"

"The right one."

"So what happens next?" he asked.

"Now? In the next minute, hour, day or month?"

"I haven't the faintest idea."

"No, neither have I," Sylvia said, rolling onto her back and looking up at the clouds moving slowly across the sky. "It'll be dark in a couple of hours or so," she said.

"So?"

"Where do you want to be in a couple of hours?"

"With you," he said.

"That's strange. If you'd asked me that question I'd have given you the same answer."

"We're here for a reason," he said.

"Are you being philosophical or practical?" she asked, not taking her eyes from the clouds.

"I know how I should answer that."

"How do you want to answer it?" she said.

"Truthfully," he said.

"Which is?"

"I don't know."

"No, neither do I."

"We're here to discuss how we are going to blow a hole in British morale," he reminded her.

"Is that so?" Sylvia asked in an Irish accent.

"It is that," Seamus replied.

"Well, what did you expect me to say? So you did?"

"That didn't sound right, so it didn't," he said.

"Neither did that."

"We're even then."

"You're right, so we are."

"Can it wait until tomorrow?"

"So it can."

Seamus put his hand on her belt buckle and began to undo it. 'Under the clouds or back at the hotel?" he asked, smiling.

"I think the hotel," Sylvia said.

Chapter Eighty-Nine

Within an hour of restarting, the search party fell upon their second gruesome discovery.

This time it wasn't by chance.

Until Ursula Dorf's body was discovered, even Inspector Jurgen Hausmann felt that maybe he had instigated a wild goose chase. However, after the discovery he believed it was only a matter of time before they found Dee Smithers

And time was all it took.

A German police officer found the second grave.

Although everyone now knew what they were looking for, stumbling on a partially covered foot and lower leg, and knowing the rest of the body lay under the soil caused one police officer to vomit in front of his inspector.

At Jurgen Hausmann's request the forensic people had remained with them. It took a few minutes to cordon off the area – only twenty or so metres from where they had found Ursula Dorf – before they set about the grisly task of uncovering the body completely, once again bagging anything they thought might be of use later.

It was nearly six o'clock.

Jurgen Hausmann stood to one side smoking a cigarette. He got no satisfaction from his intuition having paid off because he hadn't expected two bodies, and now he wished they hadn't found any.

"Do you want my people to carry on with the search?" RSM Tucker asked him.

Jurgen Hausmann dropped the cigarette onto the ground and used his heel to grind it into the soft earth. "No, RSM, there will be no more bodies."

"How can you be so sure, Sir?"

Letting a wry smile soften his lips, Jurgen Hausmann said, "Instinct, RSM. Nothing more than instinct."

RSM Tucker looked over to the screen placed round the second grave. "Do you want me to see if it is Mrs Smithers?"

"How do you feel about doing just that?" Jurgen Hausmann asked.

"It has to be done."

"Yes, it does," Jurgen said, "I did see some photographs of Mrs Smithers in the colonel's house and office, and I should be able to do it myself, but confirmation is always the best way. Both these poor women will have to be identified formally of course."

It was nearer six-thirty when Jurgen Hausmann called RSM Tucker forward. The soldiers had gone back to camp and except for a liaison officer, the military police had also gone. Under Jurgen Hausmann's watchful eye, RSM Tucker looked down at the body and quickly closed his eyes.

"My God," he muttered under his breath and nodded his head.

Jurgen thought Dee Smithers looked at peace. Like Ursula Dorf, with her eyes closed, her arms folded across her chest and her hands clasped in prayer, she really did look as though she was sleeping. Other than bruising about her throat there were no other obvious signs of injury.

"Strangulation," Hausmann said, "although I think to be more precise I ought to say she was garrotted. It's another professional murder."

The RSM turned to him. "Professional?"

"Yes, RSM – professional. These two poor women weren't murdered they were eliminated by a professional. They were eliminated in the same way Sandra Davies in *Wulfen* was eliminated." In his mind, Jurgen was now convinced they were dealing with one person for all three murders.

"You alluded to there being a connection," the RSM said as he and Jurgen Hausmann moved out of the way to allow the forensic team to carry on with its work. "But why? Why would anybody want these women dead?"

"If we knew that, RSM, we would hopefully stop whoever it is before he eliminates someone else."

Lying on the bed, Sylvia watched Seamus standing at the window.

She hadn't expected him to be so lean. There wasn't an ounce of fat on him but he was less muscular than Peter Bennett. As Seamus always wore loose fitting clothes he gave nothing away about what was underneath. She couldn't remember seeing him take any exercise but he must do something to stay in such good shape. She also liked his hair; it almost covered his ears and drooped well below collar level at the back. Yes, she thought, I like what I see. He was also a very good lover and aware that a woman's skin is a lot more sensitive than a man's, and each time they made love – it was four times now – he had caressed and stroked her until his touch alone seemed to do things to her that she had never experienced before.

She believed she was in love for the first time.

Lifting herself up on her elbows, she said, "We're not being very professional, are we?"

Seamus didn't turn round. "There will be plenty of time for being professional," he said as he moved the curtain to one side. "All the military vehicles have gone but there are still police cars there. Do you think they've found what they were looking for?"

"I've no idea, but I think I've found what I've been looking for."

This time he did turn round. He smiled. "From where I'm standing the last thing you look like is a freedom fighter."

"And from where I'm lying you look more like something out of the jungle."

He went over to the bed and sat down. Picking up her foot he gently rolled her toes between his fingers and looked into her eyes.

"You want to be serious, don't you?" she said.

He nodded. "Yes, I'm worried."

"What about?"

"This man from G2 you mentioned earlier." He ran his fingers up the inside of her calf and then onto her thigh. "Can we talk a little more about him?"

"If you carry on doing that I'll talk about anything," she said, smiling. But she was also suddenly alert. She might have said too much earlier. There had been no need. "What do you want to know?"

Seamus' fingers moved from her thigh and started drawing small circles below her navel. "Where is he now?"

"That's lovely. Where is he right now, you mean?" she asked, watching his fingers, her mind working overtime. "I haven't the faintest idea."

"No, I don't mean precisely. Is he in Germany for example?" He moved a little further onto the bed.

"Yes, he's in Germany."

"When did you last see him and when will you next see him?" He ran the tip of his middle finger up between her breasts and then down again. "Roll over," he told her.

Sitting astride her thighs he kneaded her back softly, up and down either side of her spine.

With her head on the pillow, Sylvia closed her eyes. "That's lovely too," she muttered.

"So when was it?"

"What? Oh yes, why do you want to know?"

"Now I've found you I don't want to lose you," he said.

"We're in the wrong profession for that."

His thumbs were at the base of her spine where she was particularly sensitive. She moaned, loving his touch but wishing they were somewhere else.

"We can still watch each other's backs," he said.

"You've got a good view of mine at the moment."

"I want it to stay like that." Surprisingly he meant exactly what he was saying. "So answer my question. When did you last see him, and when's your next meeting?"

"Yesterday and tomorrow," Sylvia said into the pillow, her eyes still closed. "Lower. There. Do that again."

"You saw him yesterday and you're seeing him again tomorrow?"

"Yes. Oh, that really is lovely."

"Where did you see him?"

"Not far from here."

"And tomorrow? What time and where?"

"Not far from the lake on the *Brüggen* to *Roermond* road. At ten."

"What's the purpose of the next meeting?"

"I think I've persuaded him where the bomb should go in the depot. He reckons he can get it into place so all we'll have to do is set it off. That's what we should be doing now – finding the best way in and out."

"The bomb. You say it's in a car? So it's a remote, is it?"

"Yes. And he'll give me the remote tomorrow."

"Operating distance?"

"He said about two hundred yards."

"Why can't he do it himself?"

Sylvia opened her eyes and lifting her head as best she could from the pillow she looked over her shoulder. "It's mine, Seamus. The depot is mine. That's why."

"All right, I'll go along with that for the moment." Her head dropped back onto the pillow.

Seamus lay along the length of her back so that his mouth was next to her ear. "Sylvia, listen to me," he whispered. "I think you've been so close to getting your fingers burnt already, the next time you're likely to get them bitten off."

He felt her try to move beneath him. "It's got to happen, it'll …" she started to say.

"If it can happen it will, but first I want to know more about your man from G2. I can't understand his motives, and until I do I won't let you see him alone again."

He lifted himself from her, and she rolled over onto her back. With her eyes fixed on his, she said, "You seem to be forgetting who is running this cell."

Seamus smiled. "I'm not forgetting at all, but all the best commanders listen very closely to their most trusted lieutenants. This lieutenant is telling you that I think you're in danger. I will be going with you to this meeting tomorrow."

"If he sees you he'll –"

"He won't see me," Seamus said. "But I will be there."

Chapter Ninety

"There's no chance that a mistake has been made?" Timothy Smithers asked, the numb feeling in his mind as well as in his body. He wanted to cry but the tears wouldn't come.

"No, I am sorry."

Timothy sat behind his desk, his head in his hands.

It was nearly seven o'clock in the evening and in the office with him and Jurgen Hausmann were Clive Benton and Sergeant Grossfeld.

"Where is she now?"

"She will be taken to *Mönchengladbach*," Jurgen Hausmann said.

"So far … and yet …"

"Yes, but there will have to be an autopsy and I'm afraid we will have to ask for your formal identification."

"Of course," he said, imagining a pathologist's scalpel slicing into his wife's body. He shuddered. "Did she suffer?" he asked, looking up at the other three men.

"No, I do not think so," Jurgen said.

"How was she killed?"

"We think she was strangled."

"But she didn't suffer?"

"No."

"Good, that's good," Timothy Smithers said and this time he imagined his wife gasping for breath, her faceless murderer behind her. "And you've no idea who –?"

"No, but we will catch whoever it was and bring him to justice," Jurgen said.

"You're sure it was a 'he'?"

"I'm sure your wife's killer also murdered Ursula Dorf, and yes, I am sure both were killed by a man."

Timothy looked at each of the men in turn. They were all doing their best to hide their true feelings but he could see that none of them really wanted to be there.

"There's no need for you to be here, Clive," he said. "Thank you for staying so long."

"I'll –"

"No, you go back to the Mess … or perhaps to Amy. It's been a long day."

"What about –?"

"Me? Oh, I'll be all right. I must tell the children, and Dee's mother and father, I'll …" He buried his head in his hands again. This time he couldn't hold back the tears and the sobs.

"Is there anything …?"

"No, Major Benton, unless …"

"Yes?"

"Nothing, Major, nothing."

Timothy heard Clive leave the office and then he felt somebody's arm go round his shoulders.

"I can only guess how you must feel," Jurgen Hausmann said.

RSM Tucker was in his office just down the corridor.

He wanted to be with his Commanding Officer because he needed to tell him how peaceful his wife had looked. She didn't look as though she had suffered.

He wanted to share his feelings with the other man.

RSM Tucker understood how hard a man he appeared to the outside world. That was the way he liked it. Even Inspector Hausmann had said he would scare most people. Inside though, he could be as soft as the next man. He'd been married once himself, not for very long though, and he knew what it was like to lose somebody you really loved. The loss was like having a surgeon remove a vital organ without any anaesthetic – the pain was there and it would never go away.

Stephanie had been only thirty-two when she died.

Her headaches had got worse and worse, and then after more trips to the hospital than he cared to remember they diagnosed a brain tumour. Four months later his Stephanie had died. They had met at school when they were both eleven, married when they were eighteen and he lost her fourteen years later.

Yes, he knew what it was like to lose somebody but at least his loss was down to bad luck.

Dee Smithers lost her life to a murderer … a sadistic killer.

How does anyone ever get over something like that?

Manfred Dorf sat at the kitchen table and cried.

He had felt lousy anyway, but now it didn't matter how he felt.

The bottle of *Schnapps* that was full when he started drinking was now nearly empty. She may not have loved him, but he had idolised her. He was a convenience to her but for him she was his life. Without her there was no point anymore. As long as she was there, he had been willing to put up with so much.

He didn't bother pouring the last of the *Schnapps* into the glass. Instead he lifted the bottle to his lips, his hand shaking, and drank until it was empty.

She said she had gone to see some friends in Koblenz. How do you finish up dead in woods ten minutes from where you live if you just go and see some friends in Koblenz? He had been sitting at home feeling sorry for himself when all the time she was lying in the woods, dead.

The bottle was empty, but it didn't matter.

Nothing mattered anymore …

She had treated him like a fool. Did she really think he didn't know what she was? Why else had she stayed with him

Manfred Dorf picked up the empty glass and bottle, put them in the sink and then went upstairs to his bedroom. He opened the secret compartment behind the chest of drawers in the corner of the room and took out the well-oiled Second World War 9mm Luger.

The magazine contained three bullets.

He would only need one.

Without further hesitation he cocked the pistol, put the barrel against the roof of his mouth and pulled the trigger.

Chapter Ninety-One

Not knowing how he should feel was something that was at once alien to Clive Benton.

With all his relationships, even during his marriage, he never doubted his ability to remain detached – to a certain extent – from how his partners might feel. In his opinion women expressed their feelings too readily and rarely looked at the bigger picture: they looked inwards rather than outwards.

Then he met Amy.

Amy generated feelings, emotions, questions … and doubts that he had never experienced before. He was even looking back at his previous relationships and asking whether he had been wrong and they had been right.

When Amy returned to the flat the night before, her behaviour suggested she had very recently experienced something awful, and he hadn't changed his mind. Now two women were dead … and not only dead, they had been murdered. With the discovery of Dee Smithers' body the inexplicable had become the incredible. For some reason, if it had only been Ursula Dorf then perhaps he might have already come up with an explanation; he had never trusted her, and her relationship with Manfred was strange, to say the least. But now Dee Smithers had been found …

Something very strange and sinister was going on.

But what was it?

He needed to be with Amy, to hold her and love her because she was still very much alive. How was he going to tell her what had happened? It was as though he would be telling her to pull herself together. At least she was still in the land of the living.

Get over it.

That's not how he thought but it was how she might think.

The flat was quiet. He stood inside the door and listened.

For a few seconds he thought Amy wasn't here, but then he saw the light under the bedroom door and although he couldn't hear anything he sensed she was in the bedroom. She might be resting so he wouldn't disturb her. He felt totally drained and completely exhausted, both mentally and physically. If what he believed had happened to Amy was true then that alone was enough … but being with Amy after what should have been a normal Monday, knowing that Dee Smithers and Ursula Dorf had been so brutally murdered, was too much.

He went across to the array of bottles on the sideboard, cursed when he saw the whisky bottle was empty, but selected a bottle of vodka instead and poured a generous measure. He took the glass and slumped down in a chair. Neat vodka was far from being his favourite drink but he really didn't have the strength or inclination to add ice or Coke from a bottle he knew was in the fridge, and anyway he needed the alcohol to hit him without it being watered down.

"Jesus," he said to himself, "how to go from feeling on top of the world to the depths of despair in less than twenty-four hours." He raised the glass and closing his eyes drained half its contents in one gulp.

He would go and check on Amy in a minute.

What the hell was he going to tell her?

"Clive?" Her voice was distant. "Clive?" she said again. "What's the matter?"

He took a deep breath. "I can hear you," he said without opening his eyes, the alcohol thankfully having had its effect.

"What's wrong?" Amy said again.

"It would be easier to tell you what is right?"

He opened his eyes and looked at her. Her hair was up, showing off her bone structure to its best, and her pretty ears. He liked it this way. She was wearing one of his shirts and her legs and feet were bare. He cocked his head to one side. "You look …" he started to say, trying to conjure up a weak smile.

Amy crossed her arms. "What is it, Clive? You never normally drink at this time."

"Don't I? Perhaps it's what I've been missing. It certainly helps."

"It helps what?" Amy crossed the room and knelt down in front of him. She looked frightened.

Clive stroked her cheek with his fingers. "Dear Amy," he said. "Dear poor, sweet, innocent Amy. Did I tell you this morning that I love you?" Amy nodded slowly but also frowned. He rubbed her neck gently. "You really do look lovely. I wouldn't have believed that old shirt of mine would be so … you know what I'm trying to say –"

"Clive," she said tentatively, "what's happened? You're acting very strangely. You normally moan about the sort of day you've had, but you've never been like this before. What's happened? Have they found –?"

He pulled her towards him and kissed her gently, cutting off her words. She resisted initially but then she relaxed. He loved the softness of her lips, her taste and the way she smelt. In the two months they had been together he had never known her be anything else but soft and sweet. Her perfume was always there, her breath was always fresh and her skin was always soft and silky. Even first thing in the morning she tasted of peppermint; he had no idea how she did it.

Were his thoughts incongruous after what he believed had happened to her? And what he knew had happened to Dee Smithers and Ursula Dorf?

Clive rested his forehead against hers and something very strange happened and he couldn't help himself … he started to cry.

"Clive, will you please tell me what has happened?" Amy cupped his face in her hands, her eyes imploring him to tell her the truth. "It's Dee Smithers, isn't it?"

Her face was a blur. "Yes, Dee … Dee Smithers has been found dead," he said slowly. "And not just Dee Smithers – Ursula Dorf's body was found just twenty yards away."

Closing her eyes, Leah felt as though she had just experienced an enormous electric shock. Her body went rigid, the disbelief smothered by the pictures her imagination conjured up.

Dee Smithers and Ursula dead? Ursula was supposed to be visiting friends in Koblenz, and Dee … but …?

Putting her arms round Clive's shoulders she hugged him.

When she had heard him come into the flat earlier, she had panicked. She was halfway through packing her case but she quickly pushed it under the bed before listening at the bedroom door. Because of the search, she didn't think he would be here that early, if at all. She heard him pouring a drink, then the sound of him flopping down in one of the chairs.

Now she knew why he was here earlier than expected.

Watching from *Frau* Spinks' office window as the soldiers formed up on the bottom square, and then finding out they were a search party for Dee Smithers, had registered, but not fully. Leah had her own worries: she had been raped, almost killed, threatened with the exposure of her true identity; she had left her car in the middle of an ammunition depot and was now planning her escape from her own nightmare.

Her mind raced back to the previous evening, not only to the horrors that went with it, but also to what Peter Bennett had said about Ursula Dorf and why she was married and working in the depot. At the time she thought it was another of his stories … another pack of lies.

Such situations do not exist in the real world.

She was so confused. Nothing was adding up, except it couldn't just be a coincidence.

“I’m sorry,” she whispered, “I’m so, so sorry.”

Chapter Ninety-Two

Seamus Docherty gazed at the single candle in the middle of the table, its flame providing all the light needed. Sylvia Donnelly held the glass of red wine in two hands, a smile on her face and her head slightly cocked. If asked, neither he nor Sylvia would believe or own up to the last twelve hours.

"You're a bastard, Seamus Docherty."

"I have proof of the opposite," he said. "And besides, that's not the way to talk to someone who's taken you to heaven and back on not one but on four occasions in the space of just a few hours. I was there. I heard you."

Sylvia sneered, but retained her smile. "How do you know I wasn't faking it … every time?"

"More fool you if you were," he said.

She smiled. "Well, I wasn't. All right?"

"I didn't think so."

"Smug bastard."

"Sexy bitch."

"We're supposed to be freedom fighters," she said.

"How else do freedom fighters beget freedom fighters?"

"Well, yes, but …"

"So a little practice makes perfect."

"If you say so, but you're still a bastard."

The waitress approached the table. "*Haben Sie fertig*?" she asked, not waiting for an answer before clearing the plates away.

"Coffee?" Seamus asked.

"Please," Sylvia said.

Seamus ordered. "So tomorrow we forget this ever happened, do we?" he said as the waitress left the table.

The smile disappeared from Sylvia's lips. "Forget? Why would I want to forget?"

"Because we are professionals," he said.

"If we really are professionals then we should be able to cope with this and the reason we are over here."

"What about the others?"

"Pat and Robert? As, I said – if we're professionals."

Seamus reached across the table for her hand. "You have made me break every code in the book. You realise that, don't you?"

Sylvia frowned. "What are you talking about?"

"You'll never know." Seamus wondered how the hell he was going to extract himself from his own mess, at the same time wondering if he actually wanted to. Looking at her he had the feeling that if she felt the same, telling her the truth was the only option.

If they really were in love, couldn't they both forsake their ideals and run away?

His sleep was disturbed but at least he was asleep.

Half a bottle of whisky had helped.

A man had never cried like a baby in front of her before. Eventually she dragged him into the bedroom, undressed him and put him to bed. Because he was so drunk, inconsolable and incoherent, she didn't glean any more detail about what had happened, but for him to be in such a state it had to be bad. Could it be any worse?

Leah had only met Dee Smithers three or four times but what she had seen and heard she liked. There was nothing superior about her, and Leah decided that what you saw you got, no more and no less. She was attractive in a sophisticated sort of way and was always immaculately dressed and groomed, but she seemed to make all those around her feel at ease. Leah had seen her mixing with some of the junior ranks' wives and it was as though she was their idol.

Some malicious female who was jealous of Dee Smithers' popularity probably started the rumours about her having an affair with somebody in *Rhinedahlen.* It could even be a wife of one of the other officers who didn't like her. Anyway, she didn't believe it at the time … but now? Why would anybody want to murder her? In such a close community rumours were a form of sustenance; people thrived on gossip. But murder?

People don't get murdered in sleepy hollows.

When Sam Cox had told her about the murder of a corporal's wife in *Wulfen* a couple of weeks ago, it was like reading a headline in the newspaper, when you feel sorry for the victim, their relatives and friends temporarily, but then you move on and other news takes precedence.

But when it happens on your own doorstep and not just a single murder … well? For them to be found so close to each other, you wonder if that meant there had to be a connection …

Clive rolled over on to his side, opened his eyes then closed them again just as quickly.

Although it was warm in the bedroom, Leah shivered.

What could she do? Peter Bennett had told her about Ursula Dorf's background. If it was only Ursula who had been found dead then there was a modicum of understanding – if what he told her were true. But not … Oh God! Could the connection be Peter Bennett? Only twenty-four hours ago he had his hands round her own throat and she was sure she was going to die.

She took a deep breath. It was all so unreal and yet ...

No, she was thinking only of herself. If she said anything to anybody the truth would come out and it couldn't be ignored.

What should she do?

As Leah curled up against the warmth of Clive's body, there were so many questions going round and round in her mind that she thought sleep would be impossible. She was mentally exhausted, but her eyes began to droop almost immediately and eventually she drifted into a disturbed sleep.

Tomorrow ... tomorrow she would have to do the right thing.

Chapter Ninety-Three

Peter Bennett had hidden his car a few minutes' walk from the fence that encircled Wortham Barracks, the administrative camp for the ammunition depot. He knew there were three accommodation blocks that housed the single junior ranks, but he didn't know which one his target was living in. He had therefore assumed that after the search there would be considerable nervous tension to release and where better to do that than in the NAAFI bar. A gate near the RSM's quarter that led out of the back of the barracks was unguarded and easy to climb over. The bushes to one side of the block containing the bar were in shadow.

Needing to find the female soldier who Roland Fallon had spoken to had become a necessity, not only to discover whether both bodies had been found – he had to assume they had – but more importantly what was he doing there. He might have said something to her that would give Peter Bennett some idea of what was happening. Nothing must upset the next few days – he was so close to finishing.

Once over the gate he positioned himself so that he could see the door to the NAAFI, and waited. It was nearly eleven in the evening and there was little movement. The illuminated main entrance to the camp was off to his left and a sentry was moving about at the gate, but other than that there was nothing to disturb him. He could hear the cacophony of voices coming from the open bar windows but he would give it as long as necessary.

Nothing else was going to happen tonight.

If she were in the NAAFI, he would be waiting for her.

"I'm coming with you tomorrow," Seamus told Sylvia. They were back in their room in the *Forsthotel*. Police cars remained in evidence outside and as they left their car, they could see the dim lights in the woods where the police were still working.

"I don't think –"

"There's no need to waste your breath arguing, because whether you like it or not, I'll be there."

Sylvia had never felt so contented; lying next to him in bed seemed to be so normal, and she was still what she was, he was still what he was. He was right, though. Why couldn't two people have an ordinary relationship even if their *raison d'être* was only achievable through violence. She wondered how he would respond if she suggested that after finishing what they had set out to do, the two of them disappear and leave the *Cause* to others. After all, they had done their bit. Why shouldn't they have a few years happiness?

"I'm not arguing," she said. "If I turn up with a bodyguard neither of us will see him. There will be no bomb. He will disappear and what I've been planning for so long will disappear with him."

"It won't be him that isn't seen, it'll be me. I don't trust him," Seamus said.

"I can take care of myself."

"I know you can but it all seems unreal. G2 just don't operate like this."

Sylvia traced the bridge of his nose with her finger. "I know what I'm doing but you really care, don't you?"

"Of course I care. I wouldn't be here if I didn't care."

"So I'm not just an easy lay?"

"Easy? It took long enough."

"That's true," Sylvia said. "Nobody has cared before, well not for me. They have cared whether what I do is for the good of unification, but caring for me, what happens to me, that's another matter."

"Anyway, I care what happens to you," he said, "so tomorrow morning I'll not be far from you."

"There's no need."

"I think there is every need."

Sylvia kissed him on the cheek. "That's rather sweet."

"There's nothing sweet about it. It's common sense."

"Seamus, when this is over... no, let's not talk about that yet."

After ringing his wife to explain that he wouldn't be home that night, Detective Inspector Jurgen Hausmann played the messages on his answer machine. He, like so many others, was exhausted, but he could guarantee that he wouldn't get any sleep that night. Going back to Timothy Smithers' quarter and spending another thirty minutes with him, answering as many questions as he could, had helped clear his own mind to some extent.

Ordinarily, the good colonel would have been on his suspect list, but not on this occasion.

"Hello Jurgen Hausmann," a voice he didn't immediately recognise said to him from the machine, "this is Willy Gauler in *Münster*. I did those checks you asked for and," – there was a pause – "and I think you might be interested in a name that has cropped up. Does the name Peter Bennett mean anything to you?" – another pause – "Look, it's a bit complicated.

When you get this message ring me. You have my office number and my home number is 02501 645555. Ring me at any time."

Hausmann checked his watch. It was nearly eleven fifteen, but he picked up the receiver and dialled the number. It rang three times.

"Gauler."

"Inspector Gauler, it's Jurgen Hausmann. I'm sorry for ringing this late but you know how things are."

"Only too well and I hadn't gone to bed, so don't worry. Look, this may be a long shot but does that name I gave you mean anything to you?"

"Peter Bennett? No, I can't say it does. What's the connection?" Jurgen asked.

"Well, until she was sacked from the job, Sandra Davies worked in the British Officers' Mess at the *Wulfen* depot, so I sent one of my chaps round to interview any of the locals who worked there. One of them, a *Frau* Helga Kristofferson, had more than just a little to say about the goings on in the Mess. She came up with this name. Evidently Sandra Davies and this Peter Bennett – he's a captain – had a bit of a fling when he was in Wulfen."

"Is he still there?"

"No, this is the interesting bit," Willy Gauler said. "We're going back quite a while, must be a year now, but according to *Frau* Kristofferson, the affair was discovered and he was moved very quickly to –"

"*Bracht*?" Jurgen said, interrupting him.

"You've guessed it. As I said, he was or is a Captain, and what's more, and I'll be checking the detail tomorrow, he was a bit of a black sheep. He was in trouble before he got to *Wulfen* and certainly in a good deal more trouble when he left."

"So, if we hypothesise about what you've just said, why would he go back after so long and murder Sandra Davies?" Jurgen asked.

"No idea, but it's a bit of a coincidence, isn't it?"

"It could be, yes. Is there anything else?"

"No, I don't think so. Not at this stage. I didn't hear what I've just told you myself until about four hours ago. I'll be checking for more detail in the morning."

"Well, as you said it's a coincidence, but one that is worth following up. Thanks for that, Inspector."

"Willy is my name, if we are going to work more closely together. Yours is Jurgen, correct?"

"Yes, Willy, it's Jurgen." He smiled when he remembered Timothy Smithers doing exactly the same thing. Formality bred mistrust, whereas informality lowered barriers.

"So, Jurgen, have you found your missing wife?"

“Found being the operative word,” Jurgen said. “I was going to ring you in the morning and tell you. Yes, we found her. We found her in a shallow grave in some woods between *Heidhausen* and *Kaldenkirchen*.”

“That’s not good,” Willy Gauler said.

“You could say that … and, before we found her we found another woman called Ursula Dorf, only twenty metres away. The Dorf woman, who was a Russian immigrant by the way, was stabbed, and the British woman strangled. One had been in the ground for a few days, the other only a matter of hours.”

“Hours?” Willy exclaimed.

“Yes, hours. She was still warm.”

“My God!”

“The killer left a calling card,” Jurgen said.

“What was that?”

“Both women were naked, their arms across their chests as though in prayer.”

There was silence on the other end of the phone for a few seconds. “That’s … that’s exactly how Sandra Davies was when she was found.”

“Yes I remember you saying she was naked but are you also –”

“Yes. Eyes closed, head tilted slightly forward, and the rest you can guess.” Willy said.

“We’re no longer dealing with coincidences, are we, Willy? This Bennett man could be the link. It's a long shot but ... can I ask you to get back to me if you find anything further?”

“Of course, you don’t have to ask, it will be automatic.”

“I’ll do the same for you,” Jurgen said.

“Of course.”

Jurgen Hausmann put down the phone and ran his hands over his face. It was one thing having a name, but finding the man behind the name was – he stopped, made a grab at the phone and rang Timothy Smithers.

He would get his knuckles rapped later, but under the circumstances short circuiting the system was totally excusable.

Chapter Ninety-Four

His waiting paid off.

She was in a group of five young soldiers and they were all, or appeared to be, quite drunk. It was just after one in the morning. His training and patience had kept him awake and observant. Although the transformation from female soldier – hair in a bun, wearing a beret and the very-unbecoming combat trousers and shirt – to a young woman was quite startling. Many others may not have recognised her but Peter Bennett picked her out straight away. In the dim light thrown out by the lamp close by, he saw that she was small, pretty and slim in a very young sort of way, but he had seen her face in profile and he never forgot a face.

There was no mistake.

The group passed within feet of where he was hiding. There were three girls and two young men. They were all smoking and staggering their way towards the accommodation blocks. By chance, his target and one of the other girls stopped not far away, letting the other three walk on. The other girl was taller and really skinny by comparison, her short blonde hair spiked. Both girls were wearing a lot of make-up.

"Are you gonna?" the tall girl asked the one he was interested in.

"No, not tonight, I don't think it would be right."

"Why?"

"'Cos."

"'Cos, what?"

"Well, with them women, you know, them women lying in the woods," the shorter girl said.

They were both slurring their words, the tall girl in particular. "He might not ask you again," she said.

"If he wants it bad enough, he will."

The two men and the third girl had stopped further down the road. "You two coming?" one of the men shouted.

"See, he's dead keen," the tall girl said solicitously.

"He can be as keen as he bleeding wants. He isn't getting it tonight. Not from me anyway."

"Dawn Martin," the tall girl sneered, "you'll fucking regret it"

"Maybe I will, maybe I won't but he isn't getting it, not tonight anyway."

The tall girl put her arm round Dawn Martin's shoulders and they followed the others.

"Dawn Martin," Peter Bennett said to himself. "Now that's a bonus, a real bonus."

An hour later he was still outside and not far from the main door into the accommodation block into which he saw Dawn Martin and the other girl disappear. He'd given it another hour just to be on the safe side and as he had expected, no one else left the NAAFI. His little group must have been the last. Obligingly, the front door of the accommodation block was slightly ajar, the foyer and corridors in darkness. Taking a pencil torch from his pocket he went from door to door looking at the names. The ground floor proved to be unproductive so he went up the stairs to the next floor. He knew from his time in the depot that most of the girls had their own rooms. If his luck held, Dawn Martin would be one of those.

He found her room at the far end of the corridor. Listening to the noises coming from a couple of the other rooms, he assumed that the girls concerned didn't have the same scruples as Dawn Martin.

'*Pte D Martin RLC*', it said on the white-card nameplate on the door.

He turned the handle and smiled when he discovered it wasn't locked.

The bedside light was on and he could see her clothes on a chair just inside the room. She was lying with her back to him, the duvet half covering her. The room was small and it smelt of cheap perfume.

Soundlessly he walked across to the bed.

Her skin was pale in contrast to the black hair that fell across the pillow. She was breathing steadily. Quickly sitting on the side of the bed he reached over and covered her mouth and nostrils with his hand, twisting her head so that when she opened her eyes she would see him.

Peter Bennett bent forward and whispered, "Dawn," into her ear.

Her eyes shot open and he tightened the pressure on her mouth. He could feel her lips trying to move. The look of sheer terror on her face was immediate. She tried to twist her body but he had made sure any movement would be minimal. After taking the knife from its sheath, he placed the needle sharp tip against the softness of the skin under her chin and just hard enough to draw blood.

"Hello, Dawn," he whispered menacingly, smiling at her. "Now, if you're a good girl you'll wake up in the morning and put this rather unpleasant experience down to a terrible nightmare. If you aren't a good girl it's quite simple – you won't wake up at all. Do you understand?"

Other than the unblinking terrified staring eyes, there was no reaction.

"Now, that's not very polite is it? I asked you a question. If you agree to be a good girl nod your head. If you're going to be the opposite, shake your head, you'll then feel your throat being cut from ear to ear."

It seemed impossible, but Dawn Martin's eyes opened even wider, allowing teardrops to fall from their corners. Peter Bennett moved the knife away from her chin and she nodded her head as best she could.

"Now, that's very sensible." He cocked his head to one side. "You're a pretty little thing, aren't you? Why on earth did you join the army?" He felt her lips try to move again under his hand. "No, no, I don't want an answer. Right, I am going to take my hand away from your mouth in a second, and once again you have a choice. Make a noise and this," he showed her the knife, "will sever your wind pipe and jugular vein so quickly nobody will hear a thing. Alternatively, and I would suggest this ought to be your choice ... you don't utter a sound until I want you to. Once again nod your head if you agree to be silent."

Dawn nodded, closing her eyes as she did so.

"Right, I think we're going to get along just fine." He lifted his hand from her mouth but only by an inch or so. He waited, and when Dawn just opened her eyes and looked at him he said, "That's what I like – somebody who sticks to their word." He took his hand completely away. "And another thing, I am not here to rape you or abuse you in any way, all I want is to ask you a few questions. Do you understand?" She nodded and opened her mouth to speak.

"No, not yet. You speak when I ask the questions."

After standing up, he went across to the door and slipped the latch. "Just so we aren't disturbed, although there's not much likelihood of that at this time of the morning, is there?" He smiled as she slowly pulled the duvet over her breasts. "That's good. If your modesty is back that means you're beginning to relax. Have you got anything on at all under there?"

Dawn shook her head, her eyes never leaving him. "No," she said.

"Well, as I said, I'm not here to rape you." He crossed back over to the bed. "Can I put this away?" he asked indicating the knife. "I don't want it to get in the way of our little conversation."

She lifted her fingers to the underside of her chin and they came away with a little blood on them.

"It's only a scratch," Peter Bennett told her. "Right, you can either stay as you are as we have our little chat or you can put some clothes on, whichever you feel most comfortable with. What's it to be?" She held the duvet even closer to her. "I'll take that as your answer, shall I?" He crossed his legs. "Right, you were part of the search team today, weren't you?"

"Yeah," she said.

"Good. Tell the truth all the time and I'll be out of here before you realise I've gone. You spoke to a man outside the *Forsthotel*, a tall man with longish hair. He was casually dressed."

"Yeah," she said again.

"Did he tell you who he was?"

"No."

"You mean he didn't give you his name?"

"No, I mean, yeah."

"What did he ask you?"

Dawn coughed, lifting one hand to cover her mouth. Her large brown eyes shone with health. She had freckles on her cheeks and her small round face looked as though she wasn't old enough to be out of school let alone in the army. She hadn't taken her make-up off and some of it had smudged.

"What we were doing."

"What you were searching for?" Peter asked.

"Yeah."

"And did you tell him?"

Dawn hesitated. "Sort of. He told me he was a reporter."

"Did he? Did you tell him who you were looking for?"

She hesitated again but only momentarily. "Yeah."

"And who was that?"

"Mrs Smithers, the CO's wife."

Peter Bennett nodded. "You're doing very well, Dawn. Did you find her by the way?"

"Yeah, and another woman."

"Another woman?" Peter Bennett kept his voice controlled, but felt the anger building up inside him. "Who was this other woman?"

"Ursula Dorf, the Civil Labour Officer's wife." She was watching him intently but he made sure she wouldn't sense the change in him.

"So did you tell this reporter what you've just told me?" he asked.

"Not the first time, but I did the second."

"You saw him twice."

"Yeah."

"Was he on his own when you saw him the second time?"

"Yeah, but I saw him with a woman later."

"A woman? And what did she look like."

The description Dawn Martin gave him was so detailed that he was left in little doubt about who Fallon was teamed up with. He also kicked himself for not realising the connection before. Fallon was undercover and had probably been with Sylvia bloody Donnelly the whole time he'd been reeling her in to do what he wanted. Shit! Why hadn't he showed himself before? It was Peter Bennett's turn to ask the questions and not come up with the answers. Was Fallon aware of him? The answer was more than likely yes. Fuck! Both women's bodies found and now a bloody undercover SAS prat to deal with.

Shit!

As his mind went into overdrive, he made sure his face remained expressionless. He smiled. "You've been very helpful, Dawn, thank you." He moved his hand to the top of the duvet and with one movement pulled it off the young girl. The scream was automatic but it was cut off as soon as it had started as Peter Bennett put his hand over her mouth so hard she fell back, knocking her head on the backboard.

"Now," he said, grabbing her wrists in one hand and tightening his grip, "you are a very lucky young girl. You have cooperated and for that, all you'll have left of this incident are your memories, and they are memories you will keep to yourself." He looked down her body, and the knife was back in his hand. He traced the tip from her throat, between her breasts to her navel, and then slipped it between her legs. "If you don't want to be opened up all the way down here, you'll do exactly that … you'll keep your memories to yourself. Do I make myself clear?"

Dawn looked dazed after hitting her head, but she seemed to understand what he'd said. "I … I promise," she said hoarsely.

He took the knife away. "Keep your promise because if you don't I'll be paying you another visit and, well, I think you know what will happen."

"I promise," she said again.

"Good."

Peter Bennett slowly pulled the duvet back over Dawn, then bent down and kissed her on the forehead. "You're a very lucky girl. You could so easily have been Number Four."

The tears came to her eyes properly this time and she started shaking uncontrollably.

Peter Bennett wasn't worried.

With a final smile he left her to her nightmare.

Chapter Ninety-Five

The sun was just beginning to rise as Jurgen Hausmann moved to the office window. He had mixed feelings about the forthcoming day: it could go one of two ways, either it would all be over or it was the start of something he didn't want to think about. Whichever, it was either going to be a climax or an anti-climax. Was he really any further forward? He had a name, a name that he was sure belonged to the man he wanted, the man who was clinical in the way he killed, the man who would kill again if he wasn't found and stopped.

The office door opened but he didn't turn round. "Morning Günther," he said.

"Morning, Inspector."

"Did you get any sleep?"

"About as much as you."

"Then very little."

"Or less," Günther said.

"Where is he?"

"Out there."

"But where?"

"Close."

"You have that feeling too?"

"Yes, Inspector."

"Where do we start looking?"

"God knows."

"We'd better go and ask Him then."

Peter Bennett checked the two graves.

The one now allocated to Sylvia Donnelly was untouched but fifty yards away, Leah Carmichael's needed some attention. An animal had been there during the night but no real damage resulted. Within a couple of minutes, it was ready again.

He nodded with satisfaction.

Not long now … he pictured his final victims' naked bodies in the graves ... their hands clasped and their eyes closed.

It would all be over then.

Moving silently through the woods he was looking for the right spot. It wasn't something he had previously planned so it was important that there were no more mistakes. Two to go and then he would have his freedom.

He wondered what freedom would feel like.

The voices hadn't told him.

The dining room was surprisingly full. Seamus watched as Sylvia selected her breakfast before returning to the table. There were lots of different breads, jams, cheeses, hard-boiled eggs, limited cereals, but many varieties of fruit. To drink there was coffee, tea, juices, herbal teas and milk.

He ate in silence as did Sylvia but he could guess what she was thinking.

He had heard nothing during the night, but he and Sylvia had been so involved with each other that neither had been listening for anything.

Was she really worth forsaking and risking the very reason he was here? By doing so he would be putting both their lives at risk. If their respective hierarchies discovered that they had both gone rogue, each side would take care of their treacherous behaviour.

Roland Fallon was a professional, but he was also a human being with feelings.

Having undergone the most gruelling training regime in the world, he had survived to put that training into practice. Once undercover and to maintain his credibility he had killed. He had shot, stabbed and throttled men and women and held other human beings in his arms as the lives he had taken slowly ebbed away. When looking into their eyes he said he was sorry, hugged some of them until they could no longer feel his regret, having explained their lives were the price they – and he – had to pay for the good of the long term aim.

However, this woman sitting opposite him, putting butter and cheese onto a bread roll, was different. She was from the opposite corner of society but when they had met in the centre he had embraced her rather than fought. If twenty-four hours ago the order had come for him to kill her and the others, he would have done so without flinching. She might have been one of those he had held, hugged until she died – but not necessarily.

Now?

Now it was different.

He didn't understand or want to understand.

Leah placed the two mugs of steaming coffee on the bedside table and then knelt on the bed.

He was disturbing.

She had made her decision.

When sitting in the kitchen an hour earlier watching the sun rise she realised the next few hours would determine her future. She had lied and the lying must now stop. If she was going to have a future then there must be no more lies. Maybe Clive and the authorities would believe her, maybe they wouldn't. If they did then perhaps she would be able to start again but if they didn't they would have little choice but to charge her with whatever people like her were charged with.

She could be facing a prison term.

But it had to stop. If she did what Peter Bennett wanted her to do, she would always have to live with her conscience. Fleeing the country would only bring temporary respite from the truth. Now she wanted whatever it would take to give her peace of mind. It would bring heartache for others – especially her mother and father – in the short term, but she was young and she would recover from whatever might be awaiting her.

She looked down at Clive.

His eyes flickered and he rolled onto his back. The morning shadow round his jaw was very dark. She wanted to rub her fingers over it and feel the prickles against her skin and the reality that went with them.

Could she go through with it?

Was there a chance they would believe her?

He was looking at her.

She put a hand on his chest then leant forward and brushed her lips over his. "There's something I need to tell you," she said.

Clive frowned. "Do I get a chance to wake up first?" he said, levering himself up against the headboard.

"No, because if I don't tell you now I never will," she said, reaching for his coffee and handing it to him.

"Would it help if I guessed?" He cupped the mug in his hands.

"It is too serious for guessing games."

"You ... you were attacked, weren't you?"

"Abused mentally and physically would be more accurate," she said quietly. "Clive, my name isn't Amy Carpenter, it's Leah Carmichael and I've been living a lie from the moment I came to *Bracht*."

Leah clasped her hands in her lap, lowered her head and began her story.

Chapter Ninety-Six

"Jurgen, this is Timothy Smithers."

"Timothy, how can I help?"

"The car is outside to take me to the airport. I just wanted to be sure there was nothing else I could do before I leave. I've told the Adjutant to give you as many details as he can on Peter Bennett. I've also told him to contact our Records Branch in Glasgow to see if they can give you any more information regarding his likely whereabouts."

"Thank you, I think that will –"

"I still can't believe that Bennett might be involved," Timothy said, interrupting. "He left the Army feeling very bitter but surely he wouldn't resort to murder, and if so, why my wife?"

"Maybe he hasn't, Timothy, but it's an avenue that must be investigated."

"Of course, I understand. I'll be in the UK for about a week. The children will need me there."

"I want to wish you good luck," Jurgen said, "but my choice of words does not seem appropriate."

"I appreciate what you're saying and thank you. You have my contact details if you need me."

"Yes, and I will keep you informed."

"Thank you, Jurgen. I think it's you who needs the luck."

"If he is out there, Timothy, I will find him. I can assure you it is just a matter of time. You are leaving at the right time. The press are … how do you British say it? They are sniffing around."

"I'm surprised they took so long."

"We kept it from them," Jurgen said, "but the word has got out."

"It was bound to."

"They are my problem not yours."

"Thanks. If I've heard nothing I'll ring you when I get back."

"All right, Timothy, goodbye."

"Goodbye, Jurgen."

The small village of *Overhetfeld*, which was situated about four kilometres south-east of *Brüggen*, satisfied Peter Bennett's purposes exactly. Leading out of the village towards the L373 that ran from *Brüggen* to *Schwalmen* in Holland, was a minor road called *Schwalmweg*. He drove slowly down this road, past the last of the houses and a residential camping site, then turned into a small car park on the left that was used by ramblers and fishermen.

Just beyond a small bridge over a stream, the road became very narrow. He left his car and followed this road on foot. As soon as he could after the bridge, he moved into the wood, tracking the road until he came to the L373. He waited until there were no vehicles coming in either direction and then ran across the road into the woods on the other side. Once again, he kept well inside the tree line until he reached *Hotschlagweg*, which was no more than a track leading deeper into the woods and towards the perimeter fence of the ammunition depot.

The graves he had dug were another one hundred and fifty yards down this track and fifty yards off to the right.

He was due to meet Sylvia Donnelly at ten o'clock.

After finding a slight depression from which he could see the track and the main road, he cleared a small area of leaves and undergrowth, lay down and waited.

He was used to waiting.

It was nearly eight-thirty when Leah finished telling Clive her story and she felt better straight away for sharing it with him, but she was still very worried about what he might do with the information she had given him.

She stole a glance at him.

With his head bowed, he was twisting a teaspoon over and over between his fingers.

He had let her say what she wanted to say without interruption. No doubt he was expecting her to tell him about the rape which was bad enough but the rest would have shocked him to the point of total disbelief. Using the absolute depths of his imagination wouldn't have allowed him to get anywhere near the truth.

She had been living a lie, lots of lies, and he was now part of those lies.

"I don't know what to say," he mumbled without lifting his head.

"There's nothing you can say … you can lose your temper, you can shout and bawl. I deserve everything you can throw at me, but I want you to understand one thing ... the way I feel about you has absolutely nothing to do with any of this. You were not supposed to be part of it. Us getting together happened because it would have happened anyway." She got off the bed and went over to the window. "I've told you everything up to a point," she said.

"There's more?"

"There might be." She turned round, her arms folded defensively across her chest. "I think … I think Peter Bennett might have murdered Ursula Dorf and Dee Smithers."

Clive lifted his head slowly. "You think he's the murderer? Why on earth would he do that?"

"Because he told me Ursula was a Russian agent and he's a madman, a psychopath. If it had just been Ursula, and what he told me about her is true, then perhaps, and it's only perhaps, there is some explanation for his actions. With Dee Smithers though, there is nothing. There is no motive whatsoever … and I can't think of a connection between the two, other than the obvious. When I first met him and right through to just a couple of days ago, he appeared to be perfectly normal. His ability to convince and my naivety are the reasons why I'm here – the reason why in the eyes of the law I am a criminal."

"When I came here yesterday evening I was trying to get my head round the fact that there had been two murders. Now …" he shook his head, "now … what the hell am I –"

"I was with him yesterday evening, Clive ... and … and he said it was just a threat but I'm sure he was going to kill me. But he stopped. And then he raped me."

Clive closed his eyes. "I knew ... but –"

"There's something else, Clive. I've left it until last because I can't even start to provide an explanation." She crossed back to the bed, sat down and reached for his hand. "My car ..."

"What about your car?" His expression suggested he was at breaking point. "I saw you leave with –"

"It's in the depot."

"What do you mean it's in the depot?" he asked.

Leah looked down at his fingers lying in hers. "He threatened me, said he would tell the police and the military authorities who I was if I didn't leave it in one of the open sites, where the RAF bombs are. There's a camera in the car somewhere, he said it was for –"

"Peter Bennett got you to leave the car he provided for you in the depot next to RAF bombs," Clive said slowly.

"Yes, but –"

"Jesus, Amy or Leah or whatever your bloody name is, what have you done?" Clive leapt out of bed and threw on his clothes.

"What do you mean?"

"There's only one reason he would have done that." He zipped up his trousers. "It's a bomb."

"A bomb?"

"Yes, Leah, a fucking bomb." He put on his shoes and grabbed his jacket.

"Where are you going?"

"To try to stop the biggest fucking catastrophe people round here will have ever seen … or heard," he said as he reached the bedroom door.

"And what about –"

"What about you?" He thought for a moment "I know what I ought to say but I suggest you finish packing your bag, get your pretty backside to the airport and get the fuck out of Germany."

"How?"

"I'll leave you to work that one out. Get a taxi. Some of what you have told me needs repeating to the police. It might be best if you aren't around when they come looking for you."

"But Clive …"

"There's no time for buts, Leah. Amy suited you far better." He went through the door then stopped. "When and where were you supposed to meet Bennett?"

"He was coming here at eleven o'clock."

"Here?"

"Yes."

"The man's not just mad, he's a raving lunatic. You must not meet him. Get out now."

As she heard the front door slam, Leah let her head fall onto her chest.

She couldn't go anywhere.

Now there was nowhere to go.

Chapter Ninety-Seven

"If he sees you I might as well forget what –"

"He won't see me," Seamus said.

Sylvia steered the car towards a slot on the opposite side of the car park to the only other vehicle parked with its bonnet pointing towards the stream.

"That's what you say but you don't know him," she said.

"He knows what you do but on all your previous meetings you've turned up alone. Why should he suddenly think it'll be any different this time?"

"I don't trust him."

"And neither do I but since when has trust been part of our lives? We stay alive by using our instincts not trust."

Sylvia looked at Seamus doubtfully before opening the door and getting out. "So," she said, staring at him over the roof of the car, "the last twenty-four hours have done a lot for our instincts and nothing for any trust between us. Is that right?"

He smiled. "That's not what I'm saying, but if it hadn't happened then yes, instinct would remain our only form of preservation."

"And now?" Sylvia closed the door. "Where do you and I stand now? What should my instincts tell me now?"

"That something has changed between us."

She cocked her head. "We know each other a little better, I agree, but what has actually changed?"

They walked side by side towards the small bridge. Seamus stopped her before they crossed. "How far from here is the meeting place?"

Sylvia looked over the bridge and down the road, pointing. "It's about two, two hundred and fifty yards to the main road and then another couple of hundred yards beyond that. We normally meet in one or other's car, but this time he wanted to show me something through the perimeter fence of the depot and thought being on foot would be better."

"All right," he said, drawing her back from the bridge. "Sounds a bit contrived but we can't be seen together from here on. You go and I'll follow at a safe distance."

Sylvia nodded but didn't move. "You didn't answer my question."

“I thought you were testing me.”

“I just want to know how you feel,” she said.

He took her hands in his. “Feel? Are we allowed to have feelings?” He smiled again. “Let’s put it this way, I’ve seen every inch of you, touched and kissed almost every inch of you. When you know somebody that well, it’s not so easy to look on them in the same way as you did before.”

“Seamus Docherty, that’s the biggest load of crap I have ever heard from anybody.”

“Crap it might be but it’s the best you’re going to get for the time being. Ask me again later.” He bent down and kissed her. “But,” he said once they had parted, “when did I last kiss you before something like this?”

Sylvia shrugged, tightening her grip on his hands. “You’ve answered my question with a question but it’s as good as an answer.”

“That tells me everything.”

“Good,” she said. “But not quite everything. I’m not afraid of telling you I have fallen in love with you.”

Clive Benton went straight to the guardroom and activated Operation Rose Bowl, which would mean all workers, military and civilian, were out of the explosives area within thirty minutes. The local police, military police, fire services – military and civilian – and the RLC Bomb Disposal unit in *Rhinedahlen* would also be alerted.

He refused to answer any questions. “Just do it,” he almost shouted. “Get everybody, and I mean everybody out of that depot by nine-thirty at the latest. I want a military guard on the gate and nobody is to be allowed in without my personal say so.”

“Sir,” the guard sergeant tried again, “the RSM is down at the headquarters, don’t you think …?”

“Sergeant Mathams, you do what I have ordered and don’t question me again. I’m going to the headquarters now. I’ll see the RSM there. As well as the guard on the gate, I want a vehicle control point at the top of *St Barbara Straße*, an incident control room set up here in the guardroom, and patrols put out round Wortham Barracks. Anybody who should not be in the vicinity is to be detained. Is that clear?”

“Sir,” Sergeant Mathams replied.

“The civilian police and fire brigade will be here shortly. They are to be directed to the emergency vehicle control point. When Inspector Hausmann arrives he is to be escorted down to the headquarters immediately.”

“Sir,” Sergeant Mathams said.

“I will send the Adjutant up here to take command of this end. The main incident room will be down in the headquarters.”

"Sir."

Walking along the side of the narrow road, Sylvia Donnelly was musing over things she had deduced from what Seamus had not said, rather than what he did say.

"He's as confused as I am," she mumbled to herself. "Sex is one thing, but what we experienced was something else."

When she reached the main road she switched her thoughts back to why she was here and she became more cautious. She hadn't bothered to move into the tree line. Up to that point there hadn't been any need.

She was a lone female out for a walk. What could be more innocent?

Before she crossed the main road, she glanced over her shoulder, not expecting to see Seamus but safe in the knowledge that he wouldn't be far away. She was actually quite pleased that he was there. Having operated on her own for so long it was good to know that somebody was watching her back, and that somebody really cared.

Peter Bennett was watching her before she started down the track towards their rendezvous. He saw her look over her shoulder expectantly, and then again once she was across the road. That could only mean one thing: if he had any doubts before, she had just confirmed that his precautions were justified.

Somebody was with her … keeping out of sight but still with her.

He watched her move past him down the track towards the depot's perimeter fence. She was wearing jeans, black running shoes, a cream shirt and a loose lightweight green jacket. She had tied her hair back into a ponytail. Her 9mm Beretta pistol would be hidden against the small of her back. It would be loaded and ready for use. He had never known her carry any other weapon.

He followed her progress down the track until she disappeared round a slight bend.

He switched his attention back to the road.

"I lay awake all night knowing I was missing something, Sir," RSM Tucker told Clive Benton. "You've just given me the answer … Captain Bennett. Even though it's so obvious I can't believe it."

"It is hard to accept, RSM, but it's a fact."

"Can I ask how you know, Sir?"

Clive Benton held the RSM's gaze. "At the moment I can't say, RSM. Inspector Hausmann will be here shortly. Can you arrange for him to have an office with access to a phone with an outside line?"

"I would suggest the CO's office, Sir. He left this morning for the UK."

"Yes, that makes sense." Clive Benton went over to the window and watched as cars, bikes, and people on foot streamed out of the explosives area. "I've sent the Adjutant up to the Forward Incident Control Point. Can you take command down here, RSM?"

"What about the other officers, Sir?"

Clive didn't bother to turn round. "You, me and the Adjutant, RSM, that's all we need. The rest can go to the Officers' and Sergeants' Messes and drink coffee until it's all over."

"Understood, Sir. What about the civvies?"

"Send them home. Nothing will be achieved by keeping them hanging around and this could take all day."

"And bomb disposal is on its way from *Rhinedahlen,* is it, Sir?"

"I called them from the top guard room."

"Do we know precisely where this car is, Sir?"

"In one of the RAF open bomb sites. That's all I know."

"How did it get there? It can't have been Captain Bennett. He –"

"Bear with me, RSM. It will all come out later," Clive said.

"Right, Sir. So, there's nothing else I need to know at this stage?"

This time Clive Bennett did turn round. "If there was anything else, RSM, I would tell you."

"So there's no connection between the murders and what you're telling me?"

Clive took a deep breath. "It's too early to say."

The two men stared at each other for a few seconds and then the RSM saluted and left. Clive Benton turned back to the window praying that the time he had given to Leah was enough. Perhaps if she could get to the airport she could be away before they could find her. Once back in the UK, Amy Carpenter could disappear and Leah Carmichael could emerge back into the world she should never have left.

But with Amy becoming Leah Carmichael again, if that was who she really was, he could kiss goodbye any future they may have had together.

Chapter Ninety-Eight

There he is.

Peter Bennett's mind went back to the training session when they had first been taught how to move unseen through hostile country. Silently, eyes looking out for twigs that could snap, soft ground where they could leave a footprint, broken grass stems; anything that would give their presence away. At the same time eyes shifting from side to side so that they missed nothing, saw everything.

Roland Fallon was alone and moving slowly.

There was nobody watching his back. They should never operate alone, always working as a team, each member having his own field of vision, each covering for the others.

He waited.

Another few feet and …

Peter Bennett's arm went round Fallon's neck, his knee into his opponent's back, ready for the counter moves he knew would come. The two men went down, grappling silently for supremacy, for survival. They were an equal match, but Peter Bennett had surprise on his side.

It was over in only a few seconds.

At the first opportunity, Peter Bennett cracked a heavy stone against Fallon's skull.

It took only one strike and Roland Fallon's body relaxed.

Peter worked quickly.

Gagging and tying his now unconscious opponent, he then pulled his body deeper into the woods.

"Sorry, chum," Peter Bennett whispered as he looked down on his old acquaintance, now a cataleptic adversary. "I didn't want to do that but you made it necessary because of your interference. You'll work yourself free in an hour or so but by then it'll all be over. Hope you haven't got too close to Miss Donnelly."

"Yes, I knew him Inspector," Clive said.

"I apologise for not mentioning him earlier," Jurgen Hausmann said, "but when I spoke to Colonel Smithers, we thought it best to keep the name to ourselves until something could be proven. He said he was going to ask the Adjutant –"

"I understand," Clive said.

"But now there is this other incident, it appears … well, as you are now in charge …"

"Yes, and thank you for telling me… it does look as though –"

"Would you say this man Peter Bennett is capable of murder, Major Benton?" Jurgen Hausmann took a sip of the very welcome black coffee. Adrenaline was coursing through his body but the lack of sleep still made him feel like a walking zombie. The coffee would help.

"With his background anything is possible, but murder … the murder of two women, I –"

"Do you think he might have reason to kill your Mrs Smithers? Could they have been having an affair?"

Clive raised his eyebrows as if it was something he had never considered. Why would he? "He left here a year ago. Even if they were … well, you know … why now?"

"Maybe he has been coming back," Jurgen suggested, "and they have been meeting in secret."

Clive shrugged. "What? And they had a lovers' tiff …"

It was Jurgen's turn to shrug. "It's possible." He was basing his question on the Sandra Davies murder but he didn't want to make the connection public … not yet. "And Ursula Dorf?" he said.

"I've no idea but there were rumours when he was here that they were … meeting," Clive said.

Jurgen nodded. "Thank you. May I ask you about this car bomb that could be in the depot?"

"Yes, of course, but the RLC Bomb Disposal –"

"Yes, I understand that. But may I ask how you came by this information?"

"A phone call," Clive said.

"A phone call," Jurgen Hausmann repeated. "This call was to you personally?"

"Yes."

"This morning?"

"Yes."

"Where did you take this call?"

"My office."

"What exactly was said?" Jurgen Hausmann had already decided that Major Clive Benton was lying. He would find out why but for now there were other priorities.

Clive Benton stared at Jurgen Hausmann. "Very little actually, but I can tell you exactly what was said – *car bomb, in depot, next to iron bombs* – the voice was muffled. There was no accent but it was male."

"So why did you call me?"

"Actually, the CO told me you'd called him about Bennett and what your suspicions were. I put two and two together: if he is capable of murder then a bomb in the depot was certainly within his capability."

You are still lying, Jurgen thought. "But how could he get it into the depot without being stopped and searched?"

"That's a question I've already asked, Inspector, but haven't yet come up with an answer."

Sylvia stood in the small clearing.

They had met there once before so the surroundings were familiar.

The silence was getting to her.

There was no breeze to rustle the leaves, no birds singing in the background and the main road was too far away for her to hear any vehicles.

Knowing that Seamus wasn't far away was her only source of comfort at this moment.

"Hello, Sylvia."

His voice came from behind her. She whirled round, but couldn't see him. "Peter?"

"So," he said, stepping out from behind a tree, "you decided you needed protection, did you?"

She was immediately on her guard. "What? … What do you mean?"

He stepped into the clearing. "Don't be coy with me, Sylvia. Brought your boyfriend as a safety measure, did you?"

Sylvia could feel the pistol against her back. She must time it right. Where was Seamus? How did Bennett know he had come with her? "What are you on about?" she said. "I'm here to discuss our plans for the bomb, remember?"

"Oh, yes, the bomb. Of course, and how silly of me," Peter Bennett said, taking a step closer. He held his hand out in front of him. "Your pistol, please, butt first." Sylvia's eyes narrowed. "Don't be silly, Sylvia, just give me your pistol."

"Peter, what's going on? What's happened?"

A wry smile crossed his lips. "You tell me. Why did you bring him with you?"

Sylvia shifted her feet slightly so that her weight was more evenly balanced. Something was going to happen and she wanted to be ready

"You keep on telling me I've brought somebody with me. I don't know what the fuck you're on about." She dropped her hands to her sides.

With his eyes wide open Peter Bennett followed her movement. "I can see exactly what you're doing. Just take the pistol out of your belt and give it to me butt first."

Sylvia whipped her right hand behind her, took hold of the pistol and brought it up in front of her, her other hand coming up to cup the grip.

She spread her feet a little further … she was ready for him.

"I'm impressed. That really was very good." He was about ten feet away from her, his body relaxed as he held up his hand. "Before you shoot me for reasons that aren't readily apparent, let me tell you about your boyfriend."

Sylvia extended her arms slightly, her finger taking up the pressure on the trigger. "You can fuck off."

"Sylvia! Language! I've never heard you really swear before. Is something wrong?" He edged forward a couple of inches.

"Fuck off and stay where you are," she spat at him.

"Now you're being contradictory – I can't fuck off and stay where I am."

She had never felt so scared before. She so wanted to pull the trigger to kill him but she wanted to know what he'd meant, what he knew that she didn't.

Peter Bennett dropped his arms to his side. "Now, your bodyguard – shall we give him a name?"

"Shut the fuck up."

"You don't mean that. You want to know. I can see it in your eyes." She was watching his face. "Captain Roland Fallon, Irish Guards, now SAS, and, believe it or not, part-time undercover Provisional IRA."

His words hit Sylvia like a sledgehammer.

She froze in shock and before she knew it the pistol was kicked out of her hand and he had spun her round and pulled her backwards towards him.

"Bit of a shock, was it?" he whispered into her ear. "Bit of a surprise is it to discover you've been fucked by the British Army in more ways than one. I was also SAS. Never been anything to do with the Republic's G2 set-up."

"You're lying … you fucking bastard." Sylvia was waiting for him to relax his grip just a little.

"Maybe, but in a minute's time I'll be a live fucking bastard rather than a dead fucking Irish terrorist bitch."

Sylvia struggled, kicking out with both feet as she tried to force herself backwards. But he was too strong.

She felt the blade cut into her body, followed swiftly by the pain.

"Where … where were you, Seamus?" she gasped just before everything went black.

Chapter Ninety-Nine

It was just after ten o'clock.

Clive Benton was alone in the CO's office.

After having told Clive that Sergeant Grossfeld, who was delayed by another case, was on his way from *Mönchengladbach* and would not arrive for another hour or so, Inspector Jurgen Hausmann had gone out to organise a civilian police cordon so that all access routes to the depot and its perimeter were secure.

Earlier Clive watched as two white army vehicles with *Royal Logistic Corps Bomb Disposal* emblazoned on their sides had gone into the explosives area.

A civilian police helicopter circling the depot had spotted what the pilot believed was the car they were looking for – Amy's car.

All hell would break loose when it was discovered Amy was the owner of the car and she wasn't Amy Carpenter but Leah Carmichael. He just hoped she was well on her way to the airport.

The press were in the Sergeants' Mess and Clive had made the Adjutant responsible for briefing them. The Army Fire Brigade, supported by civilian appliances from *Brüggen* and *Bracht* were lined up on the bottom square just outside the headquarters building.

With the CO away, Clive Benton was dealing with a major incident. He had informed his Brigadier in *Rhinedahlen*, who obviously knew about Dee Smithers and Ursula Dorf, and explained to Clive when they spoke on the phone that his own headquarters was also swamped by the press. If Clive needed any help then he was to ask, but from the Brigadier's experience the less people giving orders in a situation such as this, the better. He wished Clive good luck, and asked to be kept informed.

As Clive gazed out of the window only half-aware of the activity on the square opposite, he was thinking of Leah. The poor child had no idea of the seriousness of her involvement – her own story supported her ignorance and naivety. Was it her disbelief about what was happening that had forced her to tell him her side of the story, or was it her conscience? On the other hand, maybe, just maybe, it was because of her feelings for him. He had left her on her own and advised her to use whatever time she had to get as far away from *Brüggen*, from Germany, as she could. Nobody else at that stage knew of her connection but it wouldn't be long, now that her car had been discovered. Once the car details were fed into the security database, the police would be looking for her ... but the car would be recognised long before that. And what about his own involvement? By helping her, he was not just involved, he was implicated.

He needed to make sure she was no longer in *Brüggen*.

Grabbing his hat, he went out onto the square to find the RSM.

"Is everything in place, RSM?"

"Yes, Sir," RSM Tucker informed him. "Felix (a colloquialism for the RLC Bomb Disposal Team used in Northern Ireland during the troubles) are in the depot. There's a two hundred yard military cordon round where they are operating. Entry and exit to and from the explosive area are being controlled by the RMP over there," he said, pointing to two RMP Land Rovers parked at the entrance. "I'm holding the fire appliances here until we know what the situation is. It may be a hoax, but we must plan for the worst. The civvy police are putting another cordon on all roads and tracks leading to the depot. The Adjutant has the Press under control and he's also holding the ambulances on the top square, should they be needed. Yes, Sir, as I said, everything is in place."

"Excellent. I'm going up to Wortham Barracks to see for myself."

"Okay, Sir. Have you got your radio with you so that I can let you know what's happening with Felix?"

"Yes, it's in the car."

The two men saluted before Clive headed for his car. He had no intention of going to Wortham Barracks because he reckoned he had only thirty minutes to get into *Brüggen*, find out if Leah was still there, and get back before anybody missed him.

Hoping to God that Leah had taken his advice, he drove up *St Barbara Straße* towards the *Bracht/Brüggen* road.

Two German police cars with their blue lights flashing, were blocking his exit. He slowed as he approached and Inspector Hausmann, who was giving instructions to a couple of the police officers, saw him and walked over to his car.

"Are you leaving, Major?" he asked through the open window.

"Erm, no, not leaving, I'm just popping out for a few minutes."

"May I ask where you are going? I may need to speak to you."

"Erm, yes, of course ... *Bracht*. I'm going into *Bracht* to see some of the wives. They are in a bit of a panic having heard what's going on."

Jurgen Hausmann dropped onto his haunches so that he could see Clive Benton. "Far be it for me to tell you how to do your job, Major, but you are the incident commander. Should you not be with the incident and maybe send somebody else to go and talk to the wives?"

"I would, but we're a bit thin on the ground, and I thought it would be better coming from me."

Jurgen Hausmann stood up. Clive felt uncomfortable under his gaze. "As you wish, Major, I will be in the CO's office when you get back."

"Right, I'll only be a matter of minutes," Clive said.

"Of course, Major." Jurgen Hausmann stood back so that he could proceed.

At the junction Clive turned right for *Brüggen* rather than left for *Bracht*.

Chapter One Hundred

Peter Bennett moved silently but swiftly inside the tree line towards the main road. He intended checking on Roland Fallon but as he rounded the last corner he saw a lone police car parked at the entrance to *Hotschlagweg*. Its driver was leaning against the wing of the car, smoking a cigarette and looking bored. Peter Bennett went deeper into the wood and moved closer to the road and the car.

Although he couldn't see them, the sound of a couple of helicopters reached him. He thought they were over the ammunition depot and from the beat of the rotors he could tell they were moving slowly.

The police driver also heard them but after looking up just once, he stubbed out his cigarette, got into the car and started reading a newspaper. Peter Bennett watched for another couple of minutes before moving parallel to the main road until the car was out of sight. Once again he waited until there was no traffic before he crossed the road and then headed back to his car. Going back into *Overhetfeld*, he turned left onto *Dilborner Straße* and drove the short distance to *Brüggen*. He parked in the main car park just below the *Rathaus* then checked his watch.

It was just after ten thirty-five and he was due to meet Leah Carmichael in the car park at eleven. The police car he saw was now an unnecessary obstacle. Having dragged Sylvia Donnelly to her grave, stripped her, crossed her arms and closed her eyes, he covered her with earth and leaves. He put her clothes in another hole he'd prepared, then went and checked on Roland Fallon. He was still unconscious, his hands, knees and feet bound securely. But Leah's grave was not far from Sylvia Donnelly's and the police car was now blocking the track. No matter, he would kill her and then carry her into the woods well away from the police car. There would be a way.

"Four down, one to go," he said to himself as he started walking the back streets towards Leah's flat. "Where shall I go for a celebratory lunch?"

Rushing up the stairs to Leah's flat, Clive Benton was praying that she had already left and was well on her way to the airport

He fumbled for his key and opened the door.

There wasn't a sound.

Everything was as it should be but there was no sign of Leah. She must have left.

He crossed the living room to the bedroom, just to make sure.

Lying on the bed still wearing the cotton dressing gown, Leah was fast asleep. There was redness round her eyes and she was clutching a paper handkerchief in her hand. There was no sign of her suitcase and nothing to suggest she had made any further preparations to leave.

Why? Why was she being so stupid?

Clive sat on the bed and reached for her hand. He lifted her fingers to his lips. "Leah ..." She didn't stir. He gently nudged her shoulder. "Leah." She opened her eyes. "Leah, you must leave now. The police will be here at any moment."

She looked up at him, her eyes glazed, her confusion obvious. "Clive, what are you –?"

"There's no time for explanations. Why haven't you left already? You must finish packing, ring for a taxi and get as far away from here as quickly as possible." He stood up. "Better still, don't bother to pack just get the hell away from here."

"But ..."

"Leah, please, I'm deadly serious. Your car has been found and the police will trace you. You've got to get away."

Leah sat up, wrapping her arms round her knees. "That's why I'm still here. I'm not going anywhere. I am not running, Clive. If I run now I'll always be looking over my shoulder."

"That's admirable, Amy – shit, I mean, Leah – but also bloody stupid. You must go!"

"Clive, I can't. If I start running now when will the running stop?"

"But how are you going to get anybody to believe what has happened? Their imaginations won't stretch that far."

"It's the truth, Clive."

"It may be the truth, but getting somebody to believe it is another matter."

"That might be so, but it's what I'm going to do. No more lies."

"How very touching," Peter Bennett said from the bedroom doorway. "You were planning to miss our appointment were you, Leah?" He leant against the doorjamb, a mocking smile on his lips, Sylvia Donnelly's Beretta pistol in his hand.

Clive Benton recovered first. "Bennett, you bastard," he said between clenched teeth.

The smile stayed. "Hello, Clive. That's the second time I've been called a bastard in less than an hour." Clive Benton took a step forward. "No, no,

Clive," Peter Bennett said, lifting the pistol. "I would prefer it if you stayed right where you are."

Clive hesitated but then sat down on the bed.

"There's a good chap," Peter said. He looked at Leah whose mouth was still open. "Now, young lady, I want you off that bed and dressed within two minutes."

"You can –"

"More than likely, but if you're not dressed in two minutes your boyfriend here will be as dead as a dodo. It'll be a silent death and very little blood," he said as he took the knife from the scabbard behind him.

"You –" Clive started to say.

"Shut the fuck up, Benton!" Peter Bennett shouted. "Now you, off the bed and get dressed."

Leah swung her legs from the bed and slowly got to her feet. She reached for the belt round her dressing gown but then hesitated.

"This is not the time to be bashful, Leah," Peter said. "We've both seen it all before anyway, and I'm sure not very much has changed. Get dressed, Leah, and do it now."

Leah reached for her pants from the chair and slipped them on without taking the dressing gown off. Her hands were shaking and she could feel her body beginning to tremble as well. She turned her back, put on her bra and then picked up her jeans.

"She's got what most men would say is a lovely body, wouldn't you agree, Clive?" After zipping up her jeans Leah picked up her T-shirt. "To me it's just something to be used, and I certainly got plenty of use out of it, didn't I, Leah?"

"You bastard!" Clive said.

"I told you to shut the fuck up."

Leah slipped on her T-shirt and turned round. "Bastard is too good a word for you," she said slowly. She pushed her feet into her trainers.

"That might be so. Pick up your jacket and come over here," he ordered.

"What about my case? I haven't finished packing."

"Case? You won't need a case where you're going, beautiful Leah." He showed her the knife. "My little friend here is going to see to that."

Leah's eyes shot open in sheer terror. Clive suddenly leapt from the bed but Peter Bennett moved quickly and brought the pistol down hard on the side of Clive's head

He dropped like a stone.

"That was a bit amateurish, wasn't it?" Peter said, rolling Clive over with his foot. "He'll be all right – bit of a headache when he wakes up, that's all." He put the pistol back into his belt. "Right, you have an appointment with destiny, young lady." Crossing the short space between them, he took hold of Leah's arm and hurled her into the living room. First she fell against the sofa, then crashed into the coffee table.

Slowly she picked herself up but stayed on her knees with her head bowed. Her whole body was shaking and tears were streaming down her face.

Peter Bennett lifted her to her feet, put his hand on the back of her neck and whispered in her ear, "Don't worry, I've changed my mind. It'll be painless. I'm not that much of a bastard."

Chapter One Hundred and One

Waiting in a doorway opposite the entrance to the flats, Jurgen Hausmann was just about to call for back-up when he saw a man and a young woman emerge from the main door. He recognised the girl as being the one Günther Grossfeld had spoken to outside the Army headquarters two days ago.

The man was holding the girl's arm, his other hand behind her back.

The girl looked terrified.

Jurgen Hausmann was there because he had sensed that Clive Benton was lying when they met less than twenty minutes earlier. His suspicions were confirmed when he saw him turn in the opposite direction to *Bracht,* and decided to follow him. Having seen him disappear into the block of flats, Jurgen was willing to give him another twenty minutes before he went in himself to find out what was going on and who he had gone to see.

As the man and the girl began to move away from the entrance, Jurgen had to make a quick decision.

He assumed the man was Peter Bennett ... he wasn't sure but ...

The man and the girl turned right out of the flat, which meant that their backs were towards him. Jurgen drew his pistol, spread his feet, and shouted in English, "Peter Bennett, this is the police, stop where you are and turn round."

The man spun round, pushing the woman in front of him, with what Jurgen recognised as a British commando knife at her throat.

"And who might you be," he asked almost casually.

There had been a few pedestrians in the road but they had now scattered.

"I am Detective Inspector Jurgen Hausmann of the *Kriminal Polizei,*" Jurgen said, "and I am arresting you for the murder of two women named Smithers and Dorf." Holding the pistol steady in both hands he tried to assess what Bennett was going to do. He knew Peter Bennett was ex-British Army Special Forces, so he wasn't dealing with an ordinary criminal.

"That's rather presumptuous of you," Bennett said, the knife still under the young woman's chin. "May I see some identification," he added, smiling.

Jurgen Hausmann was confident that he could take this maniac out with one shot. He was so much taller than the girl and she was covering only part of his body. Her eyes told him how terrified she was. Her mouth was open but she didn't utter a sound.

"Peter Bennett, please release the girl, drop the knife and give yourself up before matters are made even worse."

"Worse? I'm not sure you fully understand what or who you are dealing with," Bennett said.

Jurgen watched the girl wince as the tip of the knife broke the surface of her skin.

"Did you say your name was Hausmann and you are a detective inspector?" Bennett said as he hooked the blade under the neck of the girl's T-shirt and sliced down the front.

Hausmann nodded, his eyes not wavering from his target.

"Inspector Hausmann, if I see your finger move, even flinch, this little bitch will die. It's as simple as that," Bennett said, his voice still clam. He drew the knife across the young woman's stomach above the top of her jeans, causing another thin line of blood to ooze from the wound.

Inspector Hausmann saw her close her eyes but tears rolled down her cheeks. Her body was shaking uncontrollably.

"If you want her dead then stay as you are, if not then put the pistol down and move away."

Jurgen Hausmann didn't flinch. "There is no escape. Please do not make me shoot you."

The sound of Sirens broke into the standoff, but Jurgen kept his eyes on Bennett.

"We seem to have reached a bit of an impasse, Inspector Hausmann. I think I may have to demonstrate that I mean what I say."

Bennett reversed his hold on the knife and as the tip of the blade entered the young woman's body just below her rib cage he simultaneously reached behind him.

Inspector Jurgen Hausmann pulled the trigger.

A small black hole appeared in the centre of the man's forehead, followed instantaneously by the report from the pistol.

Birds in nearby trees squawked their annoyance.

Almost in slow motion, Jurgen Hausmann's victim fell backwards onto the ground and the young woman fell with him, the knife embedded in her body.

Epilogue

"It wasn't that sophisticated," Captain Charlie West of the RLC Bomb Disposal Team told the RSM. "There was plenty of explosive, about two hundred pounds and all PE4, which is a bit strange but that's for the intelligence boys to investigate. The other thing that was strange was that there were no anti-handling devices. It was a remote. The receiver and detonator were in the boot behind the fire extinguisher housing, and most of the explosive was in that area too." Captain West wiped his hands on a rag. "Small car like that, all that extra weight …" He shrugged. "Anyway, it was straightforward enough. I've got to leave the car where it is for a while, and it'll need a cordon around it until it's finished with. Other than that your depot is safe again."

"Thank you, Sir. Would it have done much damage?"

Captain West threw the rag in a bin. "That's another thing. All rather strange. Although not a sophisticated bomb, if it had been put in the right place then yes, it would have been pretty horrific, but where it was?" He shook his head. "It would have scattered a few of those five hundred pounders around a bit, but none I believe would have detonated. If you want my opinion, it was what I call a live hoax … designed to keep all of us occupied while something else happened. Has anything else happened?"

The RSM looked over the Captain's shoulder towards the headquarters building. "Rather a lot, Sir, before during and after what went on here."

"Oh, what was it?"

"Can't say at this stage, Sir. Suffice to say 3 Base Ammunition Depot will appear in all the National papers back home and in Germany and not for the right reasons."

Looking about him, Captain West put on his beret. "That doesn't sound too good. Where are all the officers?"

"Read the papers, Sir."

Two Months Later

18th October 1994
Farnham, Hampshire

Dear Miss Carmichael

This is proving to be the most difficult letter I have ever had to write, and the others will be the same. Where do I start? Perhaps it would be best if I begin by saying how very sorry I am that my son was responsible for your injuries. I understand that you will recover physically. For that I must thank God, but it will obviously take time for the mental anguish he caused you to lessen. I cannot say I know how you feel bodily, but I can share the dreadfulness that will still be in your mind.

For a mother, writing about her only son in this way is a living nightmare, especially as we were once so proud of him. It is only since the police searched my house and found the diaries that the truth can perhaps be revealed. You may or may not have read in the papers what the speculators thought. Some of what they wrote was accurate but even they were unable to get into the mind of a man, my son, who had harboured such bitterness for so long. If only I had known, I may have been able to save the lives of the four women he killed and the anguish you and others have suffered.

I am not trying to provide an explanation for what he did. Explanation is another word for an excuse: there is no excuse. Perhaps you will permit me to use the word reason, because there had to be a reason no matter how twisted his mind may have been.

The police have told me he used his correct name throughout the sordid business. They have also tried to tell me that he did this because he really wanted to be stopped. He wanted somebody, anybody, to discover the truth before he carried out the horrifying conclusions to his plan that had begun at such a young age. Maybe they thought that by telling me it would make me feel better. If only I had known the truth though, it is possible I could have been that anybody, that somebody.

I am sorry I must stop for a while. I am writing from the heart and it is causing me a lot of pain. I knew it would be difficult but not as gruelling as this. Please bear with me.

It is now a couple of hours later, Leah ... do you mind me calling you that? Do you mind me trying to apologise for what my son did to you? He murdered four women, Leah, he took the life of a mother who had three young children. How can I ever come up with a reason for anybody doing that, let alone my own son?

Peter never knew his father. I can't say I knew Peter's father either. He was a stranger but an icon for a girl of my age and background. Maybe that is when it started. Maybe from the moment Peter was conceived the seeds that created him were also the seeds of his destruction, and the destruction of so many others.

He wasn't an easy child. Before he was five, he had taken me to my wits end and back on so many occasions. A single mother with a hyperactive child made sure that anybody who took an interest in me was quickly put off. From the age of five and after starting school, he changed. Academically he was streaks ahead of the other children of his age and for the first time I was able to have a life myself. However, it wasn't until Peter was eleven that I met my husband, Michael. From the moment Michael and Peter met it was as though they had always been father and son. Each doted on the other, and for a while I could not remember a time when I was so happy. Soon after Michael and I married I fell pregnant. Telling Peter that he was going to have a little brother or sister was supposed to be yet another high spot but it didn't turn out that way. Peter hadn't had a fit for nearly seven years but he had one that afternoon. I can remember it as though it was yesterday. I wasn't just scared, I was terrified.

But afterwards things did get better, or so I thought. Peter didn't have any more fits and he literally threw himself into his schoolwork. When Rebecca was born I dreaded taking her home because of what had happened, but although Peter didn't really acknowledge her presence, neither did he throw any more tantrums. His nose was always stuck in a book. He did so well at school that he eventually got a place at Cambridge. We were so proud. After that there was the military academy and although after he was commissioned he never told us what he was up to, we guessed that he was selected for something rather special. We never asked any questions because we believed that if we needed to know he would have told us, and as a mother, I'm not sure I wanted to know.

Michael, my husband, was tragically killed in a road traffic accident when Peter was twenty-eight and when, as I know now, he was in Northern Ireland. I do believe Michael's death played a tragic part in what subsequently happened. You see he was killed crossing the road and the driver of the car was a woman, and Peter's hatred of all women except me, must have increased when he lost the only man in his life whom he idolised.

Right up to two months ago, we, that's Rebecca and me, thought nothing had changed. We had no idea that he had been in trouble, neither did we know he was out of the Army. We were used to his long absences and therefore when they simply carried on, we assumed he was somewhere in the world doing whatever he had to do. He appeared every now and again, but never for very long.

Michael, God rest his soul, came from a very comfortable background and as he was the only child when his mother died and then his father, he inherited an absolute fortune (all of which I would now give up if I could go back in time). Then, and I suppose to salve our consciences, we gave Peter a sizeable allowance. We never knew where the money went, but as we never asked I suppose we didn't want to know.

Looking back, and with the advantage of hindsight, and after Michael died, I should have perhaps asked after Peter's relationships, but he never brought a girl home and neither did he ever mention even a girl's name to us. We put it down to the sort of work he was doing, and after all, we used to tell each other, there was plenty of time for that sort of thing.

Perhaps, Leah, if you have read this far, you will understand the absolute devastation we felt when just two months ago the police appeared on our doorstep to tell us that Peter was dead. Initially they told us nothing of the circumstances so at least we were able to believe he had been killed in the Middle East, or Northern Ireland or somewhere doing whatever he loved doing.

We did think the way in which we found out was a little strange but we even thought up reasons for that. Then we discovered the truth. My son was a murderer. He had killed four women in cold blood, and if he hadn't been killed you would have been the fifth ... you so nearly were. The police came with a warrant and they searched our house. They went into every room, every cupboard and every drawer. They even pulled up some of the floorboards. Secured in a locked metal box under the floorboards in Peter's room they found some of his diaries. They covered a period of eighteen years. Can you believe that, Leah? For eighteen years, my son had been writing diaries and I had no idea that he'd ever kept one.

After he joined the Army, he didn't come home very often but when he did he must have brought his diaries with him and hidden them with the rest. The most recent ones were found in a hotel room in a place called Kaldenkirchen which was not far from where three of the murders were committed.

The diaries had started two days after I told him I was pregnant with Rebecca. The entries were made weekly for eighteen years. Most of what he wrote appeared on the surface to be quite normal. He described his school years, his time at Cambridge and then the military academy. It wasn't until he was twenty that there was any indication of a problem. What he had written in December 1984 was perhaps the start. I am going to tell you word for word what he wrote:

Why are the others so blind? Why can't they see what is happening in front of their very eyes. I now know where the devil really exists. The voices have told me. The devil is in the minds of women. They are all the devil's disciples. They exist to corrupt. They are on this earth to ensure the destruction of man. I must seek guidance from the voices, and once I have what I need I will reap vengeance.

During his time at the academy, other intermittent entries were equally disturbing. It was almost as though he was searching for the key to his traumatized state. He always pledged that he would do something to prevent what he saw happening to others from happening to him. He described the relationships he saw his male friends having with girls for other than sex as giving themselves to the devil. He swore that he would never do the same.

We discovered from his diaries that he had been selected for the Special Air Service. Leah, how he managed to hide his perverted scheming from the authorities we will never know, but he did exactly that. At least his long absences were explained for us.

At one stage, he was in Northern Ireland and up to that point there was no indication that he'd ever killed anybody. He was on what he called a surveillance operation and at this point, I must repeat once again what he wrote in his diary:

Killed my first devil's disciple today. The voices told me I had to do it and I felt so elated. Sadly, five men died with her. That was not supposed to happen. The five who died were being led by the disciple I killed. Her death generated their deaths but it was not my fault. I have been given the sign. The number six symbolizes man and human weakness, the evils of Satan and the manifestation of sin. Five more devil's disciples must die to revenge the deaths of the innocents.

Leah, Peter was very ill. I can now see that he had been ill since the day he was born but as he grew older, he was able to hide it. He referred in his diaries to the voices in his head and medical experts have since tried to explain his actions with a lot of medical mumbo jumbo. All I know is that when he was twelve and he'd been seen by a psychiatrist and given many tests, all they could say was that Peter was a boy to be proud of and shouldn't be ridiculed – so much for their expertise then and now.

I don't think my daughter Rebecca or I were ever in danger but I do think we may have been the cause of his illness taking him the way it did. He learnt to hate women, except me that is ... and I hope, Rebecca. There wasn't anything in his diaries that suggested he was gay but I must warn you just in case you are told by anybody else, he did have a sexual relationship with all his victims after he shot the woman in Northern Ireland, except for one. Her name was Dee Smithers. He gave a reason. He wrote:

When I killed my first disciple, she took one of her own with her. That too must have been a sign. When I find the five disciples who are to die, one must die in a different way and she must not have tried to corrupt me. I must let the others think they have converted me to the devil before they die. Once all five are dead, I will be free.

When I write the other letters, and they are letters I must write, I will not be telling the two men who lost their wives the same as I have told you. I understand that the man who was married to the Russian woman took his own life shortly after his wife's body was discovered. How tragic. And those poor, poor children who lost their mother.

You were the lone survivor, Leah. You came close to death, but you survived and for that I am grateful. I thought, I hope correctly, that you had a right to know what drove my son to do what he did. None of what I have said has ever or will ever appear in the papers. The diaries have been destroyed. I have been able to repeat parts to you because what my son wrote will always be engraved in my memory. I will have to live with what I know, but I want what you now know to be your freedom. As your death would, in my son's mind, have given him his freedom, I want it now to do the same for you.

Having read and reread what I have written I appreciate that to anybody but you it would make no sense whatsoever. I hope I have provided the reasons why you came so close to having your young life ended by my son. As I said at the beginning, what I have written is not an explanation or an excuse. Peter was sick, very sick. His sickness can now cause no further harm.

Leah, you are young. You have your whole life in front of you. Your experiences will be with you forever but do not let them ruin your life.

In many ways, we have a lot in common.

With deepest regret but also with such joy because you survived,

Anne-Marie Warburton

Leah felt numb.

Most of what Peter Bennett's mother told her she already knew.

The reason why Leah was recuperating in a hospital in Bath and only ten miles from her parents' house in Marshfield rather than in a prison hospital in Germany or England, was because of the diaries. The Crown Prosecution Service in the UK had liaised with the German Public Prosecutor, and between them they had decided that Leah Carmichael had suffered enough. Although there was adequate evidence to charge her with any number of criminal offences – including terrorism – and her stupidity didn't absolve her of her crimes; they believed that for most of the time she didn't honestly know what she was doing. The military authorities fell into line.

What also helped Leah's case was that she was able to give so much detail of what led up to the three murders in the *Bracht* area and also Sandra Davies' murder in *Wulfen*. The authorities were particularly interested in how Ursula Ivanovitch had managed to infiltrate the British military system so easily, but it was an area in which Leah could only repeat hearsay.

At the time, Leah obviously knew nothing of Roland Fallon aka Seamus Docherty, nor did she know about the existence of Sylvia Donnelly and the IRA cell, but much of what she did know allowed the German and British police to piece together a little more of the detail.

Inspector Jurgen Hausmann visited Leah in hospital in *Mönchengladbach* before she was transferred to the Royal United Hospital in Bath. In the same way that she was able to help the police, he helped her when he explained just how lucky she was to be alive. His visits were both official and personal, although he did say the latter would not be condoned. He told Leah that his daughter Krystal was a similar age to her and there were other similarities too, so his personal visits were exactly that ... personal. He told Leah about Roland Fallon, and how after he regained consciousness he managed to untie himself. Having guessed what had happened, he then searched the area and by chance came across Sylvia Donnelly's body. She was lying in a shallow grave with her hands clasped together in prayer, her body still warm. Her clothes were found nearby. Roland Fallon, in tears, had initially told his incredible story to a lone German policeman he had found sitting in a police car not far away from where Sylvia Donnelly was murdered.

Sam Cox visited Leah in hospital on a number of occasions before she was transferred to Bath. Sam told her that everybody, military and civilian, were absolutely stunned by what had happened. Sam also related what her husband had said after Leah had joined them for dinner, and how he now wished he had followed his instincts believing that if he had he could have prevented the murders. Sam then added with a smile, that she was pregnant and perhaps she had Leah to thank for that. When she explained why, Leah managed a painful smile. When Leah asked after Timothy Smithers, Sam explained that he had been kept in England on compassionate grounds, and another officer was sent out to Germany to take command and put the depot back together again to enable it to get on with the closure programme.

Clive Benton visited as often as he could but while he waited for his new Commanding Officer to arrive he used the excuse that he had a lot to do back in the depot. Leah found his visits confusing. Although he sat at her bedside and held her hand, there was none of the intimacy she thought would be there. He seemed to have distanced himself from the fact that they had been in a relationship, and regardless of the outcome she still felt the same, but he obviously didn't. The only time she really cried was when she saw him disappear out of the ward without looking back.

A number of the German civilians also visited Leah in hospital including Fritz Breckmann, the Officers' Mess manager and Karl-Heinz Mittelwalder the *Burgermeister*. These visits meant an awful lot to Leah especially when Karl-Heinz reminded her that the invitation to go to his restaurant for a home-cooked meal had yet to be accepted.

Once she was transferred back to England and into the Royal United Hospital in Bath, the number of visits she had were restricted to her parents – who were almost constantly by her bedside – and the police who had some follow-up questions. The press, she was told, were camped out downstairs, but at her request no member of the paparazzi was allowed anywhere near her. A version of the truth had appeared in both British and German newspapers, but the press wanted more. Every time she saw the police, Leah wondered if they had changed their minds and she was going to be arrested and charged with something that would mean a lengthy prison sentence.

So, yes, Anne-Marie Warburton was right.

Leah Carmichael was recovering physically.

The knife had punctured a lung and nearly reached her heart. Had Inspector Jurgen Hausmann not shot Peter Bennett when he did the knife would have reached its target and Bennett would have secured his fifth and final victim. Evidently the scar below her ribs, which was already almost invisible, would disappear altogether. The scar caused by the cut across her tummy was also imperceptible.

She could still feel the knife cutting into her body and she shuddered when she realised just how lucky she had been. Inspector Hausmann was right. She was lucky to be alive.

But the scars in her mind would take a lot longer to heal.

Mrs Warburton's letter might help.

She hoped it would. One day Leah decided she would like to meet Anne-Marie Warburton. The words she used in her letter had come from the heart, a heart that was recovering from being broken.

Yes, Leah thought, she was still young and yes, she had her whole life in front of her.

Her parents were standing by her, albeit there was a price to pay for the horror of what their daughter had been through, and to some extent, still had to face. When they visited Leah they looked so much older and their smiles forced. Like Anne-Marie, they both thanked God that she had survived but questioned – sometimes quite openly – Leah's naiveté, and how in the first place she had let herself be so deceived. Leah tried to explain that being wise in retrospect was a trait all humans possessed, but at the time she had been so besotted with Peter Bennett that she did everything he wanted.

Leah lay quite still on her bed.

She had been told she would be going home in a week or so and would then have to face the reality of her immediate future.

At first she thought her future might include Clive Benton. He hadn't been to see her since she returned to the UK but she was now very nervous because he was due in only a few minutes.

Would his presence in any form be a constant reminder?

He was part of her life that she would never, ever forget, so how could she say he would be a reminder. She was being unfair, but she hoped the next hour or so would go well and they could part as friends. She was convinced he was coming to see her to tell her he wanted nothing more to do with her, and she wouldn't blame him. She had lied, cheated and used him as she had been used.

Suddenly he was there.

He was standing at the door, one hand on the jamb and a large bunch of red roses in the other hand. She had no idea where he'd managed to find roses in November, an incongruous thought but it didn't make the flowers any less acceptable, albeit they were a 'get well soon' gift as well as a token of what perhaps they could have had.

"Hello, Leah," he said, smiling. "I'm sorry I haven't been to see you but, well, there's a lot to tell you."

The nurse who had accompanied him to the sideward said, "I'll go and get a vase," then closed the door and left them alone.

"Hello, Clive, and there's no need to apologise. The flowers are beautiful, thank you." Leah sat up as best she could and reached for the roses. They smelt sweet and fresh. "Thank you," she said again.

Pulling up a chair, Clive sat down next to the bed and Leah moved her hand so that it was inches from his. He looked at her, lifted her hand and put her fingers against his lips. "Sorry," he said, "I'm sorry for everything."

"You've got nothing to be sorry about," she said. "None of it was your fault."

"I could have stopped him," he said.

"No." Leah shook her head. "No, you couldn't." She tightened her grip on his hand. "Anyway, that's all in the past. Tell me about you. I like that shirt. Yellow suits you."

"Leah, I had to get my head round everything, and then ... I didn't know how you would feel."

She lowered her head as tears came to her eyes.

"I've resigned from the Army and because of the circumstances I could be a civilian before Christmas."

"And ... and what about the charges against you?" she asked, as more tears ran down her cheeks.

"Dropped," he said, reaching across and wiping the tears away with his thumbs. "The German police courtesy of Jurgen Hausmann decided that because you didn't escape when I gave you the opportunity there was no case to answer."

"Everybody has been ... very understanding," Leah said.

Clive nodded. "You could say that, but the main thing is that you are going to make a full recovery."

"And then?" she asked.

"You'll be a celebrity. The German and the British press want your story, and I bet there's a publisher or two who will be clamouring for you to sign a contract with them."

"Why would I do that?" She used the sheet to wipe her eyes. Clive took a tissue from the box on the bedside table and handed it to her. "Thank you," she said.

He smiled. "You'd be rich, Leah."

"I don't want the press anywhere near me. I want to forget what happened, not recount all the gory details."

"And am I on the list of things you want to forget?"

Reaching across the bed, Leah stroked the side of his face. "I got the impression in Germany that you regretted ever getting mixed up with me." She didn't want to become too hopeful, but Clive was not behaving as he had when she was in hospital in Germany, and she could tell he was hiding something ... no, not hiding, but he was building up to something.

"I very much regret what happened to you, but as for getting mixed up with you?" He shook his head. "You're the best thing that has ever happened to me."

"But, I thought –"

"After you were admitted to hospital there was so much going on and so much to do. The police were in a frenzy and the military were dashing around like headless chickens. It wasn't just the murders, but Roland Fallon caused quite a stir and then there was Ursula Dorf – or Ivanovitch as she is being referred to now. Four women were murdered. That was bad enough but when it was discovered one was an IRA cell leader and another a Russian 'sleeper', well, all hell broke loose. Timothy Smithers was in the UK, so I became a bit of a focus for other people's wrath." Clive shook his head. "And then of course there was your attempted murder, the bomb in the depot –"

"The bomb I planted in the depot, you mean," Leah said.

"You didn't know it was a bomb."

"Didn't I? Perhaps –"

"No, Leah, you didn't know. Anyway, you said you wanted to forget, so let's discuss the future, in other words, you and me."

"My parents –"

"Are very nice," Clive said, squeezing Leah's hand.

"You've met them?' Leah asked, unable to hide her surprise. "Why would you have met my parents? What's going on?"

"We had dinner together last night and they're downstairs in Reception waiting for me to go and get them."

Leah shook her head. "I don't understand. Is there anything else I ought to know?"

"I suppose there is but it can wait."

"No, it can't! What is it?"

"I'm a bit old-fashioned," Clive said, taking both her hands in his. "I asked your father if he would object if I asked you to marry me."

"You what?"

How wrong she had been. Was her future really with him?

She wasn't sure what she was going to say, but for both their sakes she had to decide. Perhaps if they faced together what she was still going through then her recovery might be quicker.

One thing she knew for sure was that Peter Bennett had not failed: he had secured his fifth victim.

As the tears flowed yet again in anticipation of what Clive was going to say, she whispered: "Amy Carpenter was Peter Bennett's fifth victim. She is dead … but Leah Carmichael is very much alive. So ... so having asked my father, are you going to … ask me?"

Taking a deep breath, Clive slipped off the chair and onto his knees. "Leah, will you marry me?" he said, his voice breaking.

"Yes," she said. "I think I might just do that."

The End

44397479R00234

Made in the USA
Charleston, SC
23 July 2015